MW01247520

This book is a work of fiction. Names, characters, businesses, places, schools, events and incidents are either the products of the author's imagination or have been used in a fictitious manner. Any resemblance to actual persons, living or dead, or actual events is purely coincidental. All conversations, actions, and descriptions of any government figures are imagined and fictitious.

DISCLAIMER: This book contains speculative theories on the treatment of medical conditions. It is not in any way a recommendation or suggestion on a course of treatment.
CONSULT YOUR DOCTOR for any advice or treatment options for all medical conditions you or your family members may have. DO NOT rely on this book as guidance.
THIS IS A COMPLETE WORK OF FICTION AND NOT MEDICAL ADVICE.
THE AUTHOR IS NOT A DOCTOR.

MURDER AT PARKMOOR

AN AGENT WHELAN MURDER MYSTERY

KIRK BURRIS

Look for other titles by Kirk Burris.

The Agent Whelan Mysteries:
12 PILLS
MURDER AT PARKMOOR
EDDIE MORRISON

You can find purchase links on his website:
www.KirkBurris.com

Follow Kirk on Twitter: @BurrisKirk
Follow on Facebook: @KirkBurrisAuthor
Follow on Instagram: @KirkBurrisAuthor

MURDER AT PARKMOOR

KB Publishing

ISBN 978-1-7355864-2-7 Paperback
ISBN 978-1-7355864-3-4 eBook

Dedicated to my dad.

Prologue

Sophia Perkins loved dancing in the rain. She turned up the car radio when *Rump Shaker* started playing, and rolled the window down.

She ran into the center of the clearing in the middle of Scarecrow Field, a local cornfield popularized as a place for teens to make out in the summer of 1993.

Two boys braved the growing storm front and its lightning flashes to dance with her, and shake *her* rump to the seductive beats of the song.

They drank a case of "three-two" beer between them while Sophia nursed a bottle of vodka she'd brought from home, and the dancing soon became a competition for affection. After a minute, swinging fists were replaced with a baseball bat by one contender, and a tire iron by the other.

Sophia was curious to see which boy wanted her more, and allowed them to proceed, as she danced and twirled another three minutes in the pouring rain. The boys were drunk and could scarcely keep their stance, let alone strike one another with their weapons.

At fourteen, Sophia had developed nicely, and went from tomboy to every boy within a forty-mile radius of Vinita, Oklahoma, a town no one northeast of Joplin, Missouri or southwest of Tulsa, Oklahoma ever heard of. But locally, she was the prettiest farmer's daughter around. And one of the biggest trouble makers.

Her reputation for being loose was widely known and she didn't mind giving away peep shows—in beds, on hay bales, tractor cabs, or anywhere else there was a risk of being caught. She relished the attention, and garnered the name Perky Sophie, or Sophie Parks-a-lot. She liked the last one because if making out in the Piggly Wiggly parking lot didn't beg for voyeurs, then not much else stood a chance. And she loved an audience.

Boys often fought over Sophie like they'd arrived from the Gulf War, though none of them had, and few were old enough to join the service.

Most adults in the area were familiar with her situation, and her alcoholic father, and turned a blind eye when they saw her. She was pitied, and her actions considered a cry for help, though no one bothered. There was no minimum statutory age for marriage in Oklahoma, and they figured she'd be better off living under any other roof than the one she had now.

This night, Sophia was full of life—and her daddy's Smirnoff—and after watching the two boys "compete," she was worked up and ready for a winner.

She decided who she wanted to spend the rest of the evening kissing, and ran between them to declare a victor.

When retelling the story, the boys would say, "It happened so fast there was no stopping it."

The boys' weapons finally connected, but not with each other. The tire iron struck Sophia's face, tearing an enormous gash. Her bottom lip came off almost entirely, hanging by a quarter-inch of connective tissue. Twenty-eight stitches would eventually put it back on, though some would say crooked, and another thirty-four scattered stitches squeezed her face back together. The insurance company wouldn't pay for teeth, insisting they were cosmetic. Her daddy fought them for months, asking how she was supposed to eat with only her back molars and one stubborn, remaining eye tooth. They turned a deaf ear.

The baseball bat hit her in the lower back. It knocked some discs out of place, and after four months of therapy, her walk returned with a severe limp and incredible pain.

There were no more "gentle-boy" callers after the incident. Sophia kept up the narcotics longer than she should have and didn't have a problem sneaking her daddy's vodka to fill in the gap. He was usually drunk enough by nine o'clock that she could get away with stealing three fingers from the bottle without notice.

Five months later, in a shady pool hall, Sophia Perkins excused herself from a game of eight-ball, and rushed to the bathroom, blaming a polish sausage that rotated since 10:00 a.m. at the snack bar. She dropped a baby no one knew she carried—herself included—into the toilet.

The baby had his own little sausage—Italian, or Native American. She liked a couple boys from Osage County and took up with a native from Nowata more than once. She hoped it would be a particular boy who was a part of the Cherokee Nation, but she couldn't be sure. She fought to remember the names of the boys she'd shared relations with many months ago.

She picked the child up and cradled him in her arms. The hospital would soon weigh him as five pounds, two ounces. Small, yes. Premature. But not exceptional. He'd *probably* be fine.

Sophia named him Running Bear, but by the time he was three, he clearly wasn't Native American. When his granddaddy figured out he couldn't get any government money for him, he said Sophia should have flushed him and kicked them both out of the house.

They drifted north, past Quapaw and Joplin, up into Missouri. Sophie worked odd jobs—really odd. She pulled guts out of chickens at a small local farm priding themselves on their product's humane treatment. They kept them ten to a cage. The cages were three by three feet. She thought it unfair they didn't hold only nine. One little chicken shared a foot of wire to sleep at night. She'd shared worse, so she kept her crooked lips shut and cashed her paychecks.

She spent a few years as an embalmer's assistant at the busiest mortuary in the twenty-four counties spanning the fourth congressional district. The pay was better than she'd ever made. Apparently, scooping guts out of people was worth more than chickens. One weekend a month, for extra cash, she'd work twenty hours as a "port-o-potty" cleaner, which came with its own special scooping.

During this time, she volunteered at a dental school to let them work on implants for a meager cost. After two years, she wore a new smile. She wondered if she could volunteer at a cosmetic surgery school and clean up some of her scars, but they were healing well enough, and she could cover them with makeup.

By the time she landed in Kansas City in 2006, she'd regained enough confidence to find a job where she didn't have to scoop shit or body parts for a living.

The makeup counter at a local department store took a chance and hired her for extra holiday help. Eight years of scooping humbled her, and while she regained much of the beauty she'd once held, Sophia blossomed into one of the kindest persons anyone knew. Her customers were thrilled.

She made the women who sat in her chair feel like a princess for thirty minutes, regardless of their pocketbook, body shape or skin color.

Sophia openly shared her self-taught experience at hiding her own flaws, and her makeovers became so popular, she was soon invited to do them on local TV during the noon news. This led to cable and network television on a national level. Her own before and after photos were disputed online, so she started every appearance with no makeup, and mesmerized the live audiences by transforming her face in ten minutes to rival any model.

When approached by several product developers and wealthy investors to launch her own line of makeup, she jumped at the opportunity. By 2010, Forever Sophia Cosmetics was the fastest-growing company in the country. They were online, set up in department store kiosks, and in 2012, started door-to-door sales. She partnered with plastic surgeons across the country, displaying her brochures in their offices.

Annual revenue grew from 140 million in 2013 to 556 million the following year. In 2016 she launched internationally. The campaign was beyond successful and global sales in 2021 were projected at nearly fourteen billion dollars, the highest revenue of any privately held cosmetic company. Her target client always remained the "every-woman," the "plain-Jane," the "broken and scarred," the regular folks, no matter the country. Her genuine self never faltered; in interviews, on QVC launches, and TV appearances. Talk show hosts wanted to have her as often as they could.

She became a celebrity in her own right. Movie stars buttered up to her. Politicians congratulated her on the charities she started and gave to generously. Seventeen countries and counting wanted time with Sophia Perkins. And her company, Forever Sophia, became as common a household name as the Kardashians, Bobby Flay or Dolly Parton.

Enormous success and fame, coupled with her humility, left her with one genuine regret. It was the secret she'd buried on the way to the top; her bastard son. As it turned out, Running Bear was *not* all right.

Chapter 1

FBI Special Agent Thomas Whelan stood over the body of Sophia Perkins. He watched as the forensics team finished their photos and rolled her back and forth for an initial, on-site examination.

"I'm not sure if I should offer up my initial conclusion here or wait till we get her on the table," said Joe Cusack, pathologist and lead forensics agent.

"I'll allow you the right to change your findings," said Whelan. "Spit it out."

"I'm pretty sure the wounds in the back are exit wounds, matching up to the front. Maybe a long knife? Maybe a machete? Maybe…"

"Say it."

"A sword. I think she's been run through three times with a sword."

The alley in downtown Kansas City, Missouri, was poorly lit at 3:00 a.m. A light rain kept the pavement steaming as it cooled down the asphalt's August heat. Police tape shut off both ends.

"Was she killed here or dumped?" asked Whelan.

"Can't be sure. I need more light. I had two small flood lamps in my trunk. I have stronger ones on the way. I need to see how far down the blood was carried in this alley's gutter. There's not enough left here to convince me she wasn't killed elsewhere. And I'd guess about two and a half to three hours ago—twelve, twelve-thirtyish."

Special Agent Miranda Jones arrived on the scene. She wore sweat pants, and a loose ponytail bound her dark curls behind her head. "What've we got?"

Cusack filled her in.

"So," she said, "this is Forever Sophia? She lives in L.A. What's she doing in K.C.?"

Whelan shrugged. "We were able to reach her social media manager. She's in L.A. and we direct messaged her through the Forever Sophia Instagram account. There's no current promotion in the area. No family she knows of. She said Sophia Perkins was supposed to be flying out to New York at the end of the week and then to London from there."

"And *we're* working this one?" asked Agent Jones. "Are we giving up on Eddie?"

After recently working the 12 Pills Killer murders, the two agents chased leads around the country on Eddie Morrison. He was an escaped criminal who Agent Whelan locked up in April. Whelan spent two and a half years of his life gathering evidence to bring down Eddie and one of the country's most prominent drug and sex trafficking rings. He sacrificed his marriage and child to divorce over it. And worse, his previous partner was gunned down in front of him while on the case. Agent Whelan carried a personal vendetta against Eddie Morrison.

When news last month came that Morrison broke out of prison, the agents threw themselves into his recapture. Leads they trailed, however, fizzled out. The majority of Morrison's goons were either killed or also put away for life, and the survivors weren't squealing from their cells.

"We've been on him for four weeks. He's holed himself up. I've got feelers everywhere, but until he triggers a snare, we might as well work a case we can solve."

"And SAC Kendrick's okay with this?" asked Agent Jones.

"Kendrick called me himself. He was kind enough to ask me instead of ordering me. I'm okay. He's okay. If you're okay, we're good to go."

Jones patted Whelan's shoulder. "I'm okay."

She stared at her phone for a minute. "Wikipedia says Forever Sophia—Sophia Perkins—lived here from 2006 to 2010. I'm sure she has some friends in the area."

Whelan looked at the body. "And at least one enemy."

"Possibly dozens. A woman in *her* powerful position? A self-made billionaire who started from nothing? I bet she made enemies at every rung on the ladder."

"Yes. I'm sure. So, where do we start?"

"The will. Let's find out who stands to gain her empire."

MURDER AT PARKMOOR

Agents Whelan and Jones' flight landed at LAX at 2:42 p.m. Sunday. By the time they checked in at the airport hotel, rented a car, and drove across town, it was after 5:00.

"I don't miss this traffic," said Jones.

"You lived in L.A.?" asked Whelan.

"I was stationed in San Diego for a couple of years when I was in the Navy. We'd often run up to L.A. for fun. You remember what it's like being young. Hitting the clubs and watching the sunrise?"

"Sure, I did that on weekends—never," said Whelan. "I was too busy studying and wasn't especially social. I spent more time with my college professors than I did my peers."

Jones flashed him one of her famous smiles. "You've got an old soul. It's one of the things I like about you. You probably partied a lot two or three lives ago. Got it out of your system."

"Reincarnation?" asked Whelan. "You believe in that?"

"Of course. I know *I've* been around at least three times. Perhaps dozens more I can't recall."

"You can recall three past lives?"

"Yes. Hypnotherapy is amazing. I'll introduce you to my guy, and you can give it a go."

Whelan was incredulous. "Huh. I'll give it some thought. So, what was your favorite of the lives you remember?" he asked.

"Scullery maid." She said it flatly, waiting for a reaction before bursting out laughing. "We're here. Remind me again later, and I'll fill you in."

Sophia Perkins' home in North Beverly Park was everything you'd expect from someone whose personal wealth was estimated between 440 to 980 million dollars, depending on which website you landed on.

"Tax record shows she paid twenty-two million," said Jones as they parked in the driveway. "Modest."

The estate spread across two-thirds of an acre, with a large pool overlooking Franklin Canyon. There were seven bedrooms, ten bathrooms, and a chef's kitchen rivaling all the professional chefs on the Food Network.

The housekeeper escorted them out back and asked them to wait for Sophia Perkins' attorney and personal assistant to arrive with all the requested documents.

Subpoenas were issued for tax records, bank statements, corporate records, and all filings for the past five years. And, of course, the latest version of Sophia's will and testament.

They were sipping iced tea on the veranda when an older woman approached them. She appeared to be in her late sixties, and *she* sipped on whisky.

"I didn't know we had options," mumbled Agent Jones.

They stood and introduced themselves.

"I'm Sue Fielding, Sophia Perkins' personal assistant." She plopped into a large swivel glider covered with Sunbrella fabric in cornmeal blue. "It's been a long twelve hours. Forgive me," she said, raising her rocks glass to the sky before taking another sip.

Agent Whelan noted the woman's casual sweater. It showed some age and was hardly designer quality. Her pants were equally stagnant. Surprising for the personal assistant of the creator and figurehead of a multi-billion-dollar, privately held company.

Ms. Fielding perceived his scrutiny. "Oh, I clean up pretty well, Mr. Whelan. But as I said, one hell of a twelve hours. And I wasn't worried about impressing the FBI."

"It's *Agent* Whelan, Ms. Fielding, and forgive my stare. Force of habit in my line of work. You aren't what I expected."

"You mean I'm old?"

"No. I…"

"It's okay, agent, I'm old. Twice as much so today."

Agent Miranda Jones stepped in. "Ms. Fielding, how long have you worked for Sophia Perkins?"

"Since the beginning."

"2010?"

"Oh, long before then." She became teary-eyed.

Before she could continue, she was interrupted by an approaching man, flustered and balding.

"Sam Goldstein, Sophia's attorney," he introduced himself. Names were exchanged, and he took a seat beside Ms. Fielding.

"I got your call at seven," he said. "I've been putting together as much as I can for you. I think I have everything you wanted."

"Can we start with the will?" asked Whelan.

"Of course." Mr. Goldstein opened a large folder. "This hasn't been amended in over two years. I drafted the original. This is the third iteration. Would you like it read in its entirety or get straight to who gets what?"

"Who gets what," said Jones.

"Then I'll skip all the legal jargon." Goldstein retrieved a single sheet from a pocket in the left flap. "This summarizes the estate in a nutshell."

Sue Fielding sat up a little straighter in her chair and patiently held her eyes on the attorney. Whelan watched her take a deep breath and expel it slowly with a whisper.

Goldstein loosened the tie underneath his lightweight cashmere sweater vest. It looked luxurious, but Whelan was lost when it came to designers. He doubted it came from any store at the local mall.

"Okay," Goldstein started, "the sum of twenty million dollars to Grace J. Meyer."

"Her cousin," muttered Ms. Fielding.

"One million to Earl K. Humboldt," continued Goldstein.

"Her uncle, Grace's dad."

"Forty million to Sue P. Fielding. Congratulations, Sue." Goldstein put his hand on her shoulder.

Ms. Fielding began to cry. "She said she'd take care of me. I mean, I thought she would, but you couldn't be sure with that one." She raised her head to the sky. "Thank you, beautiful girl."

Sam Goldstein gave Sue time to compose herself, then continued. "One dollar to Merrill T. Perkins."

Ms. Fielding didn't offer an explanation to the agents upon the reading of the name. She appeared shocked he was mentioned it all, but then to drive the knife in deeper by explicitly issuing a single dollar left her speechless.

"And that would be?" asked Jones, directly to the attorney.

"Her father."

They were silent for a minute before Mr. Goldstein proceeded.

"The remainder of her estate, approximately six-hundred and seventy-two million dollars in value, and her entire stake in Forever Sophia, a fifty-four percent controlling interest, currently valued around seven and a half-billion dollars, goes to Running Bear Perkins."

Both agents were in the dark.

"Her son," explained Ms. Fielding.

"Son?" asked Jones. "I didn't know she had a son! Nothing I've ever read said she had any children. A son? Who's the father?"

"We don't know," said Ms. Fielding. "The only one who might is her daddy, Merrill."

"Who she left a dollar," said Whelan.

"Mmm-hmm."

Jones stood and paced the marble pavers. "Running Bear? Is the father Native American?"

"She hoped it would be, but no, he's very much Caucasian; English, Irish, some German. A mutt like most of us. A DNA exam confirmed it last year."

"*Last year?*" asked Jones.

"Yes. Sophia ran it with some of his other routine bloodwork. I guess curiosity got the better of her after all these years. She didn't tell me about it. I happened to see it on her desk one day while searching for some other documents. The girl was exceedingly private. Anyway, *not* American-Indian."

"Well, where's the son now?"

“He’s in my care,” said Ms. Fielding.

“He’s here? In the house? Why does he need your care?” asked Jones.

“No, not this one. Sophie has five homes around the country. She liked investing in real estate. He’s in Kansas City.”

Whelan stood and turned toward Ms. Fielding. “K.C.? Where Sophia was killed? And he just inherited over eight-billion dollars? I’d say he jumped to the head of the line on our ‘suspects’ list.”

“He didn’t do it. Couldn’t have. Not mentally capable.”

“How is he in your care if you’re out here in L.A.?” asked Whelan.

“Well, not my direct care. I have people with him. A full-time nurse and a doctor close by. I go back and forth between here and Kansas City once a month. Check on him. Make sure he’s stable, getting on.”

Jones’s head tilted to the right. “How does an executive assistant to Sophia Perkins come to be in charge of her mysteriously hidden child?”

“I’m not her executive assistant. That’s Sarah Williams. I said I’m her *personal* assistant. Much more personal. I’m Sophie’s grandmother.”

Chapter 2

"Grandmother!" said Jones. "You're too young!"

"I'm seventy-six. But thank you. Gave birth to Sophie's mom when I was seventeen. She had Sophie around the same age, and Sophie had Running Bear at fourteen. Lord help her. We thought *we* were too young to be mothers. Can you imagine?"

"Ms. Fielding," said Whelan, "I worked a case last year where I interviewed eleven-year-olds who were new mothers, so, yes. I can imagine a lot."

Sue Fielding didn't appreciate his candor. She wanted sympathy, and Whelan didn't have time for it. Every passing hour in the first twenty-four of a murder investigation made his job exponentially more complicated.

Jones, however, was an expert at playing on sympathy. She squatted in front of the elderly woman and placed both hands over hers. "Sue, I'm sorry for your deep, personal loss. Sophia was a national treasure. I'm actually a fan. I use many of her products. One of her foundations matches my cinnamon-bronze skin tone, and I'd be lost without her wrinkle cream. It keeps my crow's feet in check," she quipped.

"Yes," said Ms. Fielding, "I use them too. They really are miracle workers. She often brings me a bottle of her Forever Young Moisturizing Lotion along with a large arrangement of carnations. They're my favorite."

"Well, no wonder you look twenty years younger than you are!"

"You're kind. Thank you."

Ms. Fielding snapped at Whelan. "You could learn from this partner of yours. See here? Thirty seconds of kissing my ass, and I'm ready to cooperate all I can."

"You weren't before?" he retorted.

"Of course, but putting me on the defense like you did might have impaired my memory. Quite precarious."

Whelan internally debated his thoughts about her. "My apologies Ms. Fielding. I'm worried about getting back and finding your granddaughter's killer."

"Well, see there, civility reigns. Yes, let's get on with it. Ask your questions."

Jones addressed Mr. Goldstein. "Who gets the money if Running Bear dies?"

"The corporate shares would default to an even split among all the remaining stockholders."

"And how many of those are there?"

"Six. I've got them all in your document package. Contact numbers and addresses are there as well."

"Great. And the rest of Sophia's estate? Six-hundred and seventy-two million is not something to sneeze at. I've seen people murdered for a pair of athletic shoes."

"If he dies, the estate is divided between several charities."

"Who oversees that? Who's the executor?"

Mr. Goldstein paused, turning to Ms. Fielding. "Well, uhmm, with Sophia's death, Sue is."

Whelan jumped in. "And does her executorship give her the right to change those charities, at her discretion?"

"Yes. It actually allows for her, at her discretion, as you put it, to redistribute the money however she sees fit, charities or otherwise. Legally, with a bit of paperwork, it would be hers to spend wherever she wants. The charities are in place, but she could override all of it if she really wanted to."

The agents glared at Sue Fielding as if she'd been handed a felony conviction.

"What are you all implying?" she asked. "That I'd kill my great-grandson for money? That I killed my granddaughter as a means toward that goal?"

"Not at all. We're simply digesting new information, Sue," said Jones. "You were here in L.A. last night. Five nights now, I understand."

"Damn straight," said Ms. Fielding. "I expected a generous inheritance. Why would I kill her for more?"

"Maybe not more," offered Whelan, "but sooner. And as wonderful as you may appear, you aren't getting any younger."

"You're an ass."

Whelan's eyebrows popped up. "Just playing devil's advocate here. It's my job."

"I *loved* Sophie. Like she was my own daughter."

"I'm sure you did. How did *your* daughter die? Valerie? I read it was a car wreck?"

"Yes. 2013. She ran off the road one night when it was storming and the roads were wet. The hills around Mulholland are treacherous enough on a clear evening. Toxicology said she was sober. It was merely a tragic accident."

"I'm so sorry," said Jones.

"Me too. Luckily, Running Bear survived, physically unharmed aside from minor cuts."

"He was in his grandmother's car crash?" asked Whelan.

"Yes. Traumatized him for months. Didn't think we'd ever get him back to normal. Well…*his* normal."

"There was no mention of his presence in the police report."

"Good." Sue nodded with the confirmation.

"His grandfather—Sophia's dad—what happened there? Why leave him a single dollar?" asked Jones.

"Well," said Ms. Fielding, "he was a complete louse. A drunk, a cheat, could never hold a job. When Running Bear didn't live up to his namesake and Merrill couldn't collect government checks for a Cherokee bastard, he kicked them both out. Sophie never looked back. She stayed with me for a while. Her mother, Valerie, couldn't handle everything going on in her life. She was living with some man from Nebraska at the time. I owned a small farm outside Nevada, Missouri. It was perfect for a child. We raised Running Bear there for a few years, till Sophie was twenty. When it came to light the boy was…unique, well, she took him off my hands full time. But I visited often, and we always stayed close. When she became a success, and her business started pulling away too much of her time, I stepped back into the picture. And here we are."

"How is Running Bear unique?" asked Whelan.

"He suffers from an extreme case of Multi-Modal Hallucination Disorder."

"What is that?" asked Jones.

"At the risk of sounding politically incorrect; he's nuts."

Whelan drew upon his pharmacological education to offer an explanation. "MMH, if I recall, is often linked to Parkinson's disease. It can also be brought on by other disorders—for instance, schizophrenia or schizoaffective disorder."

"Bingo! Throw in derealization disorder, dissociative identity disorder, *and* he's bipolar to boot! He's basically been labeled everything the medical manuals could sort out and all the crap the journals are making up. You'd have to read through ten reams of documents to have an inkling of what Running Bear is dealing with." Sue Fielding sank deeper into her seat cushion and hung her head. "What we've all been dealing with."

She started crying. Tears fell as fast as her red eyes could produce them. And through it all, she stayed silent, not muffled but exhausted.

When she raised her head again, she said, "I need a refill. Anyone?"

"No, thank you," said Whelan.

Attorney Sam Goldstein stood to leave. "This entire package is for you. Once you've poured through it all, call me, and let me know if there's anything else you need to help."

"We need Running Bear's address, his doctors, et cetera," said Jones.

"It's all in there. Sue, you can walk me out on your way to the bar."

He held out his elbow, and she took his arm. "Hold on, Sam. Agents, I haven't told Running Bear his mother's been killed. I know you have to go speak with him. Running Bear lives in a different world than we do. I'll let the doctor explain it to you, but I don't think he's going to handle this well. I mean, worse than normal people would handle this kind of news. Much worse. Please go easy on him."

"Of course," said Jones.

"I'll phone ahead and warn the nursing staff and his primary doctor. It kills me I can't be there when you speak with him. If I could, I'd fly out with you, but I've got my hands full here."

"With what?" asked Whelan.

"Sophie wasn't my only grandchild. I had three daughters, four grandchildren, and seven great-grandchildren. The bulk of them live here in the L.A. area. I'm watching three of them now while their father's out job hunting. He can't afford a sitter."

"Why not hire one?" asked Whelan. "You can certainly afford one now."

Sue Fielding reflected a moment. "Why, yes, I suppose I can. I haven't processed all this yet. Maybe I can make arrangements and get out to Parkmoor in a couple of days."

"Parkmoor?" asked Whelan.

"It's the name of the house in Kansas City. Wealthy folks love to name their houses. Actually, I think Running Bear named that one."

Jones was curious. "With all the money Sophia made, she didn't want to help out her family?"

"No." Ms. Fielding pulled her arm away from Mr. Goldstein and took a couple steps closer to the agents.

She lowered her voice to a whisper, out of habit. "She never liked her aunts and uncles, or her cousins, except Gracie and her daddy. None of the others could help her early on when she needed it. She took it personally, though it was only a matter of circumstance. We were all poor growing up. You didn't need much to get by in the Midwest."

"Then why did they come out to Los Angeles?"

"I suppose they hoped Sophie would change her mind. But she never gave them a dime. She gave *me* a generous stipend, and I live comfortably. Haven't needed my own home for years. One of my 'assistant' duties is managing her five homes, hiring maids, cleaners, lawn care, et cetera. I would coordinate with Sarah Williams when it came to planning work-related events in the home—social parties, that sort of thing. Any-hoo, I've got a bedroom in each one and try to get to them all at least once a month to make sure they are being maintained to her expectations."

"So, no free rides for you. Sounds like you really earn your keep."

"Oh yes. I work my ass off. Did." She took a breath and a long exhale. "I suppose I'll be retiring soon enough now. Have to wrap up her personal affairs first, hire realtors to sell the other homes… Lord, maybe *not* soon enough."

"We tried to find Sophia Perkins listed in the property appraiser's office; there weren't any homes under her name in Kansas City."

"Of course not. They're under a trust. Parkmoor Properties, LLC. Can you imagine the paparazzi fest outside her door every week if they knew she owned a home there?"

"I can," said Whelan. "Her cousin, Grace Meyer, why did she get twenty million?"

"Sophie and Gracie lived together from 2006 to about 2011."

"In Kansas City?"

"Yes. Gracie helped take care of Running Bear. They all shared a small home. The girls worked jobs opposite each other, so one would always be home with him. I tried to give them a vacation once or twice a year from it. We all got on. Gracie was amazing."

"Ms. Fielding," asked Jones, "who benefits *now* from taking care of Running Bear?"

"Benefits?"

"You're the executor of his estate if he dies. Who becomes his conservator now, in Sophia's place? While he's alive? Who gets to play with his millions?"

"Billions," chimed in Whelan.

Sue Fielding looked at Mr. Goldstein. "Sam?"

"Still you, Sue. You're listed as the trustee and conservator in the event of Sophia's death. Legally, realistically, you're able to spend the six-hundred and seventy-two million however you want, immediately. It would take some time, but you could arrange for a sale of the stocks as well, cash out with over eight billion total. It's all Running Bear's money, but you control it. You get to choose how it's spent, without restriction."

Jones cocked her head toward the attorney. "And when Ms. Fielding dies?"

Sue's mouth fell open.

"It resorts to Grace Meyer. If she'll accept the role," said Mr. Goldstein.

"I doubt she'd decline," said Whelan. "But let's assume she does, or she was to die. Who's next?"

"There is no next. That's as far planned out as Sophia went."

"So then, what?"

"Then, the family would likely start fighting over it. Assuming neither Sue nor Grace made any changes before their death."

"I'm not a ghost yet," said Ms. Fielding. "Sam, we need to make some calls and start drawing up some new papers, it sounds like."

"Think about the line of succession you'd like, and get back to me," he answered. "I can have an entirely new estate plan drawn up and ready by the end of the week."

"We'll need names and numbers for those aunts and all those cousins," said Jones.

"In your package," said Goldstein.

"Please see yourselves out, agents," said Ms. Fielding. "I expect I'm going to be on the phone the rest of the evening." She disappeared inside the home with Mr. Goldstein.

When they were out of earshot, Whelan sighed. "You're the fangirl on this one. What do you want to do? Stay here and start interviewing stockholders and cousins in the morning, or fly back to K.C. and speak with Running Bear?"

"I think we can catch the last flight out. I want to talk with the kid. And something is needling me at the back of my head; Sophia's dad, Merrill Perkins. I don't care how estranged they were. You don't specifically leave someone a single dollar from your billions unless they hurt you badly. Maybe he set out to hurt her again."

MURDER AT PARKMOOR

Chapter 3

"The kid" was now twenty-seven years old. His home in Mission Hills, Kansas—one of the many suburbs of Kansas City—was what you'd expect from a billionaire. A restored mansion from the 1930s on two acres. It was a blend of rock and marble, with stunning architectural features everywhere. A swimming pool, private tennis court, and award-winning flower garden adorned the backyard. Several fountains were scattered about the grounds, the largest of which bubbled over twelve feet high near the bottom of the backyard hill beside the pool area.

"It looks like a castle," said Whelan as they parked in the large circular driveway at 8:00 a.m. Monday morning.

A young woman answered the door and asked them to wait in the foyer while she retrieved the nurse.

A marbled grand staircase twenty feet to the right wound its way up to the second floor. There was a spacious landing area halfway up before the stairs turned to the left ninety degrees and continued. A sizable tapestry adorned the wall space on the landing. Whelan guessed it was several hundred years old and contained images of knights riding off to battle.

He took to it straight away. "Impressive piece. I wonder if she's a collector?"

Jones was on a whole other line of thought. "You think Sophia greeted her party guests from up there? Waving like Evita? Toasting her guests with champagne?"

"I can't tell if you're jealous of her or…envious," said Whelan, giving her a wink.

"I would have loved to have been a fly on the wall at some of those gatherings."

"Screw that," said Whelan. "I want to be a full-blown invitee. Caviar privileges. Goodie bags. Swapping stock trades over hundred-year-old Scotch."

"Can you picture the goodie bags from Forever Sophia? The highest-end bottles of everything from her collections!" She sounded like she was fifteen instead of thirty-eight.

Whelan shook his head. This was a side to Miranda Jones he hadn't tapped yet. Their partnership was not even three months old. The attraction he felt for her early on had blossomed into a tight friendship, especially in light of Miranda's re-devotion to her relationship with Derrick Domino. They were dating for nearly three years, and things were getting back on track in an upward direction with their recent engagement.

"I'd be happy to pass on my goodie bag to you," he said.

"Perfect. I wouldn't want you to cover up those pretty freckles of yours anyway."

Whelan viewed his reflection in a large mirror nearby and studied his face. He couldn't do much about all those freckles but he flattened out his unruly reddish hair with a lick on his palm and gave a sigh. At least he'd put on some much-needed weight in the past month and was once again nearing a picture of health.

They were greeted shortly by a woman in her forties. She was clearly frazzled. Her hair was bound loosely behind her, and she wore a huge coffee stain on the front of her blouse. "I'm sorry to keep you waiting. I'm Linda O'Brien, Running Bear's nurse and the property manager." She held out her hand.

"Special Agents Miranda Jones and Thomas Whelan," said Jones, extending her hand. "Nurse and property manager? That seems like a strange combination."

"Yes. I live here full time and sort of run the estate in Sophia's and Sue's absence. The three of us who live here permanently take on whatever role we need to, really. We look out for Running Bear as our primary duty and keep the house up as best we can."

"How long have you worked for Sophia Perkins?" asked Whelan.

"Dear Lord. I actually fainted when I got the call! I can't believe she's gone!" Nurse O'Brien said between breaths. "She was an angel. An amazing, beautiful angel!" She wobbled like she might collapse.

"Ms. O'Brien, can we sit somewhere?" asked Whelan.

"Yes, follow me. I have a table set up on the terrace."

It afforded a marvelous view of the backyard, an acre of park-like, well-manicured landscaping woven down the hill. More fountains and the swimming pool were flowing clear waters into blue basins.

"This is lovely," said Jones, taking it all in.

Whelan was taking in the patio table with breakfast spread out like they were royalty. "This for us?"

"Yes. Please, sit. Help yourselves. We tend to run a little late around here. Breakfast is usually at this time, so I put out extra."

"Are ten more people joining us?"

There were platters with waffles, poached eggs over grits, and crispy bacon. A crystal bowl held a colorful fruit salad, and a huge basket containing an assortment of Danishes sat beside a pitcher of fresh orange juice and a pot of coffee. Place settings were beautiful bone-white china with pastel blue accents.

Whelan's mouth watered.

Nurse O'Brien flushed with embarrassment. "No. We don't eat like this *every* day. I just told the chef to put out a spread for six. He tends to go overboard when visitors are coming. Chad and Sylvia, the groundskeeper and housekeeper, usually join us for breakfast. They may or may not stop by with you sitting here. Chef Louie usually eats at the breakfast table in the kitchen. He's not big on conversation and prefers to watch the morning news. He's the only one who doesn't live on the property. He has a family; a wife and two boys. He comes five to six days a week. He's a gifted chef who could run a Michelin-starred restaurant if he wanted. But Sophia wanted him more, and money talks."

"We'll need to interview all of them while we're here."

"Of course."

"Oh, I hope you haven't eaten already?" asked Nurse O'Brien.

"Not like this. Should we wait for the others?"

"No, especially not Bear. He'll be down at 8:30. Please, let's *not* wait on him. I need to explain everything before he gets here."

"Bear?" asked Jones.

"His nickname. Sorry. I don't usually use it around strangers. Of course, there aren't too many people who know she has a son. Had." She broke into tears again and dotted her eyes with a napkin. "Forgive me. I'm a wreck. To answer your earlier question, I've lived here and have been his primary caregiver for nine years. Sophie went through a handful before me. Bear and I clicked, and she offered a generous salary. I have a lovely room adjacent to his. I'm part of the family now."

Whelan studied her. *Let's see if you still feel like family when you find out you've been omitted from the will.*

He began to fill his plate as Nurse O'Brien continued. "First, I haven't told him yet. I wanted Doctor Brachman to be here when I do. He's not returned my calls. Usually, he's prompt."

"So Running Bear doesn't know his mother's been murdered?" asked Jones.

"No! And I'm not sure we want to say 'murdered.' I defer to the doctor on critical news like this. I don't know if Bear would process the gravity of murder. He'd say he does. He learned a long time ago to say he understands everything you tell him. He doesn't like being patronized or spoken to like a child. He's actually brilliant. But *our* understanding, and *his* understanding, they don't always line up like you'd think."

"I read some articles online about Multi-modal hallucinations and their relativity to schizophrenia. But, please fill us in on exactly what it is Running Bear suffers from."

Nurse O'Brien took a sip of coffee and leaned back in her chair. The plush cushion nearly enveloped her head.

"Actually," interjected Whelan, "spell out the full history, if you can. We didn't get a clear picture from Sue Fielding. She said the doctor would fill us in."

"Well, I'll do my best in his absence. I came onboard when Running Bear turned eighteen. He'd been through eight doctors the decade before and given twice as many diagnoses. He went from acute psychosis to schizophrenia and schizoaffective disorder. Not extremely rare, but the severity with which he languishes is off the charts, literally, and from such a young age.

"Sophia figured out some of them, his earlier doctors, were waving their standard fees not out of compassion for them—remember, she was still dirt poor back then—but so they could use him as a means to write an article for some damned science journal. He's been written about at least a dozen times. Sophie always insisted they use a false name. Bear's mood swings became worse in his twenties, so they tacked on Bipolar disorder. Six more doctors over the following decade tried every combination of drug known to help: Chlorpromazine, Cyamemazine, Stelazine, all the phenothiazines. Haloperidol, of course. Risperidone. Quetiapine, sometimes."

Jones interrupted, "We'll need a list of all he's on and been on, if available. I can't keep up with you."

"Of course. I keep excellent records. I'll make you a copy. You see, different people's chemistry reacts in varied, sometimes dramatic ways for these disorders. There are numerous drugs, many of them outstanding, but they don't all work the same on each individual. Some make you drowsy. Some practically put you in a coma. Some are pleasant. Some have severe side effects. And Sophia…"

She took a breath before sputtering through. "Ms. Perkins went through hellacious turmoil when she had limited means and saw the toll excessive drug use took on Running Bear. When she could afford a staff to oversee him, she didn't really want him on anything but the bare minimums. If anything at all."

"You mean he's not on any meds now?" asked Whelan.

She was hesitant. "No."

"Since when? For how long?"

"About a year, maybe longer. Sophia encouraged us to 'let him have his fun' when we felt we could handle it. And we have been. Handling it."

"Fun?" questioned Jones. "Is he having that much fun?"

"You'd be surprised. He's been in a terrific place for quite a while. Anyway, we monitor him closely due to the added Bipolar disorder. We usually adjust meds depending on whether or not he's coming off a high or fighting off a low. It depends on the severity. But again, he's not really needed any lately."

“Where’s he at now,” asked Whelan.

“He’s entering a high.”

“Super,” said Jones. “If he’s entering a high, won’t it be easier to process his mother’s death?”

“Somewhat. His highs are pretty delightful, but he’s unique. He usually doesn’t go full-blown manic, but if he gets wired, getting upsetting news of this magnitude can have drastic reactions. As a rule, people who are bipolar enter their cycles slowly—days or weeks, and it can last for weeks or months. Bear can flip from joyful to furious or despondent in minutes, sometimes seconds. It takes a while for extreme, lasting depression to take over, but he can switch instantly between elation, distress and exasperation. It’s all pretty well managed currently, but you have to be prepared.”

Nurse O’Brien started crying again. “I’m sorry. Damn it. Where’s Doctor Brachman? I’m going to try him again. Excuse me.” She marched inside the home.

“Did you get all that? All those drugs?” asked Jones to her partner.

“Yes. Sounds typical. Well, the Quetiapine’s not so much, but all the phenothiazines are standard. I’m more concerned by the lack of drugs he’s on now. Apparently, he’s not on *anything* at the moment.”

“She seems distressed. Do you think it’s genuine, or is she putting on a show?”

“Can’t tell yet.”

Whelan finished his eggs and took a bite of waffle, doused with real maple syrup and fresh blueberries. “Oh my God. I need to win the lottery. I could get used to this. I think there’s a touch of bourbon in the waffle batter.”

Jones tasted hers. “Vanilla. Really superior vanilla, maybe from Mexico. I used to get the best when I was in San Diego. We’d cross into Tijuana for a weekend of partying, and there was this amazing market. I put it in all my baked recipes.”

“You bake?” Whelan was surprised.

“I make amazing oatmeal cookies. I’ll bring you a batch soon.”

Whelan shook his head. "Who would have guessed?"

He glimpsed a man staring at them from behind a large planter thirty feet away. He was crouching and eavesdropping.

"Hello?" shouted Whelan. "Please, join us."

Jones turned to get a look at him behind her. "Are you the groundskeeper?"

"No. I'm not Chad," he said. "I don't know you! Who are you? You can't be here right now. We're all in peril. The Queen is dead! Please leave!"

Nurse O'Brien came tearing out of the house, stopping at the table. She muttered sharply under her breath. "And let the games begin."

She planted her hand deliberately on Whelan's shoulder and yelled out to the man. "It's okay. This knight is from a neighboring kingdom. They're here to pay homage. This is Sir Thomas Whelan, and he's escorting Lady Miranda Jones from the…Federal Bureau of Investigation."

O'Brien curtsied before Jones. "Honored guests, this is Prince Running Bear."

Chapter 4

Agent Miranda Jones stood, shooting her partner a pleading expression. She turned to Running Bear and gave her own curtsy. Whelan stood and gave a bow.

"Please, join us," he said again.

"The Queen is dead! The Queen is dead! She was assassinated! How can you sit there and eat eggs when the kingdom's walls have been breached? The Queen is dead!"

"Shit," said Nurse O'Brien. "He knows. The Queen was his mother, Sophia."

"Running Bear, come eat." Nurse O'Brien's tone was forceful. "You didn't come down all day yesterday and didn't eat any dinner last night. You need nourishment. How can you tackle the coming battle without sustenance? These worthy loyalists are here to help find out who killed the Queen and restore your family's honor."

Slowly, the young man walked toward them. He was dressed in designer jeans, a purple polo shirt, and brown leather Skechers. His hair was about five inches long all over and curled somewhat but was cut and styled by a professional.

When he drew near, he bowed to the agents, extending his hand. "It's a pleasure. Welcome to Parkmoor. Thank you for your assistance, virtuous neighbors."

He looked at O'Brien. "Nurse Linda, please entertain our guests. I'm not up for company today." He resumed his walk toward the patio doors.

"The hell you're not!" she snapped. "You'll sit and eat and cooperate with their investigation of the Queen's death." Nurse O'Brien was overcome with emotion. She let loose some tears.

This triggered Running Bear, and he ran into her arms and began weeping like a five-year-old. Weeping became wailing. It went on for several minutes. Eventually, he was tapped and took a seat at the table. He grabbed a waffle and started eating it with his hands.

"Manners," she admonished softly.

He threw it on the plate and began dicing it up with his utensils.

"Okay, agents, let's get on with it quickly now while he's here."

Agents Whelan and Jones were totally lost on where to start.

"Your excellency," began Whelan. "My deepest condolences on the loss of your queen. Please, tell me how you came to know of her demise."

Jones gave Whelan a couple quick nods of approval. It seemed like the proper direction.

"I saw her run through three times by the dragon rider."

"You saw her killed? Where? Who was it?"

"Down by the river. They met at midnight. A secret rendezvous. They argued. He drew his sword. She was defenseless. Only a coward would cut down an unarmed woman. And the Queen! He killed the Queen!" Running Bear's calm wasn't holding. "He killed Queen Sophie!"

He stood up, pounding his fist on the table.

"Running Bear! Who? Who's the dragon rider?" asked Whelan.

"I don't know him. But he rides a red dragon! My Queen was executed by the red dragon rider!"

The man started crying again and raced inside the home.

"Will he leave the house?" asked Whelan to Nurse O'Brien.

"I don't think so. He usually hides in his room when he becomes distressed."

They sat back and reflected on the past few minutes.

"What the hell was all that?" asked Jones.

"*That* was Running Bear. And now you understand."

"Sorry, no, I don't. Everything I've read the past eighteen hours says schizophrenics manage quite well and comprehend reality for the most part, with a little extra thrown in. He's living in a whole other world!"

"It's managed with *meds*. Again, he's not on any right now. And you're wrong about living in another world," corrected Nurse O'Brien, "he's living in this one. But with a completely different perception. If he says he saw the Queen murdered, he saw it. Oh, Lord. He *saw* his mother murdered! Can you *believe* it?"

"I'm not sure." Jones was finding it difficult to respond as her mind sorted through everything.

"Well, what if you saw your own mother murdered? How would it affect you?" asked O'Brien.

Miranda thought of her mother and the last fight she had with her. *Was it by my hands or someone else's?* she wondered. "I'd be upset, of course," she answered.

"Ms. O'Brien," said Whelan, "can you please back up a notch and explain exactly what Running Bear's perception of the world *is*? If we can understand better, perhaps we can interpret what it was he really saw."

She nodded. "I'll translate where I can, but sometimes, even I can't make sense, and after taking care of him for nine years."

Nurse O'Brien took a seat again and clutched her coffee cup. The agents filled theirs and sat quietly, eyes open wide and locked on the distraught woman.

"Running Bear," she began, "loved stories when he was a child, about King Arthur and Merlin and Camelot. Sophia and Sue, his great-grandmother, well, they fed into the make-believe, as you would any child. He played with a lot of imaginary friends. Sophia played the Queen. His grandmother was the court jester. They watched many fantasy movies and read fairy tales. When he was eight, they let him watch *The Lord of the Rings* and its sequels. You know, there's a reason movies have ratings. Can you imagine being subjected to such violence at eight years old? Well, he became obsessed with them. Started devouring similar movies he could find; anything with swords, knights and dragons. They had no idea they were reinforcing the foundation that would become his real world as he grew. In *his* mind."

"They must have felt responsible," said Whelan.

"Oh yes, the weight they carried! Sophia told me once it was her biggest regret. When it became evident Bear experienced a real problem discerning reality from fantasy, they cut him off from all of it; cold turkey. But it was too late. He could no longer pull himself away mentally. Men became knights or soldiers. Women were princesses or peasants. Roads aren't asphalt; they're cobblestone or dirt. Cars are horses. Airplanes are dragons. Mansions are castles. When he sees you, his brain sublimates your clothes, and you become a peasant or, if reinforced, royalty. That's why I introduced you as a knight and a Lady. If not, his mind might downgrade you, and then he wouldn't cooperate with you. At least now, he'll respect your status and hopefully be some help."

O'Brien stared at her glass of orange juice. "And he likes magic, wizards and what-not. This OJ could be a magic potion or a glass full of poison. If Merlin or Gandalf could be involved, it gets critical attention. If it hadn't been kings and castles and magicians, it would have developed into something else. It could have been superheroes, secret agents, cowboys and Indians, anything a young child fixates on. Magic and swords are what took."

Whelan was catching up. "Then let's start translating. His mother was down by the river?"

"Brush Creek. It's shallow here, sometimes even dry. It runs along the edge of the neighborhood at the bottom of the hill. I can't fathom who Sophia would have been meeting so late at night down there."

"He said midnight. How accurate is his perception of time?"

"Pretty normal. I'm sure it was around midnight."

"Was Sophia dating anyone?" asked Jones.

"Not lately. She wasn't big on dating anyone for long. I think she always suspected no one could love her for anything other than her money. The couple of men she became somewhat serious with recently lasted less than a year. She blamed it on them. Used Running Bear's condition as an excuse. Said they couldn't handle it. One of them was a doctor. He understood perfectly and didn't let it bother him. She chased him away because, of course, he was after her millions, in *her* head. She wasn't the sort who wanted to settle down. A bit self-destructive."

"We'll need their names and contact info."

"I'll try, but the last was two years back. It's not like anyone keeps a Rolodex anymore. If it's not in her phone's address book, I can't make any promises. I can tell you, at the risking of insulting the dead…."

Nurse O'Brien cut herself off. She crossed herself as Catholics do and raised her eyes to the ceiling. "Lord forgive me."

She refocused on the agents. "She didn't have to be dating someone long before taking them to her bedroom."

"Like, a few days? A few hours?" asked Jones.

"Sometimes. I commented on it to her once. I was urging her to be careful, mind you, not judging her decisions. She explained her schedule simply didn't allow for developing a relationship, and she was a woman in her prime after all."

"Well, I think Running Bear's story plays out. She likely did have a midnight rendezvous. We know the time of death corresponds pretty well. And the sword."

Nurse O'Brien's face went white. "You mean she was really run through with a sword?"

"Three times."

"Oh my God!"

O'Brien stood and ran back inside. The agents were on her heels. She ran down the gallery to the second staircase of marble stone leading to the bedrooms in the south wing. She took two steps at a time up a flight of stairs to a middle landing area between floors. An enormous glass case hung on the wall, showcasing a collection of over one hundred swords. Some were replicas, but quite a number were authentic pieces of history. Ten years of collecting with all the money needed to buy whatever Running Bear asked for. Some were tarnished and weathered, some brand new and never used. There were broad swords, short swords, long swords and claymores. It was a monumental representation of European and Asian craftsmanship from the 14th through 20th centuries.

"You've got to be kidding me," said Jones.

"Are any of them missing?" asked Whelan.

Nurse O'Brien was frantic. "I don't know! I'm looking! I don't see any holes where the hanging hooks are. They're all there, I think. There are so many! Oh, God."

"What?" asked Whelan.

O'Brien put one hand up to her mouth, and the other hand pointed toward the bottom left of the display. There wasn't a gap, but one sword was stained red from the tip to halfway up the blade. More noticeable were the drops of blood collected on the glass bottom frame of the case.

Chapter 5

Whelan studied the sword, then turned to his partner. "You're usually prepared. Got a baggie in your pocket big enough for this?" he jested.

Nurse O'Brien mumbled through her hand. "I can get a trash bag out of the pantry."

"No, I'm sorry, Ms. O'Brien, I actually need to call in a team to do this properly. Dust for prints, collect samples—in fact, we all need to leave the area before we contaminate it further."

"We need to start interviewing the staff too," said Jones. "Going to need hair and fingerprints from all of you. This turned into a long day. I should have finished my grapefruit."

"And I don't care how upset Running Bear is. I need more answers from him, now." Whelan pointed upstairs. "This way?"

"Yes. I'll show you."

Jones held back and started dialing on her phone. "I'll catch up."

Before knocking on a door on the second level, Nurse O'Brien turned to Whelan. "Does he need a lawyer present?"

"I don't know. What made you ask?"

O'Brien shook her head and released a couple more tears. "He *sees* people. *Imaginary* people. All day long."

"And?"

"And, all *night* long."

"Ahh. You think the man he saw strike down Sophia might have been in his mind?"

"It's possible."

Whelan rolled her thought around in his head. "You think *Running Bear* killed her?"

"No. I'm saying…it's possible. Now, does he need an attorney present before you question him further?"

"Only if he's guilty. Is there anything you're aware of that would make him want his mother dead?"

"Of course not. But, in the absence of Sue Fielding's physical presence, I hold power of attorney for him. I'm asking, officially, for his legal attorney to be present before you go any further."

Whelan turned and faced Nurse Linda O'Brien full on. "I respect that. I just need to see a copy of your POA. You can call whoever you need to."

"Oh my gosh! It was drawn up years ago. I'll have to find it. Could be anywhere."

"Weren't you boasting a few minutes ago about keeping excellent records?"

Nurse O'Brien's demeanor stiffened. "I'll find it! Give me a few minutes. Go help your partner interview the staff. I need to check on him. I'll come find you, *with* your copy."

Whelan walked downstairs as the woman opened the door to Running Bear's room and disappeared inside.

He approached Agent Jones out on the terrace.

"Sneaking in the rest of your breakfast?" he asked.

She smiled. "Maybe a bite. What happened with Running Bear? You weren't gone two minutes."

"Nothing. Nurse O'Brien 'attorney blocked' me. She wants his lawyer present for any further questioning."

"Wise. When I saw that sword, my gut said Running Bear killed his mother."

"Why?"

"I don't know. I think I thought his screaming about the Queen being dead was a little staged."

Whelan recalled the famous Shakespeare quote he learned in high school. "'All the world's a stage, and all the men and women merely players; they have their exits and their entrances, and one man in his time, plays many parts, his acts being seven ages.'"

"I recognize that," said Jones. "It's from *As You Like It*."

"I think Running Bear is forever stuck in the second age; the whining schoolboy. His condition will likely never allow him to advance to lover."

"Let's hope he didn't jump over that and straight to soldier. You don't collect a hundred swords without pulling one out once in a while and playing with it, or worse."

Whelan reflected a minute before taking a swig of his cold coffee. "Running Bear's stage has been a world so apart from the rest of us, he might as well be in his own play."

"And proliferated by all a billionaire could encourage him with. He never stood a chance to come back to reality."

"You think Sophia wanted him to stay in perpetual bliss?"

"As opposed to facing what a shit-hole this world can be? Wouldn't you, for *your* child?"

"I really don't know. I think I'd want him to find happiness while understanding the truths of this world." Whelan thought of his son, Connor. He was everything to him. *Would I buy him a castle if I could? Maybe.*

"So," said Jones, "she loved him. He loved her. She gave him all he wanted. There's no motive for him to kill her."

"Not financially. He wouldn't understand the value of money in the real world. But there are other motives. Real *and* imaginary."

A man approached them from the garden. He was in his early 60s, fit and tanned under his denim shirt and jeans. He held out his hand. "I'm Chad Buckley, groundskeeper, gardener, and all-around handyman. Sylvia said you wanted to see me?"

"Sylvia?" asked Jones.

"Sylvia Moffett, the housekeeper, maid and all-around handy-woman." He smiled. "Nurse O'Brien told her, I guess. How can I help you?"

"We've got to start somewhere. Please, Mr. Buckley, have a seat. We have some questions. Have you eaten?"

By 3:00 p.m., all the staff were questioned. Nurse O'Brien brought Running Bear to the library, where the agents were waiting at a table, reading through a copy of her power of attorney for Sophia's son. Another family attorney was in tow, Adam Steiner, who took care of all affairs regarding the Kansas City estate. Along with him, was a defense attorney he recommended, Edward Toussaint. They all sat on one side of the table, with the agents across from them.

Whelan was the first to start. "We're doing this here instead of the FBI's field office out of respect to Mr. Perkins. We expect full cooperation in return. We have grounds for an arrest at this time, based on evidence, but we're hoping Running Bear will be more comfortable in his own home and can shed better light on what he saw."

FBI agent and Pathologist Joe Cusack and his Evidence Response Team Unit finished their work, and the sword was sent to the lab for immediate testing. He now joined Agents Whelan and Jones at the table.

"So," said Cusack, "the blood on the sword *is* Sophia Perkins'. The sword's hilt has been scrubbed clean, but we did pull a print off the blade. It matched Running Bear's. Hairs recovered in the area matched Running Bear, Nurse O'Brien, and the housekeeper, Sylvia Moffet. The prints pulled off the glass cabinet were Running Bear's alone."

Running Bear kept his mouth closed through all this. He focused on his lap and fidgeted with his cuticles.

Mr. Toussaint spoke up. "Running Bear didn't do this. We all know it. Ms. Perkins was found in an alley downtown. A*nyone* in the city could have done this."

"An alley downtown?" asked Running Bear.

"Yes. Sorry. We explained all this to you earlier."

Nurse O'Brien offered translation. "Another kingdom Bear. She was in between some buildings."

"They dump their chamber pots into alleys," said Running Bear. "Was she covered in piss and shit?"

The question caught everyone off guard.

"No, Bear. She wasn't."

The nurse was already losing her nerve, and they had just begun.

"Ask your questions," said the lawyer to the opposition on the other side of the table.

Jones gave a nod to her partner, encouraging him to take the lead.

Whelan tilted his head and studied Running Bear before asking, "Who's the red dragon rider? Have you ever seen him before?"

"Yes. I don't know his name."

"Where did you see him before?"

"In the house. About a week ago. He was kissing the Queen's neck from behind, in the kitchen. By the icebox. They were dressed in bathrobes and making sandwiches."

Whelan glanced at Cusack. "Kitchen."

"I'm on it," said Joe, leaving the room.

"They made sandwiches," Whelan resumed, "and then what?"

"They ate them."

Whelan prodded. "And then? Tell your story."

"And then," said Running Bear, "they went upstairs to the Queen's chamber and shut the door behind them. I listened at the door a minute, but they were quiet. I heard the Queen giggle. I felt she wasn't in danger if she was laughing, so I adjourned to my room."

"What makes you sure he's a dragon rider?"

"He was wearing a red dragon rider's outfit."

"Had you ever seen him before a week ago?"

"No."

Edward Toussaint interrupted. "This is getting us nowhere. Obviously, he's not capable of discerning *what* he really saw."

Running Bear shot the lawyer a look from underneath squinched eyebrows.

"I think he's capable of tremendous things," said Whelan.

Jones was observing Running Bear closely. She intervened. "Forgive me, but I'm curious. Running Bear, would you please tell us everyone you see currently in this room. Be honest, please."

This time Running Bear's eyes opened wide and darted toward Nurse O'Brien.

"It's okay, Bear," she said.

He stood up and walked around the table once, nervously shaking. "I see Sir Toussaint and Sir Steiner. I see Nurse Linda."

He shifted his gaze to the Agents. "I see Sir Whelan and Lady Jones."

"And?" pushed Jones.

Running Bear opened his mouth, hesitating. His gaze was locked on the opposite wall now. No one was there. He shut his eyes, squeezing out a tear which plummeted to the floor. "I see Cantor...and Marjorie." He bowed his chin.

Jones' turned her head back and forth from Running Bear to the far wall a couple of times. "Anyone else?"

Running Bear wiped his nose and scanned the room again. "No."

"Who are Cantor and Marjorie?"

He stayed silent.

Nurse O'Brien spoke on his behalf. "They've been with him a long time. He's known Cantor since he was about eight. Marjorie came along in 2015."

"So..." Jones's wheels were turning, "Cantor is his best friend and Marjorie...?"

"Marjorie is Bear's wife."

Chapter 6

Jones gawked at Running Bear. “How does *that* work?”

He stayed silent, his eyes fixed on the back wall.

Whelan mumbled to his partner, “I take it back. He *did* have his ‘lover’ age.”

“It works,” said Nurse O’Brien, “because we all allow it to. There’s never really a need for interruption in his life.”

“Forgive our interruption now, Running Bear,” said Whelan. “You seemed saddened by having to reveal your friends to us. Clearly, it upset you. Why?”

Running Bear opened his mouth to respond, then dashed out of the room.

Jones actually turned to see if Cantor and Marjorie were following him. “Wow. I’ve been delivered my first taste of how you all can lose yourselves in this setting. It’s tragic; beautifully tragic. But none of this, unfortunately, rules out Running Bear as the likely murderer. Mr. Toussaint, unless you can produce a real dragon rider in the next two minutes, we have no choice but to arrest him.”

“That will kill him!” said O’Brien.

“Will it?” asked Whelan. “I mean, seriously? When was the last time he was given the proper medications he should have and put back into reality? I think maybe it will shock him into remembering the truth.”

“It will shock him into complete withdrawal from the rest of the world! He’ll run hide anywhere his subconscious can create, and you’ll get nowhere. Your best shot at answers is to leave him here and let me work with him.”

The lawyers stayed silent, as did the agents. Everyone mulled over the best course of action.

“Why was Running Bear upset at having to reveal Marjorie and Cantor?” asked Whelan again, this time to Nurse O’Brien.

She drew a slow, long breath and held it before speaking. "He's heard people say a million times through the years, 'they're not real.' A part of him acknowledges they aren't supposed to be real. Yet they are to him. The past couple of years, Sophia was traveling every week and seeing him less and less. She wanted him to have the extra company of people he could trust. Even if they were make-believe."

"A *wife*?" asked Jones. She couldn't get her head around it. "Does he…" She let her thought trail off, possessing enough tact not to express her question.

O'Brien read her face. "Let's just say Sylvia has to change his sheets often."

Whelan mulled over her comment. "Sure going to make conjugals easier."

The nurse erupted in a hysterical laugh. "Forgive me, it's been a hell of a day. Agent Whelan, please tell me it's not going to come down to that. I mean it, you put him behind bars, he'll regress so far we won't get a thing out of him; ever. Until you're sure, beyond all doubt, please wait."

"We're still investigating. This is forty hours old now, and we do have other people to speak with."

Whelan addressed Mr. Toussaint. "I'll agree not to hold him in lockup for now and arrange for a house arrest. We do need him to cooperate. Something tells me we're far from finished questioning him."

"Then I've got some calls to make to clear my day," said Toussaint. "I'll be out back." He jerked his portly body out of the seat.

"If you need me, I'll be at my office," said Attorney Adam Steiner. "I can be back here in twenty minutes."

Nurse Linda O'Brien escorted them both out of the room.

Jones watched her partner's wheels turn, playing across his face. "What? What's going through your head?" she asked.

"Why a *red* dragon? Why not a blue one? Or gold?"

"I don't know. He sees airplanes as dragons. Maybe he likes to go to the airport and see them take off and land? If he really saw a dragon rider kill his mother, what would that be? A pilot? What airlines have red on their planes?"

"Southwest, of course, they also have blue and yellow. Emirates, Air Canada, Japan, Air Asia, Air India…Qantas…" he struggled to think of any others.

Jones was already googling airlines. "Son of a bitch. There's an airline called Cathay Dragon. It used to be Dragonair. Their logo's red."

She held the phone up to Whelan for a flash before pulling it back and starting another search. "It's a Hong Kong regional airline. Unless he's been to China in the past few weeks, I doubt it's them."

"No, O'Brien assured me earlier he's hasn't been out of K.C. for over two years. I don't think Running Bear researches airlines to know what planes might have some red on them. And from on the ground, you can't really tell. Maybe the man he saw was dressed in red? But then, pilots are usually in blue or black."

"Who else wears red?"

"In Kansas City? Are you kidding me? The NFL preseason kicked off two weeks ago. I've seen people in red multiply tenfold this month. Maybe it was a Kansas City Chief. You think Forever Sophia was dating a tight end?"

He was joking, but the thought stuck in Jones' head as she realized it could be possible. "Could be, money tends to date money. With a helmet on and those shoulder pads, I might see a dragon rider too."

"We need more definitive answers. At the moment, we can't even be sure there really *was* someone else. But let's give the guy the benefit of the doubt while talking with his family and the remaining shareholders. Anyone who might have possible influence over Running Bear is suspect right now. I'm going to check in with the office and see how many alibis the other agents on this have tracked down."

"Cannon is acting as a liaison between the office, us and SAC Kendrick. Call him directly."

Agent Phil Cannon was Jones and Whelan's most trusted agent in the office. Still in his rookie year, he'd already proven himself over many veterans. The Kansas City field office recently went through a big shake-up, with several agents dismissed from the bureau. Cannon's loyalty and quick actions were invaluable.

In addition to the many personnel changes and partner reassignments, leadership was also in play at the K.C. office. Assistant Special Agent in Charge, Henry (Hank) Monroe, was recovering from a recent heart attack. It was unclear if he would return initially, but his progress was coming along, and it was generally thought he would return for what was planned to be his last year with the bureau before retirement.

Special Agent in Charge Alan Kendrick, who headed up the K.C. office, also planned to retire in four years and was grooming Special Agent Jones to take over as ASAC when Monroe left. However, nothing was in stone, and it would all need to be run up the ladder and approved by the director.

Whelan hung up from Cannon and headed to the kitchen. Cusack was wrapping up his dusting for prints. The refrigerator and all the cabinet pulls and counters were covered in powder.

The maid, housekeeper, and all-around handy-woman, Sylvia Moffet, was standing mortified in a corner, waiting impatiently with rags and a bottle of 409. She was small in stature, but her demeanor commanded a larger sense of presence. Whelan guessed she was in her early thirties. When he looked in her direction, she offered up a polite smile. Far from wearing the stereo-typical maid's uniform, Sylvia kept her hair bound back with a scarf and wore capri pants with a short-sleeved, button-down blouse, appropriate for the hot August heat. Whelan envisioned her stepping out of McCall's Magazine from the mid-1950s. She was certainly pretty enough to be a model.

"She's efficient," said Cusack to the other agents. "I can't even pull *Ms. Perkins'* prints off anything in this kitchen, and she was here two days ago. In fact, it was a challenge getting one out of her bedroom. We can't find anyone's prints in this house who doesn't live or work here."

"If she was having sex with someone a week ago, maybe we should UV her bed," said Jones.

"On it," said Cusack. "Let me get one out of the car." He raced out of the kitchen.

"I've washed her sheets," said Sylvia, approaching Whelan. "If I'd known she was going to be murdered, I'd have done a poorer job." She bit the nail of her index finger in thought. "Sometimes, Sophia—sorry, Ms. Perkins—she encouraged us all to call her Sophia here. We really are kind of a family. Sometimes Ms. Perkins had relations by the pool. Twice I witnessed her on the double-wide chaise lounge under the cabana. I went to tidy up and clear glasses, and found her…otherwise engaged."

"And you haven't cleaned that chaise in the last week?"

"Spot-cleaned, but I might have missed something. You might still be able to retrieve your sample. The cover is removed and laundered once in midsummer and again in late fall when it becomes too cold to enjoy the pool."

"Thank you, Ms. Moffet. We'll be sure to check the area."

Sylvia sighed as she scanned all the areas ready to be mopped down. "Can I start on this now?"

"Yes, you can, thanks," said Whelan.

The agents headed to Sophia's bedroom in the home. Of course, Running Bear occupied the master suite. Sophia's room was comfortable, though, with enough room for a sitting area and an on-suite bathroom. With gloved hands, they closed the curtains.

Cusack popped in shortly, shut the door and turned out the lights. With the flick of a switch, the room was immersed in UV. Nothing was glowing; no indications of any bodily fluids anywhere. They stripped the bed. A heavy mattress pad was under the sheets; nothing. On the mattress, a faint glimmer showed up.

"That's not fresh. Likely sweat over the course of years. I'll grab an AP test and make sure, but there's nothing here."

"Let one of your team run it. And have them pull the covers off the loungers by the pool and test for semen and any other DNA. But right now, I want *you* to take a trip with me. Bring a collection kit."

"Where are we going?"

"I need Running Bear to show us exactly where by the river the Queen was run through."

Chapter 7

Running Bear was calm and surprisingly cooperative. He wanted his mother's murderer revealed. He wanted vengeance for his queen.

He led the way, with Agent Cusack, Nurse O'Brien, and Attorney Edward Toussaint on his heels. Toussaint was in a suit and tie, and the mid-August heat was causing him to sweat. His belly gave a waddle to his walk, and he didn't appreciate the steep terrain. Agents Whelan and Jones stayed back a few yards so they could talk.

"Any news from Cannon?" asked Jones.

"They've alibied the family out in L.A. and all but two stockholders. Of course, if it was one of the board members, it's unlikely they'd have done it themselves. Anyone could have hired a hitman. What's $50,000 when you think you're going to get a billion dollars more worth of shares overnight?"

"If it was a hitman, then it was someone Sophia would have liked enough to risk bringing them inside her home, her *child's* home. My guess is not. If it was someone she'd been dating a while, I could see them thinking they were going to get into her pocketbook eventually, but not a one-night stand."

"Or two," said Whelan. "I'm still wondering if Running Bear made him up."

"And he made up seeing him in the kitchen the week before? Making sandwiches? Sneaking upstairs to have sex and hearing his mother laughing through the door? I believed all that."

"Uh-huh. So did he."

Running Bear led the way down the hill beyond their backyard and across another property. They walked down Mission Drive until they reached Brush Creek.

He then took them off the road, along the creek edge, and northwest about 150 yards until they were on another road dead-ending in a roundabout alongside the creek bank. On the other side of the creek was one of the fairways for the Kansas City Country Club.

Brush Creek was fortified with concrete retaining walls along this stretch to help preserve the golf course. Running Bear pointed to the edge of one of these. His eyes went in and out of focus as he gawked at the spot indicated.

"Bear," asked Nurse O'Brien, "is someone standing there?"

"No," he said, hanging his head. "Just remembering."

"Is anyone else with us right now?" asked Whelan.

"Cantor is. I asked Marjorie to wait at home. I didn't want her seeing this again."

"Anyone else? The red dragon rider, perhaps?"

Running Bear gave Whelan a puzzled frown and cocked his head. "No. He's not here. Why would he be here right now?"

"I don't know. Returning to the scene of the crime with us?"

"With *us*? That doesn't make any sense. I doubt he wants to be discovered. Killing the Queen is grounds for beheading. I'm sure he's on the run. I bet he's several kingdoms away by now."

"Running Bear," asked Jones, "what do you suppose he stood to gain by killing your mother, the Queen?"

"Gain? Nothing."

"Do you think he thought he'd take over her kingdom?"

He thought about that. "I don't see why he would. Without a queen, the kingdom falls to me. I'm king now." Once he said it aloud, Running Bear's face began processing the weight of his new role in the kingdom. Seven different expressions crossed his brow and jaw before he owned his title.

He raised his head. "I didn't want this so early in my life. There's much to learn. But I've got help. I think I'll be a magnificent king."

"Who's helping you, Bear?"

"Nurse Linda, Sylvia, Chad…the Queen's mother when she comes. They'll all guide me. I'll work hard and be an admirable leader for my people."

"Who are your people?"

"All the people in the kingdom, of course."

Cusack examined the creek bank during this exchange. "Agents, I think this is it." He was kneeling over a spot in front of the retaining wall, collecting samples. "I'm guessing this is blood. There were showers two nights ago. Perfect night to do this. It's washed away the bulk of it. No way to be sure if this was the spot she was killed based on this.

"It was," said Running Bear. His face turned whiter as he traced the trail of stains on the ground and the concrete wall.

Cusack was studying the ground around the area. "Rain has cleared away the detail in the footprints. I'd guess we have a woman's flat and a man's boot here, but the mud's filled in the tread. I'll pull it, but I don't think we'll be able to narrow it down in the database. Maybe we'll get lucky."

Jones peered at Running Bear's loafers. She couldn't rule out his foot size as a match. "Bear, we'll need to see your shoe closet, please. Would that be acceptable?"

"Of course."

His cooperation was far from an acquittal, but it helped.

Jones whispered to Nurse O'Brien, "I'll need you to let us know if any boots are missing."

"Yes, I'll try."

"Running Bear," said Whelan. "take us through it. You followed Sophia—the Queen—down the hill, and along the side of the creek in the darkness, to this spot, where she met a secret lover who you exclusively knew about, and...what? What were they talking about before he killed her?"

"I couldn't hear anything. I was too far away, hiding behind those trees. I didn't want her to know I was following them."

"Did you do that a lot?" asked Jones. "Follow your mother without her knowing? Why?"

"I don't see her often. When she comes...." He cut himself off, choking on the last word. His eyes moistened, and he cleared his throat with a cough. "When she *came*," he corrected, "I spent a lot of time with her. I wasn't in the habit of following her around secretly. It so happens, the night I saw her in the kitchen, I'd simply come down for some water. And two nights ago, I was out on the terrace, enjoying some fresh air. Marjorie feels pent up, inside, when the Queen's in town. We like to go outside if it's cool enough and relax, listen to the waterfalls around the pool. Enjoy our own private time."

Everyone was tuned in closely.

"The Queen," he continued, "came from her chamber and sat down on the far side. She was talking on her phone and didn't see us. When she hung up, she went down by the pool and out into the yard. I was simply curious. So we followed her."

"You *and* Marjorie?" asked Whelan.

"Yes. I wish now I'd made her stay. If I knew what she'd be forced to see…." He let his building tears fall, shaking his head.

"Okay," said Whelan, "you're hiding behind the tree line with Marjorie, and you see your mother come here. Was the dragon rider with her when she came or did she meet him here?"

"He was here, waiting beside his horse."

"His *horse*? Not his dragon?"

"No. He came on a horse that night."

Whelan looked at Nurse O'Brien.

"A car," she interpreted.

"Can you describe it?" asked Jones.

"It was dark; large. I couldn't see it too clearly."

"He was waiting beside his horse and?" asked Whelan.

"And she came up to him. They kissed for a couple of minutes. Then he said something she didn't like. They argued for a minute. She turned her back, and he grabbed her; spun her around. She tried to pull free, I think. But he wouldn't let go. Then he kissed her again. She turned and faced the horse, putting her hands on it. Then…she let him ravage her."

"She *let* him?" asked Jones.

"Yes, I think so. She seemed to be enjoying it. It was dark. I couldn't tell for sure. Marjorie agreed when we talked about it later. I don't believe he raped her."

"Cusack?" asked Whelan.

"No," he said. "There was no sign of rape when we examined her. Sex possibly, yes. It matches. There was no semen inside her, though, or on her clothes. If he ejaculated, he was wearing a condom. There were no other hairs on her either. No carpet fibers. He must have placed a tarp or some kind of plastic wrap in the back of his car. Premeditated certainly. He was ready for her."

Edward Toussaint came alive. "You see! Running Bear couldn't have killed her! He doesn't drive. How in the world would he have gotten her all the way downtown?"

"Thank you, Mr. Toussaint," said Jones. "We're working on that now."

Running Bear was taking in the entire discussion.

"Nor did I fuck the Queen," he said.

Whelan swallowed a laugh, hanging his head to regain his composure. "Let's get back on track, Your Majesty. The dragon rider and the Queen finished their fun, and then?"

"And then, they talked a couple more minutes. The Queen went and stood on the bank of the river. The dragon rider removed a sword from the back of his horse. He approached her from behind, and when she turned to him, he ran her through. He pulled it out quickly and thrust again before she even had time to fall. When she did, he ran her through a third time, on the ground. She screamed. I think *I* screamed. I tried to. Marjorie covered my mouth so he wouldn't hear us. She was terrified, afraid he'd come and kill us if he knew we were there."

Nurse O'Brien put her hand on his back and swirled it around, attempting to comfort him.

"And?" prompted Whelan.

"And, he nudged her a couple of times, with his foot. I think to make sure she was dead. He picked her up and put her on the back of the horse.

He climbed in the saddle and fled." Running Bear turned, shifting his gaze to the road as if seeing it replay live before him.

"What about the sword Bear?" asked Jones.

"He took it."

"Then how did it get back in the display case?"

"I don't know. He must have come back to the castle later that night."

"With no one seeing him come," commented Whelan. "Running Bear, why didn't you tell someone what you saw immediately? Why let a whole day go by?"

The younger man contemplated his answer with a growing frown. His bodyweight shifted side to side as he balanced himself. He focused on the ground, avoiding eye contact. "Because I've been trained to doubt myself sometimes, what I see. I have to process it all. When the Queen didn't visit me in my room yesterday, I knew she was missing. And when I saw you on the veranda this morning, I knew she'd been murdered. What I saw happened, and everyone could see it!"

Running Bear stole a peek at Nurse O'Brien. "Not just me."

Whelan stared at the man, six years younger than himself but with such a disparate perception of the world. He wheeled on Nurse O'Brien. "I still can't believe you don't have security cameras on the property! What billionaire doesn't have security cameras everywhere?"

"Sophia Perkins," she said simply. "I explained all this to you this morning. She simply wanted no recordings of anything going on in the house. She never told me why, but I'm pretty sure she didn't want documented footage of Running Bear. I think it was one of her biggest fears, that the world would learn of him."

"And it would destroy her career?" asked Whelan.

"And it would destroy Running Bear. Do you know how the media would have hounded him? They would have been relentless. The headlines would read, 'Billionaire Forever Sophia's Secret Love Child Exposed. Who's the father, and how large is his inheritance?' Bear would never be able to leave the house!"

She turned to him. "I'm sorry, Bear. Forgive me. I need these folks to understand why we do things the way we do."

"I understand," he said. "Maybe we *should* announce it. Maybe they can find out who my father was."

"Bear, half of Oklahoma would be filing claims in an attempt to get at your money. Remember, the rest of the kingdoms worship paper? We've discussed this before."

"Yes. The green paper. So odd…" he trailed off, peering up the road again before moving his eyes to stare about six feet above the edge of the river. "No, he's not!" he snapped at the air.

"What is it Bear," asked O'Brien. "What did Cantor say?"

Running Bear viewed each face around him, one at a time. He stopped at the empty space above the river bank. His eyes narrowed as he glared at his friend. "He keeps telling me the dragon rider is my father."

Chapter 8

Whelan and Jones were seated at the dining table on the terrace once again. It was a little after 7:00 p.m. They were drinking fresh lemonade and nibbling on turkey sandwiches.

"Thank you, Sylvia," said Jones as she refilled her glass. "You really don't have to wait on us. You didn't have to feed us either."

"It's my pleasure," she said. "Really, we all want the same thing here. That man needs to be behind bars, and the sooner the better. You both skipped lunch. It's the least we can do to help. I'll be right inside if you need anything. I'll let you get back to work."

She scurried indoors, leaving the agents to discuss the day and formulate their next steps.

"She's pretty," said Jones.

"Is she?" asked Whelan. "I hadn't noticed."

"Not your type?" she asked without thinking.

Whelan cocked his head and raised his eyebrows at his partner. He knew she knew his type. It was someone like herself.

Her copper eyes blinked back at him, framed by ebony curls.

"Sorry," she said. "So, no one here is inheriting anything. They're all close to Running Bear and seemed to genuinely enjoy Sophia. Do you think any of them know they're not getting squat? Anyone who did would become my prime suspect."

"I don't think they've even processed that far yet. They might feel like family, but they're all employees, really. Would you expect *your* employer to leave you a gift in his will?"

"I'm expecting at least a bottle of Scotch from Kendrick," she joked.

Whelan grinned before shaking his head. "Actually, I'm stumped. I have no initial gut reactions on this one. If it's someone in this house, there's no monetary motivation. And if it's someone who stood a shot at the inheritance, none of them are in town. You think our dragon rider is a professional hitman?"

"Quite possible. Or, perhaps a scorned lover who acted out in a jealous rage."

"After knowing Sophia for a week or two? Doubtful."

A jet in the sky caught Whelan's attention as it flew high overhead. "You think there really *is* a dragon rider? Or did Bear kill his mother?"

"We need a medical opinion. Running Bear sure seemed to believe it. If it was really him, what might have triggered it? He convinced me today he loved his mother. Did he have buried hostility acting out as one of his imaginary players? I sure wish this Doctor Brachman showed up today. He's gone missing. Not at home or his office."

"Suspicious, isn't it?" asked Whelan. "Maybe *he's* the dragon rider."

"I don't think so. Running Bear would have been able to tell us. He knows who his doctor is. He was actually distressed this afternoon at his failure to show. I'm not sure if it was because he was counting on him for professional therapy or if it would help to establish his innocence."

"That's an interesting thought. He understands how serious this is for him."

"Well, he's on house arrest for now. I've got two agents showing up to guard the front and back doors tonight. I think we can wrap up and get some rest. Sue Fielding, Bear's great-grandmother, is coming in tomorrow evening. It should be interesting to see the reunion. I want to be here for it."

"Then I'll meet you at the office in the morning."

"You want to grab a drink?" asked Jones. "Josephine's?"

Josephine's Restaurant and Lounge became Miranda's new watering hole over the summer.

"Not tonight. I'm giving my liver a rest. Raincheck?"

"Any time."

Jones gathered her belongings and headed out. "You coming?"

"I want to walk the grounds once more. You go on. I'll see you tomorrow."

"Good night then."

"Night."

Whelan watched her enter the house and disappear around a wall. He sniffed the air in her wake and gave a sigh. *That ship sailed.*

He turned back, taking in the pool and manicured hedges and flowerbeds. The sun was dropping in the sky. Marble planters turned golden. As did the terrace floor. He was mesmerized by the blue waters, surrounded by green and gold with pops of color from roses, begonias and other flowers he couldn't name. Another sigh escaped as Whelan allowed a tinge of jealousy for this lavish lifestyle.

Being divorced and paying child support, gladly, didn't help. But the bureau failed to pay enough to keep their agents in anything but middle-class status. Unless he won the lottery, he'd never genuinely aspire to have this kind of luxury.

He'd recently taken a new mortgage on a small home north of Westport. It was as close to the area he really wanted to be in, Westwood, as he could afford. It was less than a mile from his partner's home, for now.

Once she married her fiancé, Derrick Domino, Miranda and her husband would likely be moving to a nicer neighborhood.

Derrick recently landed a lucrative television deal to do a series of workout videos on-air. It would also include co-sponsoring of a new, branded line of sportswear. The logo would be a play on the double-six domino across a set of six-pack abs.

Those marketing guys are clever. He'll be making double six figures to go with it, no doubt.

Whelan sighed again.

He put his laptop in his bag and walked over to the other agent sitting in an outdoor sectional against the home's back wall.

"Agent Markham?" He introduced himself to the stationed agent.

"I'm going to walk the grounds once more," he continued. "I'll let myself out the side gate to the driveway. Good night."

Whelan strolled down the walkway to the pool area. He dipped his hand in. The water was too warm for his taste. He wanted to be refreshed when he swam, at least in August.

Rounding a corner toward the side yard, he saw a light on in the utility room attached to the house. Chad Buckley was putting away some tools.

"Mr. Buckley," said Whelan. "Doing some gardening this late?"

"Howdy, Agent Whelan," said the groundskeeper. "I didn't realize 8:00 was late. As long as I've still got daylight, I keep on working."

"And what was this evening's work?"

Mr. Buckley pointed to a new flower bed. "The roses are past their prime. Getting too late in the season. I'll have to do the other three beds in the morning. I've always been fond of dahlias, and I think lavender shows beautifully with them."

"They're gorgeous," said Whelan.

"Sophia gave me free rein when it came to the gardens. Said she enjoyed all my choices." He choked up and took out a handkerchief to dab at his eyes.

"Sorry," he continued. "Damn. That hit me out of the blue. I'm still processing all of this."

"I understand. Mr. Buckley, I know you all are close here. But I wanted to give you another opportunity to express any concerns you have. You said earlier neither Sylvia Moffett, Nurse O'Brien or Chef Louie could have possibly killed Sophia. It's been a long day. You've had some time to process. Any thoughts pop up since we spoke?"

"No."

"Any new stories about Running Bear's behavior come to mind? Fights with his mother? Or any of the other staff?"

"No."

Loyal S.O.B., I'll give you that. "Have a splendid evening, Mr. Buckley."

"Thank you. Good night, agent."

Whelan glanced again at the fresh flower garden. *I wonder if Doctor Brachman's under there.*

The agents spent the following morning on the phone catching up on the extended family Sue mentioned out in California. So far, no one seemed to be here in K.C. outside of the home staff. The financial situation of Sophia's cousins was dire indeed. They could not have afforded to hire a professional killer, and their personal alibis were all checking out.

That left the stockholders. The remaining two were spoken with from Forever Sophia. Declarations were being investigated, as were financial records, both corporate and individual. Los Angeles agents were assisting. If there was a large, suspicious payment to someone, they wanted to track it down and make sure it wasn't to a hired assassin.

Jones rubbed her eyes and rocked back in her chair at the Kansas City field office. "Either someone who owned shares wanted a larger stake in the company, or it's someone here in Kansas City. Perhaps personal."

Whelan raised his eyes over his monitor. "I'm sticking with the money for now. Someone in that house thought they were in the will, or her cousin Grace wanted more, or *her* father, or Sue, or Sophia's dad, Merrill."

"You're letting Running Bear off the hook?"

"No, but I'm giving him a chance here."

"And the stockholders?"

Whelan sighed. "We'll keep tracking accounts for now, but if one of them hired a hitman, you can bet they were smart enough to hide the payment overseas. But I have a hard time believing someone who's already a billionaire would risk getting caught for murder so they could double it. I mean, yes, it's possible. But how much money does one person really need? To commit murder? I'm not seeing it."

"What about to quadruple it?" asked Jones.

"Huh?"

"Cannon's been digging into the company filings. Three of the six remaining stockholders were pressing to go public. Four more non-shareholding board members were encouraging it. Presumably, they'd be offered discounted options. Some of the projections increased the value of Forever Sophia four hundred percent within five years if they went public.

Cannon's coordinating with the L.A. office to start interviewing them today."

"Yes, he told me there were seven out of the eleven who voted for it, assuming Sophia was a 'no.'"

"Right," said Jones. "I guess they didn't really need to kill Sophia to get a majority vote and go forward then." She sighed.

"Actually," Whelan continued, "the corporate bylaws called for a two-thirds majority vote in order to offer an IPO." He worked his calculator. "Point six-four. They missed it by two one-hundredths."

"That's pretty damned close. I trust Cannon to get answers on that front."

Jones stood up and stretched.

It held Whelan's attention. "You're going to go speak with Kendrick, aren't you?"

"How'd you know?"

"You always give yourself a little 'wake-up' stretch before you report to him."

"I do?" Jones chuckled at herself. "I'll consider myself warned never to play poker with you."

"Hey," defended Whelan, "observation's my job."

"Indeed. Cannon's going to need someone proficient in accounting and corporate law to tag along. I want to see if Kendrick has someone here or if we need to recruit someone from the L.A. office to help. They need to know California law specifically, I would think."

"Have fun," said Whelan.

She forced a broad smile on her face. "Of course!"

Whelan was still chuckling to himself when Cannon bounced into the room. He appeared younger than his thirty years. His short frame with a muscular build reminded Whelan of Robin, Batman's side-kick.

Whelan always felt physically inferior in his presence. He'd take muscles over height any day, but it was all he could do to keep on a thirty-inch waist.

"You just missed her," he told the younger agent.

"We spoke in the hall. I wanted to see how it was going on your end with the house staff."

"Well, I'm leaning that direction, but who knows at this point?"

"And how are *you* doing? Generally."

Tom Whelan gave Phil Cannon his undivided attention. The last case they worked bonded the two men like brothers, and there was little time together the past few weeks as Whelan and Jones hunted Eddie Morrison, who'd escaped from prison.

"I'm okay, Phil. Moving on from it all, Eddie, 12 Pills… Settling into the new digs. Having weekly dinners with my mother."

Cannon laughed. "Awesome. How *is* Kathryn?"

"Fantastic. Ornery as ever. She's been probing about my ex ever since D.C."

"Ouch. Take a week off from her and come have dinner at my place soon. I grill a mean ribeye. Maybe we can watch a Chiefs game and catch up."

"Uh-huh, when I get a Sunday free sometime, I'll take you up on it. Maybe in 2024?"

"My friend, that's what DVRs are for!" Cannon slapped his shoulder in jest. "Have you spoken with your son lately?"

"Yes, he's getting ready for his first year in Junior High. God help me."

"He'll be fine. He has his head on straight."

"Thanks. Better than I did at his age, at least. Said to tell you to brush up on your Fortnite. He's ready for another meet-up online to redeem himself from your last match."

"Hey, the kid's gotta earn it fair and square," Cannon chided.

"I agree. He knows you don't let him win. I don't either. That's what makes it fun for him."

"He sure gives me a run for my money, though."

"That's what makes it fun for me," said Whelan, smiling.

Jones waltzed through the doorway. "Fun time's over, guys. Cannon, you've got a plane to catch, and Whelan, we've got to get back to Parkmoor. Grace Meyer, Sophia's cousin, showed up unexpectedly.

Chapter 9

"I can't believe she's gone!" cried Grace through a mouthful of Tabbouleh Salad.

Lunch was served at Parkmoor.

Whelan and Jones again graciously accepted the invitation to stay for lunch. Today was Chef Louie's Mediterranean feast.

"So, Grace," said Whelan, "we feared we might have to hunt you down. You came from Oklahoma City?"

"Flew in this morning, yes," she said. "Grandma Sue phoned me last night. I'm in shock. Who'd do such a thing? For money!"

"Well, a lot of people. You didn't need money?"

"I work as a radiologic tech at Baptist Medical Center. I make a decent salary."

"But certainly not living the lavish lifestyle Sophia and Sue were enjoying."

Grace stared at the agent. At forty-three, she carried an entire decade on him in age. She understood she was a suspect, but a modicum of tact would be appreciated. She gave him the benefit of the doubt.

"Agent Whelan, I've never once envied Sophie's money. When she hit it big, that was all her. God bless her. She earned every fucking penny. And truth be told, she did take care of me. I have a gorgeous home in a beautiful suburb, and she paid cash for that. A 'thank you' for all the help I gave raising Running Bear when she needed it."

"But she could have set you up for life without ever having to lift a finger again."

"And would have if I allowed it. I also escaped the hillbilly life, Agent. My husband is a doctor. We both work long hours but enjoy our life." She started spinning a piece of pita through the hummus on her plate. "And now, when we're ready, we'll have an amazing retirement thanks to Sophie. You can cross me off your suspect list. Now, how can I help you figure out who *did* kill her?"

Whelan smiled. He instantly liked her. This directness was seldom seen in larger metro areas, where people felt the need to be guarded and politically correct with every word.

Jones interrupted. "Grace, why do you suppose she only left Merrill a dollar?"

"Sue didn't fill you in? Merrill was a horrible dad. A drunk. Barely making two nickels a week. It didn't take much more than that to maintain the shack they lived in back in the '80s. Valerie, Sophie's mom, was smart to leave him when she did. It was a shame she couldn't take Sophie with her. But Valerie couldn't afford to provide for herself, let alone a daughter. She stayed on and off again with Sue for a long time, then got remarried. Some man in Nebraska. It lasted a few more years, until it didn't. Then she settled down outside of Saint Louis."

"Did she stay in touch with Sophia?" asked Whelan.

"Not really. Christmas cards, Birthday cards, when she remembered. Let's see, Sophie turned twenty-one in 2000. Valerie showed up with no warning and took her out to get drunk and celebrate. She crashed on the sofa and the following day disappeared without saying goodbye. Sophie said she stole thirty-eight dollars out of her purse. Real classy."

"So how did she wind up out in L.A. toting Running Bear around?"

"Money, of course. Sue kept in touch with her. It was her daughter, after all. Sophie was already making millions in 2012 before Sue clued Valerie in that 'Forever Sophia' was Sophie. I don't think it took a week for her to show up at the L.A. home, trying to apologize and butter Sophie up. She got a small apartment and worked the next few months convincing Sophie she was sincere. Sophie knew the power Merrill could hold over you, and her heart was huge. She forgave Valerie. 'Life's too short' and all that shit."

Grace put her fork down for a minute and took a sip from her glass. She leaned in after checking over each shoulder to make sure they were alone and whispered, "What woman doesn't really long to have her mother in her life and a grandmother in her child's?"

They nibbled slowly and sipped pomegranate iced tea in peace until a now recognizable voice came from the doorway to the terrace.

"Princess Gracie!" Running Bear ran toward the group and exchanged a long hug with his cousin.

She made sure to give him a low curtsey when they separated.

"Your Majesty, my deepest condolences on the loss of your queen. Her death is an immeasurable wound upon the kingdom. While she can't be replaced, your succession is a healing comfort to your citizens. I'm sure you'll rule admirably with the fairness and gentility we've come to expect from your noble family."

Running Bear began crying from the praise and respectful salute to his mother.

Grace's voice became sharper as she gripped both his shoulders and made direct eye contact with the man. "And know her death will not go unpunished. This Lord and Lady from the FBI will capture the man who tragically murdered her. They will ensure justice prevails."

"Thank you, Gracie," said Running Bear. He stood a little taller, pulling his shoulders back. "You honor our family and yours."

The two sat down and resumed eating like normal.

Jones looked at her partner, her eyebrows high on her forehead. Whelan raised his brow in return and added a shrug. Normality in this home pulsed at a different rate than the rest of the world.

Nurse O'Brien joined them, walking up from the pool area. She was putting her cell phone back in her pocket. "Agents, welcome back. Any updates?" She took a seat and began fixing herself a plate.

"I'm afraid not," said Whelan. "We've got agents investigating the board members more closely today. There will be in-person interviews out in L.A. Anything new here we should know about? Have you heard from Doctor Brachman?"

"No, and I'm perturbed. This isn't like him. He took a vacation last month. He should be in town. Hell, he should be *here*, working, helping. Lord knows we pay him enough!"

Jones debated internally whether to ask her follow-up question out of Running Bear's presence. She opted to let it fly and see everyone's reactions. "Ms. O'Brien, can you think of any reason Doctor Brachman would have wanted Sophia dead?"

Running Bear perked his head up curiously.

Grace was shocked and voiced her first thought. “Why would he? He’d lose his wealthiest client.”

“There *are* other motives for murder besides money,” Whelan stated.

Nurse O’Brien crumpled her lips before answering. “Well, I can’t think of a solitary thing. He had no *personal* involvement. At least, I don’t think he did.”

Whelan jumped on her comment. “You don’t *think* he did? What concern is giving you uncertainty?”

The nurse snapped to a defensive posture, thrown off by Whelan’s audacity and regretting voicing her thought. She chose to answer him. “Well, he held conferences with her after his visits with Bear. Those were twice a week. *Are!* If Sophia was here in person, they’d meet privately in a closed room. Sometimes twenty minutes. Sometimes an hour or more. I was never sure why sometimes it took three times as long to be briefed.”

“Was he married?” asked Jones. “*Is* he married? Damn, you’ve got me doing it. Maybe there was some *de*-briefing going on?”

“I don’t think so. He was happily married, I believed. *Believe!* What’s wrong with me? Yes. He *is* happily married. Why do we keep doing that? Do you suppose our subconscious minds think he’s been killed? Dear God! He must have been! Why else would he be missing so long?”

“Well,” asked Whelan, “how much longer would *you* hang around after *you* murdered someone?”

Chapter 10

Nurse O'Brien fell back against the cushion of her chair, staring open-mouthed at Whelan.

"I'm saying it's possible," explained Whelan. "He *could* be part of this. Why? I don't know yet. But his absence is suspicious at this point. I got an update this morning at the office from Agent Cannon before he left. Doctor Alan Brachman *is* married, and his wife has not seen or heard from him for over thirty-six hours as of 8:00 a.m."

O'Brien put her hand to her mouth. "You think he helped kill our Sophie?" She forgot Running Bear was listening to all this. "Oh, Bear. You shouldn't be here for this. Why don't you go finish your lunch in the kitchen with Louie?"

"Nurse O'Brien, you forget I'm a man. And the king now. It's my duty, my responsibility, to hear all this. I can handle it." He felt his wife Marjorie's hand on top of his own, giving a comforting squeeze.

Silence ruled the group for another minute. Smaller bites were taken with less zeal.

Chef Louie came out to see if any of the bowls needed refilling. He frowned when everyone's plates were barely touched. He picked up a chicken skewer and sniffed it, then took a bite. "It's delicious, people. Eat." He whirled around and marched back inside the house.

O'Brien came out of her stupor. "He's disgruntled easily. I'll speak with him later. So Brachman might be involved or might be dead. I don't envy your jobs."

"We'll figure it out," Jones offered, standing up. "I'm going to place a BOLO for Brachman. Excuse me." She walked down the path toward the fountains, pulling out her phone.

"BOLO?" asked O'Brien.

"Be on the lookout," clarified Whelan before turning to Grace Meyer.

"So, Ms. Meyer," said Whelan, "We got sidetracked with Valerie. You were going to tell me why Merrill was worth a single dollar. Besides being drunk and poor. Did he hit Sophia? Abuse her?"

Grace scratched her temple. "I think so. Sophie didn't talk about it. She wrote him out of her life the day she left. The strongest-willed seventeen-year-old girl I ever knew."

"He hit her," said Running Bear.

"How do you know? You were too young to remember anything Bear," said Grace.

"I remember," he said. His eyes were focused on a distant wall of the veranda. "I was sitting on the floor, watching cartoons. Mama was fighting with him. They always fought. I heard a crack and a pop. And then Mama was on the floor beside me, staring up at the ceiling. She wasn't moving. Merrill came over and started shaking her. He picked her up, and they left. He was shouting the whole time."

"Where did they go, Bear?" asked Whelan.

"I don't know. They just left. They left *me*. Siting there. Alone."

"Well, eventually, they came back."

"I guess they did." Running Bear refocused his eyes on Whelan's. "Well, obviously they did. I think stuff like that happened more than once. Not long after, though, we moved away."

"Bear, you referred to your mother as Mama, not 'the Queen.'" whispered Whelan.

Running Bear's face went blank, then filled with surprise. He rolled his eyes around the table. When they landed back on Whelan, he stated in an evident tone, "She wasn't the Queen yet."

"Of course. Excuse me," said Whelan. He stood and went to find Agent Jones.

Sounds like Merrill nearly killed her. Probably took her to the hospital. I wonder how many years they keep their records?

Jones was toward the back of the property, visiting with Chad Buckley. As Whelan walked through the gardens, he noted, sure enough, all the roses were replaced with dahlias. A different color filled each bed, with an additional flower in a contrasting or complementary color scheme. It all worked and looked spectacular.

"Mr. Buckley," said Whelan, "you've outdone yourself. The gardens are amazing."

"Thank you, Agent Whelan. How are you today?"

"Well, thanks. You weren't at lunch."

"No." Chad peered up the hill toward the veranda. You couldn't see much from this vantage. "I wanted to get these finished."

Whelan followed his gaze to see what he was watching, but he couldn't see the veranda or anyone on it from here. There were many retaining walls and raised planters among the paver-lined stairs and paths winding down to the fountains and the pool.

"Mr. Buckley was sharing his gardening tips with me," said Jones.

Whelan spotted the flower bed from last evening. "Make sure you get the brand of fertilizer."

Jones didn't envision Whelan as much of a gardener, and his comment puzzled her.

"Have you said hello to Grace Meyer yet today, Mr. Buckley?" asked Whelan.

"Not today. I heard she was coming. Does she know anything about who might have killed our Sophie?"

"I don't think so."

"Oh. Shame."

"Aren't you ready for a break? Why not join us now? Everyone else is still eating."

Chad scouted the hill again. He knew the agents were observing their every move, but temptation got the better of him. "I could use something cold to drink. Sure."

The threesome meandered up the hill, chatting about the weather. When they crested onto the patio, Chad stopped. He took a comb out of his back pocket and quickly ran a couple of swipes through his hair before continuing.

He marched straight up to Grace Meyer. "Ms. Meyer, it's wonderful to see you again." His hand was extended.

"You as well, Mr. Buckley. You're as handsome and fit as ever."

He tipped his head, his ears reddening. He turned to Running Bear. "Your Majesty," he bowed. "Good morning. I trust you are as well as can be expected today?"

"Thank you, Sir Buckley," said Running Bear. "I'm managing. Please, sit and join us for some nourishment. You appear in need of some refreshment."

Chad took a seat opposite Grace and put a chicken skewer on a plate. He poured himself an iced tea and quickly shoved a bite in his mouth.

Whelan and Jones exchanged looks. Sir Buckley was glaringly smitten with Princess Grace. Whelan wondered if the whole kingdom knew or if it was a guarded secret.

After lunch, Running Bear retired to his room until his great-grandmother arrived.

Grace and Chad took a stroll back down the hillside. He'd offered his arm, and she took it.

Jones watched like a peeping Tom from the edge of the travertine.

"Honestly, Agent Jones," said Nurse O'Brien catching her in the act, "you're like a cat, ready to pounce."

"Am I?" she responded. "How long have the two of *them* been playing cat and mouse?"

"About eight years. It's never anything more than what you see there. A silly old fart making eyes at a woman young enough to be his daughter. And she eats it up. Must not be getting enough attention on the home front if you ask me."

"I didn't," said Jones. "But thank you for your insight."

Jones turned back to the couple, but they'd disappeared out of sight. She scowled at O'Brien and headed inside the home.

After the door closed behind Jones, O'Brien walked to the edge and ran her eyes around the grounds. She mumbled to herself, "So much charm, and he'd rather waste it on a married woman." She sighed, collected some papers from the table, and headed toward her office inside to prepare for Sue Fielding's arrival.

She noted the time on a grandfather clock in an alcove she passed. She had under five hours to ready everything.

Chapter 11

Jones drove back to the office.

"So Chad has the hots for Grace. You think that's relevant to the case?" she asked her partner.

Whelan was inputting notes on his smartphone beside her. "Doubtful. Unless he's after the twenty million she's getting?"

"I think his crush has gone on for a number of years. And I don't think he knows Grace is getting twenty million. I don't think Grace knows it yet."

"She sounded confident she was getting something. Sue's going to go over the will tonight. I really want to see all their reactions."

"Me too. Specifically, O'Brien's. I'm getting an odd feeling about her."

"How so?"

"I'm not sure yet. She seemed jealous of Chad's affections."

"They've been a tight-knit group for many years. I think Chad's been there nearly eight. O'Brien longer. Sylvia's been there six. And Chef Louie three. They're bound to have feelings for one another. But I didn't get any notions of attraction from any of them, outside of Chad's for Grace, of course."

The agents were updated by others working the case once they hit the floor of the bullpen. There was nothing new to report. Subpoenas were coming in for the accounts of the shareholders and other board members. Thus far, there were no exceptional expenses or odd accounting.

Jones sat behind her desk, taking a moment of downtime. It was really Assistant Special Agent in Charge Hank Monroe's desk. She'd unofficially taken over in his place before her last case. Afraid she might jinx the recovery status of his heart attack, she'd refrained from putting up any personal photos or decorations in the private office. She took a small three-by-five-inch photo frame out of her bag and set it in the corner. It held a picture of her fiancé, Derrick. She smiled at it, reflecting on the memory of when she popped the question to him after previously rejecting at least three proposals from him.

A voice from the doorway startled her. "Agent Jones, making yourself at home?"

"Hank!" Jones shot up out of his chair and raced to shake his hand. "I was just thinking of you! When did you get back?"

He pulled her in for a hug instead.

"I'm not back. I'm done. The bureau's giving me my full pension. I've put in over thirty years, and this heart nonsense reminded me there's more to life. Like my grandkids." He picked up a photo of them on a bookshelf nearby, studied it briefly, then shoved it into an empty box he'd brought.

"Oh, Hank, this place won't be the same without you."

"No. It will be better. It'll have you. I came from Kendrick's office. The director approved your promotion. He gave me permission to tell you. Congratulations, Miranda." This time, he extended his hand for a respectful shake. "There's still some paperwork needing to be filed, but the job's yours. Should be ready by the time you wrap up your current case."

Jones was torn between joy and sorrow. The battle took place on her face.

"I'm *ready,* Miranda. Really. It's time," said Hank.

She allowed her growing happiness to win out. "Thank you. You enjoy those grandkids. Show them how lucky they are to have you in their lives."

Hank grinned. "I will. They may actually get tired of me."

The pair exchanged a last hug before she left to let him clear out his personal items.

Jones wasn't sure whether she wanted to share the news with her partner Tom or her fiancé Derrick first. She nearly bumped into Whelan, pulling out her phone to call Derrick.

Whelan it is.

She took him aside by the copy room and dropped the news. More congratulations ensued, and the pair made their way to SAC Kendrick's office to be updated.

Kendrick confirmed everything, and once Jones reaffirmed she still wanted the role, he led them both to the bullpen for the announcement to the rest of the agents.

The afternoon was spent celebrating. A bottle of fine Scotch appeared from somewhere, and the agents in the office toasted her in Styrofoam coffee cups.

Two hours later, Hank Monroe made his last goodbyes, and Jones made her way once more to his office—*her* office. She took a seat in the oversized office chair. Derrick's picture was the sole personal memento now left in the room.

"Oh shit!" She grabbed her phone and began once again to call her future husband and share the news.

Whelan spent the next couple of hours hanging out with the other agents and giving Jones some space. They'd been "partnered" a short time, and yet he already knew he would miss her by his side every day. At least he'd be able to see her often, here in the office. Seldom did an ASAC work in the field.

He wondered who his new partner assignment would be. The bureau usually frowned on permanent partnerships. They wanted agents to be flexible enough to work with anyone in the office, and often needed to combine experience from different agents for the best results on individual cases. But when the next break on Eddie Morrison came in, Whelan would be hitting the road again. And who would that be with? *Cannon? I hope so. We work well together. We can learn from each other. He's the only other person in this office I fully trust.*

Whelan shared his thoughts with his soon-to-be ASAC as the pair drove back to Parkmoor for Sue's big arrival.

"I've already suggested it to Kendrick. There aren't too many veteran agents requesting to work with rookies. I think it's a done deal," she said. "But don't be anxious to let me go. We've still got a murder to solve." She winked at him from behind the wheel.

"Never," he smiled.

They drove up to the circular area in front of the covered porch and were surprised to find a valet service was set up. They flashed their badges and insisted they would be parking a few yards from the door. Whelan gave the young man a $5 tip anyway.

"Softie," said Jones.

"Yeah, well, kid's gotta earn a living. School books cost a fortune."

Entering the foyer, Jones whispered, "Gee, I hope we're not underdressed."

Sylvia Moffett was wearing a deep plum-colored dress. Her hair was tied up in a loose bun with two braids roped across the back and pinned out of sight, and the right amount of wisp framed both jawlines. Her makeup was heavier than usual, glamorous.

"You're dressed fine, Agent Jones," replied Sylvia. "Tonight's going to be a sort of wake for Sophia—Ms. Perkins. Immediate family, close friends and everyone from Parkmoor. Since we've no idea when the body will be released from your care, Ms. Fielding thought it appropriate we don't wait any longer. There will be cocktails before dinner, and afterward, Sue plans to read the will and make some announcements.

"I wish we'd been informed," said Jones, "I could have put on a dress."

"You look lovely, Agent. Please, make yourselves at home. I've got some last-minute details needing my attention. Sue should be here soon. Hors d'oeurvres are being served in the parlor. I know you're both here in an official capacity, but please enjoy yourselves. And, of course, you're our guests for dinner."

Sylvia flitted off down the hall of the gallery to attend to matters unknown.

The "castle" was lit up like a Christmas tree in August. Candelabras were lit, sconces were glowing, and fresh floral arrangements adorned all the tables.

"They've been busy these past five hours," said Whelan. "Did you get a tour yesterday? I have no idea where the parlor is."

"No. But I hear voices this way." Jones set out down the other direction of the gallery hallway.

She was nearly trampled by two new faces dressed in formal service attire. "Excuse us, please!" hollered one of them as they flew past with trays of empty glasses on the way to the kitchen.

Another new face was stationed outside a room, holding a tray of champagne glasses filled with crisp bubbly. He motioned them inside and extended the tray. Miranda appeared like she might grab one. Thankfully, her partner took her elbow and escorted her into the room before temptation hit earnestly.

The parlor was essentially a large, formal living room. It was adorned with plush seating, fine paintings, and one wall held an enormous fireplace with a marble mantle. Side tables were scattered about, again loaded with flowers. Rich woods competed with travertine on the walls and floor, and giant mahogany rafters swept the ceiling from one end to the other.

At least fourteen faces turned toward them when they entered, then quickly resumed their more intimate conversations. Some were familiar, some were not.

More trays were offered once inside. "Remind me to get the name of the catering service," Whelan jested to his partner.

"You planning an event? Perhaps a housewarming?"

"Ha!" Whelan mentally pulled up a visual of his tiny new home and backyard. "That'll be burgers and a case of Boulevard."

"Sounds perfect to me. I'll bring the chips."

New staff walked about with various appetizers. Jones helped herself to some caviar.

A small bar was set up on one wall. The bartender, eager when they approached, seemed disappointed by their tonic with lime and Diet Coke order.

"Oh my God," said Jones, taking a bite from her first treat. "I'd always heard Beluga was best, but damn!"

Whelan was tasting some French brie. *I wonder what stock dividends I need to host a spread like this once a year?*

"Agents!" a voice behind them grabbed their attention.

They wheeled in place. Nurse O'Brien stood in front of them wearing a sequined cocktail dress.

"I was about to welcome you and tell you to make yourselves at home. Clearly, someone beat me to it." She studied the small black fish egg hanging off Miranda's lip.

Whelan pointed to his own lip where she needed to wipe.

She opted to roll her bottom lip into her mouth and lap it up with her tongue.

"Tactful," he whispered.

She whispered back, "It's three hundred dollars an ounce."

O'Brien's ears were sharp. "That brand's *twelve*-hundred. But seriously, enjoy. It's Ms. Sophie's going away party." She sniffled, dabbing her nose with a handkerchief. "Damn. It's going to be a long night." She scurried off to say hello to another face in the room.

Whelan turned to face the crowd. He recognized Grace Meyer, Chad Buckley, and of course, Running Bear, who was engaged in conversation with an older man he didn't know and the empty space to his left.

"Divide and conquer?" he asked his partner.

"Let's do it." Jones took off toward the left side and marched straight up to a group of three, introducing herself like she was long-lost family.

Whelan chuckled, then did the same with another cluster. Two were attorneys. The third was a young woman wearing a modern pantsuit in black and jade from a designer he'd never know. She shook his hand warmly.

"I'm Sarah Williams. Sophia's executive assistant. It's nice to meet you, Special Agent Thomas Whelan."

"You as well. I guess my reputation proceeds me."

She nodded politely. "Are you enjoying my soirée?"

"Tasty," he said. "You've been ignoring my phone calls for the past two days."

"I'm sorry. I've got an empire to deal with. Trying to keep this hush-hush is a PR nightmare. The stockholders are freaked out, as you can imagine. I've spent the past thirty-six hours canceling appointments with designers, corporate CEOs, the ADA *and* the NDA's national conferences, and appearances on three talk shows, two in London and another in Milan. All without cluing them in their star has been tragically murdered.

"Oh! And putting *this* together with a day's notice. Thank Sue for that one. She couldn't have waited a couple more days? The poor girl was just killed Saturday night! And flying out of L.A.X.? It's a three-hour ordeal these days. Nearly four with the moronic family in front of me. Some woman's slipper was placed on the conveyor belt for x-ray and jammed up the whole operation when it fell to the side and became caught in the mechanism. They could have opened up the one beside it, which stayed unused the *entire* time I was in line. But no. They'd rather us all smell each other for an extra forty minutes.

"And there's always some fat Indian man somewhere who still doesn't believe in deodorant. I guess that's one helpful thing, I won't have to go to Mumbai anymore. I don't care how many Bollywood films they put out a year. You can't house eighteen million people that closely without sacrifice. Forever Sophia's Eau de Toilette arrived in the nick of time."

Whelan was listening carefully and taking in Ms. Williams' body language with her racist, nervous gibber. "You don't seem terribly distraught," he said. "I mean, on a personal level. Were you close to Ms. Perkins? Personally? Intimately?"

"Of course! But I haven't had time to myself to process. Fires need to be put out before combusting the entire organization. I don't have the liberty to indulge in grief right now. Have *you* ever helped run a multi-billion-dollar corporation? Of course you haven't. The responsibility is beyond! Oh shit, here we go." She stopped cold, gazing toward the doorway of the parlor.

Whelan turned as conversations cut off mid-sentence throughout the room, shifting the attention to one seventy-six-year-old woman.

Sue Fielding, the woman who held the future of eight-billion dollars in her hands, had arrived.

Chapter 12

"It's wonderful to see everyone," said Ms. Fielding. "Please finish your cocktails and make your way to the dining room. We've broken open the finest bottles from Sophie's wine cellar to pair with dinner. Soup's on in fifteen minutes."

With that, Sue Fielding wheeled in place and strode from the room with her clutch in her right hand and a large glass of Maker's Mark over ice in her left. Her new dress was tailor-fit and hid her midsection as intended.

"The show must go on," mumbled Jones.

A voice startled her and Whelan from behind. "Grandma Sue seems nervous."

It was Grace Meyer. "I wasn't able to reach her all day. I hope she's doing okay."

"Why wouldn't she be?" asked Whelan.

"It's not like her to not take my calls."

"She's been busy," offered Jones. "Mourning. I'm unsure why the rush on all this."

"I agree," said Grace. "But I think I understand. Once this gets out to the media, the circus will be uncontainable. There won't be time for a family memorial."

She turned toward the other end of the parlor, where a large framed photo of Sophia Perkins rested on an easel. "Goodbye, dear cousin."

Grace Meyer dabbed at her eyes as she made her way out of the room.

Others began filing out. No one wanted to miss a thing at the dinner table.

Whelan snagged Running Bear's arm as he passed. "Your Majesty, if you'd be kind enough to share who it was you were talking to a minute ago? The man that slipped out of the room?"

"That was Mr. Perkins. He's not royalty. Comes from far away, outside of any known kingdoms. I'm unsure why he's here, but he says it was at the invitation of Lady Fielding. I haven't seen or spoken with him in twenty-five years."

"Mr. Perkins?" asked Jones. "Your *grandfather*? Merrill Perkins?"

"Yes. If he thinks he's going to waltz back into the family *now*, he's crazier than I am."

Whelan wasn't sure what to say. He turned to Jones for guidance. She shook her head with her eyes wide open.

Running Bear left the room laughing.

Two attorneys were sipping the last from their rocks glasses nearby as they whispered in breathy sentences. Otherwise, the room was emptied out.

Jones motioned to the photo of Sophia. "She was really something. All this," she gestured around the room, "from nothing. *Nothing!* How much of a raise do you think I'll get as an ASAC?"

"Enough to set up a fancy bar in your home like this one," said Whelan. "Minus the rest of the parlor. And the house it sits in."

Jones simply sighed.

"You walked a different path, Miranda," he comforted. "You gave of yourself to society. Service and protection of the public don't come with a lot of rewards, but the families of the victims from each piece of shit you've put away will always remember Agent Miranda Jones was there for them when they needed her."

She gaped at him, cocking one eyebrow up. "And?"

"Oh. The hard sell. *And* how much money is a life worth? How many lives have you saved throughout your career? Fifty? Sixty? I'd say those lives outweigh eight billion dollars. You're richer than you know."

She wasn't buying it. "Mmhmm. Well, I might enjoy trying on the title of Forever Miranda for a while and seeing how it feels. I'd jet-set my ass all over the world, lavish myself with caviar and champagne, attend the best parties…."

"Well, you're doing that right now. And besides, look where it got *her*." Whelan motioned to the easel.

Jones tilted her head to the side and studied the photo again. She sighed and turned to leave the parlor.

Whelan was quick on her heels. "Hey, if you still want it, go for it. She had three years on you. It's not too late. I'll post a YouTube video, and we'll have Forever Miranda in department stores before you know it!" He smiled.

Jones kept on walking. "Mmhmm." She denied him the pleasure of seeing the grin on her face.

The dinner table was set with the finest money can buy: Philippe Deshoulieres china, Waterford goblets, and Baccarat stemware, all under a French Empire chandelier spraying golden light across the table with room for up to twenty-four. It was set for eighteen this evening.

Jones wondered who made the guest list at the regular dinner parties and who didn't make the cut.

There were four seats left open, none together. Whelan took one side, Jones the other.

Shortly after they sat, the two attorneys from the parlor filed in, fresh drinks in hand, and took the remaining seats.

Sue Fielding sat at the head of the table, Running Bear filled in the opposite end. Sue rang a little bell, and a full suite of servers waltzed in, one for each guest, and set a glass of champagne in front of their chargers at one o'clock. The servers all stepped back two steps, turned, and filed back out of the room in unison.

It was like watching synchronized swimming. Whelan rated them an eight-point-six.

The dinging of a knife against Sue's glass gathered everyone's attention. She was standing, and the room was tightly focused on her.

"We're here tonight to celebrate the life of Sophia Perkins," she began. "Some of you knew her fondly, others…not so much." She shot Merrill Perkins a contemptuous scowl.

For seven minutes, Sue gave a loving tribute. Whelan's eyes went one by one around the dinner table, studying expressions and trying to determine genuine sadness versus uneasiness or boredom. It was challenging, as everyone carried some eagerness in addition to whatever else they might be feeling. *Should have eaten dinner after the will-reading. At least some of these folks could dine in peace.*

He locked eyes on his partner when he got to her seat. She was moving her eyes in a similar path, in the opposite direction. When she met up to his stare, she gave a wink.

He bowed his head then resumed his perusal of the guests. He started making notes on his phone, beginning with the guest list.

Clockwise from Sue Fielding was:

Sam Goldstein – L.A. Attorney

Unknown man in expensive suit

Sylvia Moffett – Housekeeper

Chef Louie Pirelli – House Chef

Unknown woman in cheap department store dress

Merrill Perkins – Sophie's dad

Agent Miranda Jones – FBI

Edward Toussaint – K.C. Defense Attorney

Running Bear – Sophie's son

Adam Steiner – K.C. Family Attorney

Chad Buckley – Groundskeeper, Handyman

Unknown woman in expensive suit

Sarah Williams – Sophie's Executive Assistant

Agent Thomas Whelan – FBI

Grace Meyer – Sophie's cousin

Earl K. Humboldt – Sophie's uncle, Grace's dad

Linda O'Brien – Nurse, House Manager

When Sue concluded, she held her glass high. "To Sophie."

They all took a drink except for the federal agents.

Sue then made a point of calling extra attention to Whelan and Jones. "Some of you have already met Special Agent Miranda Jones and Special Agent Thomas Whelan of the FBI. They are our guests this evening but are also here in an official capacity until they can figure out who killed our poor Sophie. Please cooperate with them and answer any questions they might have this evening. We all want the evil bastard found. Right now, our dear Running Bear is the primary suspect who evidence suggests might have killed her. Of course, that didn't happen. It's on all of us to help solve this tragedy."

Whelan and Jones nodded at the new faces here this evening which began staring at them.

"After dinner, we'll have the reading of Sophie's will, and I have a few announcements. In the meantime, I'm famished. Enjoy your dinner. Chef Louie has the evening off and is at our table this evening as part of our Parkmoor family. But, he assures me his recommendation will live up to his standards. It is award-winning Chef Jacques Fournier, who flew in from L.A. this morning and has been diligently working to prepare some of Sophie's favorite courses for our enjoyment. Bon appétit."

Another ring of the bell and the parade of black and white began again, this time bringing a silky lobster bisque.

"Tell me," Whelan whispered to Sarah Williams on his right, "who are the rest of these guests? The man between Mr. Goldstein and Ms. Moffett?"

"That's Mark Fleming. He's on the board of Forever Sophia and holds the greatest number of stock shares after Sophia. He was a big help to her early on. He quit practicing law when he saw the potential of Forever Sophia and contributed significant start-up money. Without him, no one in the world would have ever heard of Sophia Perkins. He guided her initial launch and was instrumental in obtaining favorable global licensing rights. He's single-handedly responsible for over a billion dollars more in annual revenue. He and Ms. Perkins were close friends in addition to being business partners."

She tilted her head to the right and lowered her voice even further. "This is Karen Hertzberg. Also on the board and a stockholder. Karen is head of marketing. Remember the Smooth Avocado campaign?"

Whelan's face was blank.

"Well, it was genius. A simple little visual for the Forever Sophia Avocado Mask. The commercial showed an avocado, all bumpy and gritty. The voiceover asked, 'What's hiding under *your* skin?' The second image was a perfectly smooth avocado with the skin removed. Flawlessly unblemished, creamy perfection. 'Isn't it time *you* went green?' was the tagline. Avocado mask revenues went up by 700 percent. We sold out of our entire inventory the past two years."

"I remember those commercials, the green thing, crafty," said Whelan.

"Well, last year, she suggested the *limited edition* avocado mask. The slogan read, 'After all, we have to save some for Mexican night.' Golden. The entire line was sold out three weeks before Cinco De Mayo. Anyway, she's also been on board since the early days. She was quite fond of Ms. Perkins. They lunched at least once a month at Spago or Geoffrey's and have vacationed jointly on three occasions."

"Thank you, that's all helpful. No other board members wanted to come?"

"No others were invited. These are the only two who cared about Sophia on a personal level. Don't read into that," she amended. "Everyone got along fine, but for the others, it's really all business."

"And, that woman?" asked Whelan, indicating the cheaply dressed woman at the side of Merrill Perkins. Her hair was curly, about six inches past her shoulders, and in a shade of maroon he didn't think existed since the early 80s.

Sarah Williams tilted her head up, staring down her nose at the woman who was actually picking up her soup bowl and slurping the last of her bisque over the edge.

"I'm not sure." Her disdain was evident. The woman might have been considered pretty were it not for the dollar-store makeup and discount apparel.

She was about to offer up a guess when Grace Meyer touched Whelan's arm, stealing his attention. She whispered, "That's Merrill's wife, Peggy. Been together a couple of years. I visited with her during the cocktail reception. She was kind, submissive."

Whelan was riveted on Peggy. You didn't use a word like "submissive" casually. Grace must have picked up on an abusive relationship. It fit what Sue and Running Bear previously said about Merrill. Whelan shifted his stare from Merrill's wife to the man himself.

What kind of a man could kick his daughter and grandson out of the house and never regret the loss of that relationship? I bet he regrets it now. How much do you regret it, Merrill? Enough to kill your daughter?

Merrill's sixth sense kicked in. He felt Whelan's uncomfortable gaze and turned his head to face him. He knew the agent would be cornering him soon enough for a conversation. The thought stretched his lips into a snarly grin.

Chapter 13

The second course was a trio of savory pastries.

Jones overheard the woman on Merrill's right utter, "Lemongrass." She was at least twenty to twenty-five years younger than Running Bear's grandfather, with too much mascara and a dark, purplish lipstick that failed to flatter her skin tone or her dress.

It almost matches her hair color, thought Jones, as she smiled at her warmly. She leaned her head beyond Merrill's chest and addressed the woman. "Lemongrass?"

"The flavor. It's lemongrass. I work weekends at a Thai restaurant. I don't earn much, but they let me take home free soup after my shifts. My favorite has chicken and lemongrass." She reached her hand across Merrill's chest. "Hi. I'm Merrill's wife, Peggy. Nice to mee—ow!"

Her husband quickly slapped her hand down. "Woman, don't you know you ain't supposed to reach across someone at a fancy dinner event? What the hell you watch all that downtown-abbey crap for if you're not gonna learn nothin'?"

He turned back to Jones.

"Excuse her, pretty black lady. She ain't got no manners," said Merrill. He grinned at Jones, revealing three missing teeth she spotted with a glimpse. His hair was combed back and held in place with either too much product or his body's natural grease. She suspected the latter.

Jones ignored the comment from Running Bear's grandfather. She felt sorry for his wife and smiled politely to her. "It's a pleasure to meet you, Peggy. I'm *Special Agent* Miranda Jones." She glanced at Merrill a second when emphasizing her title. "So, you work at a Thai restaurant? That's terrific. I love Thai food. I wish there was a decent one near me. Maybe you can sneak me out a few of your favorite recipes?"

Peggy smiled briefly. "I'll see what I can do." She frowned at Merrill, then hung her head and stared at her lap.

Jones detected a bruise high on Peggy's left cheek. She'd tried to cover it with some makeup, but it was showing through. Jones allowed her eyes to bounce back and forth between this husband and wife and wondered what the draw was. *How many bruises have you been forced to cover since marrying Merrill?*

"So…" Jones said aloud. She reflected all evening on the best way to approach Mr. Perkins. Accusing him of beating his wife didn't seem like the best tactic. "You haven't seen Running Bear in twenty-five years? That's a long time."

"I've seen him a couple of times. He didn't see me, though."

"How's that?"

"When he and Sophie lived with Sue on the farm. I went to visit twice. Both times, Sue blocked me at the gate. Held her shotgun on me the second time." He squinted at Ms. Fielding, his brows gathering in a V-shape. "The bitch wouldn't let me in, but I could see 'em playing in the yard. Said it was at Sophie's request. I doubt that. She begged me to let them stay when I punted them to the curb. It was for their own good. They needed to learn how to survive in the world."

"At seventeen and three years of age?" asked Jones.

"Hey," his nostrils flared as his head swung back to her, "if you're old enough to get knocked up and have a little bastard, you're old enough to raise him without your daddy's help. I kept 'em long enough. It was time."

Jones leaned back in her seat and thought about her next words. She couldn't be drawn into a heated argument. She roamed her eyes around the room, nodding her head at paintings worth hundreds of thousands of dollars, perhaps millions. "I'd say she rose to the challenge."

Merrill eased his temper, chasing her gaze around the walls. "Yep. One might say, she has me to thank."

Jones was about to defend the dead billionaire but again stopped herself. There was no suitable answer here but silence.

"I expect that's why I'm here," he continued. "When the will's read tonight, you'll see how grateful she was to her daddy. Sue wouldn't have flown us all the way up here just for dinner."

Jones smirked. *No. Dinner* and *a dollar.*

She raised her untouched champagne glass to him, making sure her partner, Agent Whelan, wasn't watching, then took a sip. One ounce wouldn't impede her. *Exceptional.*

The second course came around with a crisp chardonnay replacing all the champagne glasses. She tossed back the rest of her bubbly before they could grab it.

A wide salad bowl was set in front of her with mixed greens in a tangy citrus vinaigrette. It was lightly sweetened, and she wished she was Peggy Perkins so she could lick the bottom of the bowl.

Peggy Perkins. It was the first time she put Peggy's first and last names together in her head. *Sounds like a Stan Lee comic book character. I wonder what her maiden name was?*

Across the table, Whelan was doing his best to give equal attention to both Grace Meyer and Sarah Williams. Ms. William's fast-paced and unguarded conversation contrasted against Ms. Meyer's slower drawl and thoughtful statements. His brain was speeding up and slowing down every other minute, growing a headache in the whirlwind.

Servers dropped off the main course in time to save his neck from twisting straight off.

The conversation at the table grew eerily silent for a few minutes as the crowd enjoyed their surf and turf. It was a welcomed respite before the actual show began. The volume picked up again over Cherries Jubilee.

The last bowl was barely cleared from the table when Sue stood up. "There's cognac being served in the parlor. Freshen up if necessary, and I'll begin reading the will in fifteen minutes."

She swept out of the room before anyone else could back their chair out. Groans were heard around the table as one of the richest meals ever shared started to hit bottom. Praises for the chef were mumbled on the way out of the dining room.

Jones realized Running Bear was moving slower than his usual speed. The crowd was beelining for the bathroom, except for Whelan and Sylvia Moffett.

Jones approached him. “Running Bear, do you need help? I think you’re a little… tipsy?”

He smiled at her. “Thank you, Lady Jones. I’m afraid the King imbibed too aggressively this evening.” His eyes were watery.

“What’s wrong?” asked Jones. “Why the tears?”

“For the Queen. She would have loved this gathering, this feast, in her honor.”

“It was beautiful. Everything was perfect.” She placed a hand on his shoulder.

She was surprised when he suddenly turned into her and began sobbing. Unprepared, she simply wrapped her arms around him and let him cry.

Whelan observed Sylvia staring at them. Her eyes were moist as well, perhaps from the spontaneous display of affection. She put her head down and abruptly marched around them and out of the room.

He walked over to Running Bear and put his hand on the younger man’s shoulder. “I think the Queen would be proud of you, Your Majesty. You carried yourself well through the dinner.”

“Thank you, Lord Whelan.” Running Bear separated himself from Jones and wiped his eyes. “I’m trying, but it’s difficult. It’s really starting to sink in. I’m never going to see my mother again. The weight of my responsibilities has been consuming me.”

He checked to make sure the three of them were alone and spoke in a hushed tone. “I’m not ready to be king.”

Jones took pity on the man. “You’ll make a respectable king, Running Bear. And you’re not alone. You’ve got Nurse O’Brien, Sylvia, Chad, Chef Louie, and I’m sure your great-grandmother Sue will visit more often. Once she sells off the homes your mother owned in other cities—kingdoms—she'll probably move in here full time. Life won't be too dreadful."

"Grandma Sue isn't moving in here," he began to cry again.

He spoke to the empty space on his left. "They should know! They're here to help! Yes, they are!"

"Cantor?" asked Whelan. He picked up previously that Running Bear's demeanor toward Marjorie was much softer.

"He says not to say anything to you. He doesn't trust you yet," said Running Bear.

Jones put her hand on Running Bear's shoulder again and turned him around so she could look him square in the face. "We really are here to help you, Bear. We want to find out who killed the Queen. What doesn't Cantor want you to tell us? Why isn't Sue moving in here? What do you know?"

"She spoke with me before the dinner," he began. "She's been reflecting on what's best for me. I don't know how she's the one who gets to make all the decisions. *I'm* king now! I should be able to make my own choices."

"What choice, Bear?"

"She's not selling the castle in Los Angeles. She's selling this one! She's going to move me out to rule over the Kingdom of California and says I'll never be able to see Parkmoor or my Kansas City family again!"

Chapter 14

"She *said* that?" asked Jones.

"Yes! I don't like Los Angeles. There are too many horses on the roads, and they cough up horrible black clouds, filling the air with soot worse than dragon's breath. And in the winter, there's no snow. I tried rolling a snowman on the beach once, out of sand. A sandman."

Running Bear narrowed his eyes on Jones. "Sand doesn't roll." He let that digest for a minute like he'd delivered fresh gospel at a Sunday sermon.

She waited for a beat, then said, "No. But the castles are pretty."

"In L.A.?" asked Running Bear.

"On the beach. Sandcastles."

"They make their castles from *sand*? If they collapse as easily as my sandman did, I don't think I'd want to live in one. Lost Angels, indeed. Perhaps I should send out some carpenters, show them a few things. But *I* don't need to live out there."

Jones grinned at the twenty-seven-year-old. "I feel you, Running Bear. It's a different type of lifestyle."

She became serious, taking in the man before her, bouncing her eyes from his left to his right and back again. "I don't know what your future holds, but I will try to find some justice for you in all of this."

He took her hand and bent over to kiss the back of it. "Thank you, Lady Jones. I believe you will. Well, speaking of wills, let's not be late for the reading." He turned and exited the room.

Whelan was staring at Jones when she turned back to him. His eyebrows rose high on his forehead.

"Should I kiss your hand too, my Lady, or just keep kissing your ass?" he asked.

"My ass will do, thanks." She shoved her arm through his and peered up at his freckly cheeks. "Shall we?"

They were the last to arrive back in the parlor, having stopped at the bathroom themselves. Sue was waiting patiently, nursing another whisky.

Others were sipping Scotch or brandy. Jones wished she wasn't on the clock so she could join in on all the quality liquor. She ordered a phenomenal, aged cognac at an expensive restaurant once. She still remembered the sticker shock of seeing it on her bar bill, $110. Thank God her fiancé Derrick was courting her at the time and picked up the check.

Someone rearranged all the seating in the room during dinner to face the far wall. Near Sophia Perkin's photo, there was now a podium. The agents took seats up front, turning their chairs sideways to easily watch both directions. They wanted to read the expressions of the staff.

Sue stood, clearing her voice and walked to the wooden stand. "Thank you all again for coming. Sophia would have loved this evening. A final gathering of the troops."

Faces in the room grew confused by her statement.

"Mr. Samuel Goldstein is going to give a formal reading of the will. It should take about thirty minutes to get through it all. Please reserve your questions until the end. I'll have some clarifications and announcements to make first that might alleviate any concerns."

Attorney Samuel Goldstein walked to the podium. He clocked in at about five-foot flat, and behind the walnut box, he disappeared except for his head. It was as though he'd been decapitated right below his Windsor knot. After the first few lines were read, he realized how awkward he must appear, so he walked around and stood at the side.

The room was a captured audience, hanging onto every word, waiting for the juicy stuff.

When it came, you could hear gasps and sighs. The house staff, one by one, clued in on the fact none of them were receiving a dime. So much for feeling like family.

Nurse O'Brien, in particular, scoured at the absence of any mention.

Whelan was focusing on the newcomers, Mr. Mark Fleming and Ms. Karen Hertzberg. They perked up when it was noted Sophia's fifty-four percent stake in the company, approximately seven and a half-billion dollars, was now owned by a young schizophrenic and essentially controlled by a seventy-six-year-old hick from Missouri.

When Running Bear made no reaction to the money, Mark's attention shifted solely to Sue Fielding. Whelan was studying her too. She was a challenging read.

Mr. Goldstein concluded and sat back down as Sue reclaimed the podium.

She barely got her mouth open when Merrill shot up out of his seat. "You brought me all the way up here to tell me I'm gettin' a *dollar*? Are you fucking serious with this horseshit? I'll find me an attorney and sue the hell out of this estate."

Merrill was wild. He frantically zeroed in on the two other attorneys in the room. "You boys for hire? Get me what I'm owed, and I'll pay you double whatever this bitch is paying you!"

Mr. Toussaint and Mr. Steiner exchanged glimpses and simply shook their heads at the crazy older man.

"Merrill!" shouted Sue. "Sit down, you old fool. You're getting what you deserve. And you enjoyed a lovely dinner to boot!"

Peggy touched her husband's hand. He jerked it away and nearly struck her cheek with it. He remembered where he was before his natural reaction kicked in and got him in trouble. Instead, he marched over to the bar, yanked a bottle of whisky out and filled his glass. He made a point of slamming it back down in front of the young bartender, then took his seat. Every eye in the room was on him. No one was moving or speaking.

"Well, go on, woman!" he yelled at Sue, then took a large swig.

Slowly, the group turned their attention back to the new matriarch of the family. Sue waited an extra minute to let Merrill steep in his own embarrassment.

"So," she began, "as you can see, I've been taken care of, as have Grace and Earl." She smiled at Earl Humboldt, Grace's dad. He'd been silent through all this. He seemed surprised when it was read he'd receive one million dollars. He was simply helping his family out as any man with morals should do during those early years. Still working at sixty-five as a farmhand, he was beginning to figure out he might be able to retire. He nodded to Sue with a grateful face.

"As for you, Merrill," continued Sue, "I'm giving you $500,000. You don't deserve it, but you are family. You're Bear's granddaddy. You did provide for him and Sophie the first three years of Bear's life. I've got papers already drawn up. You sign away any other legal rights you think you have on this family, and you'll fly home tomorrow half a million dollars richer. You think you'll win more in a ridiculous lawsuit, be my guest. You'll get nothing and go through every dime you have paying some half-assed lawyer to go up against my guys."

Sue pointed toward the same two attorneys Merrill failed to recruit. They both turned toward Merrill and presented a stern, united front.

Merrill's face scrunched up, then he polished off his glass, took a deep breath, and settled more easily in his chair.

"Next," Sue began again, "I need to let you all know, there will be some changes, effective as soon as possible, with regards to Running Bear and this household. I'll be moving Bear out to California, where I've decided to stay. As soon as I can get new doctors and staff set up, everyone here will be paid a handsome severance and released from their duties. Parkmoor is to be sold."

The staff went from shock to anger. They knew they had no legal say-so, but after many years of caring for Running Bear and keeping up Parkmoor, they all felt vested in him and his well-being.

Chad Buckley was the first to speak. "What are you doing, Sue? Bear belongs here, with us. We might not be blood relatives, but we're his damned family now, for God's sake. I'm not just a groundskeeper, Sylvia's not just a maid, Louie...okay, Louie might just be a chef, but Linda's certainly not just a nurse! We're *family* to the young man." He looked at Running Bear.

Tears were streaming down young Mr. Perkin's face. "Grandma Sue, why are you doing this?" he asked again for the second time this evening. "These people *are* my family. They take amazing care of me! Why would you move me away from my home to some foreign land where they don't know me?"

Sue braced for this for two days. "Because Bear, these people really *aren't* your family. I am. And you have real family out in L.A. who would love to get to know you. Cousins you've never even met or heard of who understand blood *is* thicker than water. And my dear, sweet man, these people have *not* taken good care of you. They've allowed you to go off your meds, given in to your delusional episodes instead of making you confront reality, and they've allowed strange men to enter your home, and one of them killed your mother!"

Anger rode across Sue's face as she glowered at each of the house staff. "You should all be ashamed of yourselves!"

Chapter 15

Nurse O'Brien heard enough. She stood, beholding the other staff members, reading their emotions, before turning angrily to Sue.

"Ms. Fielding, those are harsh words. We have abided by *Sophia's* wishes. She didn't want Running Bear on a bunch of medications. He's been doing really well. He's happy. He's behaved. Even now, he's entering a bipolar high, but see how calm and reasonable he's been. It's because he feels safe. We really are a close, family-like unit here. You strip that from him now, and you'll be undoing years of work, years of therapy and growth. Your granddaughter would not have wanted him relocated from Kansas City and forced back on a regimented pill schedule with strangers he's never met."

"I wouldn't know *what* my granddaughter would want any longer," said Sue. "You've all denied me that. You think Running Bear is *safe*? Why wasn't my sweet Sophie safe?" She was becoming hysterical.

"Are you kidding me?" snapped Nurse O'Brien. "Sophia was a grown woman. We answered to *her*, not the other way around. She called all the shots when she was here. And if she wanted to bring a man home, that was her business. Not ours, not *yours*."

"Anyone allowed in this home should have been vetted!"

"Sue," said O'Brien, easing her voice, "Sophie ran at her own pace. She always did. *You* told me that once. She went ninety different directions at a hundred miles an hour. Our job is keeping *Bear* safe. And he is. Please let us continue doing so."

"You just want your jobs kept safe!"

"In the sense this has become a life we all have settled into, yes. We want to preserve what we've created here for as long as we can. And Running Bear will need us all as he processes and deals with his mother's loss. To rush him off to California right now would destroy him. Doctor Brachman would confirm what I'm telling you if he were here."

"Still missing?" Sue hissed. "I put a reward out for him yesterday. A hundred thousand dollars. I bet the fool had something to do with my Sophie getting killed."

Sue narrowed her focus on Running Bear. "You saw your mama killed sweetheart, and all that brain of yours can process is that it was a dragon rider."

She scoffed at the staff once more. "I don't think he's better off here at all. You've all gone completely mad encouraging this gibberish-nonsense. I'm tempted to have you all brought up on charges of endangerment!"

Grace Meyer stood up and took a step toward Ms. Fielding. "Grandma Sue, that's not fair. You've known how this household was run for years. You know it's what Sophia wanted. Hell, you've been here playing along many times. To act like this is all new and questionable is a little late on your part."

"Yes, Gracie, it is! Too late to save my Sophie from being killed in this circus! Sophie's gone!" She broke down and began crying uncontrollably. Then she released a loud moan and began to stumble backward. Chad Buckley raced over and caught her before she fell and eased her into a chair.

Sylvia ran to the bar and grabbed a cold bottle of water and a clean bar towel. She wet part of the towel and held it against Sue's forehead while encouraging her to take a sip of the cool water from the bottle.

Nurse O'Brien began feeling for Sue's pulse to check her vitals. "Sue, your heart rate is racing. I suspect your blood pressure is through the roof. You're flush. I think we should run you to the hospital."

"We need to finish all this," she blustered.

"Sue, we need to get you checked out. Seriously, you're not well."

"I'm fine!" she managed right before releasing an unexpected scream. It took everyone by surprise, and people jumped in their seats. She clutched at her heart. "Sweet Jesus!" she yelled.

Jones dialed 911 as Whelan, raced to Sue's side to see if he could help. While not a medical doctor, Whelan was one semester and a thesis shy of obtaining a Ph.D. in pharmaceuticals and took some medical classes in college.

"Her breath is shallow. Sue, follow my finger," said Whelan. He moved his index finger in front of Sue Fielding's face. Her eyes stayed with him for a second before drifting up and rolling toward the ceiling.

"An ambulance is five minutes out!" shouted Jones.

She noticed Running Bear was glued to his seat, staring at his great-grandmother in horror. "Bear, maybe you should wait out of the room," she suggested.

Sue braced herself on the arm of the chair with her left hand. Her right hand was being supported by Chad Buckley this whole time. He was wincing from her grip, then all of a sudden, it relaxed, and her arm fell to her side.

Sylvia was behind, trying to dab at her forehead still. Sue's neck was snapped backward, her face relaxed. Sylvia thought to move Sue's head forward so she could slip the cold towel behind her and on her neck, but she froze and screamed out. "Oh dear God!"

The crowd gasped in reaction, and Whelan yelled, "What is it?"

"Her eyes. I've seen those eyes before. On my grandmother. When she passed."

They all gawked at Sue Fielding, crumpled back in the easy chair, with wide eyes staring up at the ceiling and perhaps beyond.

"Sue!" yelled Nurse O'Brien. "Sue! Sue!" She started taking her pulse once again.

Everyone held their breath. O'Brien started shaking her head. "I believe she's gone. I think her heart failed, perhaps a heart attack." Her fingers were pressing into Sue's neck and wrist, over and over. She stopped after a few more seconds. "Oh dear Lord, she's dead. Get her on the floor! Help me!"

The men collected her arms and laid her on the ground. Nurse O'Brien began giving CPR. Whelan stayed at her side and helped her count. He took over breathing air into Ms. Fielding's lungs as O'Brien worked chest compressions. Over and over, thirty compressions and two rescue breaths. Thirty and two. Thirty and two.

The rest of the room was holding their own breaths, frozen in shock.

Half of them nearly jumped out of their seats when the doorbell's long chime rang through the house.

"On it," said Jones, racing out of the room.

She returned in seconds with three paramedics. They took over the aid from O'Brien and Whelan. In two minutes, Sue was on a gurney, with one of the men on top of her continuing compressions, as they rolled her to the ambulance to use the defibrillator on her.

"I'll go with them," said Nurse O'Brien. "Sylvia, watch after Bear." She tore from the room, racing to catch the medics.

Sylvia went and put her arms around Running Bear, still sitting on a sofa.

"I'm unsure what happened," he cried. "Is grandma Sue dead? Like the Queen?"

Chad came over, as did Grace, and did their best to comfort him.

"We don't know, sweetie," said Grace.

Even Chef Louie felt moved to come over and show support for his upset "family."

Whelan's thoughts were racing. "I need everyone to stay put in this room!" he announced.

"What?" asked Attorney Edward Toussaint. "Why?"

"Because until I figure out what just went down—" Whelan paused, staring at Running Bear, not wanting to state the obvious.

Hell, he's a twenty-seven-year-old man. Time to grow up, kid. "I need to make sure we don't have another murder on our hands. It's possible whoever killed Sophia Perkins just killed Sue Fielding, right in front of us. I'm going to need prints and DNA samples from everyone here."

Several gasps and a cacophony of snarky comments escaped the mouths in the room.

Jones was right in step. She grabbed a clean napkin and retrieved Ms. Fielding's whisky glass, thankfully not yet finished. Careful not to get her own fingers on it, she held it up to Whelan and hollered, "Kitchen!"

Whelan ran to the kitchen, searching for any signs of Sue Fielding's glasses from the dinner table. Two dishwashers were running, and a crew was wiping down the crystal washed by hand.

"Shit," he said.

"Can I help you?" asked one of the catering staff.

"Sue Fielding, her glasses from dinner! I'm looking for any of them."

The girl's head tilted slightly. "The old woman? I think she was wearing them."

"*Drinking* glasses! Water, wine, whisky—anything she took a sip from tonight!"

The server's face froze in thought, then twisted toward the clean glasses lined up on the counter, ready to be stored. "No. Sorry."

Whelan exhaled a deep breath he didn't realize he was holding. "Thanks."

He ran back to the parlor. "Nothing!" he yelled to Jones. "Did you get the bottle?"

"Got it. And I phoned Cusack. He's bringing his ERT. They will be here as soon as they can."

The room grew silent. Faces studied one another with fresh thoughts. Could they have dined beside a cold-blooded killer? Was someone in this room responsible for killing Sophia Perkins and now Sue Fielding?

Merrill wasn't the quickest on the draw, but he stood up frantically when two and two came together in his head. "Hey! I drank a glass from that bottle earlier. Should I be worried?" he asked Jones.

Her head toggled back and forth between the man and the bottle. "Shit."

She set the glass and the bottle down beside the podium and picked up her phone.

"It's going to be a long night," she said toward her partner while again dialing 911.

Chapter 16

Agent Joe Cusack, head of the forensics unit, was still collecting samples from around the home two hours later. Fourteen agents were now on the scene. Some blocked exits, some were swabbing, others were dusting for prints or taking photos. The dinner became a full-on crime scene. Sue Fielding was unable to be revived. Grandma Sue was dead, and the fate of Running Bear and eight billion dollars now sat in the hands of Grace Meyer.

"This is too much," said Grace, wiping away more tears. "Sophie? Grandma Sue? And now *I'm* responsible for Running Bear?" She turned away from Agents Whelan and Jones toward Running Bear, who was in the corner of the parlor curled up in a ball on a sofa. His right hand was tensing and releasing periodically as if someone was holding his hand and giving it an occasional squeeze.

"Well, as soon as we can figure out who killed Sophia, you have a staff of people right here who are ready and willing to help you with that," said Jones.

"Not before?" Grace asked. "What if it takes weeks? Don't these investigations sometimes take weeks?"

"Sometimes," said Whelan. "Sometimes, we catch a break." He surveilled all the activity around the room.

"You think she was killed?" asked Grace. "Maybe she had a lousy heart. A lifetime of overeating meat and cheese?"

Cusack walked up on the trio in time to catch the last question. "That didn't help her, I'm afraid. But I received a call. Toxicology showed a huge dose of clozapine was in her system. We checked Running Bear's medicine cabinet. His bottle of clozapine is empty."

Nurse O'Brien was across the room, sitting near Running Bear.

Whelan was about to motion her over but decided to move the conversation over to the sofa. He tilted his head to the others, indicating his thought. The group shifted as a unit across the floor, capturing the room's attention, and conversations quieted.

"Nurse O'Brien," began Whelan, "A substantial amount of clozapine was found in Sue. Running Bear's supply is empty. Was he out of that medication? Do you remember if there was some left?"

"I keep notes on all his dosings, but yes, he should have at least half a bottle by my recollection. It's been over a year since we took a break from them. Fifteen pills or so?"

Jones asked young Mr. Perkins, "Bear, does that sound right?"

He nodded, avoiding eye contact.

"Have you taken any lately?" she probed.

His head rattled. For a quick second, he spied the empty space adjacent to Whelan's head.

Whelan actually turned to see who was next to him before realizing it must be Cantor.

Running Bear's eyes were buried back in his lap.

"Did Cantor remember something, Bear?" asked Whelan.

"He doesn't like the pills," he mumbled in response.

"Clozapine?"

"Any of them, but yes, particularly that one. It makes it challenging for him to visit."

Running Bear looked up beside Whelan again. "Ha, ha. Very funny. Maybe I should take one now, you ingrate. Teach you to speak to the King in such a manner."

"What did he say, Bear?" asked Whelan.

Running Bear jumped off the sofa, startling the group, and got right in Whelan's face. "You know, not everything every person says is your damned business! What right have you got to come in here and stir up trouble? Everything was perfect until *you* showed up!"

Nurse O'Brien rose to her feet and put a hand on Bear's arm. "No, honey, it wasn't. Someone killed your mother, Bear, and now your great-grandmother. And as disturbing as all this is, we have to figure out who. Any information any of us have, even Cantor or Marjorie, can be useful to these agents right now. You need to cooperate with Lord Whelan and Lady Jones. The faster they get answers, the faster we can get our lives back. In whatever shape they may be."

Bear's eyes filled up with tears, but he refused to let them fall. "Cantor was being a smart-ass. He was taunting me, saying he's better suited than me to lead the kingdom. But I know how to make him disappear. Talk about an emperor with no clothes, huh?"

Running Bear's reference interested Whelan. "Keen," he mumbled.

Grace overheard him. "We read a *lot* of fables to him when he was growing up." Under her breath, she finished with, "Sadly."

Cusack took advantage of a pause in the conversation and added, "Ms. Fielding also had metoclopramide in her. Anyone here taking that?"

"What is it?" asked Grace.

"Heartburn medicine," offered Whelan, not quite sure if he remembered the drug correctly from his college classes. He turned his puzzled face to Nurse O'Brien.

"That's what it is. And no, no one in this house takes it to my knowledge."

"Grandma Sue suffered from acid indigestion my whole life," offered Grace. "Check her purse."

"We went through it at the hospital," said Nurse O'Brien. "Noted the drugs she carried, but that wasn't in there. We did find an empty pillbox. Perhaps she brought one with her and took it before dinner?" she offered to the group.

"Possibly, if she was battling GERD," suggested Cusack. "And her blood-alcohol level was hovering at point one-six."

"She liked her whisky," said Grace. "Oh! Was her whisky spiked? What was in the bottle?"

"Only Maker's Mark, in the bottle and her glass," said Cusack.

He thought to inform Merrill Perkins, who was a couple seats away, listening as best he could to the conversation. "You should be fine, Mr. Perkins. The whisky wasn't tampered with. We'll have your bloodwork results back from the lab any minute now to confirm."

He slowly relaxed his jawline. "Thank you."

The paramedics were monitoring his vitals with no signs of any issues.

"So," Cusack turned back to the huddle, "Ms. Fielding was dosed with clozapine and metoclopramide. Those drugs don't interact well. Chased with a half-dozen or so whiskies, and throw in some champagne and wine at dinner? I'd say someone knew the right medication to get her heart racing. We'll have to wait for the full autopsy to be completed, but I suspect she was already working toward congestive heart failure before this evening. That said, it was definitely the clozapine that pushed her over."

"If it wasn't the whisky, what was it in, her food?" asked Jones.

"Had to be," said Whelan. "The catering service said all but three of their servers are still here. Three left before all this started."

"Do we have their names and addresses?" asked Jones.

"For two. One of them was a new guy, Johnny. Tonight was his first gig. None of the staff here ever worked with him before or learned his last name. They said he was nervous, new job and all. The number he gave when they hired him isn't working. I'll get a trace started. I have a feeling those nerves were about more than proper table service." Whelan stepped away and dialed the field office.

"I'll confirm he's the one who served Sue Fielding," said Jones. She exited and headed toward the kitchen.

The catering staff was restless, curled up on barstools at the kitchen island or seated at the breakfast table. They were prohibited from leaving the house. They all popped their heads up when Jones waltzed in. She went straight to the manager of the catering staff.

"This 'Johnny,'" said Jones, "is he the one who waited on Sue Fielding?"

"Yes."

"And the chef?"

"Here," said a voice from behind her.

Chef Fournier stood up from his stool at the island. "It was in the food, wasn't it? That's why you're here."

"We believe so. Did Ms. Fielding make a custom order request this evening?"

"No. You all ate the same thing. So you're figuring it was either the catering fellow or me."

"Yes," Jones confirmed. "Though anyone might have had an opportunity, it's the judicious conclusion."

Chef Fournier took a deep breath and expelled it slowly. "I have my reputation to protect. How can I help clear myself from suspicion?"

"Well, the fact that you're still here and Johnny's not is a positive start. We'll need alibis for the night Ms. Perkins was killed, Saturday night. I'll have an agent take your statement. Afterward, you can go."

Jones spoke up so all could hear her. "The rest of you are free to leave. We've got prints and DNA from all of you. Thank you for cooperating. You'll be phoned if we need any further information. I'm sorry to inform you, but I need you not to travel outside of the K.C. area until this is all resolved. As soon as we have the perpetrator in custody, your lives can revert back to normal. And again, wonderful job on service this evening. We'll be in touch."

They began shuffling out of the kitchen.

Whelan arrived and took a seat at one of the stools. "I think that was enough excitement for this evening. What about you?"

"I guess. Why?" She sensed his cogs turning.

"Tomorrow, I want to take Running Bear out of here. Go by the airport. Look at dragons."

"You think that will help?"

"I don't know."

"Well, if he doesn't start delivering some amount of defense soon, we'll have no choice but to arrest him. He's all we got. You think he did it?"

Whelan dropped his arms and sighed. His eyes rolled around the ceiling. "Not one damn camera," he muttered before answering her. "My gut says no. I believe he loved his mother. There's no obvious motive. A flash of anger for getting her kicks down by the creek? I can't buy that yet."

Jones was quiet before taking a long stretch. She'd hoped to stifle a yawn but failed. "Well," she said, "I think we have another killer here from this dinner this evening. Whoever that waiter was—Johnny—he was hired by someone here."

"Based on?"

"Based on Sue's death tonight. I still leave the possibility of someone from L.A., but *my* gut says it's someone who feasted on steak and lobster this evening. They sat there, watching Sue eat, relishing the pending show of her demise." She caught Whelan's eyes. "People can really be sick fucks."

"Yep. I'm leaning in the same direction. I made a note of all the guests this evening. Except for you, me and Sue, I'm not ruling anyone else out."

"Probably not the attorneys," offered Jones.

"Agreed. Killing off your most lucrative client is not the smartest business decision."

"We'll check them out, of course, but I didn't feel a sense of familial connection from them either."

"No." Whelan started counting in his head, using his fingers to help keep track. "Twelve. I count twelve suspects then, at dinner here tonight."

Jones' eyebrows popped up. "Twelve! Dear God, we're not back to that number, are we?"

Whelan chuckled.

"Doctor Brachman!" exclaimed Jones. "We still have him as a possible suspect, unless he turns up dead. That's thirteen! Whew!"

Whelan smiled and stood up. "Thirteen it is!"

They cleared the rest of the guests to leave, giving them the "stay close and in town" warning they gave the catering staff.

Mark Fleming and Karen Hertzberg were sullen.

"With all due respect, we've got a company to help run in Los Angeles," said Karen.

"I'm sorry," said Jones. "I know this is awful. And to think you came all the way out here to pay your respects and wind up being witness to a murder." She paused, gauging their reactions. "Please, give us a couple more days at least. Can't you handle your tasks from the computer for the rest of the week?"

"We'll do our best," said Mark. He appeared disappointed in Karen's comment. "For Sophia, and out of respect to her family."

"Thank you," said Whelan.

Whelan noted Mr. Fleming's and Ms. Hertzberg's uncomfortable eye contact with each other before he crossed the room approaching Running Bear, who was curled up in the fetal position on a sofa, his head resting on Nurse O'Brien's lap. She was calmly stroking his hair. "Your Majesty," said Whelan, "we're taking our leave, but tomorrow I'll be here before eight. Please eat your breakfast early in the morning. Then I want to take you out to view some dragons."

He bolted upright on his cushion. "Dragons! Up close?"

"Yes. Might let you touch one of the small ones."

"Can Marjorie come?"

"Yes, of course. Cantor too if he'd like."

Running Bear waved at Grace Meyer, flagging her over. "We're going to view the dragons tomorrow! Can I go?"

Grace glanced back and forth between Agent Whelan and Nurse O'Brien, who offered no direction.

"I guess. Sure."

"The more, the merrier," suggested Whelan to her.

"Very well, count me in," she said. "Let's see if we can find us a red one."

Chapter 17

Special Agent Thomas Whelan pulled up to the entryway of Parkmoor around 7:30 a.m. the following day with Agent Phil Cannon in tow. Agent Jones was checking in with the team at the field office and updating SAC Kendrick.

As usual, a huge breakfast was spread out on the veranda. The agents were encouraged to join the feast. Cannon was about to sit and fix himself a plate but spotted Whelan shaking his head.

"Please understand if we decline after the poisoning at last night's dinner," Whelan said to Sylvia Moffett.

She was mortified, staring at all the warmers full of food. "I think I'll have some cereal from the pantry."

"Good idea," said Whelan.

He turned to the "King," who was slurping down the last of his orange juice. "Your Majesty. Are you ready?"

"Yes! Let's go!" He was thrilled about the adventure. If he remembered his great-grandmother was killed last night, it didn't show.

"Where's your cousin Grace?"

Sylvia commented casually, answering for him, "She said she wasn't hungry this morning." The moment she finished saying it, her eyes opened wide, and her mouth fell open with a gasp as she gaped at the chafing dish of bacon and eggs.

Whelan laughed. "Let's not convict her just yet."

The woman closed her mouth. "Of course." She walked toward the door before turning back with a red face. "Forgive me." Then she scurried through to the kitchen.

Grace Meyer stuck her head out a minute later. "You guys ready?"

The three men nodded, and the group made their way to Whelan's SUV.

The entire trip to the airport, Running Bear's face was pressed against the glass of the back window. He rarely ventured out. Seeing his "kingdom" in person like this was a treat. It was about a thirty-minute drive. As they wound up and down the hills of Kansas City's highway northward, Whelan chatted up Grace Meyer.

"So, how do you like Oklahoma City?"

"It's fine. Respectable people. Big enough to get in a headliner concert once in a while but small enough to keep our churches full of true believers."

"There aren't true believers in 'big city' churches?"

"I think they mostly go for show."

Whelan pondered that. He'd witnessed hypocrisy in churches from towns and cities of all sizes but didn't want to aggravate the situation.

"Isn't your husband thrilled to have twenty million dollars dropped in his bank account?" asked Whelan.

"Of course, but not in the manner we received it. He's sad we lost Sophie. He understands it's killing me. We were still close."

Grace's voice trailed off in hoarseness as she choked back tears. Whelan saw her face in the rearview mirror. It appeared sincere.

"My condolences for your loss," said Cannon. "I understand she'll be missed by millions, but few as much as yourself."

"Thank you, agent." Her mouth opened to express a thought, but Running Bear yelled out, interrupting her.

"There's one!" he screamed. "It's circling around to land! We must be close!"

Cannon spotted the plane in the air through his window. "What color is that one, Your Majesty?"

"I can't tell," said Running Bear. "I think it's a white dragon. Her tail is lit up with red and gold! She's a beauty."

A few minutes later, they parked outside Concourse C, and it was all the agents could do to keep up with Running Bear as he literally ran ahead to see the dragons.

Whelan guided his group to the security office where he'd made arrangements, and they were all issued badges to wear should they need to access restricted areas. The regular checkpoints at the airport were limited to access directly at each gate. Kansas City's International airport was getting a major overhaul with a brand new terminal replacing the current three concourses. It would be at least two more years before finishing the work. Concourse A was already shut down and demolished, but B and C would remain open until completion.

Once set loose, Running Bear ran to the first gate with a plane parked at a ramp. All maturity and wisdom he accumulated over his adulthood disappeared. A child full of wonder and elation danced before the agents and his cousin Grace in front of the floor-to-ceiling windows.

Running Bear turned back to them with a tear in his eye. "It's magical," he whispered.

Grace became emotional. Seeing him happy while knowing his mother was gone forever tugged on all her strings. She gave him a hug, wiping away her own tears. "Yes, Bear. Enjoy it."

As she backed away, she remembered why they were really there. She gripped Running Bear's arm and made sure she drew his full attention. "Bear, I want you to share with us what you're seeing. We're on the lookout for a red dragon today."

"Of course, I remember," he said. He took a deep breath and pulled his shoulders up a little higher, resuming a modicum of nobility. "Well, this one is a silver dragon with a red and blue tail."

It was an American Airlines 737. All of the planes were American in this section.

The group sauntered down the terminal, with Running Bear describing the planes he saw. "There's a white one with green scales and a giant Wolf on his tail!"

Again, Running Bear raced out from the others and planted his face nearly up against the glass wall.

When Whelan touched his arm, Running Bear turned around, his face beaming. "Have you ever seen a wolf that big? It can't be a regular dire wolf! It's enormous! He's howling to the moon!" Running Bear threw his head back to see if he could find the moon above. Whelan joined him in the search.

Grace and Agent Cannon stayed back a few feet, scanning the Frontier Airlines plane before them. It was an Airbus A320. Indeed, it was primarily white, with FRONTIER written down the length of its side in bold green letters. The plane's tail was painted with a giant gray wolf howling up to the sky against a starry blue background. It was the airline's theme. Nearly all of the airline's jets were painted with a different giant animal on each tail.

Running Bear was mesmerized, staring at a second Frontier Airlines A321 that pulled in next to the first. Otto the Owl was written behind its nose.

Again, Grace insisted on catching his attention. "Bear, any red dragons yet?"

"No."

She noticed the chaos of the crowds, racing, standing, drinking. Many were marching with luggage trailing behind them. Others were seated, lost in their phones. Kiosks nearby were serving coffee or beer to long lines. People were glued to barstools at a restaurant they'd passed, drinking cocktails at 8:40 a.m., perhaps so they could brace their nerves to tackle their fear of flying.

"Bear, I'd really like to understand what it is your seeing. Can you describe all this to us?"

Running Bear hadn't relayed his vision of the world to anyone in over a year. It always took him a few beats to remember other people didn't see the world like he did for some reason. This reminder usually upset him, and sometimes he refused, especially for a new doctor he didn't like. He peered into Grace's eyes. Their icy blue coolness captured his reflection and flung it back toward him.

His attention drifted back to the window, then slowly he turned his whole body in place, his eyes roving up and down and left and right until he was facing the airplanes again.

"Okay."

Before Running Bear's eyes sat a gigantic white dragon, with emerald green scales starting behind her head and running toward her tail, behind her wings, where a giant owl was perched as tall as three men. It was scanning the fields beyond.

The owl sensed it was being watched and briefly turned its head to look Running Bear straight in the eye. It decided he was not a threat and turned back to keep watch on the other dragons coming and going.

The dragon felt the shifting of the owl's weight and raised her head to meet Running Bear's gaze. A billow of steamy breath escaped her nostrils and fogged the glass. She settled back down as more passengers continued to board her. Her wings were stretched out tight. Silver scales blended with white, and her wing tips were lit with blue fire. She would be airborne soon enough.

A gentle squeezing of his hand snapped Running Bear's attention away from the window to his wife, Marjorie. She'd been standing beside him, equally amazed. It was her first time being up close to dragons.

The new young king smiled at her. She was dressed in her royal robes for this, her first outing as the new queen. She was resplendent in rich indigo fabric. Amber hair, tied into a ceremonial braid, wrapped around her head once, then trailed down her back. Her crown was thin and tasteful, the right amount of gold to highlight her stature without seeming arrogant. Three rubies adorned the crown points, one in each.

Queen Marjorie's deep brown eyes locked with his. He leaned in and gave her a warm kiss.

"Your Majesty, my love, we should recognize the people too while we're here. Your loyal subjects rarely see you," she said.

King Running Bear turned and noted the vast number of people moving about the terminal. "Yes, though many of these are guests to our land."

There were members of different kingdoms coming and going through this dragon hub. Some were dressed quite casually, visiting relatives or friends from his own kingdom. Many of them were adorned more formally, carrying or pulling travel gear behind them. A reunion of three children with grandparents they hadn't seen in ages brought tears to his eyes. For a brief flash, he remembered his own grandmother died in front of him last night. But he was here to help find who killed her and his mother. Duty called for the new king.

There were several tents pitched inside the main pavilion, selling ale and various grub. The patrons were cheerful enough. It was wonderful to see his kingdom thriving. There were booksellers, toy sellers, a paltry excuse of a medicinal supplies shop, all with store owners happily peddling their wares as people came off their dragon flights or readied themselves for a new journey.

"Should we stop and sample the street fare," asked the King to his traveling companions.

"No, thank you, Your Majesty," said Grace Meyer.

"I'm not hungry, my love," said Queen Marjorie.

As the group wandered down the terminal, Running Bear watched the circus-like atmosphere in awe. Huge awnings connected tents thirty feet in the air. Occasionally, a performer would walk by. Fire eaters, clowns on stilts, a man riding a unicycle from ten feet off the ground all went whizzing by, showcasing their talents for their King. He applauded each of them and gave an approving nod of his head.

Music played from speakers attached to the big top's support columns. Flutes carried lively melodies, cheering him, and put a dance back in his step.

And through all the joyful chaos, there were dragons. Bright yellow wyverns competed with more white dragons, some with blue and yellow tails, some with green and red.

Running Bear was fascinated by all the colors on the one at the terminal's end. The dragon raised her head, bringing it near the window and studied him. Her eye was larger than his whole head. He reached up and put his hand against the glass, separating himself from her snout. She bowed down out of respect for the King and resumed her previous stance.

"Not one red dragon?" asked Lord Whelan.

"No," said King Running Bear.

"We do have another terminal," suggested Lord Cannon.

The group moved outside. Lord Whelan flagged down a smaller blue dragon, and they all climbed on board. This one ran along the road, out from this pavilion, and circled back around to the other.

They repeated their perusal in the second dragon hub. Running Bear went through all the emotions again. He was having the time of his life.

When they exited, Whelan flagged down another small blue runner dragon, who returned them to the previous pavilion.

As they departed, Running Bear placed his hand on the side of the small dragon, behind her head, and gave her a pat. "Thank you for your service, friend."

Lord Whelan's mouth fell open.

"Running Bear," asked Whelan, "is this another dragon?"

"Yes, of course," said Running Bear.

It was one of the transport busses that looped around the terminals carrying passengers from one airline to the next.

"There are no wings," said Whelan.

"She has them tucked. She's young."

Cannon's head moved from Running Bear to Whelan, then back to the younger man. "Your Majesty, was that a *blue* dragon?"

"Yes."

"But she doesn't fly."

"She's not old enough. Her wings will spread in a few years. Right now, she has to run on the ground. We crawl before we run. They run before they fly." He appeared agitated at having to further explain himself.

A Greyhound bus was pulling up to the curb fifty yards away.

Grace Meyer clued in. "And that one over there, Bear, the silver one?" She pointed to the Greyhound.

"She's larger. She'll probably be flying in a year or two."

The group returned to Whelan's car on the lot and headed out.

"What busses in town are red?" asked Whelan. "Ride K.C.?"

"I'm on it," said Cannon. "Likely not the city bus. Those are generally blue now. There could still be a red one in service, though. I've seen them in the past. The downtown streetcar is red. Possibly that?" He was scrolling through Google on his smartphone.

They turned out of the terminal, with Running Bear's face pressed against the window, watching a dragon run faster and faster down the launch strip until she took flight, quickly rising in the sky. Her fierce roar was deafening as the massive beating of her wings carried her higher and higher.

"Marvelous," he whispered.

As they turned onto another street, the airport runway ran out perpendicular to them.

Running Bear screeched and nearly knocked the window out with his finger trying to point. "There! A red one! There's a red one!"

Whelan hit the brakes and whipped the car onto the shoulder. All four hopped out and stared at the runway.

"Where Bear?" shouted Whelan. "I don't see it."

"There!" Running Bear pointed behind the terminal.

"Son of a bitch," said Whelan, his eyes zooming in on the prize.

An Oshkosh ARV was parked in the airport emergency zone, the airport's fire truck for airline emergencies.

He did some googling of his own and found a photo. "Does your dragon rider look like this?" he asked Running Bear, holding it close.

"That's him! Well, not him personally, but that's his uniform! That's a red dragon rider's outfit! He's ready to mount her and launch."

Whelan held the phone, so Cannon and Grace could see.

It was a picture of a Kansas City firefighter, dressed in all his gear, standing on the side of a large red fire engine.

Chapter 18

Cannon researched fire stations near the residence in Mission Hills as they continued back. "There's one on sixty-third, right around the corner from the house! Station 22, Prairie Village."

"They used to have a small red dragon," said Running Bear. "But it's been a couple of years since we drove by. I bet she's bigger now."

The energy in the car picked up. For the first time, there was a concrete direction to find a suspect, besides the obvious one sitting behind Cannon.

Whelan called Agent Jones, and filled her in on their morning and new lead progress.

"A firefighter?" she repeated. "I'll be damned. I'm headed back to Parkmoor. I'll meet you at the fire station instead. I want to ambush them with Running Bear. Let's see if he can identify his dragon rider."

An hour later, Agents Whelan and Jones stood before the entire shift of Station 22 lined up for inspection. All six of them.

"I've got sixty-five men and women servicing eight towns from three firehouses across three works shifts," said the battalion chief. "If your man isn't here, try stations twenty-one and three."

Cannon was the voice of reason. "These service eight tiny suburbs. Unless we're going to assume Sophia Perkins made a habit of visiting firehouses, she presumably met the man out on the town. There must be thousands of firefighters in over a hundred stations throughout the entire K.C. metropolitan area. Are we going to drag Running Bear to every firehouse in person?"

Whelan thanked the chief, and the group huddled by his car. "Running Bear, do you remember any numbers on the fireman's hat or uniform?"

Running Bear's head fell to the side, his face puzzled.

"The dragon rider's uniform, Running Bear," corrected Cannon.

Running Bear shook his head. “No. And he wasn’t wearing his hat that night. Just the rest. He was too far away for me to read anything.”

“What about distinguishing marks? Scars? Tattoos? Do you think you could describe this fireman’s face to a sketch artist? Did you see him clearly enough?”

“I can try. Marjorie can help. It was dark that night, but…maybe.”

“Let’s get him back to Parkmoor,” said Grace. “It’s been an exciting day. We need some lunch. Have your artist come by around 3:00.”

Whelan called the office and arranged for someone to come out.

Jones sensed the dismissive tone in Grace’s voice. “Actually, we have more questions for the staff. I was heading back to the house anyway.”

Grace sighed. “Fine. But let’s give Bear a break for a couple hours.”

“I’m okay, Gracie,” spoke up Running Bear.

“I know you are, sweetie. But I’m in charge of your care now.” When the statement escaped her lips, Grace Meyer felt the weight of her new position, and tears started flowing down her cheeks. She wiped them away in embarrassment but could scarcely keep up with them. She didn’t utter a sound, but by the time they made the short drive home, she was spent.

“I’m going to freshen up and rest in my room for a few minutes. I’ll meet you all at 3:00 on the terrace,” said Grace. She disappeared, leaving Nurse O’Brien to cover in her absence.

O’Brien put her arm around Bear. “Come on, let’s get you something to eat.”

She looked at the agents, tiring for the first time of their unending presence. “You’re welcome to sandwiches in the kitchen. We didn’t know when you’d be back, so nothing is prepared.”

“We’re fine, thank you,” said Whelan. “We do need to ask more questions of everyone.”

“Starting with Mr. Buckley,” said Jones.

Down by the pool, testing the water’s pH level with a kit, Chad Buckley stood when the three agents approached. “How may I help you all today,” he asked.

"Two people died in this family in under a week, Mr. Buckley," started Whelan. "Any new thoughts?"

"No, sorry."

Jones' eyes squinted. "Grace Meyer has control over the estate now, and Running Bear."

"And his stake in the company worth billions," chimed in Cannon.

"What are you inferring," asked Mr. Buckley. "That Grace killed her Cousin Sophia and their grandmother, Sue Fielding? Right here in this house?"

"Not inferring," said Jones. "Just stating facts. Has she ever shown any desire to take over Parkmoor or Running Bear's care?"

"No," said Mr. Buckley, folding his arms.

"Ever commented about needing money or not getting along with her husband?" Jones was aware Chad Buckley harbored feelings for Grace Meyer. Perhaps he'd chatted with her about her personal life.

"No," he said again. "Grace is happily married as far as I know. As for money, Sophie wouldn't have let her hurt too much. She loved her cousin and would have taken care of her."

"How do you know?"

"Sophie—Ms. Perkins—enjoyed talking and sharing stories with me when she came. There was more than one night spent sharing a bottle of Glenlivet down by this pool. I think she took to me like a father figure in some ways."

This piqued Whelan's attention. "A *father* figure?"

"Well, I'm old enough to be her old man. She'd get drunk some nights and use me as a sounding board for how she was doing as a mother. Like we said the first day, we *all* look after Bear. I don't simply dig in the dirt and screw a loose nut around here. When Bear needs a man's perspective, Sophie encouraged him to come to me for advice. I don't know how much wisdom I really have to share, but I do my best to convey my two common cents to the boy."

Cannon chuckled at Mr. Buckley's wordplay. "We didn't get a chance to discuss the will with any of you last night, given the death of Ms.

Fielding. I wonder, how did you feel about not receiving anything from Sophia? Being as you're a father figure to her child and all?"

Chad read the young agent before answering. "We're compensated generously in our salaries. I don't think Sophie meant to slight any of us. I'm sure she thought it would be years before she would be in a position of worrying about it."

"How generously *are* you compensated?" asked Whelan.

"I was brought on at $200,000 a year. The second year I was asked to live here full time and help keep an eye on Bear. My salary was bumped to $500,000. The past three years, it's been $800,000. She said she'd give me a full million starting after ten years. It's already more than I could ever spend."

"It *is*?" asked Jones. "Sorry, but I could imagine spending quite a lot, and certainly after seeing this kind of wealth up close and personal every day."

"Well, I am *living* in it, aren't I? Without actually having it. I don't spend a dime of my salary on anything a person normally would. It's all sitting in the bank. I have no mortgage, no utility bills, no grocery bills. I have access to three cars on the property any time I want. I spoil my grandkids at Christmas a little, but otherwise, it's simply collecting interest. Unless there are plans for changes in staff around here, I'm pretty much set for the rest of my life."

"Well, there *were* plans for changes until someone killed Sue last night," said Whelan. "Sort of makes everyone in the house a suspect. The loss of $800,000 a year is a pretty strong motive for murder."

Chad Buckley drew in a breath and held it. He blew it out with a whistle. "Agent Whelan, I won't take offense to that because I know you're doing your job. But if Sophie hadn't been killed, Sue wouldn't have had any authority to close up Parkmoor and end what we all share here. And if any of us killed Sophia Perkins, we would've been biting off the hand that feeds us, literally. Thankfully, Grace plans to leave everything as it is."

"Well," Jones chimed in, "the two murders were not necessarily committed by the same person. Perhaps the second murder was inspired by the first one, unrelated to the killing of Sophia." She watched the three men before her as they reflected on the possibility.

She caught Chad Buckley's eyes. "Do you think Nurse O'Brien or Sylvia Moffett were worried about losing *their* enormous salaries? Enough to kill Sue to protect their livelihood?"

"No," said Chad defensively. "But I guess you'd have to ask them. We didn't even know about Sue's plan to close Parkmoor until she revealed it to us right before she died.

"Unless Sue discussed it with any of you ahead of the announcement last night?"

"Not me. And I'm sure Sylvia or Linda would have told me if they knew in advance."

"Thank you, Mr. Buckley," said Jones dismissively. "We'll reach out if we have more questions."

When he was out of earshot, Jones commented to Whelan and Cannon, "If the two deaths *aren't* related, then it makes sense one of the three live-ins killed Sue."

"Maybe," said Whelan. "Or perhaps they took it much more personal. I think they all genuinely love Running Bear."

"They *do* have that appearance, real or faked," said Jones.

"You don't really think the two murders aren't related, though, do you?"

"No. But we have to consider the possibility. Cannon, you hang here, speak with Sylvia. Work some of that natural charm you have."

"I have natural charm?" he asked, his cheeks reddening.

Jones flashed her pearly-whites. "And physique."

She took his tie off and unbuttoned his top two buttons. "Be friendly. Casual. She's single. You're single. Get her talking."

He smiled. "I can be friendly."

"If *he's* hanging here, where are *we* going?" asked Whelan.

"I want to get over to the hotel where Merrill's staying. Sue booked the guests from out of town at The Leonardo on the Plaza. I want to see what else she might have told Merrill in advance of last night."

"Maybe he'll be more tempted to talk now that there's no guarantee of getting the $500,000 Sue promised to pay him to go away quietly."

Chapter 19

"Nice digs, Merrill," said Jones, pushing her way inside his hotel room when he opened his door. "Posh."

"Yeah, it's all right," he admitted.

It was the utmost luxurious hotel room he'd ever stayed in. Overlooking Kansas City's Country Club Plaza, it was a one-bedroom suite, and it was clear they ransacked the minibar.

Peggy came out of the bedroom and shut its door. "Merrill, you didn't tell me we were entertaining company," she said. "May I offer you all any refreshments?"

She gestured toward the few tiny bottles of liquor on top of a desk that remained sealed.

"No," said Whelan, "we're fine, thank you."

She took a seat on the sofa and again gestured for them to sit in the living room.

"Thank you," said Jones. *You're adapting to newfound money quickly,* she thought.

"Mr. Perkins," said Whelan, "we thought you might shed some light on your perception of last night's events."

"My perception?" he questioned. "My *perception* is someone had it out for Sue. My money's on Grace. She gets it all now."

"You think Grace killed Sue so she would get the bulk of the inheritance?"

"Well, yeah. Why else kill her?"

Jones tilted her head. "Revenge. Jealousy. There are lots of reasons people kill besides money."

"Uh-huh," said Merrill, "but you gotta admit, eight billion dollars has got to be first on the list for this one."

"Perhaps."

Peggy was shifting in her seat, pressing out wrinkles on her skirt. "If you don't think Grace killed her, who do you think did?"

Whelan studied the woman. "We don't think anything, Ms. Perkins. We're collecting thoughts. What is your thought on who killed her?"

Merrill shot his eyes toward his wife, clearly intending to shut her up. She returned her husband's gaze before answering. "Well, I think—"

Her sentence was cut off by Merrill's interruption, "You don't think anything! You don't know those people. You keep your mouth shut. This is family business, and you don't know nothin'!"

Peggy closed her lips and sunk into the sofa as far as she could.

The tension hung in the room as the agents stayed silent, waiting for Merrill to take the lead in the conversation. After another minute, he delivered. "Why do you think Sophie left me one dollar? Was that to punish me? Did she want me to have to come up here and get a taste of all that money knowing I'd go home and still be dirt poor? What the hell was the girl thinking? Did I do her that much harm? Or that bastard grandson of mine? Hells bells! Am I really that big of an asshole?"

He said it rhetorically, but Jones saw Peggy's eyebrows shooting up as she gave her husband another glance.

"Again," said Whelan, "not for us to surmise. We're observers here, trying to solve a murder. Two murders now.

Jones was staring at the pair on the sofa across from her. *You need Viagra to get it up for her, don't you, Merrill?*

"I was wondering, Merrill," she started, "what did Sue Fielding tell you about her plans in advance of last night?"

"Huh?" he asked.

"She was planning on selling off Parkmoor and taking Running Bear out to L.A. Did you know that before her announcements after dinner last night?"

"No. Of course not. Did it look like I was given advanced warning?" he snapped.

"Maybe you're a brilliant actor."

"I'll be sure to submit my name for an Oscar," he said. "Sue didn't tell me nothin'! I can't believe she didn't warn me in advance she was gonna give me some money. I might not have caused a ruckus."

"You think your 'ruckus' is what gave Sue her heart attack?" asked Jones.

Merrill stopped cold. He cast his eyes on the floor, then once around the room before landing his pupils back on Jones in front of him. Her copper irises were lit up by the sun coming through the gap in the curtains.

"No. I think she was old, ate too much rich food these past few years, and clearly was on her way to drinking herself to death," he answered. "She knows who I am. Knew," he corrected.

"Apparently, so did your daughter," said Jones. "Those years you keep bragging about helping young Running Bear? She deemed them to be valued at one whole dollar."

"Well, at least Sue took mercy on me before she got bumped off," said Merrill. "$500,000 is an insult when they got as much as they got, but it'll help."

"Actually, there's no guarantee you'll receive anything now," said Whelan. "It wasn't drawn up legally and signed off on."

Merrill's face took on a confused expression before furrowing itself into a jumbled red mess. "What the fuck are you suggesting?" he screamed. "She said it! That should be good enough. I've got witnesses! You're the fucking FBI! You heard her!"

"Yes," said Jones calmly. "Agent Whelan was simply pointing out that it might be in question, given Sue's death. And the estate's control now rests in Grace's hands, as you said yourself. It's really up to her whether or not to honor that, I'd imagine. She's certainly under no legal obligation."

Merrill grew quiet and practically whispered, "I'll sue the hell out of all of them. I'll get what's mine."

"That is your prerogative," said Jones.

Peggy cleared her throat and spoke out softly. "Sounds like you better be kind to Grace. Make sure she gets you that $500,000. Maybe if you're really sweet, she'll give us a million." She winced in anticipation of being struck.

Merrill surprised her by nodding his head. "Yep. I need to get over there and butter her up. Remind her who helped raise the kid the first few years."

"Go on and ask them your other question," said Peggy to her husband. "The one you thought of last night."

"Oh, yeah! Hey," he asked the agents, "if Grace didn't want the role of taking care of Running Bear, would that default to me, his granddaddy?"

"No," said Jones. "He's a twenty-seven-year-old man. I imagine he would have some amount of say. And he made it clear in a statement last night after the funeral, he'd never see you again. So I'm guessing you're not on the list of caretakers."

"Oh." Merrill's focus drifted to the ceiling a minute and began to relax before popping to attention again. "What if Grace dies? Who's in charge of the estate and the money then?"

"I'm sure she'll set up trustees and other conservators soon enough."

"Yeah, but if she kicked the bucket before that was done?"

"Well, that's a question for the attorneys, but I suppose there would be a fight from anyone who thought they held a legitimate claim on the estate," said Whelan. "Why? Are you planning on killing Grace Meyer?"

Merrill paused in mid-thought as if actually contemplating it. All eyes in the room shifted to him.

"Of course not," he said. "And I didn't kill Sue or Sophie."

He peeped at the liquor bottles and licked his lips before continuing. "I'm simply asking a question. Someone's gunning for our family, and if they get to Grace before she sets up new trusts, I wanted to know if I owned a shot at getting more. That's all."

Jones and Whelan glared at him. Peggy stood and scowled down at the man.

"You're a monster," she said plainly, before running back to the bedroom.

The agents stood to leave.

"Someone's gunning for *your* family?" asked Whelan. "I think Running Bear might have a different opinion of who is really a part of *his* family these days."

Jones approached the older gentleman and leaned over him where he sat. Her three-inch boot heels gave her some extra confidence today. "You have a mess on your hands in there, Merrill." She shot her chin toward the bedroom behind him. "Clean it up gently because if I see another bruise anywhere on her body tomorrow, I'm coming after you for spousal abuse, even if she won't."

Jones bent down further, placing her hands on her thighs, her face inches away from Merrill's. "Whether Grace gives you any money or not, it's time for you to take a deep, hard look at yourself and the few years you have left. Grow up. Be a man. Start being a *good* man."

She walked through the doorway, entering the hallway.

"Mr. Perkins, we still need you to stay in town," said Whelan. "We're working on wrapping this up, but Sue's death has thrown an extra wrench in this. The Leonardo has a fantastic restaurant downstairs. Running Bear's estate is paying for this. Take your wife there for dinner tonight. You can bill it to the room. Won't cost you a thing to treat her to a decent evening."

Merrill's jaw tightened. He stood and locked eyes on the young FBI agent. "How dare you tell me what I should or shouldn't do with my wife." He noticed the inside of Whelan's open jacket, revealing the agent's gun, holstered in a shoulder harness.

"I won't be leaving town yet," Merrill continued. "My odds of becoming a millionaire are getting better and better." He went to the open door and held it for Whelan. "I expect I'll be seeing you at the house soon enough."

Chapter 20

Agents Whelan and Jones moved down the hallway on the second floor of The Leonardo.

"So, you went easier on Merrill there than I expected," said Whelan.

Jones raised her eyebrows. "Yeah, well, if I'm going to be an ASAC, I'd better start practicing diplomacy." She forced a smile.

Whelan wasn't buying it. "Everything all right at home? Are you getting enough sleep?"

"Everything's fine."

She knocked on another hotel room door. It was answered by Mark Fleming, Sophia Perkin's board member who attended the dinner last night.

"Oh, super, you're both here," said Jones, walking into the suite.

Karen Hertzberg, the other Forever Sophia board member, was sitting on a sofa. She stood and motioned them to sit opposite her. "I took the liberty of having a pot of coffee sent up. Can I pour either of you a cup?"

"That's the best offer I've received all day. Thank you," said Whelan. He added a splash of cream in one and handed it off to his partner. He swirled two spoonfuls in his and was about to take a sip when he stopped himself and stared at Karen.

She felt it and turned her head toward him. After a moment, she snickered at him. "Agent Whelan, you're welcome to have another pot sent up, but I assure you, this one isn't poisoned."

Karen added more coffee to her cup and took a sip. "There now. Oh, they do serve amazing coffee. Mark? You want a cup?"

"No, thank you. I don't care for any," he said, taking a seat alongside her.

Karen and the agents all froze with their cups midway in the air when he declined.

It was Mark Fleming's turn to laugh. "I can't do caffeine after 3:00, or I'll be up all night."

Whelan threw caution to the wind and took a long sip. “Very nice. Thank you both for staying in town. We didn’t get a chance to speak one on one with all the excitement last night.”

“That poor woman. That was horrible,” said Karen. “And Running Bear! To have lost his grandmother right after having lost his mother. It’s heartbreaking. I can’t imagine! We’d never met Ms. Meyer until last night. Do you suppose she’ll be an appropriate conservator for the young man?”

“My impression is she’s going to try her best.”

“That’s nice to hear.”

“Karen,” started Jones, “I understand you and Sophia were close? You socialized outside of work?”

“Yes. We bonded many years ago. She was one of my closest friends, and we shared complete respect for one another in our professional relationship. Despite some of her personal issues, she really did run the company well."

“Personal issues?” asked Jones.

“Sophia could never seem to find anyone in her private life to settle down with. Not that a woman should have to, but I think she wanted to. She dated a lot of men from many walks of life. And that’s fine, but she wasn’t as happy as someone with her success should be. There was always something missing for her. And no amount of one-night stands or short-term relationships was going to fill it.”

“Are you saying she was a slut?”

“Oh heavens, no! What an awful word. No doubt invented by a man. In this day and age, you’d think a woman should be above that. If a woman wants sexual relations without love or commitment, why do we still prosecute her? Make it dirty? It’s still a ‘boys club’ out there.”

She looked at Mark beside her. “Sorry, Mark. You’re one of the exceptions. I didn’t mean to imply anything about you. Be glad you’re married and past all that nonsense.”

“Oh, I am, believe me,” he said.

“So you’re not married, Ms. Hertzberg?” asked Whelan.

“No.”

"And you and Sophia Perkins used to go out together? Where?"

"We had lunch often, different places. And we'd hit popular nightclubs around L.A. from time to time. It's not like we're in our twenties any longer, Agent Whelan. And we're running quite a cosmetics empire. We make it out once every couple of months at best. Five or six times a year. Made. We *made* it out." She lowered her head. "I have to get used to that now."

"Is there anyone Sophia ever dated or took home in the past few months who gave you an uncomfortable feeling?" asked Whelan. "Someone who your gut told you was dangerous and might want to harm her in any way?"

"No. Not at all."

"We believe she might have been seeing someone here, in Kansas City," said Jones. "Did she mention him to you? We really need a name."

"No. I'm sorry."

"Mr. Fleming?" asked Whelan,

"She did mention to me about a month back she'd met some man here, in Kansas City. She didn't give me his name either. I didn't ask. I wish now I had. I'm not a gossipy sort, and as Karen said, there were more than a few, so I didn't get too invested when she chose to share with me. When Sophia wanted to discuss her personal life, I listened but never pushed for details."

He wheeled on the woman next to him. "Karen? She never mentioned this fellow to you she met here?"

"No. If it was serious, she would have told me. It was either new or…casual."

Mark turned back to Whelan. "I'm sorry, agents. That's the best I can do. 'Some man.'"

"Is there anyone else you can think of who might want to harm Sophia? Billions of dollars' worth of control in your company is at stake right now," said Whelan. "Personal relationships aside, that's a hefty reason for murder. Anyone we should be interviewing on the board who might have expressed thoughts about returning control of her shares back to the other board members?"

"No."

"I understand many shareholders were wanting to move forward with an IPO," said Whelan. "Sophia voted no on that. We obtained copies of your corporate documents. Are you aware the motion failed by two one-hundredths of a vote shy of the two-thirds majority your by-laws state are needed?"

Mark chuckled. "Yes. Very. We were questioned by your L.A. agents for two days before flying out here. They're diving deeply into the board members who wanted to go public. But I can't imagine any of them would commit murder to gain additional share volume. There's only so much money one person can spend in their life."

"You might be surprised by the amount of greed some people are capable of mustering," said Jones.

"Maybe."

"Perhaps they wanted to take the company in another direction and saw Sophia as an obstacle?" asked Whelan.

"No, some just wanted to take it larger too quickly. I've learned from other ventures in my life. Grow too fast, and thin walls will fall. Reinforce what you've built before expansion, and you'll develop an empire that will last forever. That's what Sophia and I were working toward. And, as Karen told you, Sophia really did run things well. I guided her, of course, but she developed a phenomenal sense of business for someone who never finished high school. She knew inherently how to market and sell herself. Without her, I can't imagine how sales will maintain like they have. Anyone involved in the company who would kill her would be removing the core of Forever Sophia. They'd be removing the moneymaker, shooting themselves in their own foot, so to speak. Doubling your number of shares means little if the share value falls to half-price."

"Do you think the entire board understands that? Feels the same way you do?" asked Jones.

"They're an exceptional group. We all get along well, share the end goal. It's the speed at which we move that is debated at times. They're smart. Yes. I think they all would agree with my assessment. It doesn't make financial sense to remove Sophia from Forever Sophia. I don't see how we're going to go on as a company." He became a little choked up. "I'm sorry. This is difficult. I loved Sophia, like a sister or a daughter. This is personal for me too."

Karen smiled bittersweetly and patted Mark's leg before speaking to the agents again. "To know her was to love her, truly."

She set her cup on the table. "We have press releases prepared. We'll say how she was really simply a spokesperson, and the quality makeup everyone has come to know will be the same. After the inevitable uptick in sales following this tragedy, we forecast revenues to fall the following fiscal year by a minimum of twenty percent without Sophia's presence. No spokesperson will ever be able to replace her. Literally or figuratively. And we all know it."

The group took a pause, giving respect to the woman who launched it all.

"Regarding dinner last night," Whelan changed the subject. "Did either of you happen to observe the man serving Sue Fielding? Could you describe his face to a sketch artist? Mr. Fleming? You were a couple seats over from her."

"I'm sorry, no," he said. "We attend quite a few functions over the course of a year, Agent Whelan, many dinner parties similar to last night. At the risk of sounding uppity, I've grown to not pay too much attention to the service staff at these kinds of things. My focus always has to be on the host or whoever the host is honoring. I couldn't even describe my own server or confidently express their gender."

Whelan's eyebrows raised slightly. "Ms. Hertzberg?"

"No. That makes us sound awful, doesn't it?" she asked.

"You live in a different world is all," said Jones.

Jones stood to leave. "If either of you thinks of any other details regarding last night or have new thoughts about who killed Sophia, please call us." She placed a card on the coffee table.

A few steps down the hall, Jones stopped and turned to her partner. "I'm getting the feeling Forever Sophia was forever a hot mess. Sleeping with strange men. Relying on older men to fill in as replacements for the daddy life failed to give her. First Chad Buckley, now Mark Fleming. I wonder how many other 'father figures' were in her life. I'll wager there were more out in L.A."

"Don't lose your fangirl status because she was a real woman with real problems. I'm developing more and more respect for her with each interview we have. To have Merrill as a dad, overcome him, then raise Running Bear to be the fine man he's grown to be, despite his obvious afflictions? I'm starting to become a Forever Sophia fanboy. How would I look in eyeliner?" he joked.

Miranda Jones studied Thomas Whelan and pictured it. "If your hair gets any longer and even more unruly, it might suit you. Can you play a bass guitar?"

"I strummed a banjo once in high school."

"Maybe you could recite some original poetry at open mike night. Wear a turtleneck?"

"It's a date."

She put her hand on his upper arm and gave a gentle squeeze before moving toward the elevator.

Her scent hung in the air as Whelan started to follow her, and it paralyzed him for the first time in a few weeks. He'd let go of any romantic feelings he'd felt for her when working their first case earlier that summer. But one whiff of her perfume mixed with her natural scent was all it took to destroy his progress in moving on from those emotions. Thankfully, he was disciplined. He bathed in the air where she stood for a few more seconds, then raced to catch up, putting it out of his head once again.

Chapter 21

On the fourth floor of The Leonardo, Jones rapped her knuckles on the door to Sarah William's room. Sophia Perkin's executive assistant wasn't answering.

"Odd, she knew we had an appointment," said Jones.

Whelan read his watch. It was nearly 4:30. "Maybe she went for an early dinner? Should we check the restaurant?"

"We can, but I doubt it. That L.A. crowd tends to eat late. *And* she's still on L.A. time. Her stomach thinks it's 2:30."

"Maybe a late lunch then?"

They checked the restaurant to no avail.

"Business center?" asked Whelan.

They found her hunched at a small desk typing away furiously on a computer. She wore headphones and needed to be nudged before she realized they were behind her.

"I'm sorry," said Sarah. "This hotel, lovely as it is, can't seem to keep a wireless signal in my room. I've been in this little mosh pit more than my bedroom the past twenty-four hours. Work is endless. You think putting out fires in person is hard? Try it from 1500 miles away! And no one knows! The second this goes public, I'll be in total crisis mode, fielding issues around the globe."

Her phone rang, and she answered it without thinking. "Sarah Williams. No. Yes. Yes. No. Three. Oh, let me check." She scrolled to a saved file on her phone. "$786,498.13. Last quarter. To Paris. Well, that flower didn't have a banner crop last year. What do you want me to tell you?"

Sarah raised her head up to the agents before her. Their faces were stoic.

"Peter, I have to go. I'm *trying* to get back as soon as possible. Four. No, Four. Yes. Yes. Goodbye."

"Forgive me. I'll put it on vibrate. Can we sit here? I've got too much work to pack up and go anywhere else. There's no one else in here. We can talk."

Whelan pulled out a chair for Jones, but she opted to sit on the adjacent desktop instead. He took a seat and scanned the desk in front of him. The contents of Sarah William's briefcase were strung out all over every inch of space. It would have been comical if there weren't a murder to be solved.

Two murders, thought Whelan. *And hopefully no more.*

"Sarah, did you happen to get a look at the waiter serving Sue Fielding at last night's dinner?" asked Jones.

"Briefly. It was him, wasn't it? Poor woman. That was awful. I don't think I've ever seen anyone die right before my eyes like that. I mean, my grandfather maybe. But he was in a hospital, and the whole family was there. He was on a ventilator, and we'd decided to unhook him after five months. The doctors said he wasn't coming back, but my mother held out hope. He took a single, shallow breath when the tube came out. For ten seconds, we all held our own breath as we waited for a second one from him. It never came. But poor Ms. Fielding! Clutching her heart like she'd been shot. Can you imagine the pain she must have been in? Well, I've never seen anyone die like that."

"Does your brain move faster or slower than your mouth?" asked Jones. "I honestly can't tell."

"I'm not sure I can either. They both tend to rattle ninety miles an hour. My mother used to say it was an awful trait. But it makes for one hell of an executive assistant. I've been with Sophia for two years. After the first month, we were clicking like Jimmy Choos. She loved that I could process what she threw at me as quickly as she could think of it. Sometimes I was even ahead of her."

She straightened herself proudly. "I hope wherever I land when all this is settled can appreciate me like she did. I'm an acquired taste, but the end results are worth it."

"And humble too," said Whelan.

Sarah eyeballed him. “There’s no room for modesty in the corporate world, Agent Whelan. Especially not in L.A.”

“I suppose not. Ms. Williams, do you think you’d be able to describe Ms. Fielding’s server to a sketch artist? We have one over at Parkmoor right now.”

“No. As I said, I saw him, but outside of a white male, thirty to forty years in age, I wouldn’t be able to recall anything. No tattoos stood out to me, though. It’s my secret pleasure, tattoos. I tend to admire the ink on others when I see it.”

She rolled up her sleeve and twisted her wrist. On her forearm, a butterfly was crawling out of a cocoon. “I’ve got more, but you’ll have to buy me a few drinks before you get to see them.”

Whelan’s eyes opened wide as Sarah smiled at him.

Jones’ focus went back and forth between her partner and the young woman. “I don’t think that’s in our daily allowance. Sarah, you’ve had a few days to process Sophia’s death. What does your gut tell you? Who killed her and why?”

She rolled her sleeve down. “Are you kidding? I have no idea.”

Jones waited for her to continue on and was surprised by her silence.

“Guess,” she ordered.

Sarah’s chin fell, her eyes distant. She let out a sigh after a minute. “I’ve been trying to figure that out since I got the call Sunday morning. Soon after they discovered her in that alley. And I understand now, she wasn’t killed there?”

Whelan replied, “No. It was right down the hill from Parkmoor.”

“So why move her? What purpose did it serve?”

Whelan’s expression grew to appreciation. “That’s the best question anyone has asked all day. Presumably, to hide the scene of the crime and any identifiers left behind. Lucky for the assassin, it was raining that night. Tire prints, footprints—washed away.”

Sarah Williams paused again, but you could see her mind working on her face. “What about questionably?”

“Hmm?”

"You said, 'presumably.' What other *questionable* reason might there be to move her to an alley downtown?"

"We're theorizing. But you tell me, Ms. Williams. You're smart. Why else would *you* move a body from out in the suburbs to the middle of downtown?"

"To keep her son from finding her in that condition."

"That was fast," said Jones. "Didn't take you two seconds."

"It took me four days. Four days I've thought about it. You asked me what my *gut* tells me, Agent Jones? It tells me whoever killed Sophia cared enough about Running Bear that they didn't want to chance he'd stumble onto his mother's own body."

"Well, if that's true," said Whelan, "then they blew it. Running Bear followed his mother down to Brush Creek that night. He witnessed the whole thing."

Sarah leaned against her chair back. More emotions raced across her face. "I didn't know."

"And I shouldn't have told you, but the more time that goes by on this, the harder it is going to be to find her killer. For what it's worth, I do appreciate your insight."

"I don't have a clue who killed her, Agent Jones." She belatedly responded to the agent's command. "My guess is someone in the family or that house. If it was someone in the company, I'd be surprised."

"No one in the company who thought they might be in her will? Get to an early payout?"

"I can't imagine who that would be. No."

"Not even you?" asked Jones.

"Ha!" Sarah roared at her. "Agent, I've not suppressed any delusions about my relationship with Sophia Perkins. We got on famously, but I was her employee. I didn't expect I would be left a dime. Never even thought about it. Until I was invited to the reading last night."

"And then?"

"Well, she *was* a billionaire. When those numbers were being read last night, I suppose there was one brief moment where I thought, *maybe*.

But then, it was over, and there was nothing, and I wasn't surprised or offended. I'm not family. I wasn't expecting anything."

"Does your contract call for a severance should you be dismissed?"

"No. And I don't like your implication. I make $180,000 a year Agent Jones. Even if I received a severance, what would it be? Six months or a year's pay? I'm going to risk jail for less than $200,000? I highly doubt it. I'll be one of the most sought-after executive assistants on the open market as soon as this is released. I'm sitting here, in the middle of the country, working my ass off to keep things afloat until the announcement. I could have bailed immediately. With my resume, I expect to be offered even more in my next position. But I'm loyal, and that's worth something still. I've given my alibis to your agents out in California. But if you need to ask me anything else to satisfy your comfort levels that I had nothing to do with Sophia's murder, please, ask it now."

"You make $180,000 a year?" asked Whelan.

"Yes. And I'm worth every penny. Sophia travels weekly. I have to travel with her. Which means no personal life. My social calendar is her social calendar. I have to be available twenty-four hours a day. It's a global enterprise. I go full steam seven days a week. This crazy energy I have? It takes someone like me to do what I do."

Whelan turned to Jones and motioned to himself. "*I* work twenty-four/seven."

Jones laughed. "As soon as saving lives becomes more important than creating exquisite makeup in a cute little compact, I'll put you in for a raise."

"Honestly, agents, I have work to do. Anything else?" asked Sarah.

"Not right now," said Jones. "And again, we appreciate your staying in town. We're working to ensure you can return to L.A. as soon as possible."

"Well then, you know where to find me. Have a successful evening." Sarah put her headphones back on and turned to her computer, where she resumed furiously typing away.

Whelan stared at the young woman. "What do you suppose she's listening to in there?"

"I don't know," said Jones, "but with her intensity, it's not easy listening."

"I can hear you," said Sarah without turning around. "And currently, it's Billie Eilish. She's on my playlist. Now please, if you're going to talk about me behind my back, do it from your car."

Whelan hopped up. "Good evening Ms. Williams."

She waved her hand in the air dismissively, and the agents took their leave.

In Whelan's SUV, he began chuckling. "I sort of liked her and wanted to strangle her at the same time."

"Partner, we are definitely in sync on that one."

"She didn't seem heartbroken over Sophia's death."

"Not terribly, no. Either she's not wired that way, or she's so busy, she hasn't allowed herself any time to process. It's been four days though, maybe she's moved on already. Would you stay upset if your boss was killed?"

"Of course! I'll give Sarah the benefit of the doubt and assume she's compartmentalizing until she can finish her job with the company."

"Very noble," said Jones. "Let's get back to Parkmoor. We should have a sketch of the dragon rider by now."

Chapter 22

At Parkmoor, Agent Phil Cannon was doing his best to chat up Sylvia Moffett. Cannon's impressive physicality didn't seem to be affecting the young housekeeper today. She was distracted and clearly still upset over the tragedy of Sue's death the previous evening.

"I can't believe this is all happening," she said to him as she poured herself a glass of iced tea out of the refrigerator in the kitchen.

Cannon was sitting on a barstool at the island. "It's a lot to take in. And you really have no idea who might have wanted Sue Fielding dead?"

"No." She took a sip and stared out the window to the Veranda, where Running Bear was sitting with the sketch artist. She couldn't make out the illustration from this angle. "I don't know why she wouldn't let us sit with him."

Sylvia referred to the FBI's demand that Running Bear be allowed to describe the killer's appearance without interruption.

"For what reason would you want to?" asked Cannon.

"Bear gets terribly nervous when forced to be alone with someone he doesn't know. If one of us were with him, he'd be able to relax, get through this process faster."

Cannon peered out the window. "I don't know. He seems pretty relaxed to me. His eyes are closed. I think he's visualizing the man. He looks calm enough."

"Really? See his fists? They're clenched on the arms of the chair he's in. He's sitting there recalling the face of the man who killed his mother. His mother was everything to him. Not the least of which, she was his queen."

Turning back to Sylvia, Cannon cocked his head, and his face scrunched in confusion.

Sylvia studied his expression before returning the pitcher of tea to the refrigerator. "I realize you don't live in our little world, Agent. This must all seem like complete lunacy to an outsider. I've been here long enough that it's perceptible to me now. Sophia was his queen. He was a prince and now a king. It's all more real to him in his head than you are.

She released a heavy sigh.

Cannon took a pause before speaking. "Do you believe it was really in Running Bear's best interest to keep him off his meds and encourage him to explore this whole fantasy life?"

Sylvia's face was blank. "I did. Now, I don't know. It wasn't my call, so I never questioned it."

"Well, question it now. Obviously, you care for the man. You all do. But what do *you*, Sylvia Moffett, really think would be the best thing for him?"

She scanned Running Bear head to toe. "I really don't know. My understanding is that it's basically two choices. We let him wallow in fantasy or a drug-induced haze that keeps his brain cloudy and wondering if it's going crazy with the few delusions that still slip in. Are you married, Agent Cannon?"

The question surprised him. "No." He flashed a smile.

"Well, imagine if you were. You have a wife you love more than anything in the world. And suddenly, she disappears. Then you see her from time to time. Perhaps across a room or walking in the street. She stops and waves at you before dissolving into nothingness as you sit there helpless. It might be weeks before you see her again. And just as the trusted people in your life have you convinced she was never real to begin with, she slips under your covers one night and makes love to you. The ensuing morning, gone…again. Is that what you'd wish for yourself? Of course not. Is that what you'd wish for Running Bear?"

"Of course not," he echoed. "Not for anyone. But, it is the way it is."

"No! It isn't!" she snapped. She gripped the counter's edge. "Right now, he's as normal as the rest of us, in a way. He has friends, he has a wife, he has his role as the King."

Sylvia stopped herself. "I can see I'm talking to a wall. Did you have any other questions? I have work to do."

Cannon stood. "Ms. Moffett, I'm sorry I upset you. You're not talking to a wall. I'm really making an effort here. When you first started here, how long did it take you to adjust to this…augmented reality existing here at Parkmoor?"

"I don't know, a few weeks, maybe three or four months?"

"I've been here two days. Cut me some slack?"

She smiled for the first time this afternoon. "Yes. I'm sorry. We're all worried for him. I know it doesn't look favorable, the sword with his fingerprints and her blood. Poor Sophia."

She started to tear up. "And now, Sue. At least there's a better suspect for her death than Running Bear. Have you not been able to track down that mystery server from dinner last night?"

"Our best people are on it. What would you guess was his motivation for killing Sue?"

"*My* guess? Goodness. Money, I suppose. Someone paid him to poison her."

"Uh-huh. Who?"

"Well, maybe—" she cut herself off. "I shouldn't be venturing a guess."

"Why?"

Sylvia's head dropped. "Because I work here. Because…the likeliest suspect is now my new boss."

"Grace Meyer?"

"Yes."

"Was that who you were going to say? A second ago? You said, 'well, maybe.' Well, maybe who? Tell me what your instinct says."

"I don't even know the man."

"Who?" Cannon's voice was loud and sharp.

"Merrill Perkins! My first thought was Merrill Perkins. I think he killed them both. Except, my head wrestles with my gut because he certainly isn't astute, and I don't think he has two nickels to rub together. So, if it's him, he must have commissioned a hitman willing to work on the assurance of a big payout down the road. And that seems unlikely. Wouldn't you agree?"

Cannon grinned. "Perhaps. Or not. You watch a lot of 'hitman' movies?"

His question didn't register, and she kept talking, thinking, out loud. "So, I have no proof it's Merrill at all. I simply…didn't like him. He gave me the creeps all night last night. I think he's here in hopes of getting rich. Isn't that sad? There's a beautiful, intelligent, creative man out there. His *grandson.* And he only came for the money. I'm glad Sophie stiffed the bastard in her will."

"See. That wasn't so hard." Cannon gave her a slight bow. "Thank you for your thoughts and honest opinions, My Lady."

Sylvia released another sigh. "You're welcome."

"I'll go check on your beautiful, creative man." Cannon exited out the French doors from the kitchen onto the veranda.

"And intelligent," Sylvia whispered.

The sketch artist, Rebecca Strathmore, was frustrated. Four pages were torn out of her book of charcoal paper. Cannon studied them, where they lay on the ground behind her. Four different men's faces were before him.

"None of these are the red dragon rider, Your Majesty?" he asked.

"No. She came close to getting it right once, but his nose was too big. Then too small. She's erased more than she's drawn. Do you have a better artist?"

Ms. Strathmore stood up after his insulting comment and threw her pad on the table. "I need some water." She jerked open the door to the kitchen and went inside.

"She's one of the best there is," said Cannon.

"Well, then, that's sad. You must not catch many criminals."

"We do all right. And we'll catch your mom's—the Queen's—killer, Your Majesty. I promise."

"Thank you, Sir Cannon. I guess we're taking a break."

Running Bear went in the other set of doors to the living room and disappeared upstairs.

Cannon picked up the drawings and laid them out on the patio table. *Four faces.*

The artist returned after a few minutes, with Agents Whelan and Jones behind her.

"I've never seen anything like this," said Rebecca. "Not in all my years. As I was narrowing in on what he was describing, he'd throw a fit and say it was all wrong. So, we'd start fresh. And again, I'd get 'close,' he'd say, before yelling at me I was off."

She brushed her fingers along one of the illustrations. They were meticulous, except perhaps in the areas where she had frequently erased to match Running Bear's ever-changing description.

Jones was studying the faces and took pictures of all of them on her phone. She began texting them. "Ron Leslie at the office," she offered to the two men as an explanation. "He can do wonders on the computer. I want him to run a composite image based on all four of these."

"Merge them all and get a winner?" asked Whelan. "Can't hurt."

"Why do you think Running Bear couldn't commit to one face?" asked Cannon.

The question seemed to stump everyone.

"Do you suppose," asked Rebecca, "his view of all of us 'real people' is constantly changing? Maybe each time he looks at us, he sees a slightly different variation of ourselves? There's a disorder like that. I can't think of the name of it."

"Prosopagnosia," said Whelan. "Highly unlikely, and there's nothing in his record."

"I think he didn't get a clear view of his mom's murderer, and his mind is trying desperately to compensate for his guilt over it," said Jones. "It was dark that night. The street lamp can throw shadows. There was a light rain. He was peeping through the leaves of a tree. He obviously doesn't know for sure what the man looks like."

"Shame," said Rebecca Strathmore. She put her pad and charcoal pencils back in her bag. "Then a fifth or sixth image won't matter. Good luck with your manhunt."

"Thanks," said Whelan.

The artist took her leave, and the three agents scrutinized the images again on the table.

"Didn't Running Bear see the dragon rider the week before his mom was killed? Here, in the house? The kitchen, I believe it was?" asked Cannon.

"Yes," answered Jones.

"Did he have poor lighting that night too?"

"No. The kitchen's pretty well lit." Jones turned toward it.

Sylvia Moffett was watching them through the panes of glass in the door and wheeled away quickly like she'd been caught with her hand in the cookie jar.

"I suspect he didn't get the best view of the man that evening either, if he was just passing by, stealing a glimpse."

"I get the feeling he steals a lot of glimpses," said Jones.

"He definitely is aware of what goes on in this house. I think either Running Bear's uncertain and afraid to commit to an image," said Whelan, "or the man he saw kill his mom down by Brush Creek isn't the same man she entertained here in the kitchen the week before."

"Or," said Jones, "Running Bear really *did* murder his mother, and he's making all this up."

Chapter 23

The three agents stood silent, intent on memorizing the images.

A splash was heard down the hill. Whelan's curiosity got the better of him, and he sauntered down the paved steps to the pool deck. Earl Humboldt, Grace Meyer's dad, was swimming a lap. When he popped up for air below Whelan's feet, the sixty-five-year-old grabbed the coping and paused.

"Agent," he said. "Something I can do for you?"

"Tell me who killed Sue Fielding and Sophia Perkins so I can get out of your hair."

"I wish I could deliver that for you. I truly do. Sue was a pistol," Earl chortled. "Despite her abruptness last night, she fostered a big heart and really loved this family."

"Were you close?"

"Can't say we were. Especially the last decade. I might speak to her once or twice a year."

Whelan took a seat in a nearby chair. "How's the water? I haven't seen anyone else in there all week."

"It's perfect. Seemed a shame to waste it. It's a hot day, and you've got me held hostage here anyway." Earl lowered his voice to barely more than a whisper. "Between you and me, I'm rather grateful. This place is ritzy, and I'm enjoying the maid service. You should see my guest room. I was never invited here before. I appreciate Sophie giving me a million bucks, but it ain't gonna buy me all this. Might as well make use of it."

"I guess so."

"Hey, what do you suppose Sophie's mansion in L.A. is like? Better than this?"

"About the same, from what I could tell. More Spanish in architecture, less medieval."

Earl chuckled to himself. "Oh, you were there, that's right. Well, it sure was some extravagant lifestyle she made for herself. Good for her."

Whelan stared at the man, sizing up his sincerity. "You're Sophia's mother's sister's husband, right?"

"Yes, Lara. She passed about ten years back. Cancer."

"I'm sorry. I understand Running Bear was in the car crash out in L.A. that killed Valerie."

"Yes."

"That was in 2013?"

"Yes."

"Why was Running Bear out in L.A. at that time?"

"Sophie was in talks with people to expand the business. She thought it would be wonderful to expose Bear to California. His delusional fairy-tale life wasn't fully dug in yet. I think she hoped he might adapt to a more manageable life out there. But, from what I understand, that ship sailed quite a few years before, and while it may visit other ports from time to time, it was never going back to its original harbor."

Whelan smiled. "No." He leaned over and felt the water's temperature with his fingers. "Pleasant. So, Valerie was out there with them?"

"Yes. Sophie needed help with Bear. She couldn't drag him around to meetings, and baby-sitters weren't sticking. She'd been through dozens. They couldn't handle Bear, or he couldn't handle them. It was a nightmare for all of them. That calamity almost ended Forever Sophia before it could really take off. But Sophie was strong. She stayed focused for the sake of Running Bear and herself, I guess. She was driven. And in a way, so was Valerie. She had everything to gain and wasn't about to run out on her grandson or her meal ticket."

"And Valerie's death was ruled as accidental?"

Earl stopped bobbing in the water and yanked himself out. He dried off and sat in a chair facing Whelan. "I'm sure you've seen the police report. What did it say?"

"It said it was an accident. No alcohol in Valerie."

"So what are you really asking me, Agent?"

"If you think Running Bear somehow caused the crash. I've not met too many twenty-seven-year-olds who were a first-hand witness to their grandmother's, mother's and now great-grandmother's deaths."

Earl stared up the hill, his face reflecting concern. "You think the boy is responsible for killing all of them?"

"I don't think anything yet. I'm gathering facts. That's one of them. How would you assess the situation?"

"I thought he was just damned unlucky."

"Maybe. Well, enjoy your swim." Whelan turned to leave.

"Agent, should I be worried for Gracie? Her safety? She plans on moving in here permanently. Maybe I should offer to move in and help. They certainly have the room."

"Grace is planning on moving in permanently?" Whelan was surprised by the statement. "I spent the morning with her, and she said nothing of it."

"Well, we spoke a while ago, and she's been on the phone with her husband in Oklahoma City. They have a lot of details to work through, but yes, I think she's moving in that direction. She doesn't want to rip Bear from his home here. Certainly doesn't want him back in Oklahoma, closer to Merrill. He's not going to go away quietly."

"Does Grace plan to honor Sue's statement about giving him $500,000?" asked Whelan.

"I have no idea, you'll have to ask her, but I think Sue had the right idea. Gonna be the only way to shut him up and keep him from becoming a pain in the ass to her and Bear."

"Mr. Humboldt," began Whelan.

"Please, it's Earl."

"Earl, if you speculated on who killed Sue Fielding, assuming it's not Running Bear, who would you say it is?"

"Isn't that *your* job?" said Earl.

Whelan grinned. "Yes. But I wouldn't be competent at my job if I dismissed the opinions of those who knew the victim. So what's yours?"

"I haven't thought about it too much, but I think it must be Merrill. Has to be Merrill."

"Because he only got a dollar?"

"Because that scumbag didn't deserve more than a dollar. I can't believe what a pathetic human being he turned out to be. When Valerie first went out with the man, we all told her he was worthless. She was a rebel, though. And he was pretty handsome in his youth when he had all his teeth. You know, I bet he gets that $500,000 and still doesn't fix his teeth."

"So he charmed Valerie, and…?"

"And it was a shotgun wedding. Lasted two years. Valerie was already seeing her second husband before she got divorced. Dropped Sophie off on Merrill's doorstep when she was about five. He didn't even know Valerie had given birth to a child. She couldn't handle motherhood back then. It got easier when her daughter was on her way to becoming a billionaire."

"And Merrill raised Sophia alone?"

"Yes. He never remarried all those years. Not too many women looking to land a man in poverty *and* a stepdaughter. About two and a half years ago, he met Peggy. She was already in poverty, I heard through the grapevine, and Merrill never told her he had a daughter or a grandson. Probably figured he'd never see either of them again, so why mention it?"

"What did Peggy see in him?"

"I don't know. I heard once she was running out of a bad marriage. The poor girl couldn't have guessed she was running right into another."

"How old is she?"

"I think…forty? No. Thirty-nine."

"And Merrill's sixty?"

"Yes. Lucky SOB. How many men marry a woman younger than their own daughter?" Earl snickered.

"You'd be surprised."

"Well, that's life."

Earl's face became serious again. "Say, you didn't answer me about Gracie. Should I be concerned for her safety around Running Bear?"

"I couldn't say, Earl. But the way I saw the two of them interact today, I'd say they have an excellent relationship."

"He enjoyed a great relationship with all three of the women in his life who are now dead too. I'm not comfortable with her being next in line."

"Again, until we complete our investigation, I really have no answers for you. They're both adults."

"I think I'm going to insist on sticking around here for a while. Help keep an eye on the boy."

"I expect that will be up to your daughter."

"She'll be glad to have me."

Whelan studied the man. He was fit. *All that farmhand work does a body good. I need to work out more. He's in better shape than me at twice my age. Healthy enough to swing a sword.*

"Well, nice talking with you, Agent Whelan," said Earl. "I want to get in a few more before I go speak with Gracie about moving in."

Earl dove back into the pool and began swimming another lap.

"Be sure to enjoy this lifestyle 'a million bucks' couldn't even begin to afford, Mr. Humboldt," mumbled Whelan. The statement fell on deaf ears amidst the splashing.

Chapter 24

Thirty minutes later, Agents Whelan, Jones and Cannon were sitting at a diner two miles away from Parkmoor going over the case.

"The L.A. office has alibied Sophia's other two cousins, and all her nieces and nephews, on both murders now," said Whelan. "Odds are, if it was one of them who killed Sophia for the money, they wouldn't have killed Sue too. They were counting on her helping them get some cash out of the estate."

"Where are we at with the missing server?" asked Jones.

"Still missing."

"We've got the dragon rider composite from Agent Leslie," said Cannon. He held up his cell phone, so Whelan and Jones could see. "You should each have it by now. I guess this is our guy. Was this Sue's server?"

They all stared into their phones.

"Maybe. I remember him as a blonde with glasses. This dragon rider is dark-haired with no glasses. If it was him at the dinner last night, he was wearing a wig and some fake specs," said Whelan.

Jones started dialing on her phone. "I'm going to get this illustration sent to the fire captains throughout the entire metro area. With any luck, we'll get a hit." She excused herself so she could talk outside to another agent back in the field office.

"I texted it to the catering service manager. Maybe she'll remember this was the guy she hired."

"So," said Cannon, "Agent Jones tells me you and I will be partnered up permanently after this case. I think that's great. I wanted to make sure you were on board with it."

"Of course," said Whelan. He paused, regarding the rookie agent, full of energy and potential. A jealous sigh escaped his lungs, and Cannon waited patiently for him to express his concern.

"I have complete confidence in you," started Whelan. "You know when I get a break on the Morrison case, I'm jumping back into that full time."

"Sure."

"It might mean weeks away from home at a time, depending on where the leads take us. I guess I'm asking if you've thought through what that means, to partner up with me and be sucked into a nationwide chase, living motel to motel and sucking down fast food with sleepless nights and potentially being shot at the closer we get."

"Bring it on."

"I appreciate your enthusiasm. I really do. But understand I have a mark on my head. The first chance Eddie gets to put a bullet through my skull, he'll take it. Or one of his goons, if he can gather a new outfit. We cleared out all of his bank accounts. Money won't come easy for him. Wherever he is, you can bet he's working on building up his cash. Speaking of which, we didn't find much in the bust. I imagine he's got a couple million dollars in liquidity—barely startup money for a guy like him."

"Okay…" Cannon was confused why Whelan was trying to talk him out of this before it was even a thing.

"So you'll have a mark on your head too. The first moment he gets wind of who I'm working with, *bang*!"

"If you're trying to scare me, I can handle it."

"I couldn't!" Whelan snapped. "It nearly destroyed me. Phil, I might appear to be Mr. Confidence on the surface, but hunting Eddie…obliterated me. Mentally. I'm not one-hundred percent yet."

Whelan bounced his eyes back and forth across young Agent Cannon's.

"Tom, I read your case file. You gave two and a half years of your life to that scumbag. I know it took a toll. We won't be going undercover. You couldn't again with Morrison if you wanted to. It will be an old-fashioned manhunt. He's the one who's scared right now. He's the one who's broken mentally. I guarantee he doesn't have anyone watching his back like you have watching yours. And if we get shot at, well, I pretty much prepare myself for that every day when I step out the door, no matter the case I'm on. It's part of what we signed up for."

Whelan darted his eyes across Cannon's, finding truth and loyalty. This agent was there for him a little over a month ago when it truly counted. He'd trusted him with his life. He hated to jeopardize his at such a young age. *Of course, he's only three years younger than me. Seems like so much more.*

"All right," said Whelan.

Cannon smiled. "Awesome, that's done. Oh, and you know those fast food joints offer salads these days? You don't have to live on a diet of greasy burgers and fries."

Whelan chuckled. "Hey, don't ruin it for me. You can eat the lettuce; I'm barely holding on to a thirty-inch waist."

"And what was your cholesterol at your last physical?"

"Cho-les-ter-ol? I'm not familiar with that word." Whelan shuddered.

Jones approached the table and slid in beside him on the booth seat.

"What's wrong?" she asked.

"Nothing," said Whelan.

"Your eyes are moist."

"I'm just sharing the love with my boy here."

Jones looked at Cannon. "Is he okay?"

"Yep."

"Are you okay?"

"Yep."

She bounced her eyes between the men. "Okay. Oh, speaking of boys, how's your son, Connor?" she asked Whelan.

"Fantastic. Can't wait to see him. I'll make a quick run out to D.C. as soon as we wrap this."

"I met up with him online last night," said Cannon. "Fortnite. He kicked my ass."

Cannon bonded with Whelan's son on a vacation trip to Grand Cayman following Whelan's last case. It was helpful to have an extra set of eyes keep tabs on his boy, growing up in Washington D.C. without a dad. His ex-wife, Georgia, was doing a tremendous job on her own. He wondered at times if he'd made a mistake moving far away from them, but then, he didn't get much time to see Connor when he was close by either.

Thank God for video phone apps and online gaming.

"Yeah, he's amazing," said Whelan. "Says he wants to be an FBI agent when he grows up. I'm somewhere between scared and terrified on that one."

"Last week, it was an astronaut. Eleven's a moody age. Next week it will be a rock star," said Cannon.

"Super. He can buy his old man a mansion to retire in." Whelan laughed with the thought.

The threesome kicked around personal stories for another twenty minutes before Whelan's phone rang.

"Merrill showed up at Parkmoor."

Nurse O'Brien was challenged keeping Merrill contained in the foyer. He kept moving down the gallery to the second stairwell leading to some of the bedrooms, including Running Bear's.

Merrill had Peggy in tow, jerking her wrist to keep up. She kept mumbling how sorry she was for the intrusion.

"Mr. Perkins, it's after 8:00," said O'Brien. "The week has been long. Bear's tired. Please, call in the morning, and if he wishes to see you then, you can join us for breakfast."

She kept checking the front door, wondering if the agent standing guard on the porch could hear her if she shouted. She was beginning to regret letting Merrill in the house.

"Lady!" he snapped. "You're not the boss of me, and you're not the boss of my grandchild. That'd be Grace. Grace! Where are you? You here?"

No one replied.

"Mr. Perkins! I may not own this property, but I live here and am still the manager of this home. And I need you both to leave! Now!"

"Bear! Grace!" Merrill's face scrunched, an unflattering mug with deep lines creasing further around reddening cheeks.

He grabbed O'Brien's shoulders and moved her physically out of the way. He ran to the left staircase at the end of the gallery and charged up the stairs, stopping at the middle landing in front of the display of swords on the wall.

Peggy chased him as fast as she could, running into him when he halted, falling to the floor in her heels.

Merrill ignored her instead of offering assistance.

He took his eyes off the sword case and turned back to O'Brien. "What the hell goes on around here?" He shouted before resuming his climb.

Peggy sat spread-eagle on the floor in front of the display case. She was mesmerized by all the shiny iron and steel. The showcase lighting reflected beams of gold onto the floor and walls at every angle, like some sort of religious altar.

Merrill shouted down at her from the top of the stairs. "Come on, woman!"

She made it to her feet and joined him on the second floor.

Nurse O'Brien ran back to the front door and stepped out onto the porch. "Agent! Agent, I need you!"

He raced inside and followed O'Brien up the second staircase to the bedrooms.

When they made it to Running Bear's room, there was only Merrill and Peggy, standing in the middle, staring with open mouths, turning in a slow circle.

The grand master bedroom of Parkmoor was a spectacle.

The walls were covered in murals. It was as though you were standing on a hillside, and in the distance, were his kingdom and two neighboring realms, each with their own castles. One flew flags over an open gate with several knights riding their horses toward the mountains. Lightning shot from one mountain peak toward the second ridge across a valley. When you got close, you could see it was two men, dressed in robes, with sparks coming out from their hands, two wizards in a battle.

Continuing on, there were small towns where people played and worked. There was a swordsmith working on building his inventory. And a pub, with a man in the window smiling at a pretty girl walking by. People were strolling on their way toward their destinies, each one with a story of their own.

As Merrill kept turning, more and more of the land his grandson saw in his head revealed itself. Two armies were battling in a valley, entire battalions on horses with spears and shields attacking one another. The detail was exceptional.

And no matter where you focused, the sky was full of dragons. Some large, some small, they flew gracefully, or were breathing fire to help out their king in a battle, or were perched protecting their cave full of gold, or were zipping in and out of the clouds, either in a duel or perhaps a mating ritual. Dragons of every color and design completed the work.

Merrill traced one up toward the ceiling, then quickly ducked before chuckling to himself. An enormous dragon filled the majority of the fourteen-foot-high ceiling, its wings spread wide and mouth open to a ball of flame. Its talons were ready to snatch its prey. The head was aimed toward the king-sized canopy bed, with reams of silk crisscrossing overhead and wrapped around the columns on each corner.

O'Brien pushed past the agent and pointed to Merrill. "Get out of Bear's room! How dare you disturb his suite."

She wheeled on the man from the FBI. He was also gaping at the world of dragons consuming the walls. "Get him out of here!"

Coming out of his trance, the agent took an arm of Merrill's and escorted him out and back down to the foyer. Peggy followed willingly.

Merrill didn't resist much until they neared the front door. "Wait a minute!"

He pulled his arm free and turned around. "Woman, you let me see my grandson! I'm not leaving, and this man has no authority to haul me away. I haven't done anything wrong."

O'Brien's jaw clenched. She yelled at the agent. "He accosted me! In my own home! Grabbed my shoulders and nearly cracked one, he was squeezing so hard. I want him arrested for assault!"

"I didn't assault her! She's crazy. You're crazy, you bitch. Bear! Grace! Dammit, where is everybody?"

"I can't leave the property, ma'am," said the agent. "I *can* call the police for you and detain him out on the driveway until they get here."

"Then do it!" she screamed. She was livid and felt violated by Merrill's intrusion into Running Bear's quarters. No one was ever allowed in his room except the house staff and Sophia.

Agents Jones, Whelan and Cannon all came racing through the front door, which stood ajar the whole time.

"What the hell's going on?" asked Jones.

The devastation of their lives this week was too much for Nurse O'Brien. She collapsed onto a bench and began sobbing, wailing uncontrollably.

Whelan approached her to offer comfort.

She screamed at him through her tears, "Please go! All of you!"

"I'm sorry. We can't. We have two murders to solve. And as much as you don't like our presence here, it was what we agreed on to let Running Bear stay in his home. Otherwise, we'll arrest him now, and we'll all get out of your hair."

Whelan wheeled around to his partner. "I'm thinking we should do that at this point anyway."

"No!" said Nurse O'Brien. "You'll undo years of work!" She wiped at her nose and cleared her throat. "Forgive me. This was the hardest week of my life."

She removed a tissue from her pocket and blew her nose, then balled it up and stuffed it back where it came from before standing to address Jones. "How can I help you this evening?"

"Our agent called us when Merrill first drove up. He suspected he was here to cause a commotion based on his behavior."

Jones wheeled on the older man. "Merrill, what are you doing here?"

"I have the right to see my grandson. And this bitch won't let me see him!"

"He's under supervised medical care," said Nurse O'Brien, regaining some of her composure. "Until Doctor Brachman surfaces, that falls to me. And I say he's had enough for today."

Whelan lowered and calmed his voice in hopes of easing the tension. "Nurse O'Brien, where's Bear now? May we speak with him, please?"

"They're all out on the terrace, finishing their dinner."

"I don't want to intrude. We'll wait here. Could you please announce our presence?"

"Consider it announced," said Running Bear, walking up the gallery to the foyer. "I needed to use the restroom. Couldn't help but overhear. Please, won't you all join us for dessert? The chef made a pie. We've enough for all."

"Thank you, Bear," said Merrill. "Don't mind if we do. We need to talk about your future."

"Perfect. I've been ironing out a few details with Cousin Grace. We have an offer for you. More than you deserve."

Chapter 25

"A hundred thousand dollars!" screamed Merrill over a slice of banana cream pie. "You've got to be joking. That's an insult. Hell, even Sue was gonna give me five times that!"

"If it was up to me, you'd get nothing," said Running Bear. "Gracie talked me into giving you something."

Merrill turned toward Grace Meyer. "You're in charge of it. How does he get a say?"

"Because I respect his wishes. It's really all his money. I'm just overseeing the estate."

"You're a little shit!" he said to his grandson. "I helped raise you the first three years of your life! And if it wasn't for me raising your mama, you'd have nothing. You'd be living in some shack in the backwoods of Oklahoma while Sophie rings groceries all day!"

The table was silent. Eyes shifted back and forth from Merrill to Running Bear like viewers at a tennis match.

Running Bear's eyes were wet. He focused them on Merrill, his brow furrowed with a growing hatred for the man. "At least she'd be alive. She was killed presumably for green paper. I'd live in a shack if it meant having the Queen back."

"For paper?" asked Merrill.

Nurse O'Brien translated for the young man. Her exhausted throat managed to whisper, "Money."

Merrill stood, licking a crumb off his finger. "My attorney will be in touch. I want what Sue promised me, or I will cause all kinds of grief. You'll spend more than a hundred thousand defending my counsel."

"And you'll still walk away with nothing, Merrill," said Grace. "Well, a large invoice from your attorney, providing you can find one who would even represent you once you explain to them what the paper says."

"The paper?" Merrill was growing agitated and confused.

Again, Nurse O'Brien reluctantly came to his rescue in hopes of expediting his departure. "The will."

Grace rummaged through her purse slung over the corner of her chair. "It always comes down to what the paper says, and that one says you get nothing except a dollar."

"Here." She threw a ten-dollar bill at him. "Ten times what you deserve. I've got all these fine witnesses that you've been paid in full. Now, if you still want that $100,000, come by tomorrow around 2:00. I'll have the paperwork ready for you to sign."

"Grandson," said Merrill, turning to Running Bear, "please, have some mercy on a poor old man."

"I did," said Running Bear.

Whelan slipped another bite of pie in his mouth as the 'witnesses' around the table uncomfortably started averting their eyes from the desperate fool in front of them. Whelan was fixated on the man, however.

Merrill sighed and walked toward the French Doors to the living room. "I'll see you tomorrow at 2:00."

He snapped at his wife, sitting frozen in her chair. "Well, come on, woman! They don't want you here neither!"

Peggy scowled at her husband, then turned her head to Running Bear. "This has been the craziest week of all our lives. I think with more time, you might come to understand your grand-daddy loves you and hopes to be in your life more now."

"Funny," said Running Bear. "He hasn't indicated it on any level, not words, not actions. You sound like a statesman."

Peggy sighed and stood. "I'm just hoping for a peaceful solution, sweetie. Good night Bear."

She headed to the terrace doors and marched past Merrill, who stood with his mouth agape.

"I'll walk you out," said Nurse O'Brien, giving his back a shove. "Make sure you don't take any side trips on your way to the front door."

When they were gone, Earl Humboldt spoke up from the end of the table to his daughter. "You handled him well, Gracie. More than the old coot deserves."

Grace sighed, gazing at Running Bear.

Sylvia Moffett, Chad Buckley, and even Chef Louie were all at the table, quietly watching the show and nibbling from their plates.

"It'll be alright, Bear," said Sylvia, breaking the silence. "I know this has been the toughest week, but it will all work out."

"I know," said Running Bear. "Cantor and Marjorie have been telling me that all evening." He stole a peek toward the other end of the table, where two empty chairs sat.

Jones ate her last bite of dessert and cleared her throat. "This might not be the best time to bring this up, but tomorrow morning, we have a doctor coming to visit with Bear."

She spoke to Grace but observed Running Bear to check his reaction. There was none.

"I was wondering when you'd get around to that," she responded. "Nothing on Doctor Brachman? He's disappeared?"

"Yes. Doctor Giuseppe Franco De Luca is a top-notch psychiatrist, a specialist in the field of schizophrenia. We need an assessment on Running Bear."

Grace sighed. "I suppose so do I."

Running Bear was fine up until this moment. "He'll assess I'm fucking bonkers!" he snapped.

He stood up abruptly, his chair falling behind him onto the pavers. "I've been through this before! I get pushed and pulled in ten different directions, and they always come back with the same answer. Nuts! Certifiable! Needs an institution. You'll not take me from Parkmoor!"

He wheeled on Cannon, who was closest to him on his right. "You try to take me from my home and you'll be sorry! I'll have a whole army siege your lands and conquer your armies!"

"I won't force you to leave, Your Majesty," said Cannon in a soothing tone. "And this doctor won't remove you from Parkmoor either. But the kingdom of the FBI has been granted extraordinary assignment on this matter, and it's a formality we must endure. Grace will be with you the whole time. And you're welcome to have Marjorie and Cantor there as well."

Cannon's statement registered with Running Bear. He grew embarrassed. "Forgive my outburst. I think I need to be alone for a few minutes."

Running Bear spoke to the empty seats, answering an imaginary question. "No, I want to be by myself for a while. Really."

He headed down the paved stairs leading to the pool.

Nurse O'Brien returned to the terrace in time to see his head bobble out of sight as he went down the hill. "What did I miss?"

"Call me Frank," said Doctor De Luca, shaking Running Bear's hand the following day.

It was 9:10 a.m., and everyone was gathered in the parlor. Agents Whelan, Jones and Cannon sat on a sofa within view of Running Bear.

The room was put back to normal following the reading of the will.

Grace Meyer was sitting on another sofa to the right of Running Bear. Nurse O'Brien was in a chair close by. The rest of the house staff and Mr. Humboldt were specifically asked not to attend.

Edward Toussaint, the family's defense attorney in Kansas City, sat beside Nurse O'Brien, recording the entire session with permission.

Running Bear did not appear nervous. He studied Frank. "You're young. Are you sure you're old enough to be a doctor?" he asked.

"I'm forty-two. How old should I be?"

"Well, Brachman was in his early seventies. All of my doctors have been old."

"Does that make them better somehow?"

"I don't know. More experienced, I guess."

"I've been practicing for about thirteen years. My approach is considered unorthodox by all those *old* doctors you've come to expect through the years. But if you'd rather not visit with me, I can make a call and get some old codger over here to test you."

Running Bear grinned. He already liked this man but wasn't ready to give a full endorsement. "Show me your arsenal."

"Thank you, Your Majesty," said Doctor De Luca. He'd been provided a case update and ordered some medical files sent over the night before.

"I'm sorry for the loss of your mother, the Queen," he continued. "I lost my mother a couple of years ago. I know it's difficult. How are you feeling?"

"I have to be strong for my kingdom."

"Of course you do, but not for me. Right here, right now, I want you to express your truest feelings. Put away the brave front you've postured for the sake of your realm for a few minutes. You lost your mom, Running Bear. How does that make you feel?"

"Sad." Running Bear squeezed Marjorie's hand. "Marjorie's grief-stricken as well. The Queen was an exceptional woman and a beautiful, competent and fair ruler."

"Sophia was more than the Queen, wasn't she Marjorie?" asked Doctor De Luca, addressing the air beside Running Bear. "She was your mother-in-law. Is your own mother still alive?"

The room perked up at this question. No one bothered addressing Marjorie directly all week. Perhaps ever.

Nurse O'Brien's head spun toward this new doctor fiercely, but she managed to keep her mouth shut. Brachman's advice was never to address Running Bear's imaginary friends directly. To do so would be an admission they were really there, which of course, they weren't. It was Brachman's hope to keep the young man more grounded in reality as he balanced his world with ours, contrary to Sophia's desire to keep him happy.

Doctor Brachman also wanted Running Bear on a vigorous dose of several medications, which O'Brien knew left Bear feeling foggy and lethargic. She embraced Sophia's house rules regarding his care once she saw how he could be managed and live a more productive life. She'd already gone against established treatments herself. She owed it to the new doctor to give him some leeway.

Doctor De Luca addressed Running Bear. "Your Majesty, please remember, I'm unable to hear her responses. I'll need you to relay them to me."

Running Bear was staring at the space two feet over from his head. "She says she died a few years ago."

"Oh, my condolences," said De Luca. "How, if I may ask?"

Running Bear paused. "A car crash."

"Oh. That's tragic. I'm sorry. Was it here, in Kansas City?"

"Yes."

"And your father, is he still alive?" De Luca asked Marjorie.

"No. He was in the wreck too."

"Both parents at once? That must have been painful."

"It was."

Doctor De Luca was studying Running Bear's body language. "And Marjorie, you're the Queen now. Are you worried about being able to handle your responsibilities?"

"No. I'm capable. I'll make an exceptional queen. The King has confidence in me."

"No doubt," said De Luca. "But how do you feel about taking over the role from your mother-in-law, who's now deceased, and by such a horrific means?"

There was a long minute before Running Bear answered on behalf of Marjorie.

"It makes me sad, of course. Sad for the King, for the kingdom, for all the help. But I'll do my best to try to live up to the standards she established."

"Sad for the help? They're just the help. Why be sad for them?"

"Because they're part of Bear's extended family."

"And he cares for them?" asked De Luca.

"Yes."

"Does that bother you?"

"Sometimes."

Running Bear's head tilted as he looked at Marjorie. "It does?" he asked her himself.

"Well, sometimes. It takes away my time with you." Running Bear continued to relay her words.

"But we're together so often! In the evenings, at meals," said Running Bear.

"I understand you have your kingly duties, but I would have you to myself all the time if I could," she responded. "I know that's selfish of me. Forgive me, Your Majesty."

"Of course, my love." Running Bear reached out and stroked a cheek that wasn't really there.

"So, Marjorie," continued De Luca, "you're jealous of the time Running Bear's extended family gets to spend with him?"

"Sometimes."

"Were you jealous of Queen Sophia? *Her* time with Bear?"

"Sometimes, I mean, no! Never!"

"Which is it, Marjorie?" prodded De Luca. "Never, or sometimes."

"She was rarely here," said Marjorie. "I would never ask the prince not to see the Queen."

"But you were sometimes jealous of the time he spent with her?"

"Yes. Sometimes."

"Enough to kill her, remove her from being an obstacle?"

"No!" Running Bear's answer for his wife came without hesitation.

Jones spoke up, disregarding Doctor De Luca's previous lecture about remaining silent during his questioning. "Marjorie, are you sure? Perhaps you were having an argument with her and struck out at her? We'll understand if you made a mistake. We all make mistakes. You can tell us."

Running Bear's eyes widened, and his gaze followed the air moving from his left all the way out the doorway to the parlor behind them.

It was clear Marjorie left the room.

"Bear!" said Jones. "What did she say?"

Running Bear leaned back on the sofa and chuckled to himself. “She said she absolutely did not kill the Queen, even by mistake.”

“And what was funny about that?”

“She also said, ‘fuck you, you prying pig.’”

Chapter 26

Doctor De Luca shot Agent Jones a fierce glance.

"Sorry," she mouthed.

"I like your wife, Bear. She's funny," said De Luca.

"She can be. She's pretty pissed at your inference she killed the Queen. She didn't do it. I would know."

"Yes, of course you would. I'm glad. Do you know who did?"

"The red dragon rider. I drew pictures. They have his picture now. *He* killed her, like I told them."

"I'm sorry you witnessed that, Your Majesty."

"Thank you."

"Bear, I'd like to talk to you about some of the medications you've been on in the past."

Whelan nudged Jones and motioned for them to leave the room while Doctor De Luca began a more detailed medical evaluation of Running Bear. Cannon stayed behind to witness the rest of the interview.

"What are you thinking?" asked Jones of her partner once they were in the hall.

"I'm thinking Bear didn't do this. His story, however far-fetched and full of imaginary witnesses, hasn't changed since the beginning. I believe he witnessed this man kill his mother. Did we get any hits from any fire chiefs about a possible match to the illustration?"

"Not yet. About half of the precincts have reported back so far."

"Did you catch what Marjorie said about her parents being killed in a car crash?"

"Yes. That was a quick response."

"I think she was caught off guard."

"How?"

"A *car crash*! Not a horse crash. Not even a carriage crash. She used the words car crash and wreck. She's grounded in reality more than Running Bear."

"Interesting. We need to mention that to the doctor."

"Yes. Let's find Sylvia while he's working with Bear. I want to confirm a suspicion I have."

It took a few minutes, but they found her dusting in the library. The walls were covered in mahogany bookshelves full of old hardbounds.

"What a gorgeous study," said Jones.

Sylvia gandered around the room. "It is, isn't it. Sometimes I forget to appreciate what we have here. It's easy to do when you're the one in charge of cleaning it all."

"I get that." Jones thought of her meager two-bedroom home in Westport. It could use a deep cleaning. Maybe she'd appreciate it more if she hired a housekeeper.

"Sylvia," said Whelan. "I've been noticing your behavior around Running Bear. You have feelings for him, don't you?"

Jones opened her eyes wide at Whelan, then pivoted her head back to Sylvia to see her reaction.

"Of course I do. He's family. We all have strong feelings for him."

"Yours are romantic feelings."

"They certainly are not!" she snapped. She put down her dusting cloth and bottle of wood oil. Her hands anchored to her hips as she struck a defiant stance.

"I beg to differ," he said. He remembered how attractive she was at the dinner two nights ago, all made up and in a beautiful dress. Every time she looked at Running Bear that evening, it was with a little too much longing. And yesterday, her comments in the kitchen about young Mr. Perkins were relayed to him by Cannon.

Sylvia darted her eyes back and forth between the two Feds a minute. "Well, if I do, what of it? I've never acted on it!"

"No?" Whelan studied the young woman. "I think perhaps I need to ask Running Bear and find out if your feelings are unrequited or if Marjorie needs to be concerned her marriage is in jeopardy."

"That's absurd! You're absurd!" she said.

"Is he?" asked Jones. "You seem shaken up by the accusation. If there was nothing there, you wouldn't be distraught right now."

Sylvia sat on the edge of a desk behind her. "It's been a trying week, Agent Jones. I *am* shaken up."

Jones shifted back to her younger partner and raised her eyebrows. *You started this line of questions, where were you going with it?* she thought.

"Ms. Moffett," said Whelan, "you've been here six years?"

"Close to seven."

"Truthfully then, how long have you been in love with Running Bear?"

Sylvia lowered her chin and sighed. She'd never told a soul about her attraction, but now that it was exposed, she started sharing eagerly. "I don't know. A year. Maybe. I was watching him one morning at breakfast. It was a normal morning, a quick meal at the island counter in the kitchen. He spilled orange juice down his shirt. I told him to take it off so I could throw it in the washer. For some reason, that morning, it…excited me. Over the following weeks, I kept seeing him in a new light. He's kind. Thoughtful. Always asking me how I am. He genuinely cares for all of us. I started being drawn to him in a new way."

Sylvia raised her head. "I know he thinks of us as 'family.' I'm sure I'm like some sister or cousin to him. He's madly in love with Marjorie. I could never replace her."

Whelan wrinkled his forehead in doubt.

"I'm sorry," she continued, "but what would it matter if we acted on it? Whose business would it be?" Her anger and defensiveness were starting to return.

"Well, it would be ours. With two murders and all. A relationship with the main suspect? That would be pretty important for us to know."

"Well, there isn't one. I'm just the housekeeper."

"Who is loved like 'family.'"

"Yes." Sylvia focused on Jones, hoping the senior agent would rescue her.

Instead, Jones decided to push her further. "Eight billion dollars is a pretty strong reason to start a relationship with someone. Love them or not."

Sylvia's head began jerking. "And as I said, we don't have one. Look, I get it. We're all suspects in this house, but you are really reaching here. Are you suggesting I tried to seduce Bear and start a relationship so I could get at his *money*? And that I killed Sophia and Sue as a means to that end? That's really rich! You've quite an imagination."

"Experience has taught us to view every angle."

Sylvia jumped up and shouted at Jones. "You've got issues! I have feelings for Bear. He doesn't have them for me. That's all. There's no relationship, and I haven't killed anyone!"

She stood there, challenging them with her face to suggest anything further to the contrary.

When the agents stood silent, she softened again. "No one here knows of my feelings. If they did, I might lose my job."

"O'Brien would fire you for loving Running Bear?"

"Maybe. But it would really be up to Grace Meyer now. And I don't know her well enough to predict how she'd react. I can't lose this job. This has become my home. And I love it here."

"What is your salary, Ms. Moffett?" asked Whelan.

"My salary? I make $140,000 a year, plus bonus."

"What gets you a bonus?" asked Jones.

Sylvia's eyes squinted at the agent. "Doing an exceptional job. Why?"

"Just curious. Thank you, Ms. Moffett," said Whelan.

Sylvia's shoulder brushed Whelan's as she stormed out of the room, leaving the two agents alone.

"Chad Buckley says he makes $800,000," said Whelan. "Quite heftier than a buck-forty. If it was brought to light someone else on staff made five or six times what I did, I might be angry enough to try and get more."

"I doubt that's public knowledge. I think Sophia was paying him to be some sort of replacement for the lack of a father or grandfather in her and Bear's life."

"Yeah. I guess I'd pay someone well too if they could do a better job than Merrill."

"Bubblegum on the bottom of my shoe could do a better job than Merrill," said Jones.

Whelan chuckled.

"So, while you were picking up on this romantic love Sylvia has for Bear, I have discerned Chad Buckley has the hots for Grace Meyer."

"And I think Nurse O'Brien is in love with Chad."

"They should change the name of this estate from Parkmoor to Peyton Place. Should we follow up on Chad's affection for Grace?" asked Jones.

"I don't think it's necessary. I'm pretty certain Grace has no idea. I'm not leaning toward him as a suspect. Are you?"

"I haven't ruled out *anyone* in this house yet."

"Well," said Whelan, "we can go embarrass him with that question if you'd like."

Jones shrugged her shoulders. "Maybe we should start rattling a few more feathers."

Her phone rang.

"Jones," she answered. "Uh-huh. Uh-huh. No shit! Really? Uh-huh. Uh-huh. Okay, thank you."

"Did we get a hit on our illustration with the fire departments?" asked Whelan.

"Isn't Cannon following up on that?"

"He is. I thought maybe they reached out to you first."

"No. That was Cusack back at the office. A full autopsy was done on Sophia Perkins. They hadn't rushed any labs because, you know, cause of death was pretty obvious."

"And?"

"And, Sophia was three months pregnant."

Chapter 27

The agents returned to the parlor about forty minutes after they left. Doctor De Luca was taking some vitals on Running Bear.

Cannon stood and joined Whelan and Jones. "He's wrapping up with a quick physical."

A few minutes later, Doctor De Luca asked Running Bear to step out of the room before providing his assessment to the Federal Agents.

Grace Meyer, Nurse Linda O'Brien, and the family defense attorney, Edward Toussaint, stayed to hear his conclusions.

"First, you've all done a remarkable job helping manage this. From what I understand, Running Bear would be challenging with a full and proper medication regimen. I'm reluctant to offer a different course of care."

He spoke to the agents, standing behind Nurse O'Brien. "He's not sleeping much lately, but that's understandable. Who would, given what he's been through? And it's pretty common when someone is in a bipolar high. I can suggest a sleep aid that shouldn't interfere with his fantasy life. For the first time in my career, I recommend not giving him any other meds. At least not at this time. I would like to evaluate him regularly, make sure there are no changes. But… I have no words."

"That's what every doctor has said through the years," said Grace. "I know early on, Sophia dragged him around and let him be poked and prodded and written up in a ton of journals. Doctors crawled out of the woodwork to jump on the Running Bear bandwagon. It was a circus until she stopped it all about three years ago. She settled on Doctor Brachman. He meshed fairly well with Bear. He cut way back on the number of meds everyone else threw at him. He disapproved of a complete removal of all meds, though. That was Sophie's doing, slowly over a couple of years, but it's worked."

Doctor De Luca agreed. "It sure has. His utter saturation into this world of kings and queens and dragons and sorcery is unparalleled. If I had met him at the beginning of my career, I might have fallen into the trap of trying to 'cure' him. But, thank my wife, I've matured in a better, more holistic direction. He's consistent and seems safe and generally upbeat and at peace, despite the loss of his mother and grandmother. My advice is to let it ride."

"I'm curious," said Whelan. "In the conversation with Marjorie, she referred to her parents' deaths in a car crash instead of calling cars horses, like Running Bear does. What do you make of that?"

De Luca bounced his eyes around the ceiling in thought before landing them back on Whelan. "I wouldn't read too much into it, actually. It's possible some of Running Bear's delusions are not as grounded in his world of fantasy as he is. There's a part of him that sees a car and knows it's a car, with an engine, and wheels—"

"And a trunk," interrupted Jones.

"Yes. And a trunk. But to separate that out versus the fictional world he's created causes stress, so his mind blanks over it. But Marjorie...Marjorie, and I suspect Cantor even more so, are links to reality his brain tolerates. They might not be fully living in Running Bear's dream world."

"Huh?" asked Jones. "They're *only* living in his dream world."

"Yes, and no. Cantor was with Running Bear since early childhood. He likely knows what a car is, and airplanes, and what money is, and can and can't buy. I bet Cantor's enjoying the sweet life incredible wealth has purchased for him, so he doesn't rock the boat very often. But Bear formed his world of dungeons and dragons well after Cantor was around. And I'm betting Marjorie, to a lesser degree, understands all that. She was here before Bear was allowed to go off all his medications and seal the deal with his hallucinations. Her mind also recognizes the reality around her."

"*Her* mind?" said Whelan. "Ironic."

"A little, yes," agreed the doctor. "Bear cognitively accepts and relies on it somewhat to help navigate the two worlds."

"What about his bipolar disorder? Any meds necessary there?" asked Whelan. He'd read up on the newer drugs on the market since his college days.

"I've seen folks with less manic tendencies manage worse on the best drugs than Running Bear seems to be with none."

He asked Nurse O'Brien, "You say he usually peaks while still in hypomania?"

"Yes."

"Very impressive. That he doesn't go to full-blown mania is incredible. Ironically, allowing him to indulge in his hallucinations is the best treatment for his bipolar disorder he could have. It keeps him happy, and happy is a beautiful thing. His wife seems to be rational. I think she's good for him."

"She returned after you left," he explained to Jones. "I am concerned over Cantor constantly playing the role of devil's advocate and encouraging juvenile behavior, but that may lessen with age. It wouldn't surprise me to find Cantor nearly out of his life in a few years. I think Running Bear's separation process from him has already started."

Whelan was trying to give the doctor's evaluation merit. "Running Bear told us three days ago that Cantor said the dragon rider—the man who killed his mother—was his father. Why would he suggest that?"

"A part of Running Bear must believe it somehow. Is it possible? Do we know who his father is?"

"No one does. Never have," said Nurse O'Brien. "Not even Sophia."

"As I said, Cantor's an adolescent. He'll likely never grow up, become a mature adult. Cantor's more of a playmate with Bear than a real friend. I expect he was teasing him, messing with his head. Like kids do."

Grace Meyer was unusually quiet.

"You have thoughts on this?" Jones asked her.

Grace was fidgeting with a ballpoint. "Perhaps. I haven't thought about it in a long time, until now."

She plopped into a chair nearby. "It's probably nothing, but about a year and a half ago, I was visiting Sophia and Bear here at Parkmoor. Late one night, Sophie and I were about three sheets to the wind, down by the pool, relaxing under the stars. She mentioned a visit at her L.A. office by someone from Oklahoma, claiming to have slept with her when she was a teenager. Now, there were a few of those through the years, so I didn't think much of it at first. There were many old 'boyfriends' looking to reconnect with her now that she was rich. But she told me this one knew she had a son. He was asking for a DNA test."

"You didn't think it was important to mention this earlier?" Jones was pissed. "Like two days ago earlier?"

"I'm sorry," said Grace. "Honestly, it didn't occur to me until you mentioned Cantor's opinion just now. I'd forgotten all about it. That's really ironic, a delusion in Running Bear's mind jogging a real memory in mine."

"Well," said Whelan, "what happened with the guy asking for a DNA test?"

"She denied having a child at all. Told him he was crazy. Of course, she *did* have a kid. I tried following up on it with her a few weeks later. She told me he never contacted her again, and she had no interest in pursuing it. She believed it was a false claim. We never spoke of it again. I mentally wrote it off. A lot of crazy people come out of the woodwork when you have this kind of money. People will say and do *anything*. It was easy to forget."

Doctor De Luca was packing up his bag and preparing to leave.

"Back to Running Bear for a second before you go," said Whelan to the doctor. "Your advice is really to let him go on as he has been? Stay here in this home as if nothing has changed?"

"Yes."

"I think with the right medication, Running Bear might recall more useful details. Don't you think his fantasy world is possibly blocking him from telling us the whole truth?"

"No. He's telling you his whole truth. You need to listen more closely. Or ask better questions."

Whelan was about to retort but thought better of it. "What about taking him out of here for a few days? It's easy to hide from it all in this lavishness. Maybe jolt him into remembering more details of the murderer?"

Doctor De Luca motioned around the Parlor, bobbing his head at the artwork and the opulence of the décor. "Living in *this* home sure beats dealing with it all in a two-bedroom ranch. I'm going to agree with what Nurse O'Brien mentioned earlier. You take Running Bear out of his safety zone, and you'll likely get a scared man who feels the need to hide further, not share more. I know you need answers ASAP, but understand the young man has barely had four days to process all this. I think he's doing amazing. And I think he should stay here. Off drugs, for now. That's my professional recommendation as your bureau psychiatric consult."

"And if you made a guess about whether or not he's capable of murdering his mother?" asked Whelan.

"Capable? Certainly. Do I think he did it? I have no idea."

"Guess."

"Guessing? No. He feels her loss. He's definitely saddened. But then, so are many people after they kill someone in a fit of rage. He understands she's dead. He doesn't seem to believe she'll magically return. I guess seeing her killed like that, first-hand, drove out any question of the possibility she might not really be gone. He's processing all of it better than many sane folks would. I'd snap if I saw my mother brutally slain by a dragon rider—or even murdered with a sword by a fireman."

"Well," continued De Luca, "I'll have my full written report to you by tomorrow afternoon. Once I replay the recorded session, I might think of something else to share, but for now, I'm ordering no changes for the young man. Have a good afternoon."

Whelan watched the doctor leave. His lips remained twisted until De Luca was out of sight.

"You okay, partner?" asked Jones. "He seemed to rattle you. I guess you were expecting him to dope up Running Bear and get some drug-induced breakthrough?"

"Maybe."

"Maybe we all were."

"I guess," said Whelan. He studied the doctor's business card.

Cannon turned back to Grace Meyer. "The man who visited Sophia in L.A. claiming to be Bear's dad, did we get a name?"

"No, sorry."

"I bet *their* offices have cameras. I'll reach out to Sarah Williams and see if we can get footage. Maybe she even has Sophia's appointment logs going back to then."

Cannon got on his cell phone and stepped out of the room.

Grace addressed Whelan and Jones. "Well, if you'll excuse me, I need to finalize the papers for Merrill to sign today. Mr. Steiner, who handles those matters, will be here any minute. Please, stay for lunch if you'd like."

"Thank you, that won't be necessary," said Jones.

"Well, I was kind of hoping you'd stick around today. In case Merrill gets violent. He's supposed to be here at 2:00."

"We'd be delighted to stay, Ms. Meyer," said Whelan.

She and Nurse O'Brien left the two agents alone in the Parlor.

Jones smiled at Whelan. "I heard your stomach growl a few minutes ago. I bet the only thought going through your head is 'what's on the lunch menu'?"

"Well, that, and when do we let the bomb drop Sophia was three months pregnant when she was killed? One of those sword injuries was in her abdomen. You suppose it was the *first* one?"

"Maybe anger was the reason for killing her after all? Instead of money?" asked Jones. "A 'fit of rage,' I think Doctor De Luca called it?"

"Possibly, but if it wasn't Running Bear, then taking a sword out of that case and planning a meeting down by the creek was premeditated. And I think if I knocked up a multi-billionaire, the last thing I'd be is angry over it."

Chapter 28

Lunch was inside today. It was getting too hot to be comfortable out on the terrace.

Whelan was disappointed when Chef Louie served up French dip sandwiches and home fries.

"Running Bear asked for it," explained Sylvia.

The entire gang was gathered around the dining room table. All the house staff, two attorneys, Grace Meyer and her dad Earl, three FBI agents, and Sarah Williams, who dropped by to fill them in on Running Bear's possible fathers from Sophia's L.A. visitors.

"So," she started after dipping her sandwich in the au jus. It hung in her hand as she spoke, waiting for her to take a breath and a bite. "I have narrowed it down to three possible men, between July of 2019 and February of 2020. James Calhoun was in July. He said he knew Sophia from high school and was desperate to see her. Sophia gave him five minutes of her calendar and then escorted him personally to the reception desk, where he was sent away with a gift basket, and when he was gone, she gave instruction to me to never let him waste another minute of her time. I take great notes. And I have an exceptional memory.

"Porter Dixon was next, in November. After sixty seconds on the monitor, Sophia called for him to come up. She cleared twenty minutes, and he went up and came down and left without saying a word to anyone. No gift basket. I can't swear to it, but I think she had sex with him in her office. He was beautiful. He was around thirty, not forty-something, but you can't always pinpoint someone's age these days, so I threw him in. If he was over forty, then we really need to find out his cosmetics routine because he was flawless."

She took a breath and barreled on, "The last guy was Bill Armstrong. Right age, right demeanor, suave without arrogance. Sophia didn't want to see him, so he waited in the lobby for over an hour until she conceded and he was escorted up, with guards, who waited inside her office. I stayed for that one too, no hanky-panky. He whispered low, and I couldn't catch it all, but he laid an envelope on her desk when he left. She threw it in a desk drawer and never mentioned it to me again."

"Low whisper?" said Whelan. "What *could* you make out?"

"Junior High, Scarecrow Field, old-times, gorgeous… He invited her to dinner, which she declined. That was it." Sarah took a bite of her French dip before the saturated tip of the bread broke away. "Oh, damn! Kudos Chef Louie. This is better than Cole's. Hey, I know innumerable foodies in the City of Angels if you need a gig after this. I'd be happy to do intros."

They all gaped at this bold woman before them, scarcely containing their scorn.

Sarah looked up with her mouth full, "Too soon? Sorry."

She finished chewing her oversized bite. "I am sorry, Running Bear, I didn't mean to be insensitive. Sometimes my voice processes faster than my head. It's often a race to the finish line."

Running Bear took the high road. "Chef Louie will always have a home here at Parkmoor, but he's not indentured. If he chooses to pursue a career elsewhere after this, he will have the full support of his King." He bowed his head to the chef, who took a seat himself after making sure they were all served.

"Thank you, Your Majesty." Chef Louie became choked up at the gesture. "I…haven't had time to even think about my future yet. For now, I'm honored to continue service here."

Whelan's eyes zipped around the table, noting everyone's expressions and how they were digesting Sarah William's information. No one spoke as they resumed their lunch in awkward peace.

Jones leaned over and mumbled in Whelan's ear, "Is she going to apologize for inferring his mother was a slut in front of him too?"

"I don't think she even realized how it sounded," he whispered back. "Have to love that L.A. attitude."

Cannon broke the silence. He was staring at his cell phone, having tapped away at it for the past two minutes. "I've been pouring through the database of firefighters throughout the entire metro area. No Calhouns, two Dixons, two Armstrongs. The Dixons are father and son. None match up with the first names, however. If we go with those, we've got three Jameses, two Jims, no Porters, two Bills and two Williams."

He tapped away again, "I think we can rule out all but two. I've got a James Carpenter and a Sonny Armstrong who might be a match. James is with Jackson County FPD, Sonny's with the KCFD, Station 53." He took screenshots and merged them in his gallery, then passed his phone around the table for everyone to view. Two men in their mid-forties were on the screen.

When the phone came to Whelan, he took out his own phone and opened up the illustration based on Running Bear's description. "I don't know. Either of these could be our guy. Either, neither. I don't know. Bear?"

He skipped the attorney and handed both phones straight over to Running Bear.

"Him," Bear said, pointing to Sonny Armstrong.

"Cannon," said Whelan, "let's call Sonny's fire chief and see what we can learn about Mr. Armstrong."

"On it," said Cannon. He took another bite of his sandwich and retrieved his phone from Running Bear before stepping out.

Running Bear's face was turning red. His eyes welled with tears, and he set Whelan's phone down with force on the table.

"Hey! Easy now," said Whelan.

Mr. Toussaint grabbed the phone, noting the illustration before handing it back to Whelan.

"I want him dead!" shouted Running Bear. "I want him strung up for the whole kingdom to see and hung until his eyes bulge out of their sockets! And his head shall be mounted and spiked at the entrance to Parkmoor as a warning to others. You don't fuck with King Perkins! Let it be known throughout the lands!"

"I knew Game of Thrones was too violent for him," whispered Nurse O'Brien.

"Come on, Bear," she said, "let's go for a walk and get some of this out of your system."

She put her hands on his shoulders until he angled his chin up. “Okay,” he said grudgingly and stood. Nurse O’Brien put her arm through his, and the pair strolled from the room.

Sarah Williams darted her eyes between Agents Whelan and Jones.

“Well, your jobs are sure fun, huh?” She was half serious, half sarcastic and wholly bewildered.

Cannon returned after a few minutes. “So, Chief Lake didn’t know Sonny. She’s got thirty-five stations under her. I spoke with Deputy Chief Parker at Station 53. Sonny William Armstrong has called in sick all week. He’s been there less than six months. Transferred from Tulsa, Oklahoma. He’s got to be our dragon rider!”

“We have an address?” asked Jones.

“Sure do.”

“We have time,” said Whelan. “Let’s take a drive.”

The warrant for Sonny W. Armstrong came through. The front door to his apartment in Lee’s Summit was rammed in when no one answered Jones’ knock. Whelan and Cannon followed her in. Three more agents were stationed out back.

Sonny wasn’t home. A thorough search revealed some hairs to pull DNA from. A box under the bed contained an assortment of old photos from a life in Tulsa, Oklahoma. Another box in the closet held a lot of paperwork. One was Sonny’s birth certificate.

“Sonny William Armstrong, Born February 21, 1978, Grove Oklahoma,” said Whelan. “This is our guy, whether he goes by Sonny, William or Bill as he told Sarah Williams a year ago February. A year older than Sophia. He could have known her. Any yearbooks or other item with a high school name on it?”

“Not so far. Sophia attended Vinita Junior High,” said Jones, “and Senior High for a few months.”

Cannon was Googling. “Vinita is about 25 or so miles from Grove. Sonny Armstrong could have moved there easily at any point in time. I’m reaching out to both schools in Vinita to see if we can track records.”

“Twenty-five miles isn’t so far. He could have met Sophia anywhere in the northeast corner of Oklahoma,” said Whelan. “Hell, it could have been a barn dance. From what Grace was sharing with me at the dinner the other night, enjoying the company of men wasn’t a new hobby for our victim.”

“We shouldn’t be crucifying the poor woman because she enjoyed sex,” said Jones.

“Not what I was doing,” said Whelan. “I was pointing out Sonny Bill Armstrong could definitely have met her. Let’s get his DNA run and see if we get a match to Running Bear.”

“We should check it against her fetus too. It doesn’t match anyone currently in the database. Maybe Mr. Armstrong fathered both her children,” said Cannon.

They all considered the possibility.

“Just because Running Bear didn’t see this guy any earlier than two weeks before he killed his mom doesn’t mean she wasn’t seeing the man off property for a few months before then,” said Jones.

Whelan started pacing the floor. Somehow it helped his mental gears turn while postulating theories. “So, according to Sarah, Sonny Bill Armstrong visited Sophia Perkins at her L.A. office in February of 2020. Presumably throws an envelope on her desk with his DNA and tells her he thinks he’s the father of her child. She kicks him out and ignores it for several months. Then sometime last year, according to Sue Fielding, she ran Running Bear’s DNA. If it matched this guy who came to see her in L.A., Sophia knew he was the father. Then what? Somehow Sonny figures out his son is living in Kansas City? So he moves here, gets a job as a firefighter, which you don’t do in six months with no experience. He’s obviously transferred from another district somewhere. Vinita? Grove? We need to blast his name and photo to the fire chiefs in northeast Oklahoma.”

“On it,” said Cannon. He pounded away at his phone screen again and walked outside to the parking lot.

"So," continued Whelan, "he arrives here, settles down, and believes he has a child somewhere in the area? Or he *knows* he has one. Maybe even where. He approaches Sophia again. A lot of time has passed. He's still fit and attractive, and he turns his charms on her again, twenty-eight, twenty-nine years later, and she gives in to him. Running Bear said it appeared she was cooperating. It wasn't rape. She enjoyed it. They argue a minute before he kills her with one of Bear's swords. Which he clearly removed earlier, so again, pre-meditated. He takes her body and dumps it downtown, returns the sword—had to have been the same night."

He stopped, waiting for his partner's thoughts on his summary.

"That all sounds plausible," she agreed.

"So then, our billion-dollar question is, who told Sonny Bill Armstrong he shared a secret love child with Forever Sophia, and how did *that* person know about Running Bear in the first place?"

"Well, if Merrill's being truthful about not knowing who Running Bear's father is—and trust me, I believe Merrill is capable of lying—then the likeliest suspect is Grace Meyer. If Sophia had ever told Sue, I think Sue would have mentioned it. And of course, *now*, we'll never know. I believe Grace knows more than she's admitting. It's possible Sophia knew who the father was all along. She might have let it slip to Grace at some point, perhaps those years they raised Bear together."

"Possibly," said Whelan. "I haven't ruled out Sarah Williams and Karen Hertzberg. Sarah scheduled all of Sophia's trips. I'm betting she knew Sophia sheltered a son here. And Karen was her closest friend in L.A. I'd bet Sophia confided in her over drinks on more than one occasion. And she stood to gain about a half-billion in share value."

"She and Fleming convinced me share value would drop next year with Sophia's death. Doesn't make sense. And Sarah Williams didn't stand to gain anything."

"So she says. I'd like to see a copy of her contract. Make sure there isn't some sort of clause giving her a severance in the event of her employer's death."

"You're reaching. I'm sticking with Grace or Merrill. This one feels more close to home."

"Maybe. My gut's not telling me anything on this one. I usually rely on trusting it. And there's one more thing not adding up," said Whelan.

"What?"

"If this Armstrong guy is our dragon rider, and he turns out to be Running Bear's dad, how the hell did *Cantor* know that?

Chapter 29

Grace Meyer stared at the picture Whelan handed her in the parlor of Parkmoor. "This is Running Bear's father? Sonny William Armstrong?"

"We think so. We're waiting on lab results now to confirm it."

The photo was of her cousin Sophia when she was fourteen, drinking beer with three other boys. Sonny was the one with Sophie's arm around his neck.

"Where did you get this?"

"From his home."

"Did you find him yet?"

"No," said Whelan. "We've got a warrant issued. What can you tell us? Did you know he was Bear's father? Did Sophia ever tell you?"

"No."

"Are you sure? Someone filled in Sonny Bill Armstrong that Running Bear was his son and was living in Kansas City."

"Well, it wasn't me! Sophie didn't know who the father was, so how could I have known?"

The agents were skeptical.

"I'm telling you the truth! Sophie didn't know! She narrowed down the possible dads to four guys. She really hoped Bear was fathered by this Cherokee guy named Light."

"Light?" asked Whelan.

"That was his last name. His first was...Oukonunaka, or something like that. I heard stories for years that he was the one who got away."

"From a fourteen-year-old?"

"What, you weren't in love at fourteen?"

Whelan pondered her question seriously. "Sorry, not till college."

"When it was obvious Bear didn't have Cherokee blood, Sophie didn't care to know who the father was. She didn't want those other boys in her life any longer, so…no DNA tests, no names, no looking back. It was her and Bear against the world."

"And you never pushed her to find out? Even during those lean years when you both could have used some extra financial support?" asked Jones.

"I didn't say that," said Grace. "I brought it up more than once over the years, but she wouldn't have it. I never knew the father's name until now."

"It turns out Sophia *did* have Running Bear's DNA sequenced last year," said Jones. "If this Sonny Bill Armstrong—now you've got *me* saying that," she said to Whelan.

"It reminds me he's going by both Sonny and Bill."

Jones absorbed his rationale a second, then continued, "If this Sonny Bill Armstrong is the father, your cousin Sophia knew it."

Grace hung her head and started to cry.

"What is it?" asked Whelan.

She wiped at her eyes. "It's all of it!" she cried. "We lost Sophie and Grandma Sue. Murdered! And by Bear's *father*? And Sophie *knew* this man was the father? It's too much!"

Grace melted against a pillow behind her on the sofa, initiating a full breakdown.

Jones threw her head to the side, motioning Agents Whelan and Cannon to give her some space. The trio retreated back to the gallery of Parkmoor.

"Thoughts?" asked Jones.

"Seemed legit," said Cannon.

"Maybe," conceded Whelan. "That leaves Merrill. One of them leaked all this to Sonny Bill Armstrong."

"They'll never admit it if they did," said Jones. "It could lead to their arrest as an accomplice to murder."

"Or, they might be a co-conspirator in *all* of this," agreed Whelan.

Cannon was left to sit with Grace Meyer in case she felt like sharing anything else after she recovered from her mental collapse.

Whelan and Jones found Running Bear in the swimming pool. He was floating on an enormous inflatable flamingo.

"Your Majesty, we need a moment, please," said Whelan.

Chad Buckley stopped trimming a nearby hedge so he could hear the conversation.

"Okay," said Running Bear. He paddled over as best he could near the edge of the pool and climbed out.

"Have you ever heard the name Sonny Armstrong? Or Bill Armstrong?"

"No. Are they brothers?"

"They're the same man."

"Ahh. He suffers from dissociative identity disorder? That's a shame."

"You know what DID is?" asked Whelan, surprised.

"Sure. I've been around a lot of doctors. They used to test me for it. Screwy doctors." He kicked the water with his foot.

"It's *one* man, who goes by *two* different names," explained Whelan.

"Yep. He's afflicted. I hope he gets better, whoever he is."

Jones flounced her curls. "He's not afflicted Bear—Your Majesty. We think it's the name of your dragon rider."

"Which one?"

"Which dragon rider? There's more than one?" asked Jones.

"No. Which name is his? Sonny or Bill? Really agent, keep up." He looked at Whelan. "And they say *I* have challenges."

Whelan burst out a laugh while Jones scoured her face. Running Bear was also chuckling. He was playing with her.

"Your Majesty," started Whelan, "we believe Mr. Armstrong knew your mother from a long time ago."

"That's subjective, 'long.' How long ago?" he asked.

"About twenty-eight years ago," said Whelan.

Nurse O'Brien's head appeared at the top of the hill. "Stop!" she screamed. She took the steps as fast as she could and was out of breath by the time she reached them.

"Stop," she gasped.

"What is it, Ms. O'Brien?" asked Whelan.

"Bear," She paused to take in more air. "Bear, can you excuse us?"

"I don't think so," he said. "I think I'd like to see what this is all about."

Nurse O'Brien grabbed her knees for support. Jones led her over to a chair at a table underneath an umbrella. She plopped down gladly.

Through heavy breaths, she begged Whelan, "Please, not yet. Not until you're sure."

"Sure of what?" asked Running Bear. He hopped off the flamingo with a splash and raised himself up over the side.

"Bear, you're dripping wet," said O'Brien. "Go grab a towel and dry off before you catch a cold."

"It's ninety-four degrees. I'm not cold." He turned toward Whelan. "Sure of what?"

Whelan caught his partner giving him a nod. "Your Majesty, we think your dragon rider is Sonny Bill Armstrong. We think he might be your father. We are waiting for confirmation."

"Oh." He nodded his understanding, then turned to his side. "Yes, yes, you did. Impressive," he said sarcastically to thin air.

Whelan took a note out of Doctor De Luca's playbook and addressed that very same air beside Running Bear. "Cantor, how did you know the dragon rider was Bear's dad?"

They all held their breath. Even Chad Buckley, eavesdropping from fifteen feet away, walked over and joined them.

"Bear," said Whelan, "we'll need you to tell us what Cantor said."

"He said he overheard the Queen and the dragon rider talking in the kitchen one night."

"Where were *you*, Bear? How was Cantor alone with the Queen if you weren't there?"

Running Bear's eyes fogged over, then he jerked his head up. "He's not always hanging out with me."

"Cantor!" snapped Whelan. "Where was Bear when you heard this?"

After a few seconds, Bear answered for him. "He says I was in the gallery, on my way to the bathroom. He hung back when we saw them while I went to take a whiz. When I came out a minute later, I returned to the kitchen. Cantor was making sandwiches for us, but the Queen and her guest were gone."

Running Bear acknowledged Cantor before turning to Whelan again. "Yes. Makes sense. He thinks the Queen heard me flush and got out of there before we could approach her. She was unaware I'd already seen them before I went to the restroom."

The group all stood staring at Running Bear. No one said anything as they each absorbed this information.

Shrugging his shoulders, Running Bear said, "Well, it doesn't change anything. Cantor's been telling me this all week. I guess he was right. Where's he at?"

"Cantor?" asked Jones.

Running Bear raised his eyebrows and lowered his chin. "*Sonny Armstrong*, my father."

"We're looking for him, Bear," said Whelan. "I'll let you know as soon as we find him."

"Thank you," said Running Bear. "I guess we're taking a rest," he said to the empty pool before marching up the hill and into the house.

"I'm sorry," said Jones. "I don't know why I continually misunderstand him."

"It's easy to fall behind," said Chad Buckley. "Bear's sharp as a tack, quick and witty. He's actually starting to warm up to the pair of you, or he never would have teased you earlier."

"I'm flattered," said Jones facetiously.

"So, that was interesting," said Whelan. "Clearly, Running Bear heard some of the conversation between his mother and Sonny Bill

Armstrong, yet his conscious blanked it out while still allowing Cantor to process it. Does that happen often?"

"Often?" repeated O'Brien. "Never, to my knowledge. I didn't even know it was possible. If Doctor Brachman were here, he'd be writing this up for another journal article. Have you two not come up with a single clue as to his whereabouts?"

"No, sorry," repeated Jones.

"I see," said O'Brien. She turned to Mr. Buckley. "Chad, be a dear and escort me back inside, would you?"

"Of course," he said.

Whelan and Jones watched the pair stroll back up to the house.

"Should we check with Doctor De Luca and get his thoughts on that?" asked Jones.

"You can, but ultimately, it doesn't matter. None of this brings us closer to finding Armstrong."

Whelan's phone rang. "It's Cusack. Whelan," he answered. "Really? Really? Okay, thanks." He hung up.

"Really-really what?" asked Jones.

"Sonny Bill Armstrong *is* Running Bear's dad. But he didn't father the baby Sophia was carrying when she was killed. I wonder if she told him she was pregnant before he ran that sword through her?"

Chapter 30

Cannon's joyful face appeared up on the veranda. "We found him!"

Whelan and Jones raced each other to the top of the hill.

"Armstrong?" asked Jones.

"Yes. He used his ATM card to withdraw $600. He must be out of cash. Twenty minutes ago, his image popped up at a convenience store near his apartment. Bought a burner phone. We tracked his movements on camera and lost him five minutes ago. But he's on foot. KCPD and several agents are scoping the neighborhood he was last seen. He's on Union Hill. Near 31st and Main."

Jones addressed her partner. "One of us needs to stay here. Merrill will be here soon. You two go. Catch this asshole."

Whelan noticed her disappointment in her own decision. "You go," he said. "This is your last case in the field. You'll be running the show from the bullpen from now on."

"Oh, for Pete's sake!" said Cannon. "I can babysit Merrill. You both go. It's your last case together."

Whelan slapped Cannon's shoulder. "Thanks."

Whelan grabbed his bullet-proof vest and tactical gear from his trunk before hopping in Jones' SUV. She took off with a squeal of the tires, then noted the tread marks on the driveway coming out of Parkmoor. "Shit. I bet I get a letter about that."

"Well, we should have answers soon enough. I'm going to miss you when you move up."

"I'll be right here."

"I know," said Whelan, "but…you know."

Partnered a little under three months, they survived a hell that forever bound them. "You getting misty-eyed on me?" she asked.

Whelan stared out the window. "Nope."

Jones patted his shoulder. "Uh-huh."

Whelan turned his head and grinned when he saw her fond expression.

Seven minutes later, they were pulling into a parking lot where four KCPD patrol cars were camped. Two other federal agents from the office were getting updates. They released three patrol cars to resume their search before Whelan and Jones could jump out of their vehicle.

"Agent Kesha Lemar," said one of the two feds, introducing herself as Jones approached.

"Yes, I know you," said Jones. "Excellent work on the Hunter case last month."

"Oh, thank you. I wasn't sure if you'd remember me. I came on in the middle of that bureau shake-up a few weeks ago."

"I remember all my agents," said Jones, owning a piece of her new role as Assistant Special Agent in Charge.

Whelan shook hands with her and her partner, Agent Ronnie Barnhardt.

"So," started Agent Lemar, "this Armstrong fellow is pretty sharp. Buy's a burner phone, but he hasn't turned it on yet. We got the serial number from the store clerk. I think he might have seen the increased patrol action. If he's smart, he knows we're waiting for his phone to ping and confirm he's still in the area."

"Where have you canvassed?" asked Whelan as he and Jones harnessed up.

"Up and down Main, three blocks north and south of 31st. KCPD is cruising the alleys and monitoring east and west. I've got four more agents freeing themselves up from the field office. Should be here…now," she finished as two more cars raced onto the lot with federal agents. Six men and women jumped out, geared up and wearing Kevlar vests.

"SAC Kendrick sent us. We're filled in. Where do we start?"

"We've got to start getting inside these businesses," said Jones. "Let's stay on foot. Radio up and stay alert. You've all got his photo on your phone. Memorize it."

She assigned a search grid and pattern for each pair of agents. She and Whelan headed south on the west side of Main Street.

As they traveled, she ran a radio check and confirmed each agent's electronic ears were working.

They popped in and out of fast food joints, a car dealership, a van storage company and were about to enter a car wash when Lemar started yelling on the radio.

"He's here! Gates Bar-B-Q! He ran into the kitchen. Shit! Watch out! Move! He's out the back door, heading east on 32nd. It's residential here. Slow down, you fucker! Shit. Ronnie go that way, 'round back!"

Whelan and Jones ran east when she said 'Gates.' They were flying down Linwood Boulevard and turned onto McGee, heading north.

Lemar was becoming winded but still reporting. "We're on Grand now, heading north. Coming up on the KCPT tower. He's heading south on Thirty-First! Oh Lord, slow down, you bastard. Ronnie! Go behind the building! I'm on Thirty-First. Suspect disappeared in front of the KCPT building. Ronnie! He's coming 'round to you!"

"Lemar!" shouted Whelan. "I'm right behind you."

Indeed, Whelan tapped her shoulder as he passed. All three agents raced onto the parking lot of the local public broadcasting building. Agent Ronnie Barnhardt came around from the other side of the building.

"Did you see him?" asked Jones.

"No! He didn't cross my line of sight."

They all scanned the parking lot. There was no sign of him.

In unison, all four agents cast their eyes on the Kansas City Public Television building.

"Shit," mumbled Jones. "Okay, Lemar, stay here. Make sure he doesn't come back out the front door. Barnhardt, circle around back again."

She gave Whelan a thin smile. "Let's go catch a dragon rider."

Whelan and Jones moved inside the building. A receptionist sat startled in her chair and simply pointed toward a door behind her to the right. Jones turned the handle and flung the door open. A bullet narrowly missed her head and struck the door.

"Shit!" she said. "Guess he's given up swords for guns."

"You!" Jones said to the woman at the front desk. "Out! Keep your hands up till you're cleared outside."

The woman took out through the front door as Whelan and Jones drew their sidearms.

Whelan went down the hall first. Sonny Armstrong was seen turning left at the end of the corridor, so they wasted no time checking the four offices between them.

Jones motioned for Whelan to move down the next hall following their suspect. At the end of this, it turned to the right. Whelan positioned himself with his gun drawn and let Jones whip out in front of him and take the lead. Another shot rang out from an open office door near the back of the building as she moved past her partner. It struck the wall beside Whelan.

A second shot hit Jones in the right shoulder, spinning her around and knocking her to the ground. She screamed out initially but quickly silenced herself.

Armstrong ran inside the office.

"Son of a bitch!" she moaned through the pain.

Whelan knelt to help her, but she pushed him back with her other arm. "I'm fine. I think it hit the corner near the vest strap."

"You *think*?"

"Go! Take his ass down!"

Whelan ran down the hall and opened the door to the room Sonny Bill Armstrong entered. He went in low, expecting another shot, which indeed came at him and hit the door above his head. Armstrong was standing twelve feet away behind a young man working on a computer. He pointed the gun at the man's head.

"Get Back!" he shouted to Whelan.

"Let him go, Sonny. It's over." Whelan had the gunman in his sights. His face looked familiar. *Do I know this man?*

"Like hell!" said Armstrong. "You get out of my way and let me go, or I'll kill him."

"I can't do that, Sonny. We need you to answer for Sophia Perkins and Sue Fielding. Why'd you kill Sophia Sonny?"

"I didn't kill anyone. I don't know what you're talking about."

"We have a witness Sonny. Or is it Bill?"

Armstrong was mumbling expletives to himself under his breath.

The young man with a gun to his head was crying but otherwise silent. His expression was growing more and more concerned with their conversation.

"Sonny, you let the man go, and I'll assure leniency," said Whelan.

Two other KCPT employees were stationed behind computers in what appeared to be a shared office space. There was another office door on the back wall in the diagonal corner. A wall of windows behind Armstrong revealed a control booth for the television station. Two men were crouching behind the division wall and stealing peeks as they dared.

There was an uncomfortable thirty seconds of silence as the two armed men squared off against each other.

The young prisoner eked out a whisper to his captor. "Please, I have a little girl."

"Then do as I say," he muttered back. "Stand up."

The man complied, and Sonny led him to the other door, walking backward with the man as a shield. He turned the handle and opened it to reveal the end of another hall and an emergency door. Sonny threw the employee forward and vanished out the door.

Whelan raced across the room. He opened the door then jumped back a step, bracing for another bullet to go whizzing by, but it didn't come.

The sound of the hallway emergency door closing identified which way Armstrong went.

In quick pursuit, Whelan bolted through the door, prepared for more gunfire. Instead, he saw Sonny pull himself over a fence plastered with high voltage signs. There was nowhere else to run.

Sonny Bill Armstrong started climbing the television broadcasting tower contained inside the fenced area.

Whelan held his gun on him from the ground. Agent Barnhardt did the same from the other side of the fence surrounding the tower. The backside was capped with razor wire so he couldn't climb over the locked gate. Agent Lemar crashed through the emergency door, running into Whelan.

"You've nowhere to go, Sonny!" Whelan yelled.

More quietly, he asked Lemar, "Agent Jones?"

"She's all right. She's going out front. I radioed for paramedics. Help's here, and more's coming."

Armstrong climbed about twenty feet up the tower before firing two rounds in Whelan's general direction. When he'd made it about thirty feet up, he jumped the five-foot gap from the tower to the station building's roof and began running west across the top of the building.

"I've got him in my sight!" yelled Barnhardt.

"Take him down!" said Whelan.

Barnhardt fired his gun, but the bullet missed its target.

"He's headed toward the front across the roof," Whelan said to Lemar. "Stay here, in case he doubles back."

"You got it."

She positioned herself beside the tower and held her gun on the visible roofline, three stories up.

Whelan ran back inside and shouted at the two men in the control booth. "Where's the roof access?"

"There isn't one. You need a ladder."

"Shit," he mumbled. No one else was left in the office.

Whelan made his way toward the front until he came across a side exit on the south side of the building. He ran out the door and faced a line of guns pointed at him by seven of Kansas City's finest.

"Federal agent!" shouted Whelan. "Hold your fire! He's on the roof."

Everyone jerked their heads up to see if they could spot him.

One police officer commented to him, "We've got the place surrounded. He has nowhere to run."

Indeed, over nine squad cars surrounded the building while they were inside. The remaining federal agents who were on the manhunt were also taking point at the entries.

A blur of a shape was seen above, jumping nearly twenty feet down from one roof level to the other. A blood-curdling scream followed.

"Sonny Bill Armstrong!" shouted Whelan.

There was no answer.

"Sonny Bill Armstrong!" he yelled again. "Do you need medical assistance?"

A weak voice was heard from the second-story roof. "I broke my leg! Here!"

Sonny threw his pistol over the roof's edge. It clattered against the asphalt in the alley.

Jones' voice rang out behind Whelan. "Good thing we've got paramedics on the way. Better get a fire truck to ladder his ass off there too," she said to one of the city officers.

Whelan turned around. "How's your shoulder?"

"Sore, but it'll be fine." She winced as she rotated her cuff, testing it. She held a Swiss Army Knife in her left hand. The pliers were drawn, and she dug at the bullet lodged in the corner of her vest.

"Another half inch and my gun arm would be out of commission," she said.

The bullet popped free. She held it up in the sunlight. "Nine-millimeter."

Whelan put on a latex glove and recovered Armstrong's gun from the pavement. "Beretta. M9, not a 92."

"Marines?" asked Jones. "You think that asshole served?

"It would have come up in his file. I'd guess some wannabe who flunked out."

Jones nodded. "Outstanding job today, Whelan."

"You too. You going to miss all this when you're in the big seat?"

Jones took her vest off and moaned as fresh blood circulated its way through her shoulder. "No, I don't think I will."

Chapter 31

"I didn't kill them!" shouted Sonny Armstrong.

He was chained to the side rail of his hospital bed. Two hours in the emergency room fixed him up with a temporary cast. He'd need a few pins in his ankle if he ever hoped to walk again. Surgery was scheduled for the following day.

Jones spit out the standard line. "Sonny, if you cooperate, we can see about getting you a reduction in your sentence."

"I want that in writing! In fact, I want full immunity before I say another word."

"Sonny," said Whelan. "you shot a federal agent."

"She's fine! Look at her." He turned his head to Jones. "You're fine, right?"

Jones winced as she moved the shoulder. The doctor x-rayed her and confirmed she'd make a full recovery. There was nothing broken. She'd be sore for a few days, but soon back to normal.

"We know you're not working alone on this," said Jones. "Someone tipped you off about Sophia's son. We have video of you visiting her out in L.A. nineteen months ago. And we know you were the waiter who served Sue Fielding two nights ago at Parkmoor, 'Johnny.' We sent your photo to the catering manager, and she confirmed you were the man she hired that morning. Apparently, she was too desperate for help to properly vet you. But your partner on this obviously tipped you off about that dinner. Is it Sarah Williams? Is she your accomplice?"

"Who?" asked Sonny. He seemed to genuinely not recognize the name.

"Sophia Perkin's executive assistant."

"I'm not talking until I get a lawyer and a plea deal. I want full immunity on this. And the ten million dollars I was promised."

Whelan whistled. "You were offered ten million dollars to kill Sophia Perkins?"

"No. I wanted the opportunity to be in my son's life and get to know him. I was offered ten million to walk away and forget I ever knew Sophia Perkins."

"Then why not take that two years ago?"

"*That* wasn't offered two years ago. *That* was offered last month."

"By Sophia?"

"Yes. Her attorney drew up the paperwork. Ask him."

"We will."

"So, why would I kill her? Who kills their opportunity at ten million dollars?"

"That *would* be counter-productive," said Jones to her partner.

She turned her head back to Sonny Armstrong. "Unless you believed you could get a lot more."

"Like a few *billion* more?" echoed Whelan.

"I haven't killed anyone. That's my story until I get full immunity and ten million dollars. Then I'll give you some answers!"

"Was it Grace Meyer?" asked Whelan. He was hoping if they threw enough names at him, he'd light up with recognition. "Merrill Perkins? Sylvia Moffett? Chad Buckley?"

Sonny Bill Armstrong crossed his arms and laid back in his bed, closing his eyes.

"Linda O'Brien? Karen Hertzberg?"

Jones stared at him a minute. He was handsome and quite fit from his years in service as a fireman. They had yet to find out which city or county he used to work for in Oklahoma.

"Sonny, where did you serve before Station 53 here in Kansas City? Where at in Oklahoma?"

He opened one eye and looked at her briefly before closing it again. "Lawyer," he said.

"Dammit, Sonny!" snapped Whelan. "Who's helping you in all this? Is someone else calling the shots? Are you just a lackey? There may be other lives at stake. If someone else dies because you failed to tell us who your partner is on this, I'll make sure you get the maximum sentence. You know Missouri has the death penalty? I'll make it my life's mission to get you first in line at Potosi Correctional!"

Sonny didn't budge.

Jones sighed and motioned her partner to join her in leaving the room. An agent was stationed guard outside, not that Sonny Bill Armstrong could escape on his own. With his leg in its current condition, he was hardly a flight risk. He would likely be in a wheelchair for several weeks.

"We're not going to get anything out of him. He's completely shut down," she said to Whelan.

"Agreed. Damn. Someone helped him commit these murders. Who else besides Grace Meyer thought they stood to gain with Sue out of the picture?"

"None of them, according to all of them."

"Well, someone sure believed they were going to get rich on Sophia's money. And if it wasn't Grace, then she's likely got a target on her back. Should we warn her?"

Jones shrugged. "I think—if she's not the accomplice—then she's already aware someone might be targeting her."

Whelan started walking back down the hall before wheeling around with a thought. "Do you suppose when Sonny went to L.A. last year, he legitimately wanted a chance to get to know his son? Or was he plotting Sophia's death even then?"

"I don't know. I keep thinking of Running Bear. If Sophia played things differently, she might be alive right now, and that boy would have a father."

"Would *you* have let him back in your life if you were in her shoes?"

Jones reflected before answering. "There are a lot of variables to consider, but I think not, if I were really in those shoes." She looked at her feet. She'd traded her flats for running shoes in the car earlier. "And if I were, do you suppose they'd be Louboutin's? I could use a few extra inches." She flashed a smile at her partner.

"Height's overrated. Let's get back to Parkmoor. Cannon was asking about you. I think he expects to see you missing your entire right arm after taking that hit today."

Jones laughed.

"And," said Whelan, "I want to hear how it went with Merrill. I'm betting he didn't walk away quietly with a scant $100,000."

Cannon gave a nod to Whelan and Jones when they entered the foyer at Parkmoor. He inspected Jones' arm. "I expected a lot more blood," he teased.

"Nonsense. I'm a tough bitch, haven't you heard?"

"I'll remember that, *boss*. Armstrong's in custody?"

"Yes. He's not going anywhere fast. That stunt he pulled nearly broke his leg off."

"Are we telling Running Bear?" asked Cannon. "Maybe we should get a positive ID on more than a photo?"

"I don't know if that's the best idea," said Jones. "Sonny's lawyered up now, and unless we can find out who his partner on all this is, he might walk. At least on the murder charges. We've no evidence connecting him. We have only the word of a bipolar schizophrenic who is also the one person we *do* have evidence against."

"This is challenging," said Whelan. "He's clearly involved, or he wouldn't have run from us, shot at us, and now be asking for immunity, which there's no way he'll ever get after killing two people and firing at a federal agent."

"No," chimed in Jones. "We're not going to get anything out of him. We're on our own for finding his collaborator. I think whoever it is instigated all this. Armstrong's barely a co-conspirator. The 'brains' behind all this is still running free."

Whelan scratched at his chin. "If Armstrong is willing to squeal for ten million dollars, he's waking up to the notion that getting a lot more out of the family isn't a guarantee."

Cannon narrowed his eyes and cocked his head. "Where did he come up with that amount?"

"Says he was promised ten million dollars by Sophia last month to walk away," said Whelan.

"You suppose that was before or after she had sex with him?" asked Cannon.

"At least twice," added Whelan.

Cannon tilted his head. "Would you be flattered or insulted by that offer? After two rolls in the hay?"

"I'm not sure," reflected Whelan.

"Hey, we've got his DNA now," said Jones. "Could have been more than twice. Did Cusack get a sample of any spooge from the chaise loungers by the pool the other day?"

"I think so," said Cannon. "I'll give him a call and tell him to run Sonny against what he collected."

"That's fine," said Whelan, "but it doesn't make a difference. We know he had sex with her a week before she was killed *and* the night of. Does it really matter if there was more? What we need is to match the father of the fetus she was carrying. Who else was in her life recently? And is *he* involved in her death in any way?"

"All the male suspects on this have moved a rung up the ladder," said Jones.

"You mentioned seeing Chad Buckley being extra attentive to Grace Meyer. Maybe she was next in line for his affections after Sophia?"

"I don't think so. No one has mentioned anything of the sort. I do remember Nurse O'Brien commenting how Sophia was getting extra attention from Doctor Brachman. Sometimes twenty minutes, sometimes an hour, she said, spent alone being updated on Running Bear's condition. My bet's on Brachman being the father of her unborn child."

"I'll see if I can gather any DNA for him and run it against the baby's. I want Cusack to run the baby's against Mark Fleming too. I'm wondering if one of these father figures in Sophia Perkin's life was a 'daddy' to her in more ways than one."

Chapter 32

"What happened with Merrill?" asked Jones.

"Nothing, yet," said Cannon. "He and his wife Peggy are still here. They're camping out in the parlor, refusing to leave until Grace agrees to give them half a million dollars. She didn't want to have them arrested for trespassing. She's letting them steep, with a bar full of liquor ten feet away, which she made known was available to them. I think she's hoping he'll get drunk enough to sign the offer for $100,000, and then it's bye-bye cousin Merrill. Don't let the door hit your ass on the way back to Vinita, Oklahoma."

"You two go check on them. I'm going to call the Kansas City attorney, Adam Steiner," said Jones. "Let's see if there was really an offer on the table for Sonny Bill Armstrong to walk away from his son forever."

Jones stepped back outside so she could speak freely. Karen Hertzberg and Mark Fleming pulled up in their rental car as she dialed the attorney's number. She hit the 'end' button on her phone after two rings.

"Agent Jones," said Mark. "We've been patient, but we really need to get back to L.A. We were given warning from a reporter they're aware Sophia Perkins was murdered. Not just dead, but *murdered!* Someone has been squealing to the press. I've got until 9:00 a.m. to give an official corporate response, or they'll leak it to the world." He read his watch. "That's barely thirteen hours."

"Sounds like they're waiting for *you* to confirm their story, or they'd already have leaked it," said Jones.

"This is awful," said Karen. "We knew it would come out soon enough, and we've been preparing, but a couple more days would have really helped. This isn't going to help your case either."

"I know," said Jones. "It won't take too long before they figure out it was in Kansas City. How much longer we can protect Running Bear after that is anybody's guess."

"Can't you get a suppression issued?" asked Mark. "I can give you this guy's contact information."

"Text it to me, I'll pass it to my boss, but putting a thumb on the press tends to blow up in your face. I've learned the hard way. It's best to cooperate, minimize the effect with intentional, downplayed information. I'd get that Forever Sophia press release polished. You want to get ahead of the circus. We're all really on the clock now."

Jones' phone rang. "It's the family attorney. I need to take this. Excuse me. Go on into the Parlor. Fill Agent Whelan in on your news."

Ten minutes later, Jones was updating Whelan and Cannon on her phone call.

"So, Steiner won't tell me anything concrete regarding a payoff to Armstrong. Attorney-client privilege extends beyond the grave, apparently. I reminded him there's an exception if a crime is involved. He said as soon as we proved Sonny Bill Armstrong committed murder, he'd be free to discuss it, but until then, we're on our own. I threatened the power of The Bureau to him, but he didn't seem impressed. I told him I knew the mayor. He said he knew the governor. It was all great fun. But after all the huffing and puffing, right before he hung up, he said that if Running Bear's real dad were really back in the picture, he can't imagine it would be for anything other than money."

"What the hell does that mean?" asked Whelan.

"Exactly. So did they offer him the money or not? I don't know. Grace is in charge of the estate now. Maybe *she* can get it out of him and tell us. Where are we at in here with Merrill's situation?"

She saw Merrill and Peggy Perkins across the room, acting like hosts entertaining guests in their own home. Peggy served Mark Fleming and Karen Hertzberg drinks from the bar.

Peggy's voice could be heard over the chatter. "You'd think they'd have a blender back there. How are you supposed to mix up anything fun? I'm dying for a frozen margarita."

"Scotch is fine, thank you," said Mark, taking the glass from her hand.

Peggy handed Karen a glass of red wine. "I don't know if this is any good. It was the only bottle I saw. They probably have themselves one of those fancy wine cellars somewhere with lots of choices."

"Thank you, I'm sure it's acceptable," said Karen. She took a sip. "Lovely."

"Well, if you'll excuse me, my bladder calls. Time for a trip to the ladies' room. Do you need to go? I can show you where it's at."

"I'm fine, thank you."

Peggy seemed disappointed to not have company. "Okay."

She brisk-walked toward the trio of agents standing by the doorway. "Evening, agents. Catch the killer yet?"

"Working on it," said Jones. "I see you're all making yourselves comfortable.

"Grace told us it was okay," defended Peggy. "I'd never drink anybody else's booze without permission."

"I understand she extended her hospitality, yes. Enjoy yourself. Say, I'm curious. Did Merrill sign Grace's offer?"

Peggy lowered her voice to a whisper. "I'm pretty smart. I know Gracie hoped we'd get drunk enough to agree to much less than what she pledged, but Merrill can really hold his liquor. He wants at least a million now, or he's going to sue for custody of Running Bear. A grandfather should have more rights than a second cousin, don't you think?"

"First-cousin, once removed," corrected Cannon.

"Huh?" asked Peggy.

"Nevermind," said Cannon.

"I think all that matters is what Sophia wanted," said Jones, "and how the estate was set up in the will. But that's really a question for the attorneys. My opinion doesn't count."

"Well, I appreciate it anyway. Thank you."

Peggy opened her mouth toward Cannon, her face a jumbled expression of various curiosities, but then her eyebrows shot up to her bangs, and she simply said, "Oh! Excuse me, if I hold this any longer, I'm going to pee myself." With that, Peggy ran out of the room and down the hall.

"Saved by the bladder," said Whelan. He patted Cannon on the back.

"She's three sheets to the wind tonight," commented Jones. "Where's the rest of the family? Still eating dinner?"

"Yes," said Cannon. "Grace didn't extend an invitation to Merrill and Peggy. She did send in some snack mix, though. Salty treats to encourage more drinking. I'd wager she tended bar at some point in her life."

"I knew I liked her," said Jones.

"What's not to like?" came a voice from behind her in the hall.

They all turned to find Earl Humboldt standing there.

"Gracie's a true gem," he said. "I was told we were having drinks in here tonight, given that company is present and all."

Earl pushed past them and headed to the bar.

"And you're not 'company' any longer?" asked Whelan.

"Well, I don't live here officially yet. Gracie's been busy with other priorities, but I think she'll appreciate the help."

"Did you help yourself to Sophia, too?" asked Jones.

"Excuse me?"

Whelan grabbed his partner's arm and shot a stern, questioning look, shaking his head.

"What?" she whispered to him. "He could be a daddy figure."

"He's her *uncle*," murmured Whelan.

"By *marriage*," she hissed back. "Oh, fine. We've got his DNA. I've got Cusack running all possible matches to the embryo anyway."

Jones raised her voice so Earl could hear her over at the bar. "I meant, have you been enjoying Sophia's *home*?" She shot Whelan a sideways glance.

"Oh, yes, thank you! It's lovely. The staff is kind, accommodating."

"Thank you, Mr. Humboldt," said Nurse O'Brien, entering the room. "We're doing our best under the circumstances."

She was carrying a glass of wine from dinner she hadn't finished yet.

Behind her came Chad Buckley, Running Bear, Sylvia Moffett, and Grace Meyer. They all exchanged pleasantries with the agents on the way in. Chad, Sylvia and Running Bear all helped themselves to a drink from the bar. Grace stayed back with the agents.

"Any news?" she asked.

"He hasn't signed it yet," said Whelan.

"Shit. Maybe I should give him what he wants and get him out of here. I actually meant on the murderer. I understand you captured him today. What did he say? Why'd he kill Sophie? Was it just the money?"

"He hasn't admitted to killing anyone yet," said Jones. "And there's no direct evidence linking him to the murders."

"Tell me you're joking," said Grace.

Mark Fleming moved by them all, his face buried in his cell phone, chatting quickly. "Excuse me," he said to them as he brushed by on his way out to the gallery.

"I wish we were," continued Jones. "I'm sorry. He's lawyered up, but I haven't given up hope yet. I can tell you we ran his DNA today. He *is* Running Bear's father."

Grace fell into a nearby chair. She started crying softly. "What sort of monster is capable of killing a beautiful soul who he knows is the mother of his child?"

She dabbed at her eyes with her cocktail napkin. "Forgive me. You must think I'm horrible under pressure," she said.

"There's been a lot of pressure thrown on you this week," said Whelan. "You deal with it how you need to."

"Thank you," she said. "You're kind. You've actually all been really wonderful this week and have handled this delicately and professionally. Thank you all."

Her tears continued to flow.

"It's our job, and you're welcome," said Whelan. "Sadly, it's not over yet. Someone close to all this tipped Armstrong off in the first place, telling him Running Bear was his. There's an inside accomplice involved.

Someone who believed they stood to gain a larger portion of Sophia's inheritance."

"Why are you telling me this?" asked Grace. "Aren't I still your main suspect? I stood to gain control over the fortune, with Sue out of the picture. And now I have. Have I somehow managed to convince you of my innocence?"

All three agents studied her.

"We go on the evidence, but no, you're not off the hook yet, Ms. Meyer," said Whelan. "I'm telling you all this because assuming you *didn't* kill your cousin and your grandmother, then as the holder of all the money, you likely have a colossal target on your back now. Once you're dead, there's no one else in charge, officially, on the record. Eight billion dollars is up for grabs by anyone who claims a stake."

Grace processed his warning and raised her head to view everyone in the parlor. "Can you protect me?"

"We'll do our best."

Whelan watched her study their faces from over twenty feet away.

He came up closer to her ear. "You're seeing them in a whole new light now, aren't you?"

"Yes. I'm family, but...Bear doesn't know me as well as he does them, the staff. It's weird. Sophie bought him a nurse, and a pseudo-father, a chef, and a pretty housekeeper... They're his family as much as me now. Have you seen the way she looks at him?"

"Sylvia? We clued in, yes."

"Excellent. You're skilled at your jobs, at observation. I haven't been around much, or I would have picked up on it before. But living here full time this week, I've seen it. She's in love with him."

"Yes," said Whelan.

"Does that make her more or less likely to have killed his mother?"

Whelan took a step back. "Now you're thinking like we do. What do you think?"

"I don't know her well enough. But I can't believe she would kill Sophie because she didn't get as much attention from Bear two days a month. Sophie wasn't here often. Plus, she'd be killing off her bread and butter."

"Plausible. And the rest of them? Tell me what you see."

Grace obliged. "I see a sweet older man, Mr. Buckley. And yes, I'm aware he cares deeply for me. I can't help that. It's been developing for years. He's respectful. He knows I love my husband, and nothing will ever come of it. I see Bear, a beautiful boy I love like my own son. He's grown into a fine man, all things considering. Sophie would be proud of how well he's handling all this. I think when it's over, he's going to need some extra comforting. Not having his mother when he enters his next down phase is going to be ugly. He may have to go back on some meds, but I'll deal with that when it comes. There's no way he killed his mother. I feel it to my core. I don't have to question it."

"And?" encouraged Whelan.

"I see a sad old man. A pathetic piece of shit."

"That one's got to be Merrill," said Jones.

"Well, it's not *my* father," Grace chuckled. "Merrill…I have no words. But I don't think he killed his daughter. As for Earl, he's been within a stone's throw of me for years. He's a wonderful man. A simple man, but those are often the best."

"He's chomping at the bit for you to invite him to live here," said Jones. "Says he wants to be of help. Does that strike you as peculiar? Perhaps out of character?"

Grace watched her father. He was cackling, telling a story to Merrill and Nurse O'Brien.

"I think inheriting wealth overnight would throw anyone out of character," said Grace. "He's able to retire now. He'll want to be closer to me. I'm making arrangements to stay here at Parkmoor and take over the responsibility of Running Bear. It wouldn't be fair to take the money and run, now would it? My dad is welcome to stay and help. I'm sure he's sincere in his desire to be of assistance. And if that comes with maid service, well, he's worked harder than most throughout his life. I think he deserves to have someone else scrubbing the toilets for a change."

She turned to Jones. “As for Parkmoor and the inheritance, I’ve got Mr. Steiner coming in tomorrow to help me draw up a new will and testament. By this time tomorrow, anyone who thinks they’re owed some of the family's money will have more than me to kill off to stand a chance at getting at it.”

Grace focused on Merrill, a frown taking over her mouth. “Excuse me,” she said to the agents before walking over to the rest of the group.

Peggy Perkins’ voice preceded her physical presence. “I hope I haven’t missed out on any fun,” she said as she entered the room.

“Nope,” said Whelan. “They’re all waiting for you before commencing in fun.”

“Maybe we could all play a game,” she mused.

“Truth or Dare?” asked Cannon.

Peggy’s face went blank before lighting up. “Ha! You’re funny!” She wheeled on the back of her heel and rejoined the rest of the family.

“Truth or Dare?” asked Jones to her partner.

“Dare,” said Whelan. “I’m questioning if any of them would say ‘truth’ tonight.”

Chapter 33

"Flies on the wall," said Jones to her fellow agents.

The three agents split up, and each joined a different conversation. Whelan came up behind Grace Meyer as she was addressing her uncle.

"Merrill, I'll give you the $500,000 if you'll sign tonight and leave here forever."

"No, Gracie. It's a million now, and if you push me any more on it, I'll raise it to two."

Grace Meyer sighed and asked her dad. "Any thoughts here?"

"Give it to him. You've got loads now. It's worth it to get him to leave," said Earl.

"Fine. Fine, Merrill! A million it is." Grace tossed back the glass of Single Malt Glenlivet she'd been nursing and reached over the bar to pour herself another. "I'll have Mr. Steiner amend the offer tomorrow, and we'll be done with this nonsense."

Merrill was pleased with himself. He turned his pride toward Peggy, but she was too busy being disgusted by his earlier behavior to give him any credit.

Mark Fleming reentered the parlor and approached the bar. "I wouldn't mind one more before we hit the road."

He commented to his fellow board member. "Karen, the team in L.A.'s been perfecting the press release all afternoon. We have it ready for in the morning. I need you to read it and sign off. It should be in your email."

"Of course." Karen Hertzberg moved to a sofa several feet away and started tapping on her phone.

Mark approached Whelan. "Twelve hours. You've got twelve hours to figure out how you're going to handle the press."

"That's what my boss is for," said Whelan. "I just need them to stay out of my way so I can keep investigating."

Jones joined them, leaving Running Bear alone on a sofa.

She viewed the glass in Mark's hand and sighed.

He caught her expression. "You want one?" he asked.

"No, thank you. On the clock." She smiled politely. "I heard you mention twelve hours. I'd better call Kendrick and let him know to expect a shit storm."

Jones left the room.

Running Bear sat quietly, listening in on the smaller conversations around him. He was about to ask if he should make a statement at the press conference, but Marjorie stopped him.

"None of that's your concern," she told him. "Focus on Parkmoor."

Nurse O'Brien was visiting with Chad Buckley. Running Bear tuned in to the pair.

"Well, I guess our jobs are secure now, anyway," said O'Brien.

"Yes. One less worry. Grace spoke with me earlier. She plans to keep us all on."

"And move Earl in. I hope he's not too picky on which room he wants. I expect Grace to take Sophia's, which leaves two to choose from, and neither is as large as yours or mine. I hope he doesn't expect us to downsize."

Chad looked across the room at Earl. He was now chatting up Sylvia Moffett and Agent Cannon. "I don't think he'll care. It's just a bed. He'll have full run of the house. He's been in the pool three times this week. I expect he'll be out there every day until the first frost, and maybe even through the first snow."

"Sophie once thought about building a greenhouse around the pool so it could be enjoyed year-round. Maybe I'll suggest it to Grace."

"That'd be an eyesore, though, in the summer."

"Perhaps something retractable?" she asked. "I know you enjoy swimming too. I've seen you down there in the evening, doing laps."

"Oh, have you now?" His eyes opened wide with amusement. "Excuse me, I need a refresher. Are you ready for another?"

"No, thank you, Mr. Buckley." Linda O'Brien's face flushed with embarrassment over his reaction to her comment. "I think perhaps I've reached my limit."

She turned to leave.

Running Bear was smiling at her. When Chad was out of earshot, he said, "*I* like swimming. We could add another pool heater if necessary. It'd be fun under the snow. Like a life-sized snow globe. Oh! Could we *make* it a globe? That would be wonderful!"

Nurse O'Brien was still red in the face. "Your Majesty, shame on you for eavesdropping."

"If you wanted privacy, you shouldn't have spoken to him six feet from your king."

"I..." She stopped herself. "You're right. I'll remember that, thank you. Excuse me, Your Majesty." She rushed out of the room.

Chef Louie Pirelli waltzed in as she rushed away. He headed for the bar and poured himself a cognac. "Something upset Linda?" he asked those gathered near.

Mr. Buckley shook his head softly. "She's fine. I think she needed some air. Nice of you to join us this evening, Chef. You don't have to rush home to the family tonight?"

"I cautioned them I might have some late nights this week. It's been a crazy one, no?" He took a long sip from his snifter and sighed.

"Indeed. You missing Sophia?"

"Of course. Signora was a beautiful spirit."

"Well, you're free now to pursue your own restaurant. I'm sure you've got plenty of capital saved, but if you need investors, I believe in you enough to be your first."

Chef Pirelli studied Mr. Buckley to determine his sincerity. "Thank you. You're kind. As I said earlier this week, for now, I'm staying here. I was resigned to be here a few more years, so... I'm lost on what to do. My boys are halfway through high school. I'd hate to uproot them right now. I think until they've graduated, I'll continue to work for young Mr. Perkins."

"The world's loss is our gain," said Chad. He raised a glass. "To fine cuisine for the foreseeable future."

Louie raised his glass. "To Signora Sophia."

They toasted and took a sip.

Sylvia Moffett was staring at Running Bear, nodding politely as Earl Humboldt rambled aimlessly through a story about Grace and Sophia when they were children.

"I didn't have any close cousins," said Cannon when he finished. "That's nice they had each other, more like sisters."

"Yes. They were tight. They have other cousins, but they were closest in age and were able to spend a lot of time together when they were in elementary school. Of course, those years raising Bear bonded them forever."

Cannon leaned in and lowered his voice. "I'm curious. How did Grace turn out remarkably different then?"

"How so?"

"Well, Sophia seems to have...gotten around more?"

"You mean she was a slut? Yes. Well, I parented my child. And Sophie got Merrill. I like to think that made a difference," said Earl. He noticed Merrill staring at them from a few feet over, so he raised his glass to the man.

Merrill raised his in return, his toothless mouth open wide and oblivious.

"And Grace never had any kids?" asked Cannon. "No grandkids for you?"

"No," said Earl. "She never told me this, but I think her husband is infertile."

"Why would you suspect that?"

"Because after they were married a few years, Gracie's personal doctor took a look at her. He said she was healthy and should be able to conceive, and I know she was trying for several years to get pregnant. Had to be him."

"Maybe he didn't want children."

"No, they both wanted to be parents. I guess now, they get to be. To a twenty-seven-year-old. At least he's potty-trained. Now, if we could rule him out once and for all as a danger, I'll feel a lot safer with my Gracie living here."

Both men were watching Running Bear, who was chatting away to the air beside him.

At some point, Sylvia tuned back into their conversation. "Running Bear is *not* a danger. To anyone."

She stood abruptly. "Shame on you."

Sylvia walked over to Running Bear and took a seat across from him.

Earl tightened his lips and turned back to Cannon. "I don't have the liberty of being confident about my great-nephew yet. I know two women I loved are dead this week. And I'm pretty sure someone in this house is responsible."

He cast his eyes back on Running Bear. He was now howling over something Sylvia said.

Cannon let his eyes roam the rest of the room. *I agree with you, Earl. Someone in this house is responsible. But who?*

Chapter 34

The guests filed out around 10:00, and the staff all retired to their rooms by 11:00, leaving Earl Humboldt doing laps with a late-night swim.

Grace thought she heard him come in around midnight and was soon sound asleep. It was one hell of a week.

Parkmoor stood quiet at 3:00 a.m. Friday morning as a lone figure made its way in the dark. A gloved hand opened the glass door of the sword display on the midway landing of the grand staircase. It took a seventeenth-century dagger encrusted with rubies in the hilt. A minute later, the figure was standing over the sleeping body of Grace Meyer.

The dagger was plunged two-handed into Grace's chest. She woke with the start of a scream but was silenced just as quickly by a pillow being shoved ferociously against her face. She wasn't sure if she would die from blood loss or suffocation first.

Grace flailed her arms in vain against her attacker, who clearly carried the advantage. Lack of air caused her to lose consciousness, and she spun dizzily into darkness.

Once Grace stopped fighting, the pillow was released. Moonlight pounded against the window shade, illuminating the cloaked and hooded silhouette as it retrieved the dagger. Blood spurted and began flowing from Grace's chest, over her limp torso and down the side of the bed, pooling on the floor.

Grace Meyer looked peaceful as the back of a gloved hand stroked her cheek once. Blood from the removal of the dagger saturated the gloved fingers. They left a streak now across Grace's face, stained bright as a cardinal's belly.

In the hallway, about to turn onto the staircase, the figure nearly ran into Running Bear, coming up from the ground floor.

Running Bear froze in fear. A flashlight was aimed brightly in his face, and a muffled voice rasped at him from the figure in the dark. "Death is but a journey, one we all must travel."

The light was extinguished, and the figure vanished as Running Bear fought to regain his sense of sight. He fumbled on the wall until he felt the light switch for the sconces lighting the corridor for the upstairs bedrooms. He took a step and tripped over an object under his left foot. He landed softly, breaking the fall with his arms, missing the tip of a bloodied blade. He bent down and picked up the rubied hilt, turning it to and fro. The red glow of the gems mesmerized him a minute. They reflected the hallway light, matching the glistening of the blood on the other end of the dagger.

His gaze was broken by the sound of Nurse O'Brien behind him. "Bear? Bear! What is that? What are you holding?"

He stood up and held the dagger toward her, hilt first, as though handing it off.

O'Brien backed up a step, her pupils dilating as they landed on the fresh blood staining the edge of the blade. "Bear! What did you do?"

"I didn't do anything. I tripped on this. It was in the hall. The wizard left it."

"What wizard?"

Running Bear peered down the corridor, then over the edge of the banister to the stairs. No one was there.

"I don't know. A wizard was here a minute ago. Must have left."

Nurse O'Brien took a step toward him and studied the sharp steel. She turned her gaze upward onto young Mr. Perkin's face. "Bear, Your Majesty, that appears to be blood. Whose blood is it? Yours? Are you injured?"

"No. It's not mine. I don't know. Maybe it's dragon's blood! We should save some. It might have magical properties. Or healing. You're a nurse! You could use it for your potions. Do you think the wizard killed it? Maybe there's a dragon up here somewhere! Let's find it."

Running Bear ran to the first door in excitement. He knocked. Sylvia answered in her nightgown. "Bear, sweetie, what's wrong. It's the middle of the night."

She noticed Nurse O'Brien standing a few feet back. "Linda? What's going on?"

O'Brien pointed at Running Bear, staring at his hand still holding the dagger, and raised her eyebrows.

Sylvia pushed Running Bear's arm, moving the dagger's blade further away from her stomach. "Bear…Your Majesty, let's put that down."

"The wizard left it for me to finish killing the dragon. We have to find it. Come with us on our quest!"

Running Bear ran to the next door. It was Nurse O'Brien's room, and she'd left the door open. He ran inside and threw the lights on. There was no dragon.

Sylvia whispered sharply to the nurse. "What's he talking about? A wizard?"

"I don't know. He might have been sleep-walking and dreaming this. I was asleep, but I thought I heard a scream, and it woke me up. I wanted to make sure *I* wasn't dreaming, so I got up to investigate. I found him with that dagger in his hand. Sylvia, it has fresh blood on it."

Both women watched Running Bear as he raced from Linda O'Brien's bedroom and knocked on another door. No one answered, so he flung the door open and flicked the light switch.

Grace Meyer's body lay still before him. He walked around to make sure he really saw what he believed his eyes were showing him. Over a quart of blood surrounded her and continued dripping onto the floor.

"Gracie?" he said. "Gracie!" He rocked her body. "Gracie! Wake up! Help! Help!"

Nurse O'Brien and Sylvia Moffett ran into the bedroom.

"Oh dear Lord!" said O'Brien. She grabbed the pillow lying beside Grace's face and jabbed it toward the wound in her chest. "Call 911!" she screamed.

Sylvia was already dialing.

O'Brien grabbed Grace's wrist with her right arm and tried to find a pulse.

"Is she dead?" asked Sylvia.

"I don't know. I can't find a pulse!" O'Brien slapped Grace's face lightly. "Grace! Grace!"

Running Bear began crying. "She's dead? Gracie's dead?" He ran out of the room.

"Help! Help!" he screamed.

Chad Buckley appeared at the top of the stairs. His bedroom was on the ground floor. "Bear? What's wrong, Bear?"

"Gracie's dead! The wizard killed Gracie! He wasn't after a dragon at all! Gracie's dead!"

Running Bear ran to Chad, wailing against his shoulder like a five-year-old. Chad held him tight and patted the back of his head. After a minute, he took a step back. "Bear, let's find out what's going on."

When Chad appeared in Grace's doorway, he saw Sylvia and Nurse O'Brien working on a lifeless body.

A couple minutes later, Earl Humboldt walked into the room. "What's all the commotion?" he said as he entered.

He was faced with the bloodied woman before him, his daughter of forty-three years. "Gracie!" He ran to her side and dropped to his knees in the crimson basin before him. He grabbed her free hand and squeezed tightly.

"Gracie, my girl. Daddy's here. Wake up, sweetie!" Tears streamed down his cheeks. "Gracie, it's your dad, honey. Squeeze my hand. Let me know you're alive, sweetheart."

With no reaction, he let go as the sound of the paramedic's siren echoed in the distance. It grew louder, bouncing off stone walls, making its way to every ear.

Two men soon ran into the room and moved the still frame of Grace Meyer onto a gurney. They took her away as quickly as they appeared while five souls gawked in silence.

It was surreal, and processing what occurred would take some time.

Earl's eyes drifted around the bed, then the floor. He stood, his daughter's life force clinging to the kneecaps of his pajamas. He continued staring wildly, at walls, at the staff, ending on Running Bear, his great-nephew who was at the heart of all the nonsense happening.

A week ago, Earl Humboldt lived quietly in Oklahoma, working as a farmhand, drinking beer with his bowling buddies, and having Sunday dinners with his beautiful daughter Grace and her husband. It was a simple life compared to the glamour and speed with which Sophia Perkins flaunted her lifestyle. He dared to think himself capable of adapting to such a life here at Parkmoor. He'd now trade his last penny for his darling girl to wake up and all of this to go away.

As his thoughts grew violent, he noticed the dagger in Running Bear's hand.

Without warning, Earl launched himself at his kinfolk. He slapped the blade to the floor with his left hand and let his fist fly against Running Bear's face with his right. "I'll *kill* you!"

Chapter 35

Twenty minutes later, Special Agents Whelan and Jones ran into the kitchen at Parkmoor, where the agents on guard corralled everyone until they arrived.

"No one came in either front or back door," said Agent Biggs, who was on entry door duty when the paramedics showed up earlier. "Once we got them all in here, Agent Tyson stayed with them while I searched the rest of the house. There's no one else here."

Jones examined Running Bear. A large shiner was developing on his left cheek near his eye.

"Who wants to start?" she asked the group. Her hair was bound in a large ponytail, and her shirt was untucked over her jeans and running shoes. They were lucky she didn't run out of the house in her nightie.

Nurse O'Brien filled them in. "And so," she finished, "Thank God Chad was in the room, or I think Mr. Humboldt might have killed our poor Running Bear."

"Poor?" said Earl. "That's ironic. That boy should be in an institution!"

"If he was," snapped Sylvia, "whose pool would you be swimming in every day?"

"You're out of line!" he roared back. "You're all crazy! Do you think you're playing a big damned game? This is real life! And my little girl has lost hers!" He began sobbing.

"Actually," said Whelan, "I got an update from the hospital as we were pulling in. They resuscitated Grace in the ambulance and are working on her as we speak. She's receiving blood. Of course, she's critical, but they're giving her a fighting chance."

"Really?" asked O'Brien. "That's wonderful."

Earl fell onto a barstool, pouring his face into his palms.

A low beeping noise could be heard coming from the counter.

"More coffee's ready," said Sylvia. "Agents? Can I offer you some caffeine?"

"No, thank you," said Jones. She had grabbed a bottle of ice coffee on her way out the door earlier.

"I'd love one, Sylvia," said Whelan. "Thank you."

Everyone was silent for a minute, processing the news that Grace was alive for the time being.

Sylvia topped off everyone's cups.

Jones pointed at the large baggie sitting on the island in front of Agent Biggs. "That it?"

"Yes. We haven't dusted it yet."

Running Bear was distressed. "I shouldn't have touched it. My prints will be on there." He sighed, seeming to understand this was detrimental for him.

"I didn't stab Gracie," he said to Jones. "I thought the wizard wanted me to kill a dragon."

"With a dagger?" asked Whelan.

"I thought that was odd at first, too, but I figured he did most of the work and saved the kill for me."

Everyone in the room turned their eyes on Running Bear after his comment.

"The *dragon*!" cried Running Bear.

He lowered his voice to a whisper. "I didn't kill Gracie. I loved her. She was my favorite princess. I'd never hurt her."

Running Bear made eye contact with each member of his "family" for a few seconds. "I love *all* of you. I'd never hurt any of you."

Nurse O'Brien put her arm around his shoulder. "We know that, Bear. And we know you didn't hurt Grace."

She turned to Whelan. "He didn't stab Grace Meyer. He wouldn't do that."

"Well, if he didn't do it," said Jones, "then someone else in this house *did*."

They all swiveled their heads quickly to one another.

"That's nonsense," said O'Brien. "None of us tried to kill Grace. None of us killed Sophia or Sue. This has all gone far enough!" she leaned on the island counter, bracing herself so she wouldn't collapse. The stress of the week overwhelmed her. She joined the others in letting the tears flow.

"I need to sit," she said.

Without permission, she marched to the living room and fell into an easy chair. The group in the kitchen all made their way behind her and relocated to comfier seating.

"If it wasn't someone in this house," continued Jones, "then you expect me to believe that someone made it past my agents and waltzed in without being seen?"

"That's exactly what happened," said Sylvia. "Bear couldn't have done this. Do you have agents at all the doors?"

"Front and back. I was told the side door in the garage always stayed bolted and the door from the garage to the house locked nightly."

"Earl," asked Sylvia, "you were the last one in. Did you make sure all the doors were locked before retiring for the evening?"

Earl Humboldt turned three sheets whiter. "Me? No one told me I was supposed to. I was in charge of locking up?" He appeared mortified.

"This isn't the Ritz," said Sylvia. "Did you think that was *my* role? Wait for you to finish your midnight dip and secure the house behind you? Perhaps you think I'm supposed to stand there while you swim, holding a fresh towel from the warmer at the edge of the pool! Why, shame on me. What horrible service you're receiving! I'm surprised you haven't complained to management. Of course, that would have been your *daughter*, now wouldn't it?"

Sylvia joined those already crying.

"Oh my God," said Earl. "I didn't know I had to lock up! The fucking FBI is here, stationed at the front and back! I didn't know there was another door to lock. Oh my God. It's my fault Gracie was attacked!"

"Everyone, take a breath!" said Whelan.

More agents soon started filing through the front door of the home. Agent Joe Cusack showed up with his forensics unit. Over a dozen agents were scouring the house.

"There are actually *four* doors," said Chad Buckley, absently voicing his thoughts aloud. "There's a cabana bath door on the lower level. It opens to a path leading to the pool. Goes right by my tool room."

Soon a forensics agent was reporting to Special Agent Jones. "The deadbolt on the side door to the garage was taped shut. The handle was jimmied to appear locked at a glance but was essentially useless. The entry from the garage into the home was the same."

Earl was sitting beside Sylvia on a sofa in the living room. "Running Bear, I'm so sorry I hit you. I was upset. I saw you with that knife in your hand. I'm sorry I thought it was you."

"Dagger," corrected Running Bear. His cheek was still sore. He stood up and walked over to him. "I…" He cut himself off.

"I need another ice pack," he chose to say, instead of forgiving him, and headed for the kitchen.

Earl stood up and thought he might follow him for a second but turned instead to Jones. "I guess that proves someone else entered the home then. He's off the hook?"

"Not at all," said Jones. "He could have taped those latches down, hoping it would look like an outside job." She waved her hand across the room. "Any of you could have."

They all stared at one another again.

Nurse O'Brien regained her composure and stood. "Well, Agent Jones, we didn't. So how do we prove it?"

"By finding the real killer."

Whelan followed Running Bear to the kitchen.

Running Bear was holding a bag of frozen peas on the left side of his face.

Whelan grinned at him. "The old frozen vegetables trick, eh?"

"It conforms better than the ice pack Sylvia gave me earlier. Agent Whelan, I *did* see a wizard. With a cloaked hood, brandishing a glowing orb shining so brightly it blinded me for a minute."

"But you couldn't tell if it was a man or a woman? No facial details?"

"For a split second, I saw the face in the dark before the orb lit up, but it was wrapped in a scarf. Then *everything* in front of me went white. He gave me a warning. 'Death is but a journey, one we all must travel.' Gandalf said something similar to Pippin in *Lord of the Rings*."

"So you think your wizard was Gandalf?"

"No. Gandalf is a fictional character. Whoever that wizard was, he was real."

"It was a *man's* voice you heard, though?" asked Whelan.

"I think so. I'm not sure, to be honest. I was so frightened. It could have been a woman's voice, I guess. Maybe an evil sorceress. It was scarcely more than a whisper. She could have stabbed me if she'd wanted me dead. I guess she specifically went after Gracie. Why do you suppose that is? Why her and not me?"

"Because all the money—the green paper—the rest of the world values, is *yours*, technically. If you were killed, it would be tied up in the courts for years before anyone got any. But with Grace gone, the money is still yours, still available, and everyone simply fights to become your guardian—your conservator. And whoever wins *that* gains control over how your fortune is spent, Your Majesty."

"Such strange practices."

"Yes," agreed Whelan. "So, it sounds like you really don't know if it was a woman or a man. Agreed?"

"Yes, I'm sorry. I really don't know."

"Did you see the wizard's eyes behind the scarf? What color were they?"

"I've been trying to remember. It happened so fast. I don't know."

"Light? Dark?"

Running Bear hung his head low to his chest."

"That's okay. Better to admit you're unsure than have us overlooking any possible suspects. Your Majesty, if you could choose anyone else besides Grace to be here with you at Parkmoor and help run things—control the green paper—who would you choose?"

Running Bear's head tilted back and forth, then he sighed. "I suppose, Chad. I feel closest to him. I trust him. I trust Linda and Sylvia too, but Chad… I think he's the wisest of them."

He lowered his voice to a murmur. "Don't tell them I said that."

"Your secret's safe, Your Majesty."

Whelan was amused by the younger man's concern for the feelings of his nurse and his maid. They truly were his family, the three of them. He believed Running Bear to be quite thoughtful and intelligent, despite his mental facilities. In another life, he'd have enjoyed being the man's friend. He thought of his mother, Kathryn, who was always equally capable of creating family out of friendships. *When life doesn't give you a family you like, go make a family from those you do*, she used to say.

But Tom Whelan was living in this reality and reminded himself to stay objective. At this time, all the evidence still pointed to Running Bear as the culprit.

Chapter 36

Jones was staring at Grace Meyer through the glass of her ICU door at the hospital. She was intubated and hanging on, still listed as critical. The dagger pierced the edge of her aorta above her heart. Were it an inch lower, she likely wouldn't have survived. The doctors repaired it with emergency surgery. Her transfusion went well, they said, no adverse reactions. It was up to Grace's body to go to work now and finish where the doctors left off.

It was before 9:00 a.m. The news conference announcing Sophia Perkins' death was scheduled to begin shortly. Jones returned to the waiting area where there was a television she could watch it on.

An armed guard was stationed outside Grace's bed. If the killer wanted to finish the job, it would be a challenge. Outside of the hospital doctors and nurses, no one but Agents Jones and Whelan and Grace's dad Earl Humboldt were authorized to enter.

Jones was up the rest of the night. She knew from past experience if she'd returned home to try to catch another couple of hours, it would have been pointless. She'd rest when the case was solved.

Derrick, her fiancé, was out of town. He'd been staying more and more in New York as his cable fitness show debuted with double the ratings expected. They ordered extra shows plus green-lit a second season. A massive bonus was written into his contract if successful, which they honored.

Both of their careers were on an upward trajectory, but she feared Derrick's might take him out of Kansas City soon. And her promotion required her to stay put, for now.

She rubbed at her neck, tilted up at the TV mounted on a wall right below the ceiling.

"Here, Miranda," said a voice from behind. Her partner, Tom Whelan, held a large cup of coffee from one of her favorite coffee shops.

"Hot with light cream." Whelan smiled at her.

He'd made it home for a fresh shower but also skipped a nap. It was going to be another long day, and he was anxious to get back to Parkmoor and see if anyone remembered anything else they might have failed to report at 4:00 in the morning under duress.

"You're an angel," said Jones. "You ready for this?" She motioned to the television.

"I'm fine. Did you speak with SAC Kendrick this morning? He's the one who will be fielding calls all day."

"He said he was forwarding them all to you," she said.

Whelan laughed.

They turned their attention to the screen when a national cable news anchor came on, announcing the press conference. The camera cut away to the media room in Forever Sophia's L.A. office. The man at the podium cut straight to the chase, starting with the fact Sophia Perkins, the company's founder and spokesperson, was murdered in Kansas City, Missouri. He quickly went into damage mode, stating sales statistics backing how well the company was doing and that nothing would change with any products or their distributors.

He soon ended with, "The makeup you've come to trust will be the same tomorrow as it was yesterday. That's our promise to you, Sophia's greatest fans. She'd want you to know you're in terrific hands. Trust that she made sure her company was run by the best in the business, and we're all still here, working tirelessly each day to bring you the finest cosmetics at the 'every person's price,' just as she wanted."

The man on the television flipped over the last of his papers. "I'll now take a few questions."

A hoard of journalists and paparazzi jumped up from their chairs, yelling over one another to be called upon. This was not the announcement they were ready for. Usually, these media briefings were held when a new line was launched or the company expanded into another country. The death of 'Forever Sophia' herself was too juicy. They all wanted to be the first to capitalize on the news.

A security officer standing on the sidelines jumped in front of the frenzy, helping get the reporters back in their seats and restore order.

The answers came off a prepared sheet, where the man was careful to read them verbatim. No question went unthought-of. "The FBI is investigating. Yes, they've made an arrest. There's a suspect in custody. No, we don't know why she was killed. No, we don't know why she was in Kansas City. It wasn't on her official schedule. No, we don't have a new spokesperson lined up at this time. We are all deeply saddened by her loss. She will be missed." He droned on for fifteen minutes.

When the questions started repeating themselves, he commented, "Please keep her family in your prayers. Thank you."

He walked off the tiny stage, and the news channel cut back to the anchor, who fumbled through a couple of minutes of awkward, unprepared comments.

"Why do you suppose they would say that?" asked Whelan. "Keep her family in your prayers. The public doesn't know she had any family. That's going to raise more questions."

"I think it's one of those things you say, you know? Even if she didn't have any children, people usually have siblings or parents still alive."

"I don't know. To me, it infers she was married or had children."

"Then maybe it's a psychological sales tactic? Keep buying Forever Sophia, and you'll help take care of the family? Forever stay a part of Sophia's family."

"Would *you* keep buying it for her family's sake? Or because you felt like you were staying in the Forever Sophia family?"

"No," said Jones. "But as long as they didn't change the quality of the products or increase the price, I wouldn't *stop* buying them either."

"Not today, but in time, people will begin to forget her. She won't be on monthly talk shows or in front of a QVC camera once a month. Eventually, her face will come down from billboards, and people won't remember that her products were created to 'hide the worst in all of us.'"

Jones' face lit up. "Oh, so you *do* pay attention to those commercials!"

He grinned. "They run a lot of them. I understand why Mark Fleming was concerned. I don't see how the company will maintain sales next year. They may have to IPO after all and go public to save it."

"Don't tell me you're back to thinking one of those board members was involved in Sophia's death so they could get their way in a vote to take the company public?"

"No. I still think it's someone who knew that with Grace out of the way, all of Running Bear's inheritance is up for grabs again, someone who was at the reading of the will. Sue Fielding would have likely allowed Forever Sophia to IPO, so killing her and giving Grace control, rules out the remaining board members once and for all in my mind. Sonny Bill Armstrong's accomplice is either in that house or staying at The Leonardo."

Jones bit her lower lip as she pondered the possibilities for the hundredth time. "We don't have any DNA from Sonny at the crime scene or in the house. How do we prove he's guilty?"

"We keep working the case. I have a feeling something's going to shake loose today. Attempting to kill Grace in the middle of the night was reckless. There's got to be some evidence we missed."

Whelan's ear picked up the words "Forever Sophia" on the television again. He turned back around to watch.

The reporter and the news anchor were having a conversation. The reporter was now positioned outside in front of the office building. The Forever Sophia logo in the company's sign on the building was strategically visible over his left shoulder. They were going back and forth over why Sophia was in Kansas City the night she was killed. The fact she lived there before moving to L.A. could easily be Googled online, so they were considering what "family" she might have there.

"Well, there's no record of her having any children," said the reporter. "Perhaps her parents live in the area?"

They continued speculating as Whelan turned back to Jones. "I knew they'd jump on that. 'Pray for the family.' You think anyone's praying for Merrill?"

"Doubtful," said Jones. "I did send one up this morning for Grace, however."

They checked in with the guard stationed at Grace's bedside and headed out for the fifth day in a row to Parkmoor.

Jones yawned as she turned over her SUV. *Someone in that house has got to break.*

On the drive over, SAC Kendrick placed a call to Jones. "Get down to the Missouri Riverfront Trail, just west of the Argosy Casino. I've got divers in the water confirming a submerged car with a license plate belonging to Doctor Alan Brachman. There's a body inside, but no way to identify it until they pull the car out. That water's murky. You can't see more than a few inches."

By the time they arrived, the Audi sedan was being hoisted out of the water by a crane on a barge off the shoreline. The operator moved it as far over a boat ramp as he could and held it until a tow truck driver could get his own chains wrapped around the undercarriage. Once lowered, the truck hauled it to dry land, and they smashed the back passenger window to allow the water to be released faster. After it dropped below the window-line, a man unlocked the door and opened it to drain the remaining water. He flicked the lock button, but it failed to operate.

He took a large gulp of fresh air before climbing inside. Once the driver's seat belt was unbuckled, he reached around him and released the door handle. The driver's body toppled to the pavement. "Shit. Sorry! Should have left him buckled in until that was open. Oh damn! It's ripe in here."

The smell of decaying flesh mixed with fish and mud, hitting everyone's nostrils. Thankfully, the water carried the bulk of it away, so it was tolerable.

Jones stood over the body. "I can't tell for sure. I think it's him. His face is starting to swell, but it's not as far along as his gut."

Cusack soon arrived on the scene. "The methane's building up in his torso but the lack of bloating in his appendages and head makes me think he's been under six, maybe seven days."

The barge captain lowered his crane to the shore and walked across like a tightrope artist. He jumped onto dry land, his first mate holding the boat's position ten feet off the bank. "I spoke with the captain of a hopper carrying grain from Kansas. He came alongside the shoreline, hitting that car. He's been on this waterway for over thirty years and knew there was something more than mud he struck. He called me. I'm the local 'rescuer of miscellaneous river objects.' Of course, I notified the police when my guys read the plate of that poor son-of-a-bitch. They got back to me right away and gave me the 'all-clear' to pull it up."

He stepped around the body on the ground. Shaking his head, he held out a clipboard. "Who can sign for receipt?"

"I guess that's me," said Jones. "Thank you for the assist."

The captain gave her a little bow and scurried back across to his boat, anxious to raise his crane and get out of there.

Cusack took the requisite photos and collected several tissue samples from different areas of the body. There was no wallet nor any papers in the glove box that were readable.

An unmarked cargo van was opened up, and a gurney was brought over to the body.

"My team's on another call. Agent Whelan, can you assist?" asked Cusack. He unzipped a body bag close to the corpse. Whelan grabbed the feet, and the two lifted the dead weight into the open bag. A little wrestling and the man was sealed inside.

"Give me an hour for preliminary findings?"

"Hurry. I need answers fast on this one. I can't hold those Forever Sophia execs hostage forever. I'm going to be losing my suspects if we don't solve this soon."

"I'll do my best. Jennie Mapleton is expeditious with her autopsies. I'll request her from the county."

They lifted the bag onto the gurney, and Cusack was soon on the road.

Jones was staring at her phone. She held it up to Whelan. "This is Brachman. This is our body. Same man?"

"I think so, but I wouldn't swear to it. He was decomposing pretty quickly in this August heat. That water temperature's got to be eighty-four, eighty-five degrees. It's not exactly preserving anything."

She stuffed her phone back in her pocket. "Let's get to Parkmoor. Cannon was meeting us there this morning. I wonder if he's getting any further than we did five hours ago."

Chapter 37

Agent Phil Cannon was not getting far at all. Three other agents were on site from the Evidence Response Team Unit. They scoured the grounds for footprints and more, hoping daylight would reveal what darkness hadn't. So far, it was a bust.

The tree line at the foot of the property below the pool area was scoured. One agent shouted out, "I've got a broken branch here. Still leaking sap. This is from this morning!" He collected the small limb and held a bright LED lamp to illuminate the shadows under the trees, hunting for fibers possibly stuck in the area. Two were retrieved.

The adjacent property below Parkmoor contained a tennis court, where two women were playing a game. Cannon flashed his credentials and inquired if they saw anyone trespassing on their property in the middle of the night. Perhaps a strange car in the street out front? Nothing. Not too many people up at 3:00 a.m.

He returned to the house. His frustration was evident.

"Not finding anything helpful?" asked Nurse O'Brien.

"We're still searching," said Cannon. He didn't want to disclose they might have a new fiber sample from an article of clothing. He was doubtful it would reveal much.

The other agents picked through the floor again in the hallway upstairs, looking to collect anything that could match what was found in the treeline. More threads were recovered, but there was nothing to be excited about until they could get them beneath a microscope. The team from 4:00 a.m. found several as well. Perhaps they would get lucky.

The ERTU agents packed up and headed out, leaving Cannon alone to continue interviews, and wait for the arrival of Agents Whelan and Jones.

Running Bear was curled up in the living room, watching television.

When Cannon approached him, he politely turned it off, as his mother taught him. "Did you see the press conference?" he asked.

"No," said Cannon. "How was it?"

"They said the Queen was murdered here, in Kansas City. It won't take long for them to figure out there's a new king now. We may soon have a war on our hands. I hope the troops are readying for battle."

"I'm sure they are, Your Majesty. Did you get any sleep after this morning's events?"

"*Events*?" Running Bear chortled. "You mean the attempted assassination of Princess Grace? Call it what it was, Lord Cannon. There's no reason to dilly-dally around the harsh truth."

"My apologies, Your Majesty. I understand your cousin came through surgery and is in recovery now."

"Yes. We were informed by the doctor. He said her odds are less than fifty percent. You'd think they'd always give someone at least a fifty percent chance. Rather cruel, if you ask me."

"Agreed. So, this wizard you saw... No further recollection of anything helpful? Eye color? The clothes? Maybe a gender?"

"No." Running Bear stared at the floor. He still felt helpless but was tired of crying over it. "He or she blinded me with that light. I've been trying to identify the voice, but even that... I couldn't tell you if it was a man or a woman. It was low and raspy."

"I'm sure they were disguising their real voice as best they could," said Cannon.

He studied Running Bear, three years younger than himself but carrying an innocence Cannon wasn't sure *he'd* ever had, even as a child.

His upbringing wasn't too far removed from Running Bear's. Cannon's parents were savagely poor and divorced at an early age. He had one brother that his father took with him and disappeared somewhere across the country. His mother became a drunk, and by the time he was old enough to conduct online searches to find out where his brother and father might have gone, she was six feet under by her own hands, and he was two years into foster care.

The internet never revealed a thing about his family. When the complete resources of the FBI's database turned up nothing on them last year, he quit trying to locate them.

"Has the dragon rider revealed any new details?" asked Running Bear.

"No. Still clammed up. Waiting for a deal he'll never be offered. Your Majesty, I'm afraid *you* are still the likeliest suspect. I have to ask, are you *sure* you saw a real person last night, here at Parkmoor? Is it possible that special head of yours created someone to cover up the fact that you were the one in Grace's room at 3:00 a.m.?"

Running Bear's wheels turned faster than Cannon would have guessed. He stood up and snapped at the federal agent.

"How dare you! Imply I'm crazy? Doctor Brachman wouldn't approve!" He strolled out of the living room toward the kitchen.

Cannon's eyebrows shot up. Given the events of the week, Running Bear was relatively calm throughout, so the sudden spark of anger surprised him.

Cannon was torn between amusement and guilt for questioning young Mr. Perkins. He wasn't a psychologist, but he knew better than to test someone with a mental disorder in that way.

Thinking to go and apologize, Cannon stood and started to follow him when Sylvia Moffett entered the room.

"How dare you!" she attacked him. "You never challenge his sanity! What did you say?"

"Uh, what did *he* say I said?"

"That you called him crazy! Then he tore out the back door and down the hill."

"Well, shit. I didn't say that. I simply asked if he was sure the wizard he saw was a real person and not just in his mind."

Sylvia froze, her face horrified. "What kind of monster *are* you? You'd better wrap this up and leave. You're causing way too much destruction here."

Cannon went from embarrassed to angry. "*I'm* causing destruction? Ms. Moffett, destruction is happening here at Parkmoor. Plenty of it. Two murders. A third attempted. In *five* days. We have tip-toed around this man and his disorders all week. We have allowed him to stay in his home when he should be locked up under supervised medical care. We—"

Sylvia cut him off, "He's under medical care! Why do you think we have a full-time nurse here? If you take him away, you'll—"

"Yes, yes, if we remove him, we'll never get the truth, and if he's put back on drugs, we'll never get the truth. We're not getting the truth now! If it were up to me, you'd all be hauled downtown and thrown in the slammer. I'm starting to think this is a conspiracy by the three of you to get that man's money."

"The three of us?"

"You, O'Brien and Mr. Buckley."

Sylvia gaped at the agent, then sat down on the sofa. She spoke through fresh tears. "We love him. We loved Sophia. We'd never…." She leaned back and let her emotions flow down her cheeks.

Cannon took a seat beside her. "Ms. Moffett, I'm sorry I yelled at you. What I should have said was, we've been lenient. Exceedingly so. And for Running Bear to stay in this home, we need you all to continue cooperating with our investigation. The more we're here, the faster we can be out of here, forever, once we find out who's helping Mr. Armstrong to kill this family."

She wiped her face with a kitchen towel she'd been holding wadded up in her fist. "That was his name? Armstrong?"

"Yes. Sonny William Armstrong. Does that mean anything to you?"

"No. I just didn't know his name. And he's in custody still?"

"Yes. Which means someone else is helping him. Someone else stabbed Grace Meyer last night. Someone close to this family, we believe."

She stood up, her composure regained. He rose to meet her gaze.

"I wish I could deliver you the answer, agent." She turned and headed back to the kitchen. At the archway, she stopped. Without turning around, she said, "I apologize too. It's been a trying week."

Sylvia left the room.

Cannon inhaled deeply and blew it out, his cheeks puffed. *And now for His Majesty. Where the hell did you go? I have one more apology to conduct.*

Chapter 38

Running Bear was pacing back and forth by the pool. His best friend, Cantor, detectable by him alone, was swimming laps. His delusionary wife, Marjorie, was sprawled out on one of the double-sized chaise lounges, sucking slowly on a margarita. She wore a beautiful one-piece swimsuit in navy. She usually swam naked at night when it was late, and it was only her and her husband. But since company was present, she dressed appropriately.

"Honestly," she was saying, "I don't understand why you don't rule them all to go away. Enough of this nonsense. They answer to you. I say, enough is enough."

Cantor overheard her and stopped swimming long enough to laugh. "He's not in charge, princess. They're running the show."

"It's 'Your Majesty,' now. I'm queen, now that Queen Sophia has passed on."

"Passed on? That sounds magical. She was murdered. Stabbed three times with one of Bear's favorite swords. Passed on? That's rich."

Marjorie looked at her husband. "Are you going to let him talk to me that way? He should show some respect."

Running Bear knew Cantor for over twenty years, well before he was a prince or a king. He was granted a lot of liberties. And while he'd never admit it to the Queen, he needed some of Cantor's bluntness right now. His perspective often served him well at stressful times in his life.

"Marjorie, sweetheart, I think it would be impolite to embarrass Cantor in front of you by a public chastising. We're in the twenty-first century, after all. A modicum of respect for his station should be honored. Please go dress for lunch, and I'll be back up soon."

"Station?" she asked. "And what would that be? Court Jester?"

Marjorie gulped down the rest of her drink and stood. "Fine. I think I'll take a nap first." She turned and marched up the path.

The two men watched her go.

"I guess you put up with that mouth because of that body," said Cantor.

"You watch your tongue!" snapped Running Bear. "You're a step away from being asked to leave Parkmoor. Even before the Queen was killed!"

"Then why haven't you?" asked Cantor.

Running Bear studied him. He sat down on the edge of the pool and hung his legs in the water. It was cool and felt refreshing in the August heat. Stripping down to his underwear, he slid into the pool and swam a couple of laps to release some anger. He stopped beside his friend and offered a belated answer.

"Because I need you. You're not afraid of me. Tell me your honest opinion. Am I crazy?"

"Of course not. You're different. You know that."

"They think I'm crazy." He waved up the hill to the house.

"Fuck'em."

"Seriously. If cousin Grace dies, we're in trouble. We're all in trouble. They'll put me in an institution. We've been down that road. It didn't end well for either of us."

Cantor sobered up. "No. It didn't. I didn't get to see you for over a year."

"I'm scared," said Running Bear. He choked up, swallowing down a lump in his throat. "Grace was my last chance of staying protected from the monsters in the world who would challenge our life here."

"Then let's pray she makes it, Your Majesty."

"I have been, old friend, nonstop." Running Bear let loose some tears. "Cantor, I miss my mother. She wasn't here much, but I always felt safe, knowing she was out there, protecting what we have at Parkmoor. I miss her loving me."

"I know, buddy." Cantor put his arm around his friend. "She was the real deal."

The two men separated when they saw Agent Phil Cannon coming down the path.

Running Bear swam to the side of the pool and lifted himself out.

"Your Majesty," said Cannon, "you're naked."

Running Bear's tighty-whities were soaked and clinging to his manhood. "Forgive me." He walked over to a chest and retrieved a fresh towel, wrapping it around his waist. He took a second one and began to dry off, sitting down in a chair beneath an umbrella.

"Actually, forgive me, Your Majesty. I wanted to apologize for my outburst earlier. I didn't mean to call you crazy. I don't believe you are. Actually, I've been impressed with you this week. It's just that, well, your view of the world is more enhanced than the rest of us."

That put a smile on Running Bear's face. "That's kind of you, Agent Cannon. 'Enhanced.' That's a polite way of describing my exceptional situation. I've been told many, many times over the years I have a gift for seeing people that others cannot."

He ignored Cantor's snickering, becoming mesmerized by the water bouncing around the pool, sunlight reflecting back in his face along the ripples edges. "Water relaxes me, calms me... The answer to your ill-phrased question, agent, is I don't know. I don't know if you would have been able to see the wizard were our places reversed. But I believe you would have."

Running Bear raised his eyebrows in an expression of hopelessness.

The sound of a bell rang from the veranda.

"Lunch is served," said Running Bear. "Agent Cannon, please, be my guest for lunch?"

"I'd be honored, Your Majesty."

The pair moved up the hill, leaving Cantor in the pool, uninvited.

Running Bear ran upstairs to dress and returned for lunch with Marjorie before everyone took a seat. Her nap would have to wait. She didn't want to miss any conversations with their guests.

It was Cannon's turn to experience the culinary skills of Chef Pirelli. A spread was laid out on the patio table. Today's slight break in the heat allowed for dining al fresco once again. The ceiling fans kept the temperature comfortable.

A chafing dish held veal piccata atop farfalle pasta in a lemon butter sauce with roasted asparagus. It was served with a Caesar salad and a basket filled with crusty baguettes.

Cannon made sure everyone at the table took a bite before he dove in. Today's company included himself, the family's defense attorney, Edward Toussaint, and regular attorney, Adam Steiner. Nurse Linda O'Brien, Sylvia Moffet and Chad Buckley were all in attendance, and Chef Louie Pirelli himself elected to join them for lunch.

After a few silent minutes enjoying the meal, Cannon realized there was an absence at the table. "Earl Humboldt, he's not here?"

"He's at the hospital. He can't do anything but sit in the waiting room," said Chad. "I tried to tell him he should stay here today, but he insisted on being there. He didn't want Grace waking up and not having any family present. My understanding of these matters is that she'll likely be unconscious for the rest of the day." He raised his eyebrows at Nurse O'Brien to see if she concurred.

"Perhaps," she said. "It could be hours or days. Until we have an update on her progress, I wouldn't venture a guess."

"What are the odds she saw her attacker?" asked Sylvia.

She was speaking to Cannon, but Nurse O'Brien answered.

"High, I'd say. I heard her scream. If she had time to scream, she might have been awake enough to catch a glimpse."

"That's awful," said Sylvia. "I can't imagine what must have run through her mind in those seconds before succumbing to the attack."

Chewing could be heard through the silence as they all conjured their own responses in their heads.

"Agent Cannon," started O'Brien, "do you have anything new to report from this morning's gathering?'

"I can't really say at this time," he said, studying all their faces for possible reactions.

Sylvia Moffett jerked her head up quickly in his direction, then swiftly turned her attention back to her plate. She was poking at her veal more than eating it. Dicing it absently into smaller and smaller bites without ever taking any.

"We do," said a voice from the doorway to the living room. It was Agent Jones.

Whelan was close behind her. He noted Cannon's empty plate.

"Gutsy," he mumbled to his colleague.

Cannon played it off, despite turning a shade paler. "I like living on the edge. I was expecting you over an hour ago."

Jones moved to one end of the table, still standing. "Doctor Brachman's car was found this morning in the river, with a body inside. We received a call as we were pulling up. It was him. He's dead. The cause of death is still unknown at this time. It would appear his body's been underwater for about a week. Hopefully, an autopsy will tell us more, but in its condition, we might not learn much."

Shocked expressions filled the faces around the table.

Sylvia jumped up from the table. "Excuse me." She ran inside, one hand on her stomach, the other covering her mouth.

"Sorry to ruin everyone's lunch," said Whelan.

"I think we were expecting he was killed," said Nurse O'Brien. "He seemed like a decent man. It wasn't like him to disappear. I held out hope he was alive somehow and still innocent of all this, but… Well, God rest his soul."

"Amen," said Chef Pirelli.

"Amen," others echoed around the table.

"So, given the circumstances, we're treating his death as a homicide unless we find evidence that can rule it out," said Jones.

"Does that mean Frank is going to be my full-time doctor now?" asked Running Bear.

"Doctor DeLuca? Would you like him to be?" asked O'Brien.

"I think so. I liked him. And he was fine leaving me off those pills. Doctor Brachman was always trying to get me to take them. They make me fuzzy. I don't like them. I didn't like him."

"Bear!" said O'Brien. "We don't speak about the dead like that in this house. Show some respect, Your Majesty!"

"My apologies," said Running Bear. He turned to his side and snapped toward the air. "Yes, yes! I know!" He turned back to the table. "Those pills also make Marjorie and Cantor disappear. They don't like to be away too long. And I miss them. I think Doctor Frank, with all respect toward Doctor Brachman, is a better fit for our lifestyle here at Parkmoor."

He tilted his head and confronted his nurse. "Wouldn't you agree?"

Nurse Linda O'Brien usually put on a brave front when under duress. She thought about her young ward, wondering if he genuinely grasped the audacity of his words. Doctor Brachman was in their lives for years. Professionally, she understood Running Bear's apathy, but personally, it was too much. Her face grimaced, and her eyes welled up with tears she refused to let fall. She blinked at the ceiling until she could get them under control, and when she became aware of them all staring at her after a minute, she stood and excused herself from the table.

Jones signaled to her partner with a nod to pursue the nurse.

In the kitchen, O'Brien was dabbing at her eyes with a kitchen towel.

Whelan was fast on her heels. "Nurse O'Brien, forgive me, but I'm curious as to your professional opinion on all that?"

She wheeled on him sharply. "On what?"

"Running Bear staying off medications."

O'Brien took an immense breath and held it. She expelled it with a sigh. "We've discussed this. This week aside, he's managing fine with no meds currently. He's happy. Parkmoor functions beautifully. Where's the harm?"

"Well, I'd agree if it weren't for three dead and a fourth fighting for her life right now, all as a result of being affiliated with Running Bear."

Nurse O'Brien scrutinized the agent. "Agent Whelan, do *you* think he should be on meds? What does all this look like to an outsider? Truly? Do you believe any of those people would still be alive if he were stoned into oblivion? Locked up in an institution?"

"Truly?" he repeated.

"Yes."

Whelan thought about it. At the beginning of the week, his initial preconception could not comprehend how someone like Running Bear would ever be allowed to live without being dosed on heavy medication. But he'd spent a great deal of time with the young man this week. He'd witnessed his personality and seen his intelligence first hand. He was witty and sharp. Traits that would have been hidden if doped up like some zombie. Whelan's medical training in college and near doctorate in pharmacology reflected a scientific mind and thought process. Those thoughts contradicted how he felt now.

He worked out his final thoughts aloud. "No. I believe the man who killed Sophia Perkins is behind bars, though we can't prove it yet, and he clearly has an accomplice continuing to attempt murder. I don't 'truly' believe Running Bear killed his mother, nor anyone else. I think these crimes are motivated by money, specifically by someone attempting to get after Sophia's. So while I keep an open mind toward every possibility until there's a finite answer, no, I don't believe Running Bear being doped up would have prevented any of these murders this week. It would in no way affect his inheritance or the chain of conservatorship over it."

Nurse O'Brien sighed. "Exactly."

Whelan leaned low, placing his elbows on the kitchen island. "Linda?"

"Yes?"

"Who do *you* think attacked Grace Meyer last night?"

"I don't know. But I honestly don't think they're in this house. I'd dig deeper into Sue's guests at The Leonardo."

Whelan squinted his eyes. *Well, of course, that would be what you'd have to say now, isn't it? The problem is, you're high on my list of suspects. You knew precisely where Running Bear's pills were that killed Sue Fielding and how to dose them. You also sat beside her at Sophia's memorial dinner. And you were conveniently right next door to Grace last night. No one else heard a scream. Were you already up, stealing a dagger from the sword case? How do I find evidence of this wizard?*

Whelan sprung upright and marched back to the living room. "I want a second sweep of all the closets in this house, the hampers and the laundry room."

Chapter 39

Agent Jones babysat everyone in the living room while Agents Whelan and Cannon, along with two others from the field office, searched the house. The Evidence Response Team already combed for signs of blood. Any visible trail of blood from Grace's room ended before the bottom step on the stairway. The trash was ransacked.

Whelan focused on the laundry room. No blood droplets. A load of whites was sitting in the dryer. Whelan removed a terry cloth bathrobe with a large hood. It smelled of heavy bleach.

"Bring Ms. Moffett!" he ordered.

Sylvia was before him in no time.

"Whose robe?" he asked her.

"Actually, that's Mr. Humboldt's."

Whelan was taken aback. "Earls? Why does it wreak of bleach?"

"I always use a lot of bleach for whites."

She seemed sincere enough.

Whelan returned to the living room. "Running Bear, Your Majesty, is this the wizard's robe you saw last night?"

"No."

"How can you be sure?" He put the robe on and pulled the hood over his head.

"I think it would have stood out, being white. Before I was blinded, I saw the cloak well enough. It was dark. Black, I think. Not white."

Whelan sighed. He took off the robe and handed it to Sylvia.

Another hour of searching returned four more possibilities from everyone's closets. Whelan donned each one.

A raincoat, "No."

Two winter coats, "No. No."

And finally, an honest-to-goodness wizard's robe, complete with sequins down the back and along the bottom in a star pattern.

"Hey! You found my costume! I haven't seen that in years," said Running Bear.

"I remember that," said Nurse O'Brien. "You were Merlin several Halloweens back. That was a fun party. Your mother dressed up as Elvira."

The staff's faces all reflected bittersweet memories.

"Was that here, at Parkmoor?" asked Jones. "I'm surprised she hosted guests here at the house. Wasn't she afraid of people finding out about Running Bear?"

"We enjoyed our share of parties," explained O'Brien. "The guest list was always for those in the know, attorneys, assistants, some of her closest friends."

"Was Mark Fleming or Karen Hertzberg at that party?" asked Whelan.

"I believe they both were, yes."

"And Sarah Williams?"

"She wasn't her assistant then. Her assistants tended to last about a year usually. Ms. Williams must be exceptional at her job. She's been on longer than any of them," said O'Brien.

"You think that's the robe from last night?" asked Chef Pirelli.

"We couldn't find any traces of blood on it," said Cannon.

Running Bear stood, his face turning red. "That's not it! Why doesn't anyone listen to me? The wizard wore his robe when he ran down the stairs! He took it with him. It's not in this house! And that's mine!"

He grabbed the robe out of Whelan's hands and sat back down, crossing his arms around it protectively.

Sylvia patted his arm. "They are listening to you, Your Majesty. They're doing their jobs, trying to find any clues."

"In my closet?"

"In case you were lying to them," she explained.

"So we're back to this?" Running bear shouted at the agents. "You think *I* killed Gracie? And Grandma Sue, and my *mother*? You're the ones who are nuts! I suppose you think I snuck out of the house a week ago and drowned Doctor Brachman too! Trust me, if I wanted that dolt dead, I would have beheaded him with a broadsword."

"Bear!" scolded Nurse O'Brien. "That's not a nice thing to say."

"Nothing about any of this is nice!" Tears began streaming down his face.

He yelled at Whelan. "You all need to leave! I command it! No more of this nonsense. Go find the Queen's murderer and leave us in peace to grieve our losses."

Running Bear began sobbing uncontrollably and buried his face in the robe he clutched.

Sylvia wrapped her arms around him and held him tight to her, shushing him softly.

Jones retreated to the kitchen, motioning her agents to follow her and give the man a break.

"We're wasting time," she said. "None of those people in that room have left this property since Grace was stabbed. There's no sign of any bloodied robe in this house. Someone else came in here, tried to kill her, and left. We have a second assassin out there somewhere."

"You're buying his story now?" asked Whelan.

"I guess I am, yes."

"Well, we've got plenty of bloody clothes. O'Brien's evening gown was covered in it, as was Ms. Moffett's. Chad's pajamas have some. Earl's is covered in it."

"And the lab's examining all of their nightclothes, trying to determine if any of Grace's blood is consistent with a spatter pattern from having stabbed her."

"They are all each other's alibis," said Cannon. "If it's one of them, the others may be covering."

"I don't get that feeling," said Jones to Whelan, her partner, for this one last case.

Whelan nodded at her. "I agree with you. I don't think Earl has it in him to stab his daughter. Even if he did, why kill the one person who would let him live here and enjoy this lifestyle? He has no other claim on the fortune. I think Mr. Buckley loved Sophia like a daughter. And I've been inclined to believe Running Bear from the start, and especially since we caught Sonny Bill Armstrong."

"We need to get over to The Leonardo," said Jones. "Let's see if Merrill's got a wizard's robe in his closet."

"This is an outrage!" yelled Merrill.

Agents Whelan and Jones were ransacking his luggage. Two other agents were going through the dumpsters behind the hotel. Cannon remained at Parkmoor to keep an eye on things.

When Jones was halfway through Peggy's second suitcase, she held up a blouse. "This is cute, Peggy. Where did you get it?" She attempted to make the battered woman feel positive about herself. She was not actually interested in her wardrobe.

"Thank you. I'm not sure, Target, I think. I've owned it a few years."

A quick search of the hotel suite revealed nothing suspicious.

"You know," said Merrill, "just because you think I'm some backwater hick doesn't mean I'm stupid. If I snuck over there in the middle of the night to stab Gracie, do you think I'd come back in here with bloody clothes?"

"We're doing our jobs, Merrill," said Whelan. "And the two of you can vouch for each other all night?"

"We were both here all night," said Merrill.

"He snores like a banshee," said Peggy.

Merrill cackled at her comment.

"I have to take sleeping pills to get through a night of it," she continued, "so I was out cold."

"She loves her sleeping pills," Merrill snorted. "I drank a few bourbons from the mini-bar, then went to sleep about a half-hour after Peggy."

"Then how can you prove you were really here the whole time? If your wife was out cold, she can't really alibi you."

Merrill was speechless for once. "Well, I guess I can't. You'll have to take my word for it."

"Because that means so much?" Whelan snarked.

"How is Grace doing?" asked Peggy.

"Well, I'm glad someone in this room has a heart," said Jones. "She's in critical condition, but of course, we're hoping for a full recovery."

"If she wakes up, she might be able to identify who tried to kill her," said Peggy.

"That's what we hope for."

"I'll put her in my prayers."

Peggy spoke to her husband with disdain. "Merrill, you could at least pretend to care about your niece and show some respect in front of these kind agents."

"They're doing their job. I don't need to pretend nothin'. Besides, she's my niece by way of marriage. A crappy marriage, long over. We're not really kin."

"You and I are related by marriage. What if that was me layed up in a hospital bed? Would you send a prayer up for me or hope I die so you can cash in that big insurance policy?" Peggy was heated.

She looked at Jones. "It's funny to him because he took out a $25,000 term policy on me when we got married and said if I wanted one on him, I'd better work some extra shifts to pay for it."

Peggy shouted at Merrill, "And what did I do, *darlin'*?"

Merrill started laughing, "You picked up two weekends a month at Tom Tom Thai!" He continued gut-busting himself into a frenzy.

"Hang in there," said Jones to Peggy, patting her shoulder.

Peggy grunted and saw them to the door.

Next up were Mark Fleming and Karen Hertzberg. Whelan took Mark's room while Jones searched Karen's. No bloody clothes or wizard's robe were discovered in either. Both of the board members spent the entire time on their cell phones, fast-whispering to others on the board with suggestions on how to put out the fires stirred by today's news.

Before the agents moved on, Mark grabbed Whelan's arm and whispered over his cell phone, "We're flying home tonight. Either arrest us now, or you can deal with our attorneys. We've been patient out of our respect to Sophia, but we're needed back in L.A."

"I understand," said Whelan.

"Agent, we do wish you all the best in your hunt. We want justice for Sophia as much as you do. If there are any new developments we can help you with, please call."

Whelan left the room and met up in the hall with Jones. They headed to Sarah William's room. Sophia Perkin's executive assistant was beside herself.

"It's a total shit storm," she said, watching the television. She kept flipping back and forth through cable news networks. They were all covering the death of Sophia Perkins every few minutes.

"My phone won't stop ringing. I've fielded calls from journalists, paparazzi scumbags, and at least three board members who seem to think I work for them now! My contract was with Sophia, not the company. Two job offers already came in, and four more headhunters called, hoping I'd sign with them so they can make an easy commission off me. Thank God Sue put our rooms all under her name, or they'd be knocking on my door. Didn't you find the murderer already? Mr. Armstrong? Why are we still being held prisoners here? I desperately need to get back to L.A. This isn't working here any longer. I need computer access twenty-four-seven! You know, I knew this would be a tough day, but God help me!"

She stopped long enough to take the last sip from her coffee cup. When she tried to pour more, the pot was empty. A second empty pot sat beside it. She dialed room service and ordered a third.

Whelan filled her in on the happenings at Parkmoor overnight.

"Grace Meyer, that kind woman from Oklahoma?" Sarah seemed genuinely shocked. She was barely sitting on the edge of a chair in her suite. "How many is that now? Three? Killed in that house in the past week? If you have Mr. Armstrong in custody, then someone else tried to kill that woman last night. That poor man, Running Bear. I can't imagine what I'd be going through if someone killed three people I loved in my family. I know he's 'peculiar.' Is he processing all this? I mean, I don't even know why I care. I guess these years of seeing Sophia speak fondly of him have me concerned for him somehow. Vicariously empathizing on behalf of a now-dead former employer. Boy, is my life fucked up or what?"

Whelan and Jones were expecting her to start another tirade, but she was quiet, hoping one of them would give her an answer to what they supposed was a hypothetical question.

"I've seen worse," said Whelan.

"I bet you have. In another world, I'd love to hear about it over drinks, but I'm living in this hell right now. Go ahead, search. Do what you need to do." She turned back to the television and started flipping the channels again.

The fourth room inspection of the day again revealed nothing.

Whelan and Jones met up with the other two agents in the lobby. The hotel dumpsters contained no wizard's robe, so Jones ordered them back to Parkmoor.

Jones started rubbing her shoulder where she'd been struck by Sonny Bill Armstrong's bullet the day before.

"Still sore?" asked Whelan.

"You wouldn't believe how much. I think it would hurt less if the bullet went through me."

"Doubt it. I've been shot twice, and it was hell both times."

"Really?" asked Jones. "I didn't know that. I'd love to hear about it over drinks, but I'm living in this hell right now." She was mocking Sarah Williams' words.

Whelan smiled. "It's a date. Now, how do we wrap this up? Who do we shake to get some answers?"

"The only one we can, Sonny Bill Armstrong."

"He's lawyered up."

"So, his lawyer can be there. I want to see how the news of Grace's stabbing affects him. And the fact that she's bound to wake any moment and deliver us a name."

"I thought the doctors said it could be hours or even tomorrow."

"They did. But Sonny doesn't know that."

Chapter 40

"The doctors think Grace will wake up today," Jones lied to Sonny Armstrong. "And when she does, we'll know who tried to kill her."

Whelan stood in the corner of the interrogation room, watching his partner lay the invitation.

"So," she continued, "either we get your testimony now, and you deliver the name of your accomplice in all this, or we'll have *your* name from *them* by the end of the day. I'm giving you the first shot here. And the first one to cooperate with us will be encouraged leniency at sentencing by the Bureau."

Sonny whipped his head around to his attorney.

Ron Davis, Attorney at Law, rolled his eyes. "Agents, we need guarantees, in *writing*. I've told you this. My client's told you this. If the Bureau wants to *encourage*, it should be now, to the D.A., for complete immunity of my client before he agrees to cooperate with you."

"And ten million dollars," said Sonny.

His attorney jerked his head toward him.

"You're not getting any money from us," said Jones. "I highly doubt the Perkin's estate will cough up a dime after killing off Sophia and Sue."

"Didn't do that," said Sonny.

"Oh, and Doctor Brachman," added Whelan.

"Who?" asked Ron Davis. He looked at his client again, his eyebrows raised.

Sonny Armstrong squinted at Whelan. "I don't know a Doctor Brachman."

Whelan obliged the man with a photo from his phone he'd taken down by the river.

Both Sonny and his attorney took a quick glimpse then averted their eyes. Sonny waved it away like he was dismissing a pawn to its death.

Whelan thought of Eddie Morrison, the man who killed his last partner and who he spent nearly three years of his life working to capture.

Sadly, Eddie's recent escape still plagued his nightmares. "Sonny, the last man I put away for three murders, received three life sentences." He omitted the rest of Eddie's charges or the fact he was now on the loose.

"Are you threatening my client, Agent Whelan?" asked Ron Davis.

"Golly, not at all. I simply felt obligated to relay the facts of his predicament and how cooperating right now could really be a benefit." Whelan locked his eyes on Sonny's. "Three. Life. Sentences."

Sonny didn't flinch. Someone did their research when recommending Ron Davis, the number one defense attorney in the Kansas City area for the past four years.

After a staring contest between the two men went on for over two minutes, Jones broke the silence with a buzz on her phone. "She's awake!"

"Excellent!" said Whelan. "Sonny, you've got until we can get to the hospital to take my offer for leniency. I'd say, about eighteen minutes."

Sonny frantically addressed his attorney, "Ron?"

His head was oscillating calmly. He wasn't buying her bull.

Jones ignored Ron's expression. She turned to her partner. "I wasn't bluffing, Whelan. She's really awake! Let's go."

She stormed out of the room.

"I guess I was wrong," said Whelan to Sonny. "You don't even get one minute."

Whelan followed his partner's cue and raced out the open door, commenting to the defense attorney on the way. "Better ready your client for the realities of the justice system."

In their absence, Sonny again opened his eyes wide to Ron Davis.

It was Ron's turn to pucker his lips inquisitively to an empty doorway.

In the hospital, Jones was nurse-blocked by a large woman with a thick Croatian accent. "You no come in now, she resting."

"I need one minute, then she can rest the remainder of the afternoon," explained Jones.

"Only doctors!"

"Listen here," Jones glanced at the nurse's name tag, "Petra, I can have you removed, or you can step aside for sixty seconds. I won't upset her."

"She sleeping! Go 'way. Come tomorrow."

An ICU doctor was coming out from behind Grace Meyer's curtain. "She actually *is* sleeping right now. I can't authorize waking her."

"More lives are at stake," hissed Jones. "I just need a name!"

Whelan slipped around the nurse's station from the other side of the corridor. While Jones was arguing her position with the medical staff, he crept behind the curtain and approached Grace Meyer. Her intubation tube was removed. She was hooked up to multiple IV bags, and at least eight cords were coming from different parts of her body and attached to machines monitoring every possible vital they could record.

He put his hand on her arm, barely touching it. "Grace," he whispered.

She gave no response, so he shook it gently. "Grace. Grace, I need you a minute."

Her head tossed back and forth lightly. The expression on her face was painful, grimaced. It appeared she was having a nightmare.

Whelan focused on keeping his voice calm and soothing. "Grace, it's Tom Whelan. I need you to wake up for a few seconds."

Her head froze in place, and her eyes popped wide open, startling the agent. He took a quick inhale before finding his voice again. "Grace!" he whispered. "Grace, it's Tom. I need you to tell me who stabbed you. Who did this to you?"

Grace didn't speak at first, then the hoarsest sound came from her lips.

Whelan couldn't hear, so he put his ear close. "Repeat that Grace, I couldn't make out what you said."

The woman mustered the strength to raise her neck half an inch, and a slightly louder mumble reached Whelan's ear. "Didn't see."

She relaxed against her pillow as tears gathered in her eyes. They fell unwiped onto her cheeks.

Whelan grew to like Grace Meyer this week, and her present circumstances clearly excused her as a suspect. He touched her arm again. "It's okay, Grace. Get some rest. I'll check on you tomorrow. Running Bear's safe. Your dad's safe. Everyone else is fine. Sleep Gracie. I'm sorry I woke you."

He grabbed a tissue from a nearby box and dabbed softly on her cheeks until they were dry.

Grace closed her eyes. Whelan threw open the curtain and came face to face with Earl Humboldt. He was holding a cup of coffee. Grace was sleeping peacefully.

"Agent Whelan, I take it someone informed you she woke up earlier?"

"Yes."

Earl was perturbed. "I get you need to do your job, but can't you give her even one day to recover?"

"We're concerned someone else might be in danger."

"Who would that be? At this point? Running Bear?"

"Possibly. Depending on who's involved."

Earl nodded. "If you'd been here two hours ago, I'd be ripping you a new one for disturbing her. But right now, I'm elated she's going to be all right."

"So am I, Mr. Humboldt. Sincerely."

"Did you get your answer?" asked Earl.

"No. She didn't see who it was."

"Damn."

The two men watched her breathe for a minute.

"Are you planning to return to Parkmoor today?" asked Whelan.

"Tonight. The doctor upped her medications a bit, so she'll sleep through the rest of the day and night. And I'll be no use to her exhausted.

At least I was here for her when she woke the first time. She was scared. I saw it in her eyes. She didn't understand what had happened. That awful tube was in her throat. Surprised all the nurses!" Earl chuckled. "She's got a lot to live for now."

"She didn't before?" asked Whelan.

"Well, of course, but now, her life is about to change forever."

"Yes. Both of your lives. We want to make sure she'll be around for a long time. We'll keep a guard stationed outside her doorway."

"You really think the killer would come here and try to murder her again?" Earl's face took on fresh worry for his daughter.

"Possibly."

"Then I appreciate you having someone here. Thank you."

"Of course. Have a good evening Earl."

Whelan left the room and motioned to Jones, who was still arguing with Nurse Petra in the hallway. The doctor was nowhere in sight.

Jones saw her partner leave and stopped mid-sentence. She turned and left the ICU area, meeting up with him in the corridor outside ICU. "Well?"

"She didn't see who it was. I told her to rest. We'd check on her tomorrow. Maybe she'll remember something when she gets her energy back. She was having a restless sleep, perhaps reliving it in a nightmare."

"If she's reliving being stabbed, perhaps she'll recall the face of her attacker as well."

Whelan nodded.

"I saw Earl slip in. How's he holding up? Any revelations?" asked Jones.

"No. Just a father concerned for his daughter. I think it's safe to cross him off our suspect list. If Grace died, he'd have no ultra-posh lifestyle in front of him. And I believe he loves her deeply."

"Yes. That's admirable."

Jones thought about her own father. She swayed her head, curled locks bouncing on her shoulders, putting her past out of her mind the best she could. It left her agitated. Her head started shaking again, thinking of the man in holding.

She turned and started marching down the corridor. “I guess that Sonny-of-a-bitch Armstrong gets one more night of rest.”

Whelan picked up his pace. “Miranda, what if Grace never remembers who stabbed her? What if she really didn’t see who it was?”

Jones stopped abruptly. “That’s not an option right now.”

She wheeled on the balls of her feet and continued tromping toward the exit. “No way I’m letting Sonny Bill Armstrong take the fall alone. Someone else is going down.”

Chapter 41

Agent Phil Cannon hung up his cell phone. Running Bear and the staff of Parkmoor were fixated on him. “Good news. Grace Meyer woke up once today and is doing well. They’ve already taken her intubation tube out, and she’s breathing fine on her own. She’ll require extensive rest over the coming days, but the doctor says she’s strong and expects a full recovery.”

“Oh, thank God!” said Nurse O’Brien. “Praise Jesus. I’m going to put on a pot of tea to celebrate.” She stood and left the living room.

“She celebrates with tea?” asked Cannon.

“Yes,” said Sylvia. “She takes it with Irish Whiskey.”

She grinned and looked at her watch. “I think we could all use a cup after the past twelve hours. It’s close enough to 5:00. Might as well treat ourselves to happy hour.”

Cannon turned to Running Bear. “Your Majesty, Grace didn’t see who stabbed her. The identity of your wizard remains a mystery.”

“Perhaps she’ll recall when she’s more rested.”

“Perhaps. Well, I’m going to get out of your hair for the rest of the evening,” said Cannon. “I’ll be by in the morning after breakfast to give you an update. As always, if anyone thinks of anything new, please call us immediately.”

“Thank you, Agent Cannon,” said Chad Buckley. He shook the younger man’s hand and left the room.

Sylvia escorted him to the front door. She frowned when she opened it and was reminded there were still agents stationed at the front and back of the home to keep an eye on their coming and going.

“You know,” she said, “I know it’s only been three days we’ve been blessed with these—guards—but it feels like an eternity already. “I’d never do well in prison.”

Cannon tilted his head. “Do you expect to be *going* to prison, Ms. Moffett?”

"Of course not! I was just thinking out loud. It feels like they're monitoring us, like Parkmoor has become *our* prison."

"You're free to leave the house whenever you need to. They're here to *protect* you, not hold you captive." Cannon was genuine with his comment.

"And keep an eye on us."

"You understand Running Bear is on a sort of 'house-arrest'? Under normal circumstances, he would have been brought in and held as our prime suspect in the death of his mother. I think these guards are a small price to pay for his being able to stay here while we continue our investigation and search for Mr. Armstrong's accomplice."

"Who you wouldn't even have if you *had* arrested Bear initially!" she hissed.

She was jittery, shifting her eyes from Cannon to the agent on the porch.

Cannon again tried to make the young woman feel better about the situation. "Until we can confirm who else is involved in these killings, these 'guards' should make you feel safer. Shouldn't they?"

"If you say so. Good night Agent."

"Good night Ms. Moffett." Cannon headed to his car, nodding at the other agent on the way.

By the time he made it to the field office, Agents Whelan and Jones were already there.

"Terrific news about Grace Meyer," Cannon said, walking into Jones' office.

"Yes," said Jones. "With any luck, she saw who stabbed her and will be able to recover her memory after more rest. How did it go at Parkmoor today?"

"Fine. Nothing new. They are all relieved to hear about Grace, of course. Running Bear was content. He wanted to see her but understood she would need a quiet evening to begin recovery. His understanding of the way the world works sometimes is so…normal. You forget he's living in a whole other world in that head of his."

Whelan agreed. "I thought the same thing two days ago. He's surprisingly…composed."

"Right?" said Cannon. "Say, Sylvia Moffett was acting odd as I was leaving. Said she felt like a prisoner with our watch on the house. I tried to make her feel better, but I think I failed."

"It's strenuous to live through all this," said Jones. "We've been an additional interruption to their quiet little world. On top of two murders in the family. The distance a little time will provide down the road should make them grateful for our handling of all this."

She sighed and darted her eyes across the floor, landing at Whelan's shoes. She moved her questioning gaze up to his face.

"You're doing great, boss," he said. "I wouldn't handle it any other way. And SAC Kendrick has full confidence in you."

"Thank you."

Her neck spiraled her head in circles as she tried to release tension. "You boys care to join me for a drink? I'm taking a couple hours of downtime and heading to Josephine's. There's not much else we can do this evening. We all need some rest so we can process with fresh thoughts in the morning."

"Sounds good to me," said Whelan. "I haven't eaten all day, and Fridays are prime rib night. Phil, you in?"

"I could eat," he said.

The threesome made their way to the restaurant and secured a booth in the back providing some amount of privacy. Two bottles of wine and three full bellies later, the conversation flowed.

Whelan felt brave enough to ask Jones a question he'd been holding for a while. "So, is Derrick moving to New York? What does that mean for the two of you?"

Miranda Jones was typically private, but these two men proved to be the truest of confidants and friends this summer. "I really don't know."

She flagged the waitress over and ordered a Maker's Mark on the rocks. "You boys want anything?"

They declined.

"I suppose we're in a 'wait-and-see' mode. I'm thrilled for Derrick. He works his ass off. I wouldn't want a little thing like our getting married to hold him back. If our roles were reversed, I wouldn't want him holding me back."

"I don't understand why he can't film his new show here in K.C.," said Cannon. "How much could really be involved in making fitness videos?"

"You'd be surprised. It's much cheaper to have him there than fly and house seven or eight of them here. There are lighting people, film people, sound people, coordinators, other trainers, and they're trying to line up a list of celebrities for a spin-off. And of course, they're either already in New York or fly there all the time. It's all just easier. They're really doing high-quality productions. It's not like a Jane Fonda workout tape from the 80s anymore."

"Who?" joked Whelan.

"What's a 'tape'?" asked Cannon.

"Ha. Ha," she snarled at Whelan. "You're five years behind me. Quit making me feel old. We're in the same generation."

"Well, I always feel ten years older than my age anyway. I'm just catching *you* up to me."

They both adopted frowns then turned their heads to Cannon in unison.

"How do we catch *him* up?" asked Whelan. "I've got eight years with the Bureau. Jones' got nine. The FBI puts some lines on your face."

"Where are your lines, rookie?" teased Jones.

Cannon grinned. "Nope, I'm planning to stay young forever. My new partner here can take all the stress and fractures. I'll stick with facial scrubs, and when the time comes, there's Botox."

"How metrosexual of you," said Jones.

Whelan feigned being hurt. "Your *partner* can take all the stress? Gee, thanks for watching my back! Is this a done deal, or can I still switch? Agent Lemar seemed pretty street-smart yesterday. I want to team with her." He winked at Jones.

"You remember who has your back when the chips are really flying," said Cannon.

They all laughed.

Jones ordered another Maker's Mark.

Whelan frowned for the first time all evening. "Should we be concerned by the amount of alcohol you've been drinking lately?"

Miranda gripped the table's edge before popping her eyebrows and pulling in a deep breath. "I'm fine," she exhaled. "Truly. Why do you think I've been working on all these yoga techniques? I'm trying to supplement alcohol with meditation, but deep breathing doesn't kick in as fast as two fingers' worth of whisky. Really, I'm good."

She patted Whelan's arm and sat up straighter in the booth. "So, what's our next step toward finding our accomplice in these Parkmoor murders? What does your gut tell you at this point?"

"Mine's confused," said Whelan. "I would normally have a feeling about someone by now, but I'm not feeling any of them. I think we're whittling down the suspects, though."

"My gut says Sylvia," said Cannon. "She's acting a little strange."

"You're upset because you couldn't cajole her the other day," said Jones.

"She's *cajoled* with Running Bear," said Cannon.

"Maybe I've seen too many M. Night Shyamalan movies, but I keep thinking it's going to wind up being Marjorie," said Whelan.

They all pondered Running Bear's imaginary friends as suspects.

Jones broke their thoughts. "Oh! Cusack called me today. He believes Doctor Brachman's death was caused by the drowning. There was an impact at the lower back of the skull, but this likely just knocked him unconscious. It definitely didn't kill him. At least he was out cold when his lungs filled with the Missouri River."

"Let me add that to my timeline on Sonny Bill Armstrong," said Whelan, typing on his phone. He liked to keep his cases updated in the cloud as new information came in.

"Repeat what you've got there, chronologically, for Armstrong," said Cannon.

"Sure. Sometime in 1993, Sonny and Sophia hooked up, and Running Bear was born on November Fifteenth. Sonny's not in her life for twenty-five years until February of 2019, when he shows up in L.A. with a sample of his DNA and tells Sophia her son is his. Sophia doesn't bother checking on that for a few months. Then Sonny moves from Tulsa to Kansas City six months ago and gets a job at a local firehouse. Presumably, he knows his son is living here. He probably approached Sophia multiple times, left her messages or somehow contacted her, maybe threatened her. She must have realized his being here physically meant he was serious. So she gets the DNA test and knows the truth. Sonny says he wanted to be in his son's life. Now, whether or not that's because he wanted to be a father, or he wanted access to all that money, who can say for sure?"

"I can," said Jones.

"Maybe he wanted both. Then at some point, Sophia grows concerned he'll wreck her life by spilling it to the press. She offers to buy him off. Ten million dollars."

Each of them considered what ten million dollars would mean to them.

Whelan continued, "So they meet up at least twice, perhaps more over the past four weeks. A spark is rekindled between them, and they start a brief affair. But either Sophia wasn't feeling it, or Sonny was playing her all along, but last Saturday, he sees her a final time, before killing her, unknowingly in front of his own son. So much for starting up a fatherly relationship now."

"At least with Running Bear," said Jones. "I'm guessing Sophia told Sonny that night she was pregnant and that it wasn't his this time."

"Another child and baby-daddy would only complicate matters," said Whelan. "With the family, with the inheritance, with Running Bear."

"Then why not take the ten million?" asked Cannon. "If all he really wanted was money, why not take it? I think he must have really wanted to get to know his son."

"Or he wanted a lot more," said Jones. "Why settle for ten million when there will be over eight billion up for grabs? A court would seriously consider granting conservatorship to a parent, despite what the will says. It's a gamble and a fight, but it's possible."

"Well, not now. Even if we can never pin the murders on him, shooting a federal officer will put him away for a while. He doesn't stand a chance at getting involved in the estate now," said Whelan.

"Which is why he wants ten million *now* to squeal on his accomplice," said Cannon. I'm guessing he's regretting not taking that payday and walking away when he had the chance. This has become messy for him."

"It's messy for Running Bear and Grace Meyer, too," Whelan noted. "And the rest of those folks at Parkmoor."

"Who is *not* messy for, right now?" asked Jones.

Whelan scratched at his scalp, digging out an answer. "Merrill. He's sitting back watching the show, waiting for his paycheck. Which Attorney Steiner refused to write today given Grace's attempted murder overnight."

"Then I'd say it just got messier for Merrill too."

"Did we ever figure out if Sonny Bill Armstrong went to school in Vinita, Oklahoma with Sophia?" asked Cannon. "Junior High? Maybe Senior?"

"Not yet," said Jones. "The schools are supposed to get back to us, but no word yet. I know it seems like days already, but we only notified them yesterday. We've known about Sonny for less than thirty hours."

"I think I'd like to get down there and put some pressure on them," said Cannon. "And it's time for a visit to Tulsa. We need to talk with the firefighters in his last station. See who knew him well and learn what we can about his life there. We're not getting anything out of the crew at Parkmoor. Whoever's helping Sonny probably knew him in Oklahoma. What did the background checks on the staff come up with? Any of them ever spend time in Northeast Oklahoma?"

"Not that I saw," said Jones. "But you're right. The two of you get to Tulsa, then up to Vinita. See what you can dig up on Sonny Bill Armstrong.

It's possible someone in that area tipped him off that he fathered a child with Sophia Perkins. We need to know who."

Chapter 42

Unable to gather information online regarding which fire station Sonny Bill Armstrong worked out of, Special Agents Whelan and Cannon met with the director of the Tulsa Fire Department at its Headquarters. He directed them to Station 37, near Bixby, Oklahoma, on the south end of town.

“Didn’t know him personally,” said the Station Chief. “I came on three months ago. But you’re welcome to speak with the crew.”

It was a small firehouse with one engine, no ladder truck, and one EMS truck. There were three teams of six working 24/48 shifts. Shift changes were at 10:00 a.m. It was 11:15 now.

Two men remembered Sonny Bill Armstrong.

“He was here for about three years,” they said. “Didn’t share many shifts, but he had a girlfriend, Diedre Owen. She’s here at the 37, well, on another shift.”

“What do you recall about him yourselves?” asked Whelan.

They ricocheted their answers off one another.

“He was okay.”

“Quiet. Did his job.”

“Not much sense of humor, but polite enough.”

“He blended in.”

“Came from… Grove?”

“That sounds right. Might have been with Claremore before that? He was never in one place long.”

“Moved around a lot. Unusual for a firefighter. You need more, go talk to Diedre.”

“Yeah, talk to Diedre. She’ll know him better than anyone.”

Whelan obtained a list of addresses from the Station Chief and set out to find Deidre Owen. Her roommate directed them to a lounge where she bartended to pick up some extra cash during her off shifts.

They navigated to a seedier part of town, and when they entered the parking lot, Cannon's face lit up. "This is a strip club! Look at all the cars! And before noon on a Saturday. So much for 'family' day."

"Oh, now, I'm sure it's just because they have cheap lunch specials," said Whelan.

After his eyes adjusted to the low light inside, Cannon's face showed genuine shock by the two women currently on center stage. They weighed around 170 pounds and churned out six kids. Each.

Whelan patted his shoulder. "Better luck next time."

"The only strip club I was ever in was in Vegas, for a friend's bachelor party. This place is a lot less…." He fought for the right word.

"Less?" suggested Whelan.

"A lot less."

The majority of men in the joint were hovering below the performers, so plenty of seats remained open at the bar.

Whelan took a seat.

"What'll you have," asked the woman serving. She was much more fit than the strippers and wore a tight blue t-shirt and jeans. She was in her early thirties and was surprisingly attractive and wholesome, given the environment, but Whelan knew not to judge books by their covers.

"Have any food?"

"Nope. You want Charlie's. Up the road. We just have drinks."

Scrutinizing the two agents in their suits, she summed up they weren't here for the showgirls. "Two-drink minimum," she said.

Whelan and Cannon pulled out their ID in unison and flashed their badges.

"You're Deidre Owen?" asked Whelan.

"Maybe. What did she do?"

"She might have dated Sonny Bill Armstrong a few months back?"

"Ha!" she spit. "Sonny was a regular roll in the hay. Dating implies he was generous enough to buy me dinner once in a while. I'm pretty sure I paid for more booze and weed than he ever did. All he ever bought were cheap burritos from Tijuana Timmy's across the street. $6.95 gets you two and a bag of chips."

"Tijuana Timmy's?"

"Run by a little Mexican guy named Timas. He's actually a pretty nice guy. Comes in here once in a while. Tips well. His food tastes amazing going down, but coming back up? Uh-uh. And it always comes back up."

"Thanks. We'll find another place for lunch. Deidre, Sonny's in trouble. What can you tell me about him?"

"What did he do?"

"Suffice it to say he'll be going away for a while," said Cannon. "Ten to twenty. If he's lucky. Maybe for life."

"No shit?" Deidre whistled. "He ran hot, that one. Great in the sack, but his temper got him in trouble a lot."

"Is that why he moved around so much?"

"Maybe. They don't like firing firefighters, and to my knowledge, he never broke any laws. They 'encouraged' him to find another station where he might fit in better. One day, he up and disappears. No word to any of us. And the chief won't say where he went to. I asked around, and I don't think he's in Tulsa anymore."

"Kansas City," offered Whelan. "You know why he'd go to Kansas City from here, Deidre? Does he know anyone up there?"

"Not that I know of, no. Kansas City, huh? Well, good for him. Or, apparently not. Ten to twenty, maybe life? Did he kill someone? I warned him that temper of his would come back to bite him in the ass."

"What did he do here, in Tulsa. What kinds of things did you see him lose his temper for?"

"Lots of things, but it was kind of hidden if you weren't watching him close. At work, he played it cool, and I used to think he was clever at hiding it. But when we were off duty, he'd get ugly sometimes. Yell, curse. I saw him beat a dog with a stick once. 'Cause it was barking. I mean, dogs bark. You don't have to go wailing on the poor thing. Another time, he smashed someone's headlights out on their car. He wouldn't tell me whose it was. Said they had it coming. Once he got it out of his system, he'd be fine the rest of the night. Actually, better than fine. On nights he was mad, the sex was amazing. But, I guess it's that way with all guys."

"It is?" asked Cannon, genuinely intrigued.

"Sure, baby. You look like you could use a lesson or two. What makes *you* angry?"

She asked Whelan, "You taking a rookie under your wings? Either you got a big heart, or you pissed someone off."

Whelan laughed as Cannon's jaw dropped. "Deidre, we're on the clock. Did Sonny have family here, in Tulsa?"

"I'm not aware of any."

"Did he grow up here? Where did he go to school?"

"I think he was from Vinita. Played football in school. I saw some photos once. I think it was a Vinita High uniform. I used to cheer for Tulsa when I was in school. We played them sometimes, but Sonny was ahead of me a few years. Uniforms change, but, yeah, try Vinita."

Cannon recovered himself and asked, "Deidre, why was Sonny 'encouraged' to find another firehouse? Why didn't they want him at the 37 any longer?"

Deidre Owen wrapped her arms around herself and gave a squeeze, her chin toward the floor. When she brought her eyes back up, she was more guarded. "We were told not to talk about it."

Cannon mustered up some of the charm Jones told him he possessed and leaned against the bar top. He took his voice to a throaty whisper and gazed into her eyes. "Deidre, please, it might be important. I can't discuss my case, but please trust me. There are other lives still at stake right now."

"Really?" She was hooked.

"Yes. You might be our one shot at saving them."

"Me?" She paused. "Gimme a sec." She walked to the other end of the bar and opened a beer for a man running low, then returned.

Turning to make sure no one was within ear-shot, she leaned over the liquor bottles and rested her arm on the bar. "Word around the rumor mill is that he hit some broad. He denied it, but she accused him, and after an investigation didn't reveal nothing concrete, he was given a paid severance and a letter of recommendation if he would move on from the 37, regardless. I thought he was innocent. A lot of girls around here will say anything to get a man in trouble. I figured she lied 'cause they fought or something. But if you're telling me he might have killed someone? Now I'm not sure. Maybe she was tellin' the truth."

"Who was she? Do you have a name?"

"No. And the thing is, she didn't file a police report. Just waltzed in one day and went straight to the battalion chief, and spills her guts. I asked Sonny who she was, and he told me to mind my own business but swore he never hit no one."

"Why not file a report with the police?" asked Cannon.

"Right?" agreed Diedre. "Unless you're making the whole thing up. So I figured she wanted to hurt him but not send him to jail or nothing. He high-tailed it out of there with eight weeks' pay, and no one's heard from him since. We were told to let it go. So we did. You want a name? Talk to Captain Ramsey. He was there when all that went down."

Whelan threw a five-dollar bill on the counter and thanked her.

Cannon gave a polite nod.

"You sure you don't want to stick around and get fired up, cutie?"

He took a step back. "Another time."

Returning to the firehouse, Agents Whelan and Cannon drove through a fast-food drive-through in a better part of town and picked up two dozen tacos.

They dispersed them among the firefighters. Saving the last for the station chief and Captain Ramsey, who was called in on his day off.

The chief was perturbed by their presence for the second time that day. "We're not allowed to discuss it," he claimed, chomping down on his third beef taco with extra hot sauce. He shot the captain a look, effectively ordering him to keep his mouth shut.

"If you knew about this, why didn't you speak up earlier? Save me from two hours of running all over Tulsa," said Whelan.

"I really don't know the details. I was given a file and an update when I came on here, and the official word is Sonny Armstrong was innocent, and it's not to be discussed any further. With anyone."

Whelan ignored the chief and turned directly to the Captain. "We could drag this out. Take you to the nearest field office. That would be Oklahoma City. We should have you back by tomorrow afternoon," said Whelan.

"There's a Resident Agency for the FBI right here in Tulsa," snapped the chief. "Guys, we're doing our job, obeying orders."

"And we're doing ours," Cannon barked right back. "We're racing the clock and trying to save lives in an active case. We need a name. And we never heard it from you."

"You never heard the name Margaret Gilroy from me?" said Captain Ramsey. "Fair enough. Have a good day, gentlemen. Oh, and if you want to bribe me with tacos, get them from Tijuana Timmy's."

"You're familiar with that area?" asked Whelan. "Maybe I should have given you twenty singles for across the street. It would have cost me less than lunch."

"Nothing wrong with showing moral support for one of my firefighter family members," he snickered and walked out.

"You happen to *never see* Ms. Gilroy's address?" shouted Cannon to his back.

He stopped and turned to them before letting the door shut. "Actually, no. But she was from Vinita."

Chapter 43

Jones was sitting in SAC Kendrick's office.

"I have information in the Eddie Morrison case," he told her. "But you need to keep it mum from Agent Whelan until you finish your investigation into the Forever Sophia murders."

"Sir," she started. "Eddie killed Whelan's last partner, Agent Pierson, right in front of him. Tom gave up his whole life hunting him. Some idiots either *let* Eddie escape or *helped* him escape from prison."

"I understand all that."

"Sir, Alan, you can't really expect me to keep anything from my partner regarding Eddie Morrison."

"You're his ASAC now, so yes, I can. I know you and Whelan went through hell this summer, but if you want a seat in the big chair, you're going to have to make a lot of hard decisions. There's a reason we keep a respectable distance from the agents under us. We ask them to put their lives on the line every day. And, sometimes we have to keep things from them. A certain amount of impartiality helps. It's too late for you to avoid getting close to Whelan. Your role will be onerous. I need you to tell me you can handle it."

Miranda Jones bit her lower lip and let her mind race for three seconds. She pulled her shoulders back. "Yes, sir. Of course."

He threw a folder on the table in front of her. "That's got the details. You can go over it later. Put it in your desk or file cabinet, and lock it for now. Morrison was seen last week in Iowa. Surveillance tracked him to a farmhouse about fifteen miles southwest of Cedar Rapids. Resident agents surrounded the farm. There were two SWAT teams on the scene. The house came up empty. The two women and three farmhands who lived there claim they never heard of Eddie Morrison. They were interrogated for two days, but there's not a shred of evidence that puts him there."

"Then how the hell was he tracked there?"

"A car with plates belonging to one of the women was seen in video footage the day before, with Eddie at the wheel. Facial Recognition picked it up randomly. Camera footage shows him at a grocery store, where he shopped for ten minutes, then headed out in the direction of the farm, about three miles up the road. The car was there. But no Eddie."

"Is there camera footage anywhere on that three miles of…?"

"State Road 151. And no."

"They bungled it. They shouldn't have pounced on the house! They should have laid a trap. Damn it. Whelan's going to flip!"

"Which is why we're not telling him. Eddie Morrison's gone. Again."

Miranda was heated. She jumped up and paced the floor a minute, staring at the carpet. She stopped and jerked her head up. "Last week? What day last week?"

"Wednesday."

"Wednesday, *ten days* ago Wednesday?"

"Yes."

"Alan, we were still on that case! Sophia Perkins hadn't even been killed yet. Why the hell weren't we notified?"

"A.D. Caulfield called me himself," said Kendrick. "First, Morrison was spotted outside our jurisdiction. You guys were given a lot of leeway for over a month, and he felt it was time to move you to new assignments."

Jones grew cold and gave her superior an icy glare. "If Whelan and I were still on this, we'd have Eddie in jail right now. He tracked him for over two years. He knows how he operates, how he thinks. How to be patient."

"That's the problem. They didn't want the two of you spending another two years tracking him. We don't have the resources. And you're needed here now. Welcome to management."

Kendrick's face was full of frustration. "Sorry, Miranda."

She walked to the doorway and turned back. "I get it, Alan. But you *know* me. And you're getting to know Whelan. You should have insisted we were allowed to take the lead with that new intel. That was wrong, and you know it. And now Eddie's God knows where."

SAC Kendrick sighed. "Yes. Next time we get something on Morrison, maybe Caulfield will listen. But Agent Jones? Not a word of this to Whelan. No need to throw him off his game right now during this current investigation."

Jones glared at her long-time friend and commanding superior before conceding. "Yes, sir."

She marched to her own office and quietly shut the door. She kicked her shoes off and took a seat on the floor, folding her legs up into a full lotus position. She inhaled with long, deep breaths and released them slowly, preparing herself for a twenty-minute meditation session. It was either this or go around breaking things. *Maybe I'm growing.*

Her eyes popped open with the thought of her partner racing around northeast Oklahoma.

Nope. Put it out of your head Miranda. Breathe. In. Out. In. Out.

She managed eight minutes of silence before her phone rang. It was Merrill Perkins.

Damn. Duty calls.

She answered the phone, "Special Agent Miranda Jones."

"Agent Jones? This is Merrill Perkins. Peggy and I are with Earl at the hospital. Grace woke up. She's doing swell. She's giving us our million dollars. The family attorney, Mr. Steiner, should be here in two hours with the revised contract. Then we'd like to go home. I got my weekly poker game tonight I'd rather not miss, and Peggy has to go to work. Until the check clears the bank, I don't want her missin' any hours."

"Very thoughtful, Merrill. I'd hate for you to miss out on your free bowl of soup, too."

"Right, so can we go? That hotel is first-rate, but I'm bored as all get out. We're packed and ready. We stopped by to wish Gracie a quick get well and finalize all this, then we're heading to the airport."

Jones took a breath and exhaled slowly. "No, Merrill, I'm sorry, we haven't cleared you yet. I need you to stick around a few more days. Please."

She wasn't sure she sold her feigned politeness and didn't much care.

Merrill mumbled away from the phone's speaker, "She's not letting us go. We're stuck here."

Earl's voice could be heard in the background. "Well, you're not prisoners. She can't hold you here. It's illegal. Ask Mr. Steiner what the law says."

"We're going home, Agent Jones," said Merrill back into the phone. "I'm taking Earl and my grandson to lunch since it's the last time I might ever see him. The contract will be here to sign by the time we return, then we're catching a 3:00 plane. You want more from us, come to Oklahoma."

The line disconnected.

"Shit."

She dialed Whelan and filled him in on Merrill's plans.

"I'm headed over to the hospital now to talk with Grace Meyer. Perhaps a good night's sleep jogged her memory on who stabbed her."

"We're on our way to Vinita," he replied. "Talk soon."

Jones hung up and checked in with SAC Kendrick before heading out to Mission Hospital.

Earl Humboldt touched the arm of his pride and joy, Grace Meyer, with tears in his eyes. "I'm delighted you're doing alright, sweetheart. It was a scary few hours yesterday."

She was still frail. Her pain medication left her groggy, but she was awake and glad to see him.

Merrill, on the other hand, wasn't a welcomed sight. She managed a hoarse whisper. "One million, and you walk away forever. You give up any claim to Running Bear or his estate. That's the way it's drawn up."

"I get it," he said.

"You have no legal stake and are lucky to be getting anything at all."

She coughed, and Earl rushed in with a cup of water.

"Take a sip, sweetie," he said.

He scowled at Merrill. "Why don't you two wait in the hall. I'll be out in a minute, and we'll go grab a bite while we wait for the lawyer."

Merrill grabbed Peggy's arm, and the pair disappeared behind the curtain.

"Gracie," said Earl, "I hate to ask you this, but do you recall who might have stabbed you yesterday? Is nothing coming to you yet?"

"No, dad. I didn't see anything but a pillow coming toward my face. I'm sorry."

"Don't be sorry, sweetheart. It's fine. I know those federal agents will want to question you today. You tell them that and tell them you have to rest, and they have to leave, just like that. They have no right to drill you for more information you don't know. You hear me, sweetheart? Don't let them torture you for hours."

"I'm all right, dad. Let me rest a bit? Go to lunch. In fact, go back to Parkmoor and take a nap afterward. You look like you haven't slept."

"No, I haven't since you got stabbed. Maybe I will. I'll be back before dinner to check on you."

She nodded, then shut her eyes.

Earl went to the hall and found the guard who was supposed to be watching her. He waited until the man was safely standing back in front of Grace's room before turning to Merrill and Peggy. "Where's Running Bear? I thought we left him out here in the waiting area?"

"He wasn't here," said Peggy. "Probably went to pee."

She sat down in one of the eight chairs in the little make-shift area cut into a recessed section of the wall and rubbed at her neck. "I'm exhausted. All you boys go to lunch. I'm not hungry. I'm going to grab a coffee from the cafeteria and read my romance book a while."

"You had coffee at the hotel," said Merrill. "Why don't you come with us? You didn't eat much this morning."

Peggy lowered her chin and gawked at her husband. "We don't all need 2000 calories at every meal. And if I'm supposed to fly back down to Tulsa and then drive to Vinita and make a 5:00 shift so I can wait on people who tip like shit for two dollars and thirteen cents an hour, I'd better get some more caffeine in me."

She winced, expecting him to slap her as usual when she spouted off.

Merrill let loose a gut-busting whoop. "Fine, you ain't hungry, no reason to throw money away."

Earl said a silent prayer of gratitude he had experienced a better life.

Running Bear rounded the corner down the hall and approached the group. "This medical facility is amazing. You should see the modern advances in the equipment they have. I saw a woman get what they call an X-ray. It showed her ribs! Can you believe it?"

"I'm not even gonna ask where you were," said Merrill. "Somewhere you shouldn't have been, no doubt. Boy, let's go eat. You need to say goodbye to your granddaddy. Your cousin Grace isn't gonna let us see each other no more after today. What are you hungry for?"

Running Bear looked at Earl and Peggy. Peggy shook her head, flipping a page in her romance.

Earl spoke up. "Bear, why don't we go grab a pizza? You like pizza?"

"Love it. I want one with shrimp scampi on it. Louie makes the best scampi."

Earl blinked at him. "Well, today, we're going to see how we do with pepperoni. Okay? Let's go, guys."

Earl took pity on Peggy. He was sure she was really hoping to take a breather from Merrill for a couple of hours. "I'll bring you back a slice?"

"Thank you," she responded.

As the three men walked down the hall, a team of doctors and nurses rushed toward them with a patient on a gurney.

The trio flung themselves tight against the wall until they passed. Running Bear took off down the hall before the older men could say a word, chasing the emergency responders.

"He might need an X-ray!" he yelled back.

Merrill stopped and motioned to his disappearing grandson before turning to Earl.

"You sure you really want to live with *that*? If you're smart, you'll cash out like me and head home."

Earl crinkled his lips and began slowly walking back up the hall in search of his great-nephew.

Chapter 44

Agents Whelan and Cannon were heading north on Interstate 44, approaching the Vinita exit.

"Is that a McDonald's over the highway?" asked Cannon.

A large structure spanning the distance across the Will Rogers Turnpike formed a bridge with a giant golden arch. There was parking on both sides of the highway, north and southbound.

"Huh," Whelan commented.

They exited a mile later and traveled along the historic Route 66, the main road into town. It made a sharp left downtown, where yet another McDonald's took over a corner.

"I think it's time to buy stock in Mickie-D's," mumbled Whelan.

The GPS led them to the high school. Several cars were in the lot, thankfully. Whelan was afraid it might have been shut up, given it was Saturday. But he saw two more cars pull in and realized there was football practice. A woman was in the administrative office, and within twenty minutes of flashing their badges, they were flipping through yearbooks from the mid-90s.

"Here," said Whelan, pointing to a photo from a 1994 book. "That's him, William Armstrong."

He flipped to the index, then over to the football section. "There he is again. Played varsity his sophomore year."

The woman helping, Leslie Smith, took a peek. "Oh, he's a cutie. I bet he was popular."

William Armstrong was in yearbooks for 1993 through 1995, but not 1996.

"Must have moved," said Cannon.

"Or he didn't graduate," said Leslie. "We aren't exactly setting state records for graduates here, I'm afraid."

"So he was here, for at least three years," said Whelan.

He started flipping through those same yearbooks, searching for a Margaret Gilroy. She wasn't to be found.

"Younger? Older maybe?" They went through the books from 1985 to 2005 with no results.

"Damn," said Whelan. "Maybe the Junior High?"

"Middle School. It's a middle school here now. Ewing Halsell," said Leslie.

Whelan opened the 1994 yearbook. He flipped to the Freshmen section and found Sophia Perkins. He studied the portrait of the young, future self-made billionaire. All the hopes and possibilities a teenager dreams about were made a reality by the young woman against impossible odds. The picture in the yearbook was horrifying. It was taken two months after the accident in the summer of 1993. Whelan traced the stitches holding her cheeks together. The crooked dangling lips, barely held on by more stitching, were closed tight, hiding a toothless mouth. Her physical and mental pain showed in the photo.

"She was beautiful before she got knocked senseless," said an older woman's voice from Whelan's left side. "I told her to use the previous year's photo for the book, but her daddy wanted a record or some such bullshit."

He turned to find a Native American woman in her mid-60s. Her hair was long and dangled behind her back in a thick braid, primarily gray. She smiled and held out her hand. "I'm Atsila Redbird. Welcome to Cherokee Nation."

He extended a warm handshake. "Special Agent Tom Whelan with the FBI. This," he motioned to Cannon, "is Special Agent Phil Cannon. Cherokee Nation?"

"You're in its heart. Over a third of our class here in Vinita is Native American. Thank you, Leslie," she said to the other woman.

Leslie retreated to another room.

"You knew Sophia Perkins?" asked Cannon.

"Taught her, yes. I've been here a long time. I'm the principal now. You here about her death?"

"Yes. You saw that?"

"Can't escape it. It's been running non-stop on all the cable channels since yesterday morning. When I walked in, I expected you were with the press. That's why I came in today. At least three have called and warned me they're sending reporters. I've been making them wait until the weekend. Didn't want our students distracted on a school day. Should be here around 1:00."

It was 12:40 p.m. now.

"And you remember Ms. Perkins from 1994?" asked Cannon.

"Yes. Beautiful child, until that summer day. I had just transferred from teaching at the Junior High. I taught her both years there, History and Social Studies, and her first semester freshmen year. When she dropped that kid, she also dropped out of school. What a difference a summer can make in the life of a teenager." She reflected on unshared memories and took another peek at Sophia's picture in the yearbook, grimacing with thoughts of the past.

"So you met her father, Merrill Perkins?" asked Whelan.

"Yes. He never came to parent-teacher conferences. Never came to anything school-related. But I was fond of Sophie and went to her home after the accident to check on her a couple of times. Merrill was quite…challenging. Always smelled like a cross between his cattle and his rye field. He still lives out there, about ten miles up the road, but his farm has gone to shit."

Cannon grinned. "You have a sharp memory."

"Yes. And she was memorable. Do you know who killed her? I guess you don't, or you wouldn't be here."

"We're looking for connections," said Whelan. "We have a man in custody, but there was someone else involved. Can you recall anyone in her life from that time who might want her dead now for any reason?"

"No. Of course not. She was popular before the accident. Afterward, well, not as much."

"Do you recall any names from the early 90s of boys or girls who she hung out with? Any friends who still live in the area?"

"Not that I'm aware. I don't think true friends were in her cards back then. She was a free spirit. I hope she's been dealt better hands since."

"Boyfriends?" asked Cannon.

"Plenty, but none of them serious either. She was known as a party girl. I could smell liquor on her breath once in a while. I blamed the father, never her. She was delightful under that facade. The attention she wasn't getting at home, she grabbed from the boys in the school. At least, I hope she wasn't getting that kind of attention at home. Sometimes I wondered."

The two agents reflected on Merrill for a minute, with renewed vile at the thought.

"Borrow that yearbook, would you?" asked the principal. "I don't want the reporters posting that picture of her all over their media outlets. Return it sometime when you get a chance to drop it in the mail. And if that page is missing, I'll understand you were doing your duty."

Whelan ripped out the page with Sophia's photo on it. He scanned the index to see if she was anywhere else in the book. There was no other mention of her.

He handed it back to Atsila. "Consider it borrowed and returned." He folded the page up and put it in his inside coat pocket.

"Thank you."

"Did you ever know a Margaret Gilroy?" asked Whelan.

"That name doesn't ring any bells. Did you check the yearbooks?"

"Yes. Didn't see any. Perhaps she attended another school. Is the Middle School open today for any reason? I'd like to stop by and go through their records."

"No, but let me call the superintendent and see what I can do." She stepped into the hall and started dialing on her cell phone.

Whelan asked Leslie for copies of the files on Sonny Bill Armstrong and Sophia Perkins. "And double-check for a Margaret Gilroy, please."

He checked his notes on his phone from earlier in the week. "Also, can you pull anything on an Oukonunaka Light?"

"I'll see what we have."

Whelan returned to the yearbooks and started flipping through them. The page he wanted was torn out. He laughed at himself and removed the sheet with Sophia Perkins on it. The other side contained the 'L's. Third from the top was Oukonunaka Light. He was handsome, with long black hair and wore a traditional Cherokee buffalo skin coat handed down to him from three generations. He appeared proud.

She returned from the copier with three folders. "No Gilroy. Are you sure she attended here?"

"No, I'm not. Thank you."

He flipped through the transcripts briefly. Sophia's was one page. She made a 'C' in Home Economics and a B in Art. The rest of her classes, for her one semester, were 'F's.

Sonny Bill Armstrong was a decent student. He averaged a three-point-two over his four years. Oukonunaka Light was a four-point-zero. His file also contained his certificates for class valedictorian and consecutive years on the honor roll. There were letters of recommendation from several teachers for colleges and three copies of acceptances to ivy league schools.

Whelan grabbed the yearbook for 1997 and went straight to the senior photo of young Mr. Light. His hair was cut short, and he was wearing a navy suit, fashionable for the late '90s.

"Conformist?" asked Cannon.

"Maybe. I didn't walk a mile in his shoes, but I'm guessing they weren't moccasins by the time he graduated.

Principal Redbird returned. "They're going to meet you there and open the office for you."

"Thank you," said Whelan. "Mr. Oukonunaka Light. What can you tell me about him?"

Atsila studied the two yearbook photos, freshmen and senior. "It's not easy being a minority. Ever. Not in the 90s and not now. Kids can be cruel. We offer counseling for our young Cherokee family, but they are often subjected to ridicule and harassment. It's disgusting. We all share one roof. You'd think in this day and age we'd be past all this."

She sighed. "Mr. Light was a brilliant young man. I think he went to Harvard? Might have been Yale? I can't recall. Last I heard anything about him, he was getting a doctorate in internal medicine. One of our few exceptional success stories."

"We haven't been able to find anything on him. Any idea where he lives now?"

"No. Sorry. But I heard through the grapevine once that he changed his first name to Konun. Easier for his patients to pronounce, I guess. Try that name."

"I will, thank you. How about Sonny William Armstrong? Do you have any recollection of him?"

Atsila thought for a moment. "His name rings a bell, but I can't recall much. Did he play football?"

"Yes," answered Cannon.

"Well, I didn't follow the athletics department too much. My goal in the early days was to increase attention and funding to the creative arts. If I'd known how fruitless it was going to be…well, I'd have done things differently. This school has always placed a priority on football. The coach back then has long been retired. I'm not much help to you, I'm afraid."

"You've been wonderful," said Whelan. "Thank you for all your help Principal Redbird. Good luck with the press today."

"Thanks, I'll need it. Agent Whelan? I hope you catch your killers. Sophie deserved so much better than to go out like that. She still had a lot more to give."

"That's the plan."

A media van pulled up in the parking lot, and a reporter and her videographer were collecting their gear. She spotted the two agents and ran over to them as Whelan unlocked his car door. They hopped in before she could reach them and Cannon let the tires squeal as they made their get-away.

On the way to the middle school, Whelan powered up his laptop and researched Oukonunaka Light in the bureau's database once again, now that he had a new first name to go on. He located Doctor Konun Light in Chicago, privately practicing medicine with a small medical group where he was one of the partners. He had two kids and loved boating and basketball, according to his bio. His hair was still cropped short.

A couple of phone calls confirmed he was in the office all week but was currently unavailable.

"Please have him return my call ASAP," commanded Whelan.

A search through the records at the middle school didn't reveal anything else new. Sophia Perkins, Armstrong, and Light all had files, but there was no mention of Gilroy.

The agents drove by Merrill Perkins' farm. Nothing to see. A rundown shack in the middle of a field of drought-ridden soil. Two cows roamed a thirty-acre fenced lot, munching on weeds and a few strands of rye that hadn't flourished in years. They watched the agents drive slowly by, and Cannon swore he saw a plea for help in their eyes.

The clock on the rental car read 1:20 p.m. Whelan's foot pressed harder against the gas pedal. "If I floor it back to Tulsa, we might be able to catch that 2:25 flight back to K.C."

"We're through here?" asked Cannon.

"You holding out a lead on me?"

Cannon sighed. "I guess we're through here."

Whelan nodded absently. "Let's get home."

Chapter 45

Jones made her way to the ICU ward at Mission Hospital. Grace was asleep in her bed. Her face was contorted, likely from a nightmare.

Jones debated whether or not to wake her but decided to let her sleep.

She headed inside the ladies' room and nearly ran into Peggy Perkins, who was on her way out.

"Agent Jones! You startled the life out of me!" said Peggy, clutching her heart.

"I'm sorry," said Jones. "It couldn't happen in a safer place." She smiled at the woman, a year older than herself but who seemed fatigued.

"Peggy, give me two minutes in here and then I'd like to talk to you."

"If you're trying to convince me to stay, you don't have to twist my arm. It's Merrill who's bored. I'm enjoying the hotel life. I'd move in forever if it was up to me."

"Where *is* that husband of yours?"

"All the boys went to grab a bite. I didn't care to join them. Watch them rub their crotches and talk trash? I get enough of that back home."

"That sounds awful. Peggy, not all men are like that. I doubt Earl Humboldt is or Running Bear. Are you hungry? I haven't eaten today. I could use a bite. Why don't we try the cafeteria?"

"I got some coffee. Honestly, their food doesn't look so great. I'm fine though. Earl was sweet enough to call me and see what kind of pizza I liked. He's going to bring me some. They're at Waldo Pizza? Do you know it? You could meet them there. Maybe convince Merrill somehow to stay a few more days?"

"Yes, I'll run over there. It's about ten minutes southeast. You're sure you don't want to join me? Sitting around a hospital isn't much fun."

"It beats sitting around Merrill! You go on, see if you can get him to let us stay. We're supposed to be on a plane home in two hours, and frankly, I'm not ready to go back to work."

"I'll do my best," said Jones. She slipped inside the restroom while Peggy repositioned herself in the waiting area outside ICU.

Fifteen minutes later, Jones plopped beside Merrill Perkins in a booth at Waldo Pizza. "What's up, Merrill?"

"Agent Jones! You're a lovely sight. Help yourself to some pizza."

"Thanks." She grabbed a napkin and slice of pepperoni. "Merrill, what's your hurry to get home? Your money from the estate will take time to wire. Why not at least wait until Monday or Tuesday? I might have more questions you can help answer."

"Ask away," he snickered.

"Well, I don't know them yet. Investigation is a patience game sometimes. I just have to wait for the killer to slip up." She narrowed her eyes as she stared into his.

"Lady, I ain't got nothin' to slip up from." He took a sip of beer.

"Agent Jones," said Earl. "Please, let him go. As much as it's nice to see family, once every twenty years is enough in this case."

"How about you, Your Majesty?" asked Jones. "You tired of your grandfather too? Or would you like to have more one-on-one bonding time?"

Running Bear glanced to his left. It was an empty seat, but Jones was clued in it wasn't empty to him.

"Cantor? Or Marjorie?" she asked.

"Marjorie. She says he's free to leave. He paid homage to my mother, and she'd rather not smell him any longer."

Running Bear was honestly relaying her comments and hadn't intended to insult his grandfather.

"Excuse me?" Merrill snapped.

Jones turned back to him and sniffed. "You do run a bit ripe, Merrill. At least you'll be able to afford better deodorant now. Look, you're never going to make a 3:30 plane, stay until Monday, and if I don't have all my questions answered by then, you can go home."

She didn't expect she'd have much more from him with another day and a half, but it was a last-ditch effort. She'd figure out another reason to keep him around on Monday if necessary.

"Well, it's nice to be wanted by *somebody*," he pouted. "Okay, pretty lady, you win. Do you want to come by later for happy hour? I'm buying."

"Thanks. Maybe I will. Let me call the hotel and make sure your room is resecured." She stepped out to the sidewalk.

Earl sighed. "Merrill, go home. She can't make you stay."

"She's not. I'm offering. Two more nights of comfy living is fine. Besides, like she said, I'm not gonna have the money in the bank today anyway. Might as well enjoy the swank life till I can buy it for myself."

"Fine, you're right. Two more nights won't kill anyone," said Earl.

Running Bear waved over their waitress. "Miss, thank you for your service. I'm sure you're honored to have the king in your establishment, but we really must be going. There's a woman in need of this pizza. Could you please find some parchment so we might bring it to her?"

"I'll get you a to-go box," she said. She smiled at him, assuming he was flirting with her in some way or another.

"Splendid."

Earl bobbed his head fondly at Running Bear. "I think we're going to get along fine, Your Majesty. We'll see what we can do this fall about closing in that pool so we can swim year-round." He slapped the young man's shoulder.

Running Bear lit up like a little boy on Christmas morning.

The group returned to the hospital and checked on Grace, who was still asleep.

Earl glowered at all her IV drips and whispered, "She's not used to being doped up like this, poor thing. Let's let her rest."

Jones came across Peggy at the nurse's station, staring at a large bulletin board.

She smiled at the agent when she turned around. "This is a busy place. Did you get him to let us stay?"

"I did," said Jones. "At least you get a comfy bed for two more nights."

"Oh, bless you!" She reached in and surprised Jones with a hug.

Merrill walked up to them. "Where's that attorney? Steiner? Ain't he supposed to be here by now?"

"He came by, but I told him you were running late, and he got all upset and said he wasn't going to wait on you all day and he'd meet you tonight at Parkmoor." Peggy cleared her throat. "So, I guess it's a good thing we're staying another couple of nights."

Merrill frowned at the logic. "He *knew* we was leavin'!"

"But, we're staying now, so, where's the harm?"

"Woman! I oughtta…!"

"What, Merrill?" asked Jones. "You oughtta what?" She positioned herself in between the spouses and gave Merrill her best "I dare you" pose.

It worked. He backed off. "Yeah, fine, we're stayin' anyway."

He turned to Running Bear down the hall. "Boy, I guess we're joining you for dinner tonight. Better let that cook know to put on a fancy spread. You've still got family in town."

Running Bear approached his grandfather. "I've upheld my familial responsibilities. Dinner was never part of the arrangement. We shared our one final meal. I think we're set for another in—"

He cut himself off and asked Earl. "Twenty years was it?"

Earl nodded.

"Twenty years," he finished revolving back to Merrill. "Goodbye, grandfather."

Merrill was speechless. He gathered his wits as Running Bear headed down the hall.

"Wait, boy! What about Steiner? He's got my paperwork!"

Running Bear paused and turned back. "He works for me now. I'll make sure he's there at 7:00 p.m. with your papers. I wouldn't be late this time if I were you."

They were quiet as Running Bear disappeared around the corner of the hallway.

"Well," said Earl. "He's not gonna drive himself. I told Grace I'd go get a nap and check on her around dinner time."

He chased after Running Bear.

Merrill turned back to his wife. His confusion developed quickly, turning to anger. "Woman!"

He caught Jones moving out of the corner of his eye.

She tilted her head to the right and struck another challenging stance.

"Let's go!" He headed down the same corridor as the other men went.

"Peggy," said Jones, after Merrill was out of earshot, "if you need another room tonight, I'll make sure one gets booked. I can't guarantee it will be at The Leonardo, but somewhere safe and away from Merrill. I don't know why you put up with that nonsense, but you don't have to."

"I'm fine, agent, really. He's not so bad. Bark's worse than his bite and all. I'll be alright. But thank you." She gave the agent another hug and left.

Men that liked to bully women irritated Jones more than all her other peeves. Growing up, she'd seen a fair amount of that from two of her uncles and vowed she'd never again be a victim of physical abuse. She took in a deep breath and held it for a count of ten, then exhaled as slowly as possible. Nurses flitted about her as she stood in the middle of the hall, breathing herself into a calmer disposition.

Again, it was her phone's ring that brought her out of her trance. This time, it was Whelan.

"Hello, partner. Where are we at?"

Chapter 46

Agents Whelan and Cannon were back in Kansas City. Whelan filled her in on his day in Oklahoma, and Jones relayed all she knew.

"Meet me at my place," said Jones. "If I don't get a load of laundry in the washer, I won't have any clean underwear tomorrow. We'll compare notes there."

By 4:00 p.m., the agents were sitting in ASAC Miranda Jones' living room. It was a small home in the Westport area of Kansas City. She wasn't the best housekeeper and was too tired to care. A pile of junk mail was moved to make room for Cannon to sit in a recliner.

"Sorry, the shredder's broken, and I don't like for my name to go in the waste can. Can I offer you boys a beer?"

"I'm fine, thank you," said Cannon.

Whelan took an iced coffee and shared their day in Oklahoma. "So," he concluded, "we're waiting on a call from Oukonunaka Light to see if he remembers Sophia Perkins or Sonny Bill Armstrong. According to Grace Meyer, Sophia hoped Mr. Light was Running Bear's father."

"Any idea who fathered the child she was pregnant with now?" asked Jones.

"Not a clue," said Whelan.

"I followed up with Cusack today," said Cannon. "Lab results confirmed it was *not* Doctor Brachman. If she was having relations with him during those longer 'update' sessions, they were using birth control."

Jones exploded, "Oh shit!" She jumped up and ran to the bathroom.

She returned shortly with a sigh of relief. "I thought I forgot to take *my* birth control this morning," she explained. "Not that it would matter. Derrick's out of town more than in town lately."

"Give it a few weeks before you get yourself too worked up about moving separate directions," said Cannon. "If it's meant to be, he'll find a way to work out a schedule affording him more time with you than without you."

"We were stretched thin as it was with *my* schedule. Now his has quadrupled in the last month, and neither of us is ready to hang up our career for the other."

"A little time apart will allow for reflection on whether you're still a fit for each other."

Jones focused on the man eight years her junior before turning to Whelan. "Wise, this one. I think I'm leaving you in capable hands."

"I know you are," said Whelan. "It's poor Phil who drew the short straw."

He smiled at Cannon as he answered an incoming call. It was short and informative.

"That was Tamara Baker at the office. All the remaining alibis for the rest of the board members checked out for what it's worth. The L.A. office also confirmed Mark Fleming and Karen Hertzberg arrived back home last night. Sarah Williams is still here at The Leonardo."

"She's the highest-strung personality I've been around in a while," said Jones. "It really tests my ability to zen."

"She's still on my short-list," said Whelan. "She might not fit the profile, but I can't rule her out given her unfettered access to Sophia the past two years. Thoughts?"

Cannon stood up and stretched. "I don't think she would have given us Sonny Bill Armstrong's name if she was involved. I've mentally checked her off."

"Unless she's throwing him under the bus?"

"He'd likely have evidence connecting her. Phone and text records, if nothing else. It's unlikely."

Whelan's frustration was making him antsy. He jumped up and paced the floor a minute. "I'm going to head back to the office. See if bouncing any of this off the rest of the team gives me thoughts in a new direction."

"I'll go with you," said Cannon. "My car's still there."

"Let me get my wash in the dryer, and I'll be right behind you," said Jones.

As she moved her laundry from one machine in her basement to the other, she wondered what more she could get out of the staff at Parkmoor.

Running Bear was sitting on the pool edge with his feet dangling in the water. His wife Marjorie was swimming laps in front of him.

"I wish you'd put on a swimsuit," said Running Bear.

"They're so confining," said Marjorie. "No one else is here right now. Besides, you're the King. You set the rules. If it bothers you, keep them from joining us. In fact, why aren't *you* joining me now?"

She splashed some water on him and giggled as she swam away with a proper backstroke. Pausing halfway across the pool, she grew lost in the clouds.

"Do you think Earl can really get a glass enclosure around the pool this fall?" she asked.

"I don't see why not," said Running Bear. "I see them in magazines. It's possible. I'll put Earl in charge. He likes to swim as much as I do. He'll make sure we're swimming in the snow come January."

She completed her lap then walked up the ladder at the other end, bouncing her nakedness in the way she knew he enjoyed before wrapping a large towel around her. As she passed by him on the way back to the house, she planted a kiss firmly on his lips, then climbed the path up the hill.

The roar of a dragon grabbed his attention. It was silver with red and blue scales on its tail, flying high above. He watched it until it was out of sight.

It reminded him of his father, the red dragon rider. He fought this week to put it out of his head, but it visited him in his nightmares and made him sick to his stomach when he dwelled on the fact that his father killed his mother. *Do I have that in me? Would I be capable of killing a family member?*

Without the ability to perceive the value of money, he could not grasp it as a motivation for murder.

The wizard who killed Princess Gracie must have put a spell on the red dragon rider to have him kill my mother. Who's the wizard, and why is he after me? Is he someone I know and trust? Those regents from the kingdom of the FBI seemed to think it was someone close to our family, perhaps someone right here at Parkmoor!

He reasoned in and out of possibilities as to why Nurse O'Brien or Chad or Sylvia or Chef Louie would want to kill Grace Meyer. *There's no way it's Earl. Gracie's father couldn't be the wizard. Could he?*

Earl was the only new face in the house since his mother died. The rest he knew for years. Earl Humboldt lingered as a strong possibility. *It has to be someone else, some stranger we don't know. But why? For green paper?*

Running Bear returned to the house and entered the kitchen. Chef Louie was prepping for dinner, slicing raw vegetables on a cutting board.

Sitting at a bar stool on the island, Running Bear watched him chop with skill.

"What are we having tonight?"

Chef Louie smiled. "I thought I'd make a ratatouille. Chad brought these beautiful zucchini and squash from the vegetable garden. I bought some eggplant to go with them."

"Chad has a vegetable garden?" asked Running Bear. "I've never seen it."

"It's on the side of the house. The main flower beds he keeps full of flowers for you and your mother to enjoy." Louie choked up and corrected himself. "I guess, for *you* to enjoy, Your Majesty."

Running Bear walked around and gave the chef a hug. "Do you enjoy the flowers, Louie?"

"Oh, yes. They're beautiful."

"They're for all of us now." Running Bear sighed. He grabbed a slice of raw zucchini, popping it in his mouth as he left the kitchen and made his way to the parlor.

It was approaching 5:00 p.m. Happy Hour would start soon. He didn't feel very happy today. Grace's attack left him scattered and unsure. *What's happening? First the Queen, then grandmother, and now Princess Gracie? Why are we under siege? What have we done to deserve this?*

He approached Sylvia, polishing glassware at a side table near the bar.

She stood when he entered and gave a nod of her head. "Your Majesty. How are we today? Can I make you a cocktail?"

"No, thank you, Sylvia. You may have one if you'd like. I'm…worried. About Gracie."

"I hear she's doing wonderfully. Should make a full recovery and be joining us here at Parkmoor permanently soon. If that's what you still desire?"

"Yes, of course. I love Gracie. But…"

"But she's not your mother," said Sylvia. Her face grew concerned.

"I miss her." Running Bear released a tear. Once the first one was free to fall, others gathered and felt empowered to do the same. Within seconds, the waterworks flowed down Running Bear's face like never before.

Sylvia ran and wrapped her arms around him. "It's okay, Bear, get it out. I miss her too."

The pair buried their heads in each other's shoulders and cried until exhaustion nearly knocked them over. They sat on a sofa and wiped away their pain.

Running Bear smiled at the housekeeper. "Thank you. You're an excellent friend in addition to a fine maid."

Sylvia beamed. "Thank you, Your Majesty. I think of you as a wonderful friend too, in addition to being a fine king. I hope that is all right?"

"Yes, of course."

Running Bear viewed Sylvia in a new light for the first time since she began working there. He stood abruptly. "I have to go. Carry on."

He fled the room, leaving a puzzled Sylvia to resume her duties.

Nearly running straight into Marjorie as he rounded the landing on the stairwell, Running Bear yelled at her. "Watch where you're going! You should be more alert when in the King's presence!"

Marjorie's mouth fell open, and she stood speechless as Running Bear bolted past and ran up to their bedroom. He slammed the door behind him.

How is it that Sylvia understands more than my wife that I'm missing my mom?

He stripped and hopped in the shower, turning the water as hot as he could stand. It beat on his back as more tears flowed and mingled above the drain.

Depleted of all energy, he collapsed on the bed afterward and let his mind go blank. Sleep began to envelop him, and he allowed it. *A nap before dinner should clear my head. I need to pull myself together. The kingdom still needs me. Gracie needs me. Who in the hell is the wizard?*

Chapter 47

Chad Buckley shook Running Bear's shoulder over an hour later. "Your Majesty, Attorney Adam Steiner is here with the paperwork. Your grandfather should be here in thirty-five minutes. Please get dressed and come downstairs."

"Thank you, Chad. And thank you for your vegetables. I had no idea you were growing them. They're beautiful. I can't wait for dinner."

Chad was taken aback at the unusual display of gratitude over a simple zucchini. "Thank you, Bear. It's my pleasure."

He stood to leave. "Do you have a favorite vegetable you'd like to see planted?"

Running Bear gave legitimate thought to his question. "I'm rather fond of pumpkin pie and Autumn's around the corner. It would be fun to see some of those growing. Feel free to use one of the flower beds closest to the veranda. And any other winter squash Chef Louie would like to have is fine too."

"Yes, Your Majesty. That *would* be fun." Chad left with a broad smile.

Running Bear dressed and managed to make it downstairs within ten minutes.

It was 6:32, judging by the grandfather clock in the gallery.

You've got twenty-eight minutes, Merrill, or your deal is off.

He entered the parlor, where everyone was gathered with drinks in hand. He marched straight up to Adam Steiner and held out his hand. "Great to see you again. Please make yourself comfortable here at Parkmoor. I trust we're taking first-rate care of you?"

The family attorney wasn't used to dealing with Running Bear as the head of the house, and his new demeanor threw him for a loop. "Thank you, Your Majesty. Yes, I'm fine. Everything is in order. We're waiting on your grandfather."

"If he's not here by 7:01, you can rip it to shreds, and he can fight for it. In court."

He caught Sylvia's attention. She was wearing a lovely evening dress. His face asked her if that was the correct phrase to use, and she nodded politely.

"Very good, sir," said Steiner. He headed to the bar and helped himself to a refill.

Nurse O'Brien approached the young man. "Bear, how are you feeling? I heard you took a nap? That's not quite like you." Without permission, she touched the back of her hand to his forehead to see if he was running hot.

"I'm splendid, thank you. You're particularly fetching this evening, Linda."

She blushed, unsure where this praise was coming from. "Thank you, Your Majesty. I haven't worn this in a while. It's from the back of my closet. I'm glad it still fits."

Nurse O'Brien went over to Sylvia. "What's gotten into him this evening?" she whispered.

Sylvia smiled. "We shared quite the cry earlier. I think the first genuine, heartfelt one since his mom was murdered. I suspect he's feeling renewed with energy, is all."

Nurse O'Brien leered at the younger woman and raised her eyebrows. "And that's *all* you shared? A cry?"

Sylvia turned her head and feigned shock. "Ms. O'Brien! Shame on you. Of course. He's a married man."

She walked over to her Earl Humboldt and politely made small talk so he would feel like part of the Parkmoor family.

Nurse O'Brien mumbled to herself in Sylvia's absence. "And all the movies he watches have some king or emperor who cheats on his queen with a whore."

She turned her gaze to Chad Buckley and allowed herself to pine for the man whom she'd known for years and who endured his own crush on

Grace Meyer. She spoke aloud to herself again. “Oh, dear. Perhaps we’re no better than one of his movies after all.”

In the hotel room at The Leonardo, Peggy Perkins was having a hell of a time with her husband, Merrill. He was already drunker than usual by 6:30, and she was trying to get him to the car. “Come on, you wanted to stop by the grocery store before we head over to Parkmoor. You’re going to give Running Bear a nice bottle of wine as a goodwill gesture. If you don’t hurry up, we’ll be late.”

“Yeah, yeah,” he slurred. “I think you’d better drive.”

He handed her the keys to the rental car and walked out to the hallway.

“Merrill! Put your shoes on!” she yelled. She picked them up and threw them at him one at a time, the second one hitting his leg.

He finished dressing, and they were on their way. It didn’t take him sixty seconds to pass out against the passenger door. After a few minutes, Peggy found an empty space and parked. The sudden stopping of motion woke Merrill from his slumber.

“Where are we?” he asked. His bourbon was burning his stomach, and bile crept up his throat. He swallowed it back down and took a sip from a bottle of water Peggy brought.

“We’re at Price Chopper! You wanted to give Running Bear a gift. What’s wrong with you?”

His noggin was spinning. “I wanted to give him a gift? He’s got everything he ever needs. He should be giving *me* a gift!” When his head hit his chest, he snapped his neck back quickly, fighting off more drunken sleep.

“You know what? I’ll go pick something out. You’d better keep your ass here in the car and keep napping before we get there.” She slammed the door when she got out.

Merrill's head hit his chest again, and he slid over to the side, leaning into the car door. His snoring began, and Peggy swore she heard it through the cracked window all the way across the parking lot. She trotted along in her four-inch heels, her oversized purse slung over her shoulder.

She mumbled expletives the whole way, cursing her husband and hoping the choices that led her to this point in her life weren't a mistake.

Inside the Kansas City field office, Whelan was going over notes in the bullpen from each agent involved in flushing out leads. He tried to connect anyone to Sonny Bill Armstrong or pinpoint evidence that might identify them as the mystery-wizard who attempted to kill Grace Meyer.

His watch read 6:45. In eight hours, he'd officially clock in an entire week on the case. Sighing, he plopped into a chair and stared blankly at a computer screen. His phone rang, showing a number he didn't recognize.

"Agent Whelan," he answered.

A voice on the other end started out shaky. "Hi. Uh, I was told to call this number? The FBI wanted to speak with me. This is Doctor Light."

Whelan's spine straightened, and he snapped his fingers to catch Cannon's attention. He put the doctor on speakerphone, and the bullpen quieted. "Doctor Light, this is Special Agent Thomas Whelan with the FBI. You're Oukonunaka Light? From Vinita, Oklahoma?"

There was silence for a few seconds, then, "Used to be, yes."

"That's right, it's Konun now. Doctor Light, I'm working a homicide investigation. Sophia Perkins. You knew her in school?"

"Oh. Yes."

"You knew she was dead?"

"I saw it on the news last night, yes. It's tragic."

"Were you close?"

"I guess that depends on how you define 'close.'"

"Did you sleep with her?" asked Whelan.

"A couple of times. We were kids, both of us young. I think I was fifteen? You don't believe I had anything to do with her murder, do you?"

Whelan chuckled to himself. People always felt the need to clarify their innocence. "I'm gathering information. Do you have any reason to want Sophia Perkins dead?"

"Heavens no! She was a sweet girl."

"She was sweet on you, I hear. Hoped you were the father of her baby."

More silence. "She had a *baby*?" Doctor Light managed to spit out in a whisper.

"Relax, Doc, you're not the father."

"Oh, thank God!"

"Doctor Light, I'm searching for people who might still be connected to Sonny William Armstrong. Were you friends in school?"

"Yes. In Junior High. We hung out on occasion. Gosh, I haven't heard that name in many years. We lost touch in high school. He was into athletics, I developed an interest in science. I think he moved to Chelsea the summer before his senior year. I never heard from or saw him again after that."

"Did both of you have an interest in Sophia Perkins at the same time? In Junior High?"

"I suppose, yes. I think a lot of boys did. She was…popular."

"Yes," said Whelan. "I understand she was promiscuous. Who else might have enjoyed a special relationship with Sophia that you can recall? I need names."

"You mean aside from every boy at Vinita Junior High? And some from the high school? Go down the roster. I'm sure you can obtain one from the school."

"We have that, and we're making calls. But given Sophia's more intimate attachment to you, I was hoping someone particular might strike you as having an extra interest in her."

"No, sorry."

“Perhaps someone who might want to seek revenge for anything she’d done?”

“I can’t recall that she was anything but kind to us. If you want people who hated her, don’t look to the boys. Look to some of the girls.”

“Why is that?” asked Whelan.

“Well, she slept with half their boyfriends. Not too many girls were engaging in sexual relations at that age. They usually maintained some semblance of morality, at least until high school.”

“Any girls' names who stand out to you?”

Doctor Light was silent on the other end. “No, sorry. That was such a long time ago, and I did my best to get the hell out of there when the chance came. I was an oddball.”

“In what way?”

“I knew I wanted to expand my education and personal growth beyond what that area offered,” he said guardedly, trying to be politically correct.

“You didn’t want to come home and treat your Cherokee Nation family once you became a doctor?”

“I’m not ashamed to be Cherokee,” he said. “But I didn’t feel any desire to return to a town that will never outgrow six-thousand people. I developed an appreciation for other cultures besides my own. I prefer not to be prosecuted for it.”

Doctor Konun Light was growing agitated.

“Fair enough,” said Whelan. “We aren’t able to gather any family information for Sonny Bill—William—Armstrong. His parents are listed as deceased. We haven’t been able to track any siblings, or aunts, or uncles. No cousins. Do you know of any?”

“He has a sister. She was four years younger than him. As for aunts and uncles, I don’t recall hearing him mention any ever. But what fourteen-year-old really pays attention to that sort of thing? I didn’t. We weren’t that close. We drank a little beer we took from our folks on the weekends once in a while, harmless fun. Like I said, by the time we got to high school, we were clearly on different paths.”

"What was his sister's name?" asked Whelan.

"Maggie, I think."

"Maggie, as in short for Margaret? Was it Margaret Gilroy?"

"Gilroy?" asked Doctor Light. "No. I don't know her middle name, but it was Margaret Armstrong."

Whelan's gears were churning at full speed. He remembered contemplating Sonny Bill Armstrong's face in the interrogation room and thinking he seemed familiar somehow. "Doctor Light, did Margaret ever go by another nickname besides Maggie? Did she ever go by Peggy?"

"Yes, she did. I remember her being called that when she was in elementary school. But by the time she hit seventh grade, she preferred Maggie, though her family still called her Peggy sometimes, out of habit. It was around the time I lost track of Sonny in high school. I certainly didn't keep tabs on his little sister."

"Thank you, Doctor Light. If we need anything else, we'll be in touch."

Whelan hung up the phone and spun his seat around to face the nine other agents who were now gathered around his chair, including Cannon, Jones, and SAC Alan Kendrick.

"Peggy Armstrong!" said Whelan. "I just realized why Sonny Bill looks so familiar! His sister is Peggy Perkins!"

Chapter 48

Peggy Perkins threw open a side door on the large building in front of her. But it wasn't Price Chopper. It was Mission Hospital, where Grace Meyer was recovering. She entered through a section of the hospital she'd noted earlier that morning while campusing the place when everyone went to get lunch. She'd also memorized where the hospital cameras were and the closest restroom to slip into once inside without being seen on video surveillance.

She pulled on a pair of surgical gloves and closed herself inside a stall. When she stepped in front of the restroom mirror five minutes later, she was wearing a doctor's lab coat, white pants, white tennis shoes, and her normally wild and bright maroon hair was bound tightly and tucked underneath a black wig, which was pulled into a bun in the back and jammed full of bobby pins. A large pair of glasses completed her ensemble.

She took her bag, now containing her original outfit, and hid it beneath the trash bag inside the receptacle mounted to the wall. A final check on her appearance reminded her to wipe off her excessive lipstick. *God, I hate that color. Never again soon!*

A hospital name tag she'd swiped from a doctor's lounge earlier while scoping the place out was pinned on her white medical coat. It read, Dr. Amanda Breyers. The backside contained a magnetic strip. She took a deep breath and opened the door to the bathroom.

She slowed her pace as she walked down the hall so as not to draw attention. She nodded kindly when others acknowledged her. When she made it to the nurses' station in the emergency room, she swiped the tag on the reader outside the locked medication storage room and braced herself to hear alarms and whistles. She wondered if armed guards might rush her and tackle her to the ground.

Instead, she was greeted with a beep and a click of the glass door, allowing access to rows and rows of medication. Peggy ran her eyes over them as fast as she could until she spotted what she needed. She grabbed a bottle of morphine and a bottle of pentobarbital. They were shoved in her doctor's coat pocket along with two syringes. Another door was at the other end of the room. She exited there and walked through a different corridor on her way to the ICU.

Slow down!

Her nerves were in overdrive. She forced shorter steps.

As she rounded the corner to the ICU, she saw the guard in the hall who was supposed to be standing at Grace's curtain. It was the same man who was there at lunchtime. He'd even visited with her in the hall six hours ago. He looked right at her.

She froze.

He gave her a smile, then returned his gaze to the television above the waiting area. No sign of recognition was on his face.

She walked right by him, noting some college football game on the screen.

Entering the ICU, Grace's curtain was near the door. She pushed it back slowly. If there were any doctors or nurses with Running Bear's cousin, she was prepared with an excuse and would return in a few minutes. There were none. Grace was asleep, so she hurried to complete her task.

First, she flipped a few switches on the monitors recording her vitals, then took out the bottle of morphine and withdrew 200 milliliters. She injected it into the port of the IV at Grace's wrist. Then she took a side clamp off the catheter tube and moved it three inches up. She locked it, then ran her fingers up the line eight inches, drawing the roller clamp with her. This moved all of the saline out of that section of the catheter. She clamped it in place.

Peggy took out the bottle of pentobarbital and withdrew the entire contents, injecting it also, this time filling the available space in the catheter. She set the drip rate to the maximum allowed on the infusion pump the catheter tube ran through, then removed the side clamp and released the roller clamp. The unit began flowing again.

That should hit her in about twelve minutes. Give me enough time to get out of here before her heart stops.

Experience gave her a pretty accurate gauge of timing.

Once back in the bathroom, she slipped into her other clothes and stuffed the lab coat, badge, and empty bottles and syringes into the bottom of the trash, covering them with paper towels. Her hair was mussed from the wig, which she pushed to the bottom of her purse along with the latex gloves. She tossed her real hair with her fingers a minute until it regained some volume.

She snuck out the way she came in and was back in the car in no time. Her watch showed seven minutes had transpired. It was 7:15. Merrill was still out cold.

As she started the ignition, she allowed herself a smile. She'd soon be at Parkmoor, and eight billion dollars would be up for grabs.

A few minutes earlier, Agents Whelan and Jones were racing to Parkmoor as Agents Cannon and Lemar were racing to the hospital. They were connected via their cell phones' Bluetooths and could hear one another through their car speakers.

"I saw Peggy at the hospital five hours ago," said Jones. "I can't reach Earl. He was going back around dinner time to check on her."

As Jones drove, Whelan researched Peggy Perkins, a.k.a. Margaret Gilroy, Maggie Armstrong, and Peggy Armstrong, so far.

"We took prints from everyone the night Sue Fielding died. Peggy's weren't in the system," he said. "She either remained aloof all these years, or had someone scrub them from the database."

"It's easier to stay hidden in the backstreets of Oklahoma," commented Jones. "Now we have some names to work with."

"I've found her as Margaret Armstong in some newspaper articles," said Whelan. "She's been a busy woman. Margaret Armstrong left Vinita, Oklahoma and attended the University of Tulsa. She got her degree in nursing! She graduated in 2005 and married a man named Jeff Cambridge that same year. Make that Doctor Cambridge. They were married for…four years I think." He typed away at his laptop.

"She's educated?" asked Jones. "She's been playing like she's some dumb hick!"

"Manifesting the role," said Cannon.

Whelan continued, "I've got an obituary. Doctor Jeff Cambridge was killed in a car crash in 2009. Fell asleep at the wheel, coming home from a late shift at the hospital one night. 'Survived by his wife, Maggie Cambridge.'" He kept typing.

"Okay—wedding announcement. Margaret—Maggie—must have moved to Oklahoma City and began working at "Oak City" General Hospital. In 2010, she remarried. This time it was a hospital administrator named Edwin Luge." He paused as he continued typing and searching articles.

"Luge?" asked Jones. "Not Gilroy? Interesting. You know, those hospital administrators make the big bucks. Often more than the doctors."

Agent Lemar agreed. "Mmmhmm. Sounds like she's a gold digger."

Whelan turned his laptop so Jones could see the photo of Peggy and her second husband attending a charity fundraiser in 2011.

"She's beautiful!" said Jones. "And with blonde hair! She cleaned up damned well with some money. I wonder why she gave that up? And to marry *Merrill*?"

Whelan continued searching. "Not Merrill. Robert Bakersfield. Edwin Luge died in a house fire at their home in Oklahoma City. The newspaper says they think he fell asleep with a cigarette in his mouth."

"And where was Maggie?" asked Lemar. "She too fashionable to die in a house fire?"

"A late shift at the hospital. She was on duty in the ER when they brought him in, fried to a crisp. It caused her to have a breakdown, and she resigned to cope with the magnitude of it all."

"So, how long before she married Bakersfield?" asked Cannon.

"I'm searching… Found her! Apparently six months," answered Whelan.

"That's a whole lotta coping right there," said Lemar. "Mmmhmm."

"She's on the society page of the Wichita Eagle in a 2012 article. 'Whirlwind romance leads to marriage for Wichita Boeing Plant Manager.'"

"Wichita!" exclaimed Jones. "Sounds like she's working the whole Midwest."

Jones peeked at the screen. "She's a brunette in this one," she said for the benefit of Cannon and Lemar, who were nearing the hospital.

Whelan continued and flipped to another window on his screen. "I'm bookmarking all this. Wow! That's a lot of flowers."

"Did you find a wedding photo?" asked Cannon.

"Funeral. Bakersfield died of a heart attack in 2015. Survived by his wife, Margaret Bakersfield. No children."

"Thank God," said Jones.

"Amen," echoed Lemar. "So we're not looking at a gold digger here. We have ourselves a black widow."

They all grew silent, pondering the implication.

"Found her again in Tulsa, 2017," said Whelan. "Married to Frank Gilroy, a mechanic. They got hitched at his auto shop because he was too busy to take time off for a proper wedding and honeymoon. And she's back to calling herself Peggy with this one. And she's blonde again!"

Jones peered at the screen in Whelan's lap. "Cute picture. The groom's in coveralls, and Peggy's in a matching jumper. I don't get it. She goes from doctors and administrators to a mechanic?"

"There's a lot of money if you own the shop," said Cannon. "Any of you had a car worked on lately? It's ridiculous."

"A whole franchise of shops!" said Whelan. "Their website boasts, 'Eleven locations in three counties.'"

"How did she kill this one?" asked Lemar.

"Give me a minute," said Whelan. He clicked in silence, then, "Accident at the shop. A customer's car slipped off a lift, crushing his vertebrae. He was turned into a paraplegic. His pain management proved too much to bear, and he died by self-inflicted overdose in 2018."

"I'm guessing he had some help from Nurse Maggie Kevorkian," said Lemar. "So, that was number four. I don't get it. She inherited the wealth and presumably insurance settlement money from several men. She must have millions. Why keep doing it? When is it enough?"

"I'm guessing when she lands eight *billion* from Merrill's daughter's estate," said Whelan.

"And maybe not even then," said Cannon. "Profiles for black widows frequently indicate it's not just about the money. It's the thrill of killing and not getting caught. She made it through four of them. And no one is going to miss Merrill. He might be number five once she secures her inheritance."

"Or number six," said Jones. "Her initial background check came back with a last name of Johnson. I thought it was her maiden name, but now I think there must have been another husband in there somewhere. Probably her first, before she got her nursing degree, and before she started going by Maggie again. Peggy. Maggie. I wonder if she suffers from some sort of split personality? She could be more delusional than Running Bear."

"Black widows often do have deep psychological issues," said Cannon. "All that role-playing is more than some latent desire to try out their acting skills. She'd blend right in at Parkmoor and work her way into that family's hearts."

"Already started," said Jones. "She's got that sweet, 'poor little me' routine down pat."

Jones grew red the more she thought about Peggy's innocent act and stepped on the gas. "That tramp had me feeling sorry for her! I guess I might take a little slapping around, too, for an eight-billion-dollar payout after a few years! She knew who Merrill's daughter was when she met him."

"*Before* she met him," Whelan agreed. "At some point, Sonny Bill Armstrong told his little sister about sleeping with Forever Sophia. And he would have known who Merrill Perkins was."

"So she finds Sophia's dad," continued Cannon, "probably in a bar some night, gets him liquored up, and he confirms he has a daughter named Sophia."

"And," Jones added, "at some point shortly after that, Merrill lets it slip he's got a grandson. I bet Peggy's the one who pushed her brother to go out to L.A. with a sample of his DNA and try to get in with Sophia. It took another year, but it eventually worked."

"So I'm guessing it was Peggy who talked Sonny out of taking the ten million dollars to walk away?" asked Cannon.

"Yep," said Whelan. "After screwing up his position with the Tulsa fire department with her bogus accusation, she set him on a course that would take him down a treacherous rabbit hole. She's more dangerous than the Queen of Hearts. She probably could have had half that payoff, five million, but it wasn't enough for her. Her mind's set on billions. I wonder if Sonny Bill Armstrong will squeal on his sister now?"

"We're pulling up to the hospital," said Lemar. "We'll check on Grace Meyer and get back to you soon."

"We're a half-mile from Parkmoor," said Jones. "Merrill's supposed to have signed for his million dollars at 7:00. I'm guessing he's still there, with Peggy in tow. I bet she's somehow convinced him to hold out for more and tries to delay the signing again."

She hung up the phone. "What do you think, Partner? You ready to take this bitch down?"

Whelan's clock on his SUV's dash read 7:15. "Yes. I hate to play devil's advocate, but without Sonny Bill Armstrong's testimony against his sister, we may never be able to prove any of this. All we have is conjecture."

Jones sighed. "I'll make it my life's mission."

Still seething with anger and frustration, she wheeled into the circular drive in front of Parkmoor's front entry and clobbered the brakes. "Remind me to give up Thai food!"

Chapter 49

Agents Cannon and Lemar rushed inside the hospital and to Grace's room in the ICU. The officer stationed at her curtain checked their badges and let them through.

"Has anyone else been here in the past couple of hours?" asked Cannon.

"Doctors and nurses. No visitors."

Grace Meyer was still sound asleep.

Agent Kesha Lemar took a hard look at the woman in the bed. "Her breathing's really shallow. I helped take care of my granny when I was in high school. She's barely taking a breath."

She glanced at the monitors still attached to Grace's body. "Her heart rate down's to thirty. That's getting dangerously low!"

Cannon studied the monitors. "If I'm reading this right, her blood oxygen level is down to eighty-one. Is she in trouble? Don't these things have bells and whistles when your readings aren't normal?"

Lemar studied the machines. "Someone's turned off the alarms." She hit a button, activating them, and they started ringing out loud warning signals.

"Get help!" yelled Cannon. He scanned Grace up and down, thinking about Peggy Perkins and what she could have done earlier that would take effect now. She was a nurse with medical knowledge beyond Cannon's training. A drip from the IV bag with saline snared his attention. It was half full.

It's in her bag!

He followed the flow to the back of Grace's right hand. Unsure how to stop it, he grabbed the tube below her wrist and gave it a yank. The IV needle was ripped from her hand. The vein started spurting blood everywhere, much of it on Cannon's shirt and suit jacket. It sprayed his neck as he clamped his hands over it, saying a prayer for her not to bleed to death.

The curtain was whipped back behind him.

Earl Humboldt was standing there, his face contorted with horror at the blood-covered agent holding his daughter's hand.

"What in God's name have you done?" Earl screamed.

"I'm trying to save her!" Cannon replied. "I think she's been given something in her IV. Get help!"

Earl was frozen. He couldn't accept this man covered in crimson from his child wasn't trying to hurt her. "Stop it!" was all he could manage.

The curtain was whipped back again, and two nurses and a doctor ran in. Lemar was right behind them.

Cannon let go as they took over, and Lemar grabbed Earl's arm.

"Let them work," she said.

"Don't touch me!" he yelled. "Oh God! Gracie! My darling girl. Please don't die, Gracie. You're all I have."

He shouted at Cannon. "What did you do?"

Tears welled in his eyes and fell to the floor. A river was soon streaming down his face.

Lemar felt sorry for him. "Mr. Humboldt," she said softly. "Let's sit in the hall and let them work. I'll explain what happened."

He allowed her to guide him to the chairs in the waiting area and collapsed into a seat behind him. She sat with him as he hung his head.

"Oh God. Oh God," he repeated in a low whisper.

Cannon walked further down the hall to call Jones and give her an update.

Jones hung up the phone from Cannon. She was standing in the parlor at Parkmoor along with the entire household. They were all waiting for the arrival of Merrill and Peggy Perkins.

"Grace is in trouble," she whispered to Whelan. "Let's not further upset them until we get a medical report."

She gave a quick summary to Whelan of what Cannon told her.

The agents arrived ten minutes earlier. They chose to fill in everyone at Parkmoor regarding Peggy's connection to Sonny William Armstrong and her likely involvement in the deaths of Running Bear's family and Doctor Brachman. They needed to question everyone about Peggy Perkins, given the new light shining on her. What did they know about her? What had they heard discussed? Did anyone witness her anywhere in the house she shouldn't have been? Could it have been her that Running Bear saw in the hallway dressed up as a wizard?

They were all in shock, and no one could offer much in the way of information. Their answers were as vague as the questions. "Nothing. Not much. No. Maybe."

Running Bear kept himself muffled the whole time. He walked to the bar and poured himself a glass of scotch. He turned and faced the room with all eyes on him. "So my dad *and* my aunt killed my mother, my grandmother, my doctor, and attempted to kill my cousin. Do I have that right?"

Jones raised her eyebrows high and sighed. "Yes, Your Majesty, you have that right."

He looked at his wife, Marjorie, whose pained expression and visible tears simply angered him more. "And my aunt married my *grandfather*? And presumably, they've had relations. Isn't that incest? Is my family truly this deranged? Is this why I'm *special*?"

The group took a beat, with no one moving or volunteering an answer as they digested it was Running Bear's aunt who orchestrated the nightmare they were all living through.

Nurse O'Brien straightened her shoulders and marched up to the young man. She took both his arms in her hands, forcing eye contact. "No Bear. Your dad's sister is not related to your grandfather. If your dad and your mother ever married, she would have simply been an in-law. There's no incestuous relationship, sweetheart. And they have nothing to do with your extraordinary state of being. You are exceptional because you are kind and generous, and despite the revelations of this week, your mother raised you to be the wonderful man you are today."

The pair hugged, and both returned to a sofa and took a seat. Marjorie leaned her head on his shoulder and sniffled her tears to silence, meeting the austerity of the room.

At 7:25, the doorbell chimed. It rang loud throughout the house. For once, the sound of chatter over drinks in the parlor didn't drown out its eerie echo as it reverberated off marble walls and floors.

Sylvia Moffet was startled and let out a little gasp. When the group all turned to her, she stared back at them curiously.

"Oh!" she said. "That's *my* job! Sorry." She left the room to let them in—Running Bear's alcoholic, abusive grandfather and his murderous aunt.

She couldn't bring herself to make eye contact when she answered the door. Staring at the floor, her hand shaking on the door handle, she said, "Please, come in. They're all waiting for you in the Parlor. I believe by now you know the way."

Merrill Perkins was given a dose of methamphetamine by Peggy on the way from the hospital to help him wake up. She told him it was aspirin and would make him feel better, and boy did it ever. He strutted in like a prize-winning turkey at the state fair. He was here to claim his million-dollar stake in his dead daughter's fortune.

Peggy Perkins wore a smile and kept up with her husband's step. She was here to make sure he *didn't* sign so they could claim the more massive stake of billions to come.

When the pair walked into the parlor, their faces were met with frowns and tears.

"Why so glum?" asked Merrill. He turned to his grandson. "Boy, with all you got, you'll never miss a million dollars."

He scanned the room, his eyes narrowing in on Attorney Adam Steiner toward the back. "Now, where's that contract? Let's get this over with."

Peggy was about to interject with her prepared statement, but Running Bear cut her off by jumping up from the sofa. "You're late, grandfather. You blew it! There's no money for you."

On the inside, Peggy was jubilated. She didn't have to use her prepared speech about why they shouldn't sign. She didn't have to pretend to care about wanting to be a part of the family, how they hoped they could become legitimate grandparents to Running Bear and be in his life more.

On the outside, she managed to put on a puzzled expression and feigned disappointment as she turned toward her husband.

"Now, boy," started Merrill.

"Don't *boy* me!" yelled Running Bear. "Don't speak to me ever again, you baboon imbecile! I don't know if you're involved in my mother and grandmother's deaths or not, but to sit idly by and allow it to happen right under your own nose! Shame on you!"

Merrill was confused. He took a step back as his grandson approached him, three shades of red from his forehead to his chin.

"You're a despicable swine of a man!" continued Running Bear.

He turned his head to Peggy. "And you! Where's your wizard robe tonight? Where's your dark magic? What defense are you prepared to offer for your crimes? How could you have killed my family? And all for green paper? You will be executed for your atrocities! I'll swing the sword myself at your beheading, *Aunt* Peggy!"

Peggy Perkins froze in shock before whirling in a circle near the center of the room, comprehending the harsh reality they all knew who she was. Their sad and angry faces made sense now. She stopped her roving eyes on Jones.

Jones stared back, an icy cold gaze that nearly cut the woman in half. "Peggy Perkins," she announced, "you're under arrest for the murders of Sophia Perkins, Sue Fielding, and Doctor Alan Brachman. And the attempted murder of Grace Meyer. Turn around and place your hands behind your back."

Agents Whelan and Jones took a few steps in Peggy's direction.

The woman turned and ran out of the room. She remembered the closest door was out the garage at the end of the gallery. She ran to the door and jiggled the handle. It didn't turn. Of course, her tape keeping it unlocked was long removed, and a key-required deadbolt was installed.

When she turned back to run toward the front entrance, the entirety of the parlor was now spread out in the gallery in front of her, blocking her path. They also cut off the doorway to the kitchen. She abruptly turned and raced up the steps of the second grand staircase. On the middle landing, she flung open the glass door to the sword case and grabbed the first sword she thought she'd be able to swing, an artillery shortsword from nineteenth-century France.

Running Bear was still quite angry, and before the agents could stop him, he ran up after her, two seconds behind. Marjorie grabbed his wrist and tried to restrain him. He ripped it free without even acknowledging his wife.

When Peggy turned around with her sword in hand, the sight of her nephew startled her, and she jumped back a step. It gave the man time enough to reach his hand in the case and remove a wakizashi sword from seventeenth-century Japan.

Running Bear pointed it at her chest, and Peggy used her shortsword to bat it away, then quickly raised it again. The weight of the iron surprised her, but she managed with two hands to swing it wildly in the direction of the man. He easily countered her attack and struck at her sword, foiling her move.

She swung several more times, trying to strike her nephew down. Running Bear had training and practice, and the benefit of being robust. Each strike was knocked away effortlessly. Under other circumstances, he might have enjoyed sparring, but he was angry, and this was an actual duel. A bona fide opponent was before him, desperate and wild.

"Running Bear!" she screamed at him. "Put that down, and let me explain! I haven't killed anyone! I *am* your aunt, but it was Sonny who killed your mother. Not me! I'm innocent."

"You pulled all the strings!" he yelled back. "You did this! And it was you who tried to kill Gracie!"

He struck at her sword once more, knocking it to the side, and before she could raise it back up in defense, he moved in and held the edge of his sword against her throat. She struggled to move her arm and swing the point of her shortsword toward Running Bear's back, but he saw her maneuver and kicked the sword out of her hand. She screamed in pain.

Running Bear pressed the edge of his wakizashi further into her neck, breaking her skin across two inches.

She screamed again. "Stop this, please! Someone! Help me! He's going to kill me."

"You're damned right I am. Now admit your sins against the family!"

Tears were streaming down Running Bear's cheeks.

Agents Jones and Whelan were at the foot of the staircase. Their weapons were drawn and pointed at the pair on the landing.

"Your Majesty!" shouted Whelan. "Don't do it. She's not worth it!"

Running Bear positioned himself behind his aunt, still holding the blade at her neck.

He whispered in her ear. "You've taken everyone from me I loved most."

Peggy could scarcely take a breath or speak. As she drew in air to voice her reply, his sword dug further into her neck. Blood was raining down on the marble floor at their feet.

She managed to eke out a response in a last attempt to save herself. "Yes, it was me. I had your mother killed. I'm sorry."

"And?" he whispered.

"And your grandmother," she echoed.

"And?"

"And Doctor Brachman."

"And Gracie?"

"And I stabbed Gracie," she repeated. "And pretended I was a wizard when you saw me in the hallway. Please don't kill me, Running Bear. I'm your aunt. I'm family!"

She matched his tears, and they both cried furiously.

"You don't deserve to live!" he growled.

"Your Majesty!" shouted Whelan. "Even the King is not allowed to commit an execution without a fair trial by the Royal Court! She must go before a judge! If you do this here and now, *you'll* be the one locked in irons! Please, Bear! I beg of you!"

Running Bear eased the sword a quarter-inch against Peggy's neck and pressed his lips tight against her ear. "Why? Why did you take my Queen? There was everything left to live for."

Peggy Perkins' voice was hoarse. She pleaded again, this time to the agents. "He has no idea what he has here. He can't even appreciate the life that billions of dollars could give. It means nothing to him."

Jones slowly took the steps, one at a time toward the couple. "Peggy, this young man knows exactly what he has here. And he knows you took so much of that from him."

She spoke softly to Running Bear. "Your Majesty, please, release her to my charge, and I promise she'll pay for the deaths in your family."

Running Bear's eyes were fixed on Whelan. He moved them to Jones, then danced them between the agents. He lowered his sword from Peggy's neck and backed up a step. "You're right, Lord Whelan. She isn't worth it. Please, make sure she and my father face the judgment they deserve."

Whelan ran up the steps and cuffed Peggy Perkins. "They'll both pay, Your Majesty. Justice *will* be served."

Nurse O'Brien wrapped a bar towel around Peggy's neck when they reached the bottom of the stairs. She conducted a quick assessment and determined the gouge wasn't deep enough to have nicked anything vital. Soft tissue and a little muscle, but she'd heal fine with a few stitches. She tied the towel tight, nearly choking the woman.

"It's for your own good," O'Brien hissed at her. "Be grateful."

Jones read Peggy her Miranda Rights in front of seven witnesses on the way through the gallery. In the foyer, she paused to see if her partner was behind her.

Whelan was speaking with Bear down the hall. She opened the front door and marched Peggy to her SUV.

The agent stationed at the porch opened the back door. They secured Peggy, and the agent climbed in next to her from the other side.

Jones returned to the house to grab Merrill.

Whelan was locking Merrill's hands behind his back when she entered. He was also read his rights, though, at this point, they had no idea whether or not he knew of Peggy's actions. He was blithering on about his innocence and seemed legitimately shocked at his wife's exploits.

"You're lucky, Merrill. A few more weeks and she would have set her sights on you," said Jones.

"Huh?"

He was yet to be informed of her colorful history of husbands.

The other agent guarding the back of the house was called to the front, and they placed Merrill in the back of his car.

"What were you telling Running Bear?" asked Jones of Whelan.

"How proud I was of him, of his ability to reason, and that he made the right choice. I confirmed what O'Brien was telling him earlier. That's he an amazing man with a future ahead of him, even if he couldn't see it right now. In time, he'll heal from the pain of his losses. He has an amazing support system right here. I think he'll be okay."

"I think he will, too," she agreed. "Let's call Cannon and check on Grace Meyer. I hope Running Bear has at least one real family member left in his life."

Chapter 50

A week later, Grace Meyer was being released from the hospital. Thanks to the quick action of Agent Cannon, the pentobarbital that started entering her system was negligible. The doctors were able to counteract its effects, as well as the large dose of morphine, and prevent any permanent damage. Her heart was healing nicely, and tests indicated she'd be fine.

"They have me on bed rest," she told Whelan when he stopped by the house the following day. "But I'm feeling much better. Really. You just missed my husband and father. They were here all week. They flew back to Oklahoma City this morning to start wrapping up our life there. It will take a while, but we plan on staying at Parkmoor. Everyone here has been amazing. I could never disrupt Running Bear's life and the family he's made here."

"What will you do about the L.A. crowd?"

Grace sighed. "One step at a time. There's so much to understand. I don't know how Sophie did it."

"She hired and accepted help. Make sure you do the same."

"I will, thank you. Agent Whelan, I read the coroner's report on Sophie. Did you all know she was pregnant?"

"Yes. I'm sorry we couldn't tell you. The father might have been involved in her murder."

"I understand. And I also found out it wasn't Mr. Armstrong. You don't know who it was?"

"Not a clue. There's a whole city out there. Sophie's dead. The baby's dead. Does it even matter at this point? He obviously wasn't involved seriously, or he would have made an appearance over the past two weeks."

"I guess you're right. Probably never know. And I've already decided it's for the best. I'll die with that secret. No one else here knows. Running Bear doesn't need to spend his life questioning what it might have been like to have a young brother or sister around. It would only haunt him. Please swear to me you won't tell him either."

"It's not my place. I swear."

Grace smiled and nodded.

"And *you* promise *me* you'll get some security cameras up around here," added Whelan.

"Already ordered."

The 'family' of Parkmoor was sitting around the table on the Veranda, enjoying a fine lunch as usual. Grace insisted Whelan stay for lunch, and the pair joined the others outside.

"Lord Whelan," said Running Bear, "we'd like to thank you again for all of your work last week helping to secure my dad and aunt. I'm still working through some of it, but Doctor DeLuca has assured me that it should play no bearing on my role as king. My name's not tarnished."

"No, Your Majesty," said Whelan. "I think you should be proud of the Perkins name. Your mother was more than a corporate success. She inspired millions of women and men around the world. Her gift of helping others will be remembered in dozens of kingdoms, and I believe her generosity of spirit will live on in you. As you reflect on everything over the coming months, and you will, remember you have her kind heart and soul."

Marjorie cried at Running Bear's side. Whelan's considerate words were appreciated.

Running Bear patted her hand. He looked around the patio, wondering if Cantor would show up for lunch. He'd been around a lot less this past week.

"Agent Whelan," said Chad Buckley, "do we have any word on what will happen to Bear's aunt? Or his dad?"

"I can tell you it will be a court battle. The siblings have turned on one another. Peggy's claiming that her brother was the mastermind behind the whole plan. Sonny Bill Armstrong says she's the one who conjured up the dream of becoming billionaires. He's hired an attorney, independent of hers. That's usually a good thing for cases like this. When the culprits fall in opposite camps, their stories fall apart, and the truth usually prevails. Of course, Peggy will fight the charges all the way, and she has money. She's hired a top attorney. At some point, you'll all be required to testify."

"Gladly," said Sylvia Moffett. "We'd be ecstatic to help put her away for as long as the law allows."

Everyone agreed.

Nurse O'Brien took a bite of chicken cacciatore. "Delicious, as usual, Chef Louie."

The chef started taking his meals with the rest of his Parkmoor family, feeling more bonded after the week's tragic events. "Thank you, Linda."

He turned to Whelan, "What about Merrill? Is he going to jail? Did he admit any involvement?"

"He's pleading ignorance of his wife's crimes. Given her sordid past and history of dead husbands, I'm inclined to believe Merrill was just another victim of Peggy Armstrong. In a way, so was her brother."

Whelan focused intently on Running Bear, "But don't feel sorry for your dad. Ultimately he made his own choices. He needs to own responsibility for his actions and pay the price."

Running Bear agreed. "You're wise, Lord Whelan. You sound like you're ready to rule a kingdom. I understand there's plenty of them out there. I get to stay in mine now."

"Excellent, Your Majesty."

After a quick plate, Whelan stood. "Well, I have to go. Don't anyone get up on my account. I'll see myself out."

They all stood regardless and raced to shake his hand or give him a hug. "Thank Yous" were issued all around again.

"And be sure to thank Agent Jones and Agent Cannon for us as well," they said.

Whelan smiled at the group. He would miss them. They were remarkable people, emotional and quirky, as any family is, but full of love and loyalty.

He headed back to the officc. He hadn't intended to stop by Parkmoor but couldn't help himself. Ordinarily, he didn't check up on cases once resolved. But these people impacted his heart.

He pushed the 'phone' button on the car's steering wheel. "Call mom," he said.

Two rings later, Kathryn Whelan answered the phone. "Tell me everything!"

Cannon looked up at Whelan when he walked into the bullpen at the field office. "That was a long lunch break. You bring me back a sub?"

"Oh, uh…I'm sorry. I plum forgot."

Cannon opened up a bag of chips on his desk. "No problem, these will tide me over."

He walked by Whelan on the way to the breakroom to grab a bottle of soda. "I smell Italian food," he mumbled, sniffing the air around his new partner.

"Really? Huh…" Whelan chuckled and headed to ASAC Miranda Jones' office.

"Well, you're fitting right in," he said when he stuck his head in her open door.

"It's getting there," she said. She was hanging a picture on the wall of a zen garden somewhere green with mountains in the background.

Whelan grabbed the other side and helped navigate it to the hook. "Would Kendrick not let you put one of those on the rooftop?" he joked.

She paused and opened her eyes wide. "That's a brilliant idea!"

Grabbing a Post-It, she jotted down his suggestion and pinned it to her rolling corkboard. There were photos of someone else's case plastered all over it. Dead bodies competed with close-ups of explosive devices for space.

Whelan was glad it was not his case for once. He and Cannon finished up another tidy murder case over the past week, and he was in the mood for something less bloody.

"Any corporate espionage cases we can work?" he asked.

"No, sorry."

Jones sat at her desk, appreciating the personal furnishings she'd added over the past week. She seemed pleased with it all.

"Oh, here," she said, pushing a tin box toward him.

He opened it to find a dozen fresh-baked oatmeal cookies. One bite, and he was impressed. "Exceptional vanilla. I can taste it. These are amazing, thank you."

"You're welcome. And none of that partially hydrogenated crap. All butter. And you could stand to gain a pound. Me, on the other hand, I put in thirty extra minutes on the treadmill."

He curled one side of his mouth. "You always look exceedingly fit, to me."

ASAC Miranda Jones pulled a file out of her desk and viewed her old partner with the new eyes of a superior. She'd be forced to consider him through these eyes from now on. And she was always aware in the back of her mind that she had Whelan to thank for saving her career, and her life, earlier that summer.

Screw it, she thought. *I'll work on balancing it all out later.*

She threw the file in front of him. "Whelan, Eddie Morrison was almost captured three weeks ago. Here are all the details. I need you to read through it and postulate where he might be now. Get back to me ASAP with your theories."

Whelan's mouth fell open, but he managed to snap it shut. "How long have you been keeping this from me?"

"About ten days. We needed to close the Perkins case cleanly and with clear heads."

Whelan nodded. "I understand, boss."

He started to walk out when she called to him.

"Tom, I am sorry I couldn't tell you sooner."

He started to respond, but simply nodded instead, then left the room.

In the hallway, he took a deep breath. He counted to ten and released it slowly like he'd seen Jones do a hundred times over the past three months.

Indeed, it wasn't as fast as whisky, but it worked to calm him.

Whelan found his new partner sipping a cola and downing the last crumbs from his one-ounce bag of chips. He patted Cannon on the back. “Partner, let’s go get you a sub. We’ve got some reading to do. You might just get your manhunt sooner than later.”

THE END

Thank You

Thank you for reading **MURDER AT PARKMOOR**! I hope you enjoyed it. Did you guess the killer before the big reveal?

I had a wonderful time writing this for you, and if you haven't read **12 PILLS** yet, you're in for a treat. You can pick up a copy of that and more from the links on my website, http://www.kirkburris.com.

If you enjoyed this story, please tell your friends and family, and most importantly, **leave a review** on the site where you purchased this book! Reviews go a long way to help indie-authors like myself build an audience so we can keep writing for you.

Lastly, the third book in the Agent Whelan Mystery series is out now! It picks up the pace dramatically in true, action thriller style. Pick up **EDDIE MORRISON**, available in paperback or digital eBook format. Learn the history of Eddie and Agent Whelan, and hold on to your seat!

Eddie has kidnapped Connor, Whelan's son. Out of options and with no clear alliances, a desperate Eddie is making deals with the devils in order to secure a future for himself, from a mysterious sex trafficker in Miami, to an old drug runner in the Louisiana Bayou. Every minute wasted is another minute Eddie Morrison comes closer to taking another life, and the death toll is rising faster than the Mississippi. The criminal Whelan thought he knew, is proving to be a psychopath hell-bent on destroying Connor from the inside out, and is breaking the minds and spirits of both father and son.

Grab your copy of **EDDIE MORRISON** today!

Have a blessed day!

Kirk Burris

Made in the USA
Monee, IL
13 July 2025

20857949R00198